DJ KRIMMER JOE ARDEN

Dedication

For every soul who's ever watched something precious slip through their fingers and didn't pretend it didn't hurt. You are not broken for grieving. You are brave for remembering.

"If there's a book that you want to read, but it hasn't
been written yet, then you must write it."
–Toni Morrison

"We die. That may be the meaning of life. But we do
language. That may be the measure of our lives."
–(also) Toni Morrison

Warning

Welcome to the OtherWorld. We hope you enjoyed your time in the mortal realm, and look forward to assisting you as you navigate the remainder of eternity. Please be aware that the ride you are about to embark on is not without its dangers. Management insists that you keep your arms and soul inside the book at all times. As a reminder, this story may not be suitable for passengers with heart conditions–just ask Rue–or broken funny bones–just ask Kane.

Please obey all posted signs throughout your journey. Before we begin, please ensure that you will not have any issues dealing with the following:

Graphic Violence
Strong Language
Descriptive Sexual Content
Dark Humor
Death. All Kinds. Everywhere.

If this adventure is not right for you, that's completely understandable. Management respects your wishes and hopes you enjoy your new forever in The Nothing.

For those ready to venture forth, the story is about to begin ...

For a full list of triggers and content warnings, you can visit:

TheRealJoeArden.com
Or
AuthorDJKrimmer.com

Playlist

String Quartet No. 3 "Mishima": VI. Mishima/Closing, Philip Glass, Carducci String Quartet

Youth, Daughter

Dead Girl Walking, Heathers Original West End Company

Heathens, Twenty One Pilots

Don't Fear the Reaper (Re:Imagined), Denmark + Winter

Pale Moonlight, Dayseeker

People Are Strange, The Dead South

Nothing Changes, Hadestown Original Broadway Company

D.D., The Weeknd

Villain, Stella Jang

Save My Soul, Big Bad Voodoo Daddy

Dead Man's Arms, Bishop Briggs

Where Did You Sleep Last Night - Live, Nirvana Unplugged

My Body Is a Cage, Arcade Fire

When Our Wings Are Cut, Can We Still Fly?, Kronos Quartet

Breathe Me, Sia

The Night We Met, Lord Huron feat. Phoebe Bridgers

As the World Caves In, Matt Maltese

Only Love Can Hurt Like This, Paloma Faith

Glitter & Gold, Barns Courtney

Eulogy, grandson

Wake Me, Bleachers

Prologue

PLAGUED FROM THE START

KANE

Northern France – Around Three Hundred Years Ago

AN ONE DIE OF A BROKEN HEART?

It's a question that echoes in the minds of many, a desperate plea, a whispered cry into the void, a silent scream reverberating through an aching soul's hollow chambers. It is a question that, if asked in a social setting, I would've gladly debated intellectually.

Metaphorically, I can think of many lives lost to that most romantic of conditions: a broken heart. Passions burn, love dies, and along with it the lives of so many rakes and damsels of stories past. But can a feeling affect the body to such a degree that it could change function? To push the query even further, could a sense of over-whelm be so seismic as to cease the beating of the heart?

As a learned medical professional, I feel I should have the answer, but I ask not as a physician or a scholar–no, I ask as a wretched soul, barely clinging to existence. A man undone.

Grief is not sorrow. Sorrow is a guest who will leave. Grief is a parasite–it latches on, it feeds, it remakes. It is a rot that eats away at you and leaves only a husk. It is the weight pressing down on my chest with every breath, my dark shadow beside me, whispering I will never be whole again.

And so, this doctor, a master of the science of the soul, postulates that though heartache might not be the direct cause of death, it can serve as a catalyst, slowly chipping away at our will to live. It is a relentless torment that never ends, gnawing away at our very being until we are nothing but an empty shell. Like an executioner's blade, it cleaves the soul from the self, leaving us gasping for air as our heart slowly withers away and sends us to our final resting place.

I never thought I would be forced to grapple with such questions personally. I never imagined these musings would be more than a scholarly pursuit or piece of theological training. As a man of noble birth, I was raised by proud and honorable parents, who provided me with an education that paved the way for success in my career in medicine. My life was built on discipline, devotion, and love so consuming that I feared it might one day swallow me whole. But never, not in my darkest nightmares, did I imagine that love would be the very thing to unmake me.

Isabelle. My Izzy. For nine years, she's been the breath in my lungs, the fire in my veins. A beacon in the darkness of this cruel world. I worshipped her body and soul, moving the moon and stars to bring her joy. What was gold? What was power? What was *anything* compared to the way her laughter warmed my heart? I did all of this gladly because I belonged to her.

But she did not belong to me.

"Was." The word is familiar yet foreign as it stumbles from my lips.

Isabelle *was* my wife.

Isabelle *was* my everything.

Isabelle *was* my light in the dark.

Now ... she is not.

Heartbreak is a whoreson dog. And any doubts about my love for her were rendered insignificant when rage consumed me, blinding my reason and pushing me beyond the brink of sanity. It is a bitter truth: life is not fair. Never once did I stray, not even a glance. Why would I when perfection waited for me in our home? How could she? How could *they*? After everything I'd done. All I'd sacrificed.

A darkness plagues our world again. Death looms at the forefront as a constant threat amid chaos and desperation. This sickness came like a black tidal wave, sweeping through the fetid streets, leaving behind piles of rotting bodies. The wails of the dying have become a mournful song I am unable to escape, driving doctors like myself to the brink of madness. Even worse, fear has turned brother against brother, causing people to suspect even a simple sniffle as a sign of illness. My professional duties have always been clear: rid the body of disease and save souls. Keep in line the humors and maintain the earthly balance of body, mind, and soul.

But nothing in my years of healing my fellow Parisians prepared me for this pestilence. Entire families are dying slowly, in the tens of thousands. People are locking themselves away in fear and choosing to take their mortality into their own hands rather than waiting for the illness. Villages have been quarantined and then buried alive. The torments are great; the answers so very scant.

Add to that unthinkable anguish the horrors I witnessed after coming home from my tour. Doctors are not above our fellow men, and many of us have succumbed to the illness; therefore, a rule was established. After our missions, we had to confine ourselves before being allowed to go home to our loved ones.

That in-between time seared deeper than any fire nature could forge. Do not underestimate the torment of prolonged isolation. I was locked away, unable to communicate with the outside world, unable to know how Izzy fared. The ache of the unknowing was a physical weight. Stone upon stone heaped upon my chest as I waited to see if I would show signs of the very disease I had been sent to help eradicate. And if I did demonstrate even a hint of the plague, my fate would be sealed. No goodbyes, last touches, or final moments of connection with my beloved. When I look back, perhaps that would have been the better course for my days.

The reality instead was this: after being cleared from my fortnight-long solitude, free of disease and desperate for connection, I made for the home my toils and labors had paid for. I raced to the entrance to hold my wife, to see my beautiful Isabelle, to feel her warm embrace once again. As I burst through the door and stepped inside, the sight I found left me speechless.

The woman I loved was not waiting for me, not in the way I had dreamed, not in the way I had prayed.

Our bed …

Our bed!

Her body was entwined with his—my brother—a pair of unholy serpents coiled in coitus. My mind couldn't comprehend what I was seeing. The balance I sought in my patients and myself faltered, splintered, and finally broke.

Betrayal. Anger. Heartbreak.

A storm raged inside me, swallowing every ounce of logic, every shred of reason. My hands trembled, and my vision clouded as I found I could not make sense of it all.

But, as I had seen in countless cases over my storied career, madness makes no room for reason, and I could feel—physically feel—something snap inside of me. The calm, understanding man I had always been, he was gone, replaced by a monster filled "from the crown to the toe-top full of direst cruelty." The scene before me blurred as I saw nothing, but heard everything. Every scream, every cry, every desperate gasp for air filled my ears, fueling my fury. At that moment, I could only listen helplessly as my world shattered into a million pieces.

My brother got away, only briefly, and that was when it all changed.

"Kane! Let him go!" Isabelle cried, but it never reached me. How could it? She had killed the man she was yelling at. He was no more. There was no longer a heart inside the chest upon which she pounded. I was bereft of soul.

Isabelle stood between us as he lunged for me. He shoved her out of his way and tackled me to the floor. I wasted no time grabbing him and rolling until I was on top, pinning him down. I gripped fistfuls of his hair as I begun to slam his head into the stone flooring until his body went limp.

I wiped the blood off my hands as I stood and walked over to Izzy, who lay on the floor now, evidently cowering.

"How could you?" I hissed while glaring at her form.

"I've devoted my life to you. I've loved you with every-thing I had, and you betray–" I froze as I looked at her still-motionless body. "I-Isabelle?" I whispered while kneeling beside her. I turned her over, and a sob wracked through me. "No."

Blood ran over her pale skin and into her yellow hair. She must've hit her head on the edge of our coffer when my brother pushed her.

She is gone. She is gone. Isabelle … *my* Isabelle is … gone.

"No, no, no, no." That one word is all I can manage, a futile and desperate plea to an unresponsive universe.

Passion overcame me, sending me spiraling into rage. The results of my mania lay before me. My moist eyes caught a glimpse of the small knife Isabelle kept on her bedside table. For her protection, I insisted, not knowing she was safe in the arms of another.

But death? Oh, cruel Death! I never wanted you to come for her. Murder, unintentional and borne from pas-sion, lay doubly on my hands now. The hands that pull closer and closer to that gleaming silver knife.

What have I done to deserve this? To deserve the be-trayal of my brother and wife, my family by blood and marital bond?

Nothing. I've done nothing to deserve this fate, and it is nothing I am left with. One cannot take anything from nothing.

I stare at the shining blade, feeling the weight of guilt and regret crushing down on me. Thoughts swirling and slicing through my brain: *I do not want to die, do I? I could easily cover up this murder and continue living my life as if nothing ever happened. This plague has claimed so many souls that lay piled in the streets. How easy it would be to add two more to the countless number. I could hide behind my professional facade and return to the streets, offering help and healing to those in need.*

Yet deep down, I know I can never truly wash away the stain of blood on my hands.

My eyes stare at the grotesque and tangled mocker-ies of the love I once knew. I could dress them, I suppose. The old Kane would have. It's disrespectful to leave them naked and soaked in blood. Maybe I've been afflicted with the disease after all. Perhaps it has been eating away at my brain. Or maybe they really did break me when I lay witness to their sinful dance. Whatever the cause, I can no longer be bothered. They are no more–two decaying corpses.

And I–well, I am no longer a man. I am aftermath. I am ruin itself.

And the aftermath doesn't heal. It haunts. Ruins do not heal.

I am nothing, yet I still breathe. The words whisper tauntingly in my brain. Over and over and over again. *Nothing. Nothing. Nothing.*

And in that instant, I know. I know I will never be free from this moment, clear of this pain, or rid of this reality. I grip the blade tightly in my fist. It's almost as if the silver edge sings to me now–enchanting notes of freedom and release.

My eyes scan the carnage that surrounds me one last time. *There is nothing left for me here. Nothing. What waits beyond the waking life? What sits past the veil of life's fleeting breath? What lies beyond?*

Tempus ut de. *Time to find out …*

With one swift motion, I stab the small blade into my carotid artery with lethal precision, crashing my whole world into immediate darkness.

Chapter One

THE END

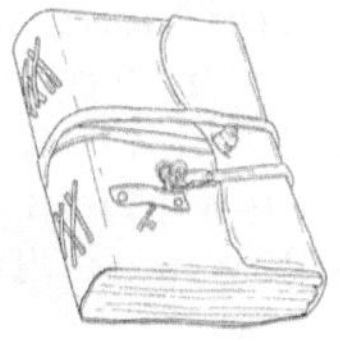

RUE

Present Day

"Hello?"

My voice whispers through the void landing like a single droplet of water at the bottom of a well. It vanishes without so much as an echo, devoured by the infinite dark pressing in from every direction.

I blink. Or try to. It's hard to tell if my body's even moving. Hard to tell if I have a body at all. I feel suspended, somehow stitched into this silence.

Where am I?

What happened?

Logic tells me I should be panicking. But there's no pounding heart, no hitch in my breath. Nothing inside me stutters or shakes.

I frown, slowly concentrating enough to raise my hands to my chest, feeling the fabric of my dress, the memory of skin beneath it. I press down hard. There's no thud. No flutter.

Nothing.

Oh.

Oh no.

My fingers rise instinctively, clawing at the base of my throat, scrambling for purchase against a reality I can't yet bring myself to believe. They tremble as they press into the soft space just beneath my jaw, searching desperately for the familiar double thump of a life still present, still fighting, still mine.

But there's nothing.

A foreign sound escapes me. It's brittle and breathless. The noise goes nowhere. It vanishes before it can mean anything.

The cold doesn't settle on my skin; it sinks beneath it. It seeps into my bones and coils low in my stomach, then higher, weaving its way into my chest, into the space where my heart once lived. I can feel it curling around my ribs like ivy growing wild in a graveyard, making itself at home in the hollowness left behind.

That's what I am now.

Hollow.

The sensation is so new, yet somehow so obvious.

I am *gone.*

There's no panic. No flood of adrenaline. Not even a jolt of fear to cling to. Because panic would mean my body's still trying to protect me. Fear would mean there's something to run from. This is complete stillness.

And I know. I know it now, in a way I can't unknow.

I am dead.

The thought sinks heavily into me, like the last lingering note of a somber song.

There is no bright light. No tunnel. No warm embrace waiting just beyond the veil.

Darkness.

The pitch blackness of a moonless night.

I wrap my arms around myself–or at least, I think I do. I can no longer feel my body in the way I used to. It's like hugging smoke.

My knees hit the ground, and I welcome the fact that I can feel the impact, but am terrified by the awareness that it does not make a sound. I curl forward, pressing my forehead into the earth, but nothing can relieve the burden that I alone must carry.

It's me.

It's what's left of me.

I open my mouth, but I don't know what to ask for. Help? Forgiveness? A second chance?

I need guidance. I need someone to help me navigate this. I don't know how to do whatever this is.

But there is no one.

It's not the sharp, specific pain of acute injury. It's not even the broad, dull ache of grief. It's something deeper. The kind of pain that hollows you out and leaves you feeling like a jack-o'-lantern in mid-November.

This isn't what I thought death would be. I thought I'd feel a release. Peace. Some kind of weightlessness.

Instead, it's as though I'd been erased so gently that I didn't even notice until I was wiped clean from the page.

I tilt my head back, eyes searching for anything, but I am surrounded by a uniform blanket of nothingness.

I'm alone.

Utterly, completely alone.

And that breaks me.

I open my mouth again, and this time, the word falls out on a sob I can't quite make. "Please?"

I don't know who I'm asking.

I force myself to look up as the suffocating blackness around me begins to shift, like ink in water–thinning at the edges, rippling into shadows that stretch and lean without form. Shapes that almost look human if I stare long enough. But they keep slipping away the moment I try to name them.

I take a cautious step forward. The ground beneath my feet is solid but my feet are numb.

The emptiness is unbearable. An endless desert of loneliness. No one to say my name. No one to say goodbye.

No gates to enter. No bridge to cross. No warm hand reaching through the dark.

Nothing.

"I don't understand," I whisper, but the void offers no answers.

"I DON'T UNDERSTAND!" The near roar that leaves me is a raw voice I barely recognize as my own.

The black begins to pulse, and I see a light. Not white, not golden.

A flicker. A shimmer.

It's ... purple.

The air catches in my throat.

The light pulses once, twice, and I move toward it without thinking. Without fear. Because fear requires the possibility of loss, and right now, I'm not sure if I have anything left to lose.

I reach out, my fingers brushing the edge of the glow.

And warmth floods through me.

First like the gentle heat of the sun peeking out from behind a cloud, then like the scalding energy of a crackling fire, and finally the all-consuming burn of memory. That memory takes the shape of smell: fish, tarred rope, and salty air.

I choke on the sound that leaves me.

"Dad?" My voice cracks, the word torn straight from the center of my soul.

The scent of long days at sea and callous, oil-stained hands invades my mind. It's really him! I scramble forward, reaching for the glow, my entire being lunging forward, *toward him.*

But a force hits me in the chest like the earth itself now denies my existence. The stab to my solar plexus feels absolute and final.

I gasp, my hands grasping at the thin air. My chest caves as the pinprick of soft light begins to recede.

"No!" I croak, the word jagged and torn. "Please don't go!"

I reach for him again with everything I have left–my arms, my voice, my soul.

"Please, don't leave me. Please." My pathetic cries award me no sympathy. "Help me. Please, Dad?" My voice breaks around his name, splintering into a million lost moments of love and laughter.

The warmth fades as the last candle burning in my room full of shadows begins to flicker.

The essence of him vanishes. The scratchiness of his beard against my forehead disappears. The sound of his sonorous laughter falls silent in my mind.

I try to sob, but my body doesn't remember how to cry. The grief just presses out through the seams of me stretching the thread.

Then I feel the sensation of something brushing my cheek.

So soft. So impossibly gentle that I think I imagined it. A ghost.

A sharp yanking seems to pull from the center of

me, more forceful than the gentle feeling from before. It wraps around my ribs like barbed wire ripping me apart.

The space around me splits open, and I fall. Plummeting headfirst in a weighted free fall through an infinite chasm that feels as though it has no beginning and never ends.

Amid the grief and the loss and sorrow coursing through my mind, I return to the same question I had when this all began.

Where am I?

And I voice the same sad, simple word that wants nothing more than to be answered. "Hello?"

Chapter Two

CHECK. MATE.

RUE

Three Hours Before the Present

"**D**ON'T GO EASY ON ME JUST BECAUSE I'M AN OLD MAN, KID." GG squints across the chessboard at me, his liver-spotted hand hovering above his rook like it's a nuclear trigger.

We're playing in the rec room of Sunset Gardens, a senior community center. We're surrounded by floral wallpaper in a maudlin shade of beige that makes it look as though the repeating pattern of daisies never knew color. The gentle wheezing sound of oxygen tanks fills the space with a distant white noise.

"GG," I say patiently, "you tried to castle into check five moves ago. I'm doing you a mercy."

He harrumphs. "A mercy? You calling me weak?"

"I'm calling you old, GG. Weak came with the upgrade."

He snorts. "You know, I fought in a war."

"And I've fought for the remote at a local bar during the playoffs, so really, we're both soldiers."

That earns a huff of laughter. He finally moves his bishop, eyeing me like he expects it to bite.

"Checkmate in three," I announce.

"You're a menace," he grumbles.

"And you're a glutton for punishment. Want to go best out of five?"

He waves me off and starts setting up the board again. "You're gonna have to pry this win from my cold, arthritic hands."

"Don't tempt me."

Across the room, Selma is crocheting something with yarn that is *aggressively* purple, watching us with the smug expression of someone who has read the end of the book before anyone else.

I glance at the clock. "I've got to go soon, Selma," I call over. "Are you ready for our literary showdown next week?"

She perks up. "Of course. We're still reading *Rebecca*, right?"

I flip my shoulder-length hair from my face. "Obviously. I have strong opinions about Mrs. Danvers, and I need someone to validate my rage."

"I've got opinions about *you*, Miss Rue." She smirks while pointing her hook at me.

"Those don't count. You're biased. You like me."

She makes a noncommittal sound that's somewhere between a scoff and a purr. "You bring me peppermint tea and books with bite. You'll do until Liam is ready for my bath."

I wiggle my brows at the woman while giving her a suggestive grin. "Now, Selma, you haven't been pulling out those old photos from your twenties to seduce the poor man, have you?"

Selma claps her arthritic hands together as she lets out a laugh. The nurses around me smile softly.

I know I'm one of the only visitors these seniors get. They come here because their kids put them here while they're working—like an elderly daycare. Or, in GG's situation, he comes because he's lonely. The problem is that most are lonely, old, tired, and no one wants to engage in conversation. That's where I come in. I somehow became the social butterfly of Sunset and now come weekly to hang out with the group. Well ... I try to. Sometimes, I have to skip a week if I'm too tired. But I'm coming next week for sure. I never miss book club with the 1950s ex-pinup-star Selma. I'll be honest; I've seen the old photos, and she was a solid ten.

"All right, you all try to behave while I'm gone," I

warn while grabbing my coat off the back of GG's chair. "Same time next week, GG?"

He nods. "Bring your A game, girlie. I'm training for this one."

"Bring your glasses, GG. Would hate for you to not see my victory." I give him a small kiss on the cheek before heading to the front doors.

I grab my phone and order a rideshare before going to sit on the bench and wait. I miss driving. It's funny because I actually hated it growing up. I blame it on living with my mom in Chicago and then with my dad in New Orleans when he was home on shore leave. When my doctor told me last year that I couldn't drive with my new medication, I was honestly happy because it meant no more stressing in traffic. But now I realize it's just another slice of freedom this illness has stolen from me.

Looking up, I smile at the skies, which threaten rain. I hope it's a cleansing downpour; this humidity is making it even harder to breathe.

I jump as my phone buzzes in my hand and roll my eyes sarcastically when I see who's calling–*Mom*.

I swipe to answer and hold the phone to my ear. "Rue Chamberlain. Reporting for emotional whiplash."

There is a tired exhale of breath before my mom's refined voice responds, "Is that how you answer the phone now?"

"It is when the caller ID says Guilt Trip."

"You named me that?"

"Originally, it was Supreme Overlord of Guilt, but I opted for brevity. Plus, every time I see the name, it really raises the stakes of answering. *Guilt Trip. Accept or decline?* Hmmm."

"I'm touched," she deadpans.

"It was either that or Warden."

She sighs, but I can hear the smile behind it. "Are you coming straight home?"

"I mean, I was planning to stop for a margarita and a motorcycle tattoo, if that's what you're asking."

"That's *exactly* what I'm asking. You've got that look in your voice again."

"That's not how voices work."

"It is when you're my daughter. I know your *I'm about to make a bad decision* tone."

"Relax. I'm coming home. Chess with GG. Sass from Selma. Nothing illegal or remotely dangerous."

"Yet."

"You're very comforting, Mom."

"That's what they say in all the parenting books. Be deeply supportive and vaguely threatening."

I exhale a laugh and glance to see my rideshare has arrived. I place my earbuds in as I head to the back of the white sedan.

"You feeling okay today?" she asks, the softness slipping in like a shadow beneath the sarcasm.

"I'm fine," I say. Which is mostly true. Or at least true enough for now.

There's a pause, just long enough to say *I know you're lying, but I'll let you have it.*

"I'm making soup," she announces, and I let out a polite sigh.

I'm trying to stay chipper and witty, but I'm actually exhausted.

"The air is the consistency of soup, almost the same temperature too. Why on earth would you make that right now? Also–and this is even more important–you can't cook!"

She snorts. "You don't need to be a Michelin-starred chef to use a can opener and the microwave. Now get home before it goes cold."

"Just make sure you don't put the can in the microwave, Mom."

She sighs good-naturedly, then hangs up.

The call ends just as the clouds break. A soft drizzle begins, dotting the window as the driver pulls away from the curb. The rain drums steady on the roof of the car, soft and rhythmic, like fingers tapping out a lullaby.

I let my head rest against the cool window and try to anchor myself in that sound. It's easier to focus on something external than the ache in my chest or the knots in my mind.

I reflect on the day as the rain beats out its natural rooftop rhythms.

Sunset Gardens smelled like pear and lavender hand lotion today.

GG tried to cheat at chess again, and I let him.

Selma made me cry laughing with her deadpan review of our book club pick: "Too many feelings. Not enough murder." I brought her orange chamomile tea, and she called me her "little weirdo sweetie."

That's something, isn't it?

That should be enough.

Lives touched and impacted. Doesn't matter for how long, does it?

The car turns onto Main Street, tires hissing over wet asphalt. I squeeze the edge of my dress and watch the blurred shapes outside the window. Lights smudge like watercolors. The world is still moving. Always moving.

Do they laugh with me because they care or because they feel sorry for me?

I shake the thought off like a drop of rain, but it clings to me. The driver hums along to a song I don't know. His voice is off-key, but he makes up for it with confidence.

Will they still laugh like that when I'm gone?

I try to hold on to the warmth I felt leaving Sunset Gardens–the old fingers squeezing mine, the way Selma winked at me like we shared a secret. I tell myself that matters.

But even this most recent memory has a shadow behind it.

If I disappeared tomorrow, would the world just ... keep turning like I was never here?

I clench my jaw and shake my head, trying to scatter the thoughts like leaves in the wind. They don't go far. They never do. But I know the difference between despair and surrender. I don't want to die. I don't want to run out of time before I've said what I need to say.

Outside the window, Saint Rienne slips by in softened colors. It's a town most would overlook on a map–tucked just north of New Orleans, hidden somewhere between myth and memory. It's the kind of place that feels dipped in nostalgia, even while it's still happening. It's a patchwork of wrought iron balconies, rainslicked cobblestones, and pastel buildings that look like they've been washed and repainted a dozen times by ghost hands. Spanish moss drapes the live oaks like tattered lace. Bougainvillea vines cling to painted brick, their blooms bright against the grey.

A trio of old women huddles beneath a shared umbrella, arguing in French over pastries in a bakery window. A jazz quartet plays under the green awning of a coffee shop, undeterred by the weather, their brass notes curling into the mist like a hymn for the dying day. Tucked between the café and the bakery like a secret the street's trying not to tell, a voodoo shop leans slightly to one side–its shutters half closed, its windows fogged with time. Purple candles burn low behind the glass, their flames barely flickering, and a faded, painted sign hangs overhead that simply reads *OPEN*, as if it has always been and always will be.

I watch the beads of rain race each other down the glass, tracking them like constellations I'll never name. Each street we turn down carries its own memory–festivals, open mics, ghost tours, bookstore signings I was too tired to attend. Places I said, "I'll go next time." But time is a shrinking thing now. It used to stretch before me like a runway, but now it folds inward like origami.

Still, I love this place. I love the crooked windows and patina and all the wrought iron. I love the scent of jasmine in the rain and the way even the cemeteries here feel strangely alive.

It's beautiful in that noble way that old things are beautiful–in their resiliency, the effortless way in which they still stand. Still try.

Kind of like me.

I press my forehead to the cool glass and let the world blur, everything softened by the downpour and my own fraying focus. The fog on the window blooms beneath my breath.

This town has always felt like a prelude. A half chapter before the story cuts off. I don't get the next act. Not really. Not the one with road trips, promotions, or heartbreaks that take years to recover from.

And I'm not bitter about that. Not exactly. I've made my peace with the horizon.

But sometimes, when I let myself think too long, I ache for a version of me that never got to be.

I don't need statues. I don't need my name etched in gold. But I want someone to read my words one day and pause. Just for a moment. And think, *She was here.*

I close my eyes and whisper to the rain, "Let that be enough."

It takes a little over an hour before the car slows in front of my house. Porch light still burned out. The mailbox leaning. My home. My graveyard of unread books and unfinished stories.

I open my creaky door with all the subtlety of a haunted house attraction. I wince and slip off my shoes, inching past the umbrella stand and coat rack with the delicacy of a cat burglar.

My goal: get past the kitchen undetected, avoid cold canned soup, and bypass a mom-ologue until she leaves for the airport and goes back to her loft in Chicago for another art exhibit.

I pause my ninja-like movements when I hear the family grandfather clock begin its hourly intoning. After six dull strokes, the silence is filled by her voice in the kitchen.

"No, she's just been so tired lately." I hear her padding around in the kitchen, putting dishes away. "I know it's expected," she continues, "but that doesn't make it easier to watch. She keeps pretending it's fine, and I keep pretending I believe her."

There's a beat of silence, followed by a brittle laugh.

"Yes, I know it's her choice. I know. But some days, I just want to shake her pretty face and say, *Stop being so damn stubborn and come back home with me.*"

My stomach twists. My fingers tighten around the strap of my bag as I lean against the wall and close my eyes.

Ugh, Mom.

She sounds like someone who's trying not to drown while being stuck in the middle of the ocean. She's been begging me for two years to move to Chicago with her permanently. I can't leave this home though. I won't. Always the stubborn one, she stated she would move here then. That idea lasted a week, and we were at each other's throats. My mom needs the busy city, the high fashion, the eccentric art scene. She needs skyscrapers, concrete, and stainless steel. I like … well, I like chess with GG, book club with Selma, and the cobblestones.

Still, I love my mom dearly, so I square my shoulders and do what any emotionally unstable, terminally ill twenty-six-year-old would do in this moment of quiet vulnerability.

I drop my bag, lie flat on the living room rug, and fold my arms over my chest in what I consider to be excellent corpse formation.

Mom rounds the corner thirty seconds later and gasps like she's discovered a body.

"Rue! What on Earth–don't do that!" she shrieks, pressing a hand to her heart like I shaved five years off her life. "Honestly, darling, it's so morbid."

I crack one eye open. "You should probably see someone about those lines once you get back home," I state dryly as she rears back, turns to the mirror hanging by the door, and begins to pull her face taut.

She gasps again–genuinely scandalized–still tugging at her temples like she's trying to reverse time. "Excuse me?"

"I'm just saying"–I keep my tone bored and flippant, which only fuels her annoyance–"you're already behind in the race. Let's not throw in the towel completely."

She glares at me, and I give her a smirk before sticking out my tongue.

"You are an insufferable child," she mutters, turning fully toward me, causing her ridiculous number of bracelets to clink together, sounding like a one-woman percussion section.

"And yet here you are. Still visiting. Must be the charm." I wink, causing her to roll her hazel eyes.

She releases a sigh. It's classic Cerulean–over the top, theatrical, and dramatic.

"I'll have you know, these"–she gestures to her face–"are your fault."

I sit up slowly; there's an odd pain in my chest, but I ignore it, keeping my smirk intact. "Really? I always assumed they were from that yoga retreat where you 'found yourself' as well as a third-degree sunburn."

"Rue." Her voice drops to a deadly octave. "We do *not* speak of Arizona."

"Oops."

She swats at me, laughing, and it hits me—how much I miss this. The noise and the nonsense, the joking and smiles. Now I'm left with these small rays, followed by the way she looks at me when she thinks I'm not paying attention. Like she's trying to memorize every detail in case it's the last time.

I know the look. Because I give it to myself in the mirror more often than I care to admit.

She crouches beside me, smoothing stray pieces of orange-and-black hair behind my ear. "It's bad enough I'll have to see you this way one day far too soon. Let's not do the dress rehearsal."

"I'm just figuring out the best arm placement," I mumble, feigning nonchalance. "Over the chest seems a bit judgy, like I'm eternally disappointed about something."

She snorts. "You're right. Maybe this." She flips up both middle fingers in a neat double salute.

I cackle. "Mom, can you imagine the funeral?"

"I insist. If I have to live through that unimaginable day, I'm getting *some* artistic input."

"You'll be too busy cashing in on my ghost to worry about my corpse pose."

She clasps her hands to her chest. "You wound me."

"Ha! You exploit me."

She pulls me into a careful hug—tight enough to feel like something, gentle enough not to hurt.

"I love you, Rue," she whispers into my hair.

I freeze, just for a moment. Rarely do Mom and I say that we love each other, not because we don't. It has just never been our dynamic. That was something Dad and I shared.

I smile. "Feelings make you wrinkle. Careful."

She pulls back with a watery laugh, and the pain

behind her eyes nearly knocks me over. "You are incorrigible."

"I love you too, Mom."

She checks her phone. Her ride's here. I escort her to the door.

She pauses, and the look on her face is almost one of fear. "I could stay."

"And miss your exhibit? What would the community think?" I smirk playfully.

"Fuck them." Her words catch me off guard. "Tell me to stay, Rue."

It's not a demand; it's nearly a plea. One I can't answer because if I look at her and tell her that my heart is racing like a hummingbird's wings and my literal bones ache, she would stay, and her memories would be forever tainted with the pain I endured every day. No, that's not the story I want her to tell. I won't allow it. I just need a couple of weeks to relax in bed, and then she can come back.

"Mom, go," I insist. "Go mingle and let everyone be dazzled by the great Cerulean Oaks. I'll be here."

"You'll text me?" she urges, ignoring the driver honking his horn.

"I always do."

"And you'll eat?"

"Yes. Probably not that soup though."

She exhales before leaning in and giving me a brief hug. Pulling back, she looks at my hair as she shakes her head. "You and your crazy colors. It looks like a pumpkin vomited."

"Bold words, coming from the woman who once paid how much to glue faux fur on a canvas and called it a 'critique on contemporary mores.'"

We share a laugh before the driver honks again.

"Rue," her voice cracks softly. "You know that I... well–"

Giving her my best smile, I wave with both my hands. "I know. Go. Before your driver leaves and you're stuck haunting me."

She grins. "Don't tempt me," she calls back as the door clicks shut behind her.

And I drop my smile.

Just like that, the act is over. No audience, no reason to pretend. I wrap my arms around myself as I sit on the couch, staring at the blank TV screen.

She's scared. I know that.

So am I.

Chapter Three

MARRIED TO THE JOB

KANE

One Hour Before the Present

"**A**ND ANOTHER THING!"

The woman hurls her phone at me. I don't flinch. I don't move. I merely tilt my head, watching with faint curiosity as it passes clean through my incorporeal form and hits the wall with a delicious *crack*. Her eyes go wide. Her mouth snaps shut.

Finally, some peace.

Most stop screaming after that–nothing humbles the recently deceased like throwing a tantrum at someone who can't be touched.

I cross my arms and exhale through my nose. Not out of necessity, just routine.

She's still breathing heavily, which is rich, considering her lungs are currently more memory than matter.

Rolling my eyes, I remind myself why I'm here. *She has to cross over.*

And I'm the one assigned to make that happen. *Lucky me.* Reaper, death guide, post-life concierge–whatever one wants to call it, it's my job. And apparently, because nobody likes an unhappy soul, I have to do it with something resembling a smile. It's in the *Reaper Regulations Guidebook*.

Which I find absurd, of course. I died centuries ago, and any customer service I had left in me evaporated somewhere between the devastation of the plague and the invention of social media.

It's not that I hate the job. I simply loathe the part where the living assume I care about their problems. Like they're the only ones.

Crossing my legs, I lean back against the wall and wait for her to finish reattaching her ego. She's one of the loud ones. A lot of them are at first. Mortals cling to their sense of importance, right up to the moment they realize the universe didn't even pause to mourn them. But I've been doing this long enough to know how it ends. And in the meantime, I listen to them wail about meetings and latte orders and unfinished business, as if their entire life wasn't already a montage of things left undone.

This one is particularly dramatic. Or maybe it's her knock-off shoes that are especially loud on the marble.

Either way, she's annoying, and she's chewing up her crossover countdown.

From the moment of death to the final chance to decide, souls are given a small window to make a large decision. It's not arbitrary, nor is it symbolic. It is some cosmic law carved into the marrow by Time herself. A brief sliver of time to choose whether they'll come with me to the OtherWorld or stay tethered to this one.

If they follow, they cross. If they refuse, they remain.

Not alive. Stuck. Anchored by unfinished business, delusion, or plain old stubbornness. They are left to wander between the cracks of this world until they become nothing but noise in a hallway or a cold spot in someone else's memory. They think they're clinging to some perceived purpose, but really, they're circling the drain.

Ghosts mostly. Souls, if you're feeling romantic.

I try not to feel romantic. It never ends well.

The window closes quickly on the mortal's final decisive action, and once it snaps shut, there is no reopening it. At least not from me. That's above my pay grade.

I'm just the usher. *The collector.* The one with the clipboard and the coat and the polite apathy that comes from watching a thousand versions of the same story unfold over and over again.

And she's spending hers yelling about a meeting. A *meeting.*

Every second ticks inside my head like a metronome. A countdown. She has very little time, which she is flagrantly wasting.

Will she realize nothing she's clinging to matters anymore? Can she let go of a life that no longer belongs to her? Will she take control of the last thing she has any actual control over?

Most of them take it down to the wire. Something always trips them up–denial, regret, panic.

Occasionally awe. But never peace. Peace is earned, not granted.

And this one continues ranting and employing projective phone technology.

Pity.

"The next time someone decides to pull me out of a meeting for something so frivolous–" she begins again.

I sigh. Loudly. "You were giving a PowerPoint on quarterly projections. You'll forgive me if I don't hold a vigil."

She freezes. Her head turns slowly, like a broken doll, eyes narrowing. "A lot is riding on that pitch."

"And now you're dead," I reply dryly. "Which, if I may, slightly outweighs the importance of your Q4 pitch."

Her mouth opens and closes, resembling a fish out of water, like she's trying to remember how to breathe in a world where the rules have changed without her permission.

"Don't be ridiculous. I'm not dead, you cretin."

Name: Katherine Sinclair

Age: 54

Occupation: Media executive

Time of Death: Four minutes and seventeen seconds ago

Cause: Sudden cerebral aneurysm while micromanaging a meeting and eating a turkey sandwich

It's shocking how many times turkey accompanies a death.

I don't need the file really. I know her type. They come through all the time—tightly wound, high-achieving, over-caffeinated mortals who thought legacy was something they could brute-force into permanence.

And yet here she is. Already halfway to translucent.

She's pacing. Well, not pacing—her feet make no sound, and she leaves no mark—but she performs the *idea* of pacing like a windup toy let loose on a countertop.

While every case is *technically* unique, I've watched the denial cycle play out through so many faces that it's become background noise. Still, I'll give her some credit—this one manages to lace her denial with such pure, un-diluted rage that it almost makes me nostalgic.

Almost.

"I assure you, Ms. Sinclair, you are most certainly dead," I say, glancing at the clock on the wall, hoping she'll get the hint. "Now, are you prepared to come with me so we can begin your intake process? Your case-worker in AfterLife Processing, or ALP, is waiting to help you get assigned and settled into your new reality in the OtherWorld. Or are we planning to spend the rest of your final minutes playing corporate charades?"

She stiffens like I insulted her stock portfolio. Her eyes flare with fresh indignation, dark with the kind of contempt only executives and reality TV judges can properly conjure. "I can't be dead. I have too much to do."

Ah. The classic. *Everyone's too important to die.* As if mortality consults their calendars.

"Listen, ma'am—"

"*Ma'am*?!" she barks, eyes snapping like a hinge about to break. "Oh, I don't think so. You're not going to sweet-talk me into anything, Mr. Men's Suit Barn. Who is your supervisor?"

Suit Barn? This is a double-breasted, custom-tailored Cifonelli work of art.

I suppress a smirk. "I answer directly to the division head, but I promise you there is nothing my boss can do for you that I cannot. Including keeping you from haunt-ing the sixteenth floor of your office building forever like a boardroom poltergeist."

Her lips part in protest, but I hold up a single hand.

"Do you know what happens if you don't make a

decision soon?" I glance at the clock on the wall for her benefit again. "Time is unforgiving, Katherine. She waits for no one."

Her brow twitches.

"A decision will be made for you. And that decision involves you spending the rest of eternity here. You linger. Pointlessly. No function, no impact on the world around you. You become a ceaseless, passive observer of a story that has moved on without you. Now, I can make you cross over. My boss would prefer it actually." I think about the Death-issued reaper blade in my pocket and the carnage caused in the past by its edge. "But, Kat, call me old-fashioned. I think when faced with your final free act, I should do your legacy the honor of allowing you make the call. For better or, as it's looking in your case, for worse."

A flicker of uncertainty cuts through her fury, but she masks it with practiced bravado.

"Okay, listen," she tries again, voice shifting gears, angling into the slippery silk of the bargaining phase. "You might not know this, but I'm a very important person. Lots of people depend on me. I've got teams, clients, investments. I just turned fifty, so clearly, there's some sort of misunderstanding happening here."

I lift a brow, dry as dust. "*Fifty-four* actually. Naughty fib, Ms. Sinclair."

She flinches.

I press the advantage, voice smooth as a scalpel. "Your daughter just started her freshman year at NYU. You missed her last call, by the way. Your ex-husband remarried a yoga instructor, who owns a gluten-free bakery and has very flexible morals. And you? You buried yourself so deep in quarterly forecasts and executive strategy meetings that when your body hit the ground, no one even heard the thud for a solid three minutes."

Her mouth falls open.

"In case you're wondering," I add casually, "that was long enough for your assistant to send two instant messages, reschedule your calendar, and wonder aloud if she'd get a promotion now."

Silence swells like a tide.

And in that stillness, the final layers of her ego begin

to splinter. Not enough to break her, not yet. But it's starting. They always do, right around the metaphorical moment that the window is about to seal and they realize there is no turning back.

Her voice, when it returns, is smaller. "So, that's it then? That's how I go?"

I shrug, straightening the collar of my suit jacket. "You could have gone in your sleep. You could have gone holding your daughter's hand. You went screaming about a slide deck. I don't make the rules. I just collect and cross."

She blinks and shakes her head.

"Window's closing," I state.

She'll either choose to come with me—accept the ending and begin what comes next. Or she'll spend the rest of her afterlife screaming at her own reflection in the glass of an elevator no one rides anymore.

"The choice is yours, Katherine, but remember, the clock ticks down the same, and once it reaches zero, there's no turning back."

I drink in the look on her face like a sommelier savoring a rare vintage. Shock, disbelief, outrage—it's all there, pouring from her wide eyes.

"How *dare* you speak so disgustingly about my life? My–my legacy!" she snaps, and the air itself seems to tremble with her indignation.

"Respectfully, Ms. Sinclair," I sigh, ready to move this along, "get over yourself."

She opens her mouth again, stunned.

"We all go in the end," I continue smoothly. "Some with grace. Some kicking and screaming in fake heels that aren't fooling anyone. You, so far, are doing neither with any real flair."

Her shocked silence is gratifying, if only for a short time.

"But look on the bright side—crossing over doesn't have to be your finale. In fact, if you come with me, you'll continue your existence in the OtherWorld. And while I can't tell you exactly what it will be for you, it'll be better scenery than this beige purgatory of recycled air and motivational posters."

I gesture to the office around us, an echo of her

once-treasured kingdom now slowly losing its definition as her presence fades.

"So, what do you say?" I ask, voice lilting with theatrical charm. "Ready to shuffle off this mortal coil and get out of this glorified filing cabinet?"

Her lips twitch, and for a moment, I think she might laugh. But instead, she exhales a soft, crumbling breath. "I can't leave," she murmurs. "I have shows in production. Teams that need me. I have stories left to tell. So much still inside me. It can't end like this. It's too–" Her voice cracks. "It's too sad."

Ah. Depression. Right on cue. They always hit this phase hard when the denial starts to lose its sheen.

I try to give her descent the courtesy of my full attention–weepy revelations do so love an audience–but the subtle buzz from my Tombstone Phone cuts through the moment like the blade in my pocket. I glance down, expecting a passive-aggressive reminder about paperwork from one of the interns.

But no. It's Big D himself.

Big D: What is taking you so long? Check in immediately. —Big D

I straighten, my spine stiffening on instinct. Even in death, some names command obedience.

Katherine's voice drifts in again, low and shuddering, somewhere between grief and self-pity. "I just … I wasn't finished. I had more to give."

"They always do," I mutter under my breath.

Aloud, I say, "Ms. Sinclair, that was my boss–"

"Your boss from the underworld *texts* you?"

"It's timeless technology," I deadpan. "And it's the OtherWorld, not the underworld. I mean, it is below us, but Corporate didn't like the optics. Now, I really must attend to this urgent matter–"

"I just *died*," she snarls, voice rising. "I'd say that's pretty fucking urgent too!"

"To you, yes," I reply coolly. "It's a personal crisis. But cosmically? It's just another Tuesday. Now listen. Your window is closing. Your soul's still soft enough to mold, but the clock is ticking, and I'm done begging."

With a flick of my wrist, a smooth ivory card appears between my fingers. I hold it out like an afterthought.

"This is your intake information. Present it to the clerk in the AfterLife Processing Department. They'll assign your file and start your transition paperwork. With this card, you'll avoid the lines and get preferred treatment. I know how important that is to you."

She stares at it, back at me, and crosses her arms, which are already beginning to grey at the edges. "No."

My phone buzzes again.

Big D: Now. —Big D

"Fuck," I mutter, the word coated in venom as I lower the card. "Ms. Sinclair, this is not a negotiation. If you don't accept this card *right now*, your essence will remain tethered to this floor for eternity, not in power, not in glory. You'll be trapped. A pale echo. An office ghost."

"I belong here," she declares, smug and absolute. "This is *my* building."

"Was," I correct coldly. "It *was* your building."

But the decision's already been made. I watch as her figure begins to unravel, her arms fading into the air. Her feet lift an inch off the floor, and her final hues of living color fades to grey. She's chosen the static. The slow fade. The purgatory of her own ego.

Another soul lost.

"Good luck with the rest of your afterlife, Ms. Sinclair," I say, tucking the card back into my coat pocket. "Try not to knock too many staplers off the desks. Some people here still have real work to do."

I shake my head in frustration. Big D won't be pleased. Then again, neither am I.

Since my untimely and particularly theatrical exit from my waking life centuries ago, I've spent the afterlife punching the celestial clock for the grandest bureaucracy you've never heard of–Death's Door, LLC.

Not sure why he would need to limit his liability. Not like anyone can sue him. Big D's idea. "Branding," he called it. It was supposed to make the business of dying sound modern, efficient, and palatable to recently crossed souls, who were choking on their own fragility. People get too many trophies nowadays.

I'm the Lead Reaper of the Natural Causes Division. Fancy title. No pension, no benefits—just an eternity of peeling souls out of failing meat sacks and sending them through to AfterLife Processing with a nod and a folder full of postmortem paperwork. Before this, I served in Atrocities, followed by Overkill. Both were less than favorable departments. No rules, no order. It was constant screams and chaos. I clawed my way out of those trenches to a brief stint in Accidents to where I am now.

The deaths I handle are mostly quiet. Bedside exits. Sleep-softened farewells. Gentle handovers at the end of a long line of mortal days. I get the occasional resistant soul, but, hey, fear of the unknown and all that. I get it.

I work alone. That's not a policy; it's a preference. No rookie reapers bumbling into mortal bedrooms with their blades still sharp and their consciences intact. No bright-eyed interns asking me how to "ease the client's transition." I'm not a fucking doula. It's death. It's supposed to be hard.

A few associate reapers report directly to me. Or they try to anyway. I'm what you would call a hands-off boss. I also generally don't bother learning their names because most of them don't last long.

My tenure has paved a path to crushing boredom and ceaseless ennui. The only thing I've learned in my centuries of unliving? Nothing matters.

Bleak but true, to paraphrase Big D's favorite band, Metallica.

Musical taste aside, I don't actually despise Big D. He's always liked me. Took a shine to me the second he assisted in my crossing. I still remember the pints of blood spilling into the cracks of the wood of my home's floor. He stood over me like a shadow wearing a crown. Told me I had moxie as I choked on my own pride.

He gave me the job before my body cooled. Didn't even send me to ALP. Said he could "sense something" in me.

Daryl. That's his real name. Not Death, Doom, or Damien. No, no. Just Daryl. And if you ever call him that to his face, make sure you've already picked your replacement because your second death won't be as pleasant as your first.

Since his promotion to the position of Death, D doesn't

work crossovers anymore. He's too important, he claims. More like too busy trying to look busy, but, hey, he took over the top spot, so we play by his rules.

This conversation is probably going to require my undivided attention, and while the living can't see me, I can still hear them, so I decide to head to the roof.

I step into the service elevator and take it up. It's not a gentle ride. This rickety box jerks me to the top like I've been hooked and reeled by a novice fisherman. Transporting would have been much smoother, but that's reserved for trips between worlds and case arrivals. Once I'm here, it's mortal means of conveyance for this guy.

After several shuddering seconds, I find myself on the rooftop of Ms. Sinclair's high-rise building.

The moment I'm alone, I press the flame-red Call button on my phone's display.

It doesn't ring. It never rings.

He always answers instantaneously.

He's always there, waiting.

"Kane."

My name isn't spoken; it's *summoned*. Death's voice isn't loud; it doesn't need to be. It pours through the line like chilled syrup, seeping beneath the surface of my skin.

"Where the fuck have you been?"

The profanity doesn't dull the gravitas. If anything, it's worse. Casual authority is the most dangerous kind.

"I called as quickly as I could," I state. "And respectfully, sir, you don't have to sign every message *Big D*. I know who you are."

"I'll do whatever I want, Kane. And you will do whatever I ask. Now, where are you?"

"Just finished with the Sinclair case. Or rather, she finished herself." I sigh, jaw tight. "She didn't cross. Your message cut into the last sliver of her window."

"So, you lost another one?"

I wince. It isn't a question.

"Married to the job, boss," I answer coolly. "Now she gets to spend eternity wandering the carpeted halls of the Titan Media headquarters as a uniquely vengeful, spreadsheet-obsessed ghost."

A coiled silence springs out between us.

"Unbelievable." The word drops like a gavel. Not yelled or barked. Just delivered. "You would think after the mandatory seminar I just held about better reaper/reapee relations, you would've had this one in the bag."

"No one was tearing this woman from this place."

Big D exhales slowly, like the world's about to end and he's been through it before. "Your ARVD case has gone into transition early. Unrelated to her condition, but still a heart issue. But that's not the point. The point is you need to get your ass over there and extract the soul before you lose two souls in one day. Deliver her to AfterLife Processing yourself if you have to. That's your job. Collection."

I nod barely. "Understood."

He keeps going. He always does. "I hate this atrocious era. Technology has turned into a curse. Ghost hunters, spirit videos, EMF readings posted to social media—it's a circus. The moment a soul lingers too long, someone snaps a video. The footage gets filtered, slowed down, and then goes viral. It was all fun and games when the cat was in the vase. Now, the living are starting to ask questions they have no business asking. That's when the Weaver Sisters get twitchy. And when they get twitchy, I get calls. I hate calls, Kane."

I say nothing. Not because I agree, but because I've learned it's less work to let him wear himself out.

He continues with that smooth, suffocating timbre only Death can pull off. "Your job is containment. Not curiosity. It's really not difficult, Kane."

I pinch the bridge of my nose—harder than necessary.

"Yes, sir. I've got it. You can count on me," I state before disconnecting the call.

It's a lie—maybe. Or maybe not.

Depends on what I do when I get there.

Name: Rue Chamberlain

Age: 26

Diagnosis: Unknown heart disruption

Status: Premature crossover in progress

Last Words: Mayday.

I nearly drop my tombstone when I see her photo.

I know her.

The girl from that community center in New Orleans. She was there while I was handling a reap. Not my own case. It was actually a cleanup from my former junior reaper, who left half the soul flailing and screaming in the body. It was a mess. I remember threatening to shove the whiny reaper wannabe into The Nothing for such a heinous mistake when I saw *her*. She was talking to someone about a du Maurier novel, and it caught my attention. Well, that, and her contrasting orange-and-black hair and that long black dress with green combat boots.

Her eyes stopped me. Not because they were beautiful–though they were–but because they held something I could not recall seeing before. Her stormy-grey eyes were steady, unafraid, and as she looked right at me, I felt it rattle something loose in me. A thread pulled taut across ages, finally giving way.

Okay, she didn't actually see me, but seemed to *feel* my presence. Most can't. We are trained to slip in and out undetected. Some say that very few can feel us, and when she looked right at me, mere inches from my face ... I don't know ... it was an unsettling moment that I've been trying to forget. And now she's my next case.

Big D's threatening directive plays in my mind. Failing to cross two souls in a single day would be unprecedented for me, and not without its consequences.

But something in me–something buried and rusted over from centuries of blind obedience–doesn't seem to care about that right now.

Maybe it's instinct. Maybe it's idiocy. I'm not sure I know, but the feeling hits me like a slap across the face and cannot be denied.

I'm tired of being a lackey for the bureaucrats of the OtherWorld, and there is something different about this soul, I could sense it even in that briefest of moments.

I grit my teeth and vanish in a pulse of light, knowing full well that this is going to come back to bite me.

Chapter Four

STONE-COLD

RUE

Thirteen Minutes Before the Present

I INHALE SHARPLY AS I COME TO. LOOKING AT MY PHONE, I NO-
tice I've been asleep on the couch for over an hour.
I wish I could say it helped, but it didn't. The silence
settles in around me, heavy but familiar.

I pass through the kitchen, my socks whispering
over the tiles–and pause.

All the cabinets are open.

Plates are stacked in strange little towers, teacups
balanced like they're part of some abstract sculpture. It's
not my handiwork, and while Mom is known for her theatrics, she's more "crushed velvet and socio-commercial
criticism" than "poltergeist performing art."

I sigh. "I'm not in the mood for you today, asshole."

Something whooshes by my left ear, and a ceramic
plate shatters against the wall with theatrical flair.

"Oh, for fuck's sake," I mutter, flipping the ghost my
most expressive middle finger. "We get it. You're very
scary!"

I've grown up with this ghost. As a child, it was my
imaginary friend. Never could see it or hear it, but they
would make themself known. As I grew, I heard from
them less and less. Then my parents split up, and Mom
and I moved to Chicago. I would come down here during
my dad's offseason, and it was rare that the ghost would

pop up. But since Dad passed two years ago and I moved down here permanently, the jerk has become a daily nuisance.

I make my way toward my bedroom, which is on the main floor now because the stairs and my body no longer negotiate terms. So, now, I try to limit the times I have to exert myself on those stairs. The last thing I need is to get dizzy and fall. It has happened before.

I enter my newly appointed first-floor bedroom, hopeful I'll return to a normal baseline after some rest. My body aches, and I feel the tightness in my chest. I press my hand just below my collarbone, rubbing in slow circles, as if I can ease the pressure lodged there. It doesn't help much. It never does. But the motion is muscle memory now, an old habit at this point.

Inside my room, I close the door with a soft click and lean against it. The wood is cool against my spine. I close my eyes. Just breathe.

The exhaustion isn't just physical; it's cellular. Fatigue that hits marrow deep. It never leaves.

Something soft brushes against my ankle. I open my eyes to see Esther–the true queen of this house–twining around my legs. She headbutts me once, then plops dramatically onto her side, tail flicking.

"Well, hello, Miss Sass," I murmur, bending down slowly to stroke her soft fur. "Can I tell you a secret?" I pick her up and nuzzle her nose as I whisper, "You're the only creature I like haunting this place."

Her presence brings a sense of comfort, a reassurance that I'm not alone in this struggle.

She purrs–a declaration of her loyalty, her unwavering support.

I lie on top of my bed, and I stare at the ceiling. My soul hurts today. I miss my dad.

My gaze drifts to the wall across from me, where books line the shelves like old friends. These books have always been my refuge, a secret society that my dad gave me the password to many years ago. But the escape of fantasy feels fraught right now in the face of my bleak reality.

My journal rests solidly on the nightstand. I derive comfort simply from seeing it sitting there, existing.

I reach for it, the cracked leather cover soft and worn from years of use. The weight of it in my hands is not just physical, but a reminder of the significance of writing in my life. The pages are dog-eared and ink-stained, filled with poems and stories I have not dared to speak aloud.

The act of writing, of pouring my thoughts and feelings onto the page, is a form of therapy for me, a way to make sense of the chaos within. Words matter, and they outlive our physical form. Someone, someday, might read my thoughts and think, *I get her.*

And if they don't?

Well, Poe only made nine bucks off "The Raven," and look how that turned out.

I flip through the pages, scanning some of my own words.

I scribble a few notes in the margins of one of my works in progress, then close the notebook reverently.

Esther curls beside me, and I press the journal across my traitorous heart like leather-bound armor. The weight of it settles my breathing. Another sharp ache pulses behind my sternum, and I rub at it again, slow and firm.

My heart will fail me sooner rather than later. An unfortunate genetic curse handed down to me by my dad.

I think about what will happen to this house when I die. A thought occurs to me, and I can't help but chuckle. Mom will absolutely turn this place into a haunted artist retreat the second I'm gone. She'll swan about in chiffon, sighing dramatically as she tells guests about the tragic daughter who haunts her own home.

And you know what? She'll make it beautiful.

I close my eyes and focus instead on the thunder as it booms and rolls across the roof like a haunted orchestra with no conductor. Each lightning strike is a dramatic crescendo, each raindrop a melancholic note. It rattles through the bones of the house, deep and rhythmic, and I let it settle into mine.

Some people flinch at storms, but not me. I've always loved them. There's something romantic about the way the sky unravels and demands attention. Storms don't pretend to be anything but what they are. They come undone in a furiously loud sight. I admire that frankness.

There's a strange kind of peace in it too–the way the air stills before the crack, the hush that makes even the ghosts pause. Thunder reminds me that the world's still turning. That a force that has seen generations come and go still thrashes and breathes and sings.

I inherited this old Victorian home after my father passed away, just like I inherited his heart condition. Heart and home–both faulty, stubborn, and prone to giving out when you need it most. The house is an elegant, crooked thing–paint peeling in places, windows warped with time, shutters that groan when the wind kisses them just right. It leans a little to the left, like it's tired of standing, but hasn't quite given up. But in its imperfections, it holds a unique charm that I've come to appreciate.

It suits me.

The gables are sharp and spired, slicing into the sky like ink strokes on parchment. The porch wraps around like a warm embrace that never lets go, and inside, every creak of the floorboards sounds like a story being retold. My dad always said the house was a living thing–breathing through its vents, sighing through its rafters. I didn't understand what he meant until the first night I slept here alone and realized I could hear it in my dreams. This sense of connection with the house makes me feel like I truly belong here, bringing me comfort in times of solitude.

I love this place, even if it's falling apart. Actually, I love it *because* it's falling apart in places. It reminds me of Dad and me.

That's why I don't mind the storms. They make the house feel less empty. They fill it with something electric and alive. And on nights like this, when the thunder hums in the walls and the wind sings through the chimney, it feels like the house remembers us both. Like it's keeping the rhythm of two hearts–one gone too soon, one not far behind. Our house, with its unique character and the memories it holds, becomes a place for me to reflect and feel connected to my past.

Esther stretches beside me, her little body curled tight against my hip. She's the only other creature who knows how to be still with me through all this noise.

I run my fingers through her fur as lightning flashes against the window and casts spidery shadows across the ceiling.

"I think I need some fresh air." I smile softly, giving her one last scratch as I stand. "A little family reunion at the cemetery."

Esther gives me a small, chattery meow as I make my way from my room, through the kitchen, and toward the back door.

The sky splits open with a crack of lightning just as I push open the door. Rain spits gently against the porch, not yet a downpour, but steady. That kind of quiet, persistent rain that seeps into your bones before you even realize it.

Esther follows me to the edge, her tail flicking with unease. She might be okay with storms, but that doesn't mean she wants to be outside during one.

"I'll come back if it gets bad," I promise her, which is most likely untrue. Honestly, I want to go to the cemetery and stay there until dawn.

I step barefoot into the yard, the grass cool and overgrown beneath my feet and completely drenched. The smell of wet earth rises around me—moss and old stone, iron-rich soil and something faintly sweet, like honeysuckle clinging to decay, a funeral bouquet left too long in the sun.

The family plot is small. Maybe a dozen headstones, all of them crooked. Some are so old that the letters have worn away entirely, names swallowed by time.

I've walked this path so many times that it's etched into my muscle memory.

The mindlessness of my meandering brings comfort now.

I keep walking.

The fog is low, snaking through the trees. Rain needles my skin. My dress clings to my legs as the wind tugs at the hem. I feel a bit like a ghost wandering through the dead.

My fingers dance over the top of each concrete slab, names so old that not even the stone remembers them anymore. Several of the family headstones have faded to the point that they can no longer be read. Grey stone swallowed by erosion and moss, stories lost to time.

Then I arrive at my destination—the plot I always land on whenever I make my way to the Chamberlain family resting place.

"Hey, Dad," I whisper, pressing my forehead to the cold marble. "Miss me?"

The vines have grown thicker, with green tendrils curling around the base, as if they're holding it steady. Like they won't let it fall, even if everything else around it does.

I brush away the wet leaves. "I know you never cared much for appearances, but I like your plot to look good. And you can't do anything to stop me."

I let out a laugh that sounds like a wet sob. I wait for Dad to respond. I know he won't, that he can't, but I always like to leave a little room for magic.

Once the silence has stretched like taffy, I confide in the best listener I have ever known, in life and the afterlife. "I don't know what brought me out here tonight, Dad. I can't put my finger on it, but I can't shake this feeling. It's a bit like foreboding or melancholy maybe. Anyway, you always told me to trust my instincts, and something told me to come out here and let you know just how much I miss you.

"I do, Dad. I miss you so much that it's like I can feel it."

Naming the sensation brings it into being, and a sharp pang hits my heart, followed by a tingling sensation running down my right arm. I flex my fingers.

"I wrote you something a while ago, and it plays in my head all the time. It's one of the only sonnets I've written that I have memorized. Can I read it to you, Dad?"

A crack of lightning floods the world in an instant of light, which feels like an answer to me. As the rain continues to fall, I share my words with my dad.

"I wrote this one while wrestling with the whole uncertainty of the ARVD thing. This is called 'Present.' "

PRESENT

How could I not want a gift that you gave
Me, even if it arrived in pieces?
Glue them together in gold so I save

The story of those imperfect creases.
Wonder with glee what is wrapped up inside.
It's the thought though that's truly the treasure.
A present speaks loudly what you never hide.
That your feelings for me are past measure.
Why is it then that you look rather sad?
You gave me your heart. I know it's broken.
Enough for me that it came from you, Dad.
In my chest beats a love that's unspoken.
Carry your memory in this cage of bone.
The heart we share means that I'm always home.

I finish the memorized passage and take a moment to try to unscramble my warring emotions. My gently falling tears mingle with the gently falling rain. Missing this man hurts so much. What has always been emotional pain takes physical form in this moment and stuns me out of my reverie. There is nothing metaphorical about the sharp stab that spikes in my heart. The erratic beating of my chest sends me into a panic attack.

The immediate sensation hits hard, like a punch behind my breastbone. I fall forward with a gasp, hand flying to my chest.

"Oh fuck. Fuck."

It's not a pinch anymore. It's a vise. It's a warning bell.

It's my body telling me, *This is happening.*

I press my palm flat to my chest and then drag it across to my shoulder, trying to ease the pressure. It only spreads. Fire under my skin. My breathing quickens, but nothing fills my lungs.

Panic continues to rise.

"What's–" My voice shakes. "What is this? Owww."

I curl sideways into the wet grass, rain slicking down my neck, cold mixing with heat, the thunder overhead so loud that I feel it in my teeth.

My vision blurs.

"I–I don't–"

I want to go back. I want to go home. However, I no longer know where that is. My body feels foreign. Like it's closing in on itself. Like every cell is packing up and leaving without me.

"Not yet," I whisper. "I still have–I haven't finished–"

Another sharp pulse in my chest. My arm goes numb.

I turn my head, straining to see my father's stone through the curtain of rain. It's the only one still upright. Still whole.

I think of his voice on the boat, of the calm way he'd teach me how to steer when the waves got rough.

"Now remember"–I recall the advice he gave me as a girl with the nickname only he ever used–"OO-bee, if you ever need help and you're too far out, use the radio and call out one word–Mayday."

"Mayday," I croak now, rain filling my mouth. "Mayday. May–" The word dies on my tongue. A stillness sweeps in behind it.

And then nothing.

Chapter Five

FREE WILL COMES AT A PRICE

KANE

The Present. Again.

I'VE EARNED MY STRIPES. STITCHED THEM ONTO MY COAT through centuries of servitude. But I'm feeling reckless today. Culmination of ages of mind-numbing repetition perhaps, but I'm not following the ledger this time. I'm not crossing Rue Chamberlain. Not yet anyway.

Not because I care or because I'm some sentimental fool.

I've been going through the motions for centuries, and I want to see what happens when the motion stops.

So, here I am—ankle deep in weeds, standing on soggy soil outside a Victorian manor house that looks like it was sketched by a madman with a laudanum addiction. The place looms against the dark ominously. The kind of house that feels like it's watching you back.

Behind it, the family cemetery broods. Wrought iron fencing curves around the graves like ribs around a broken heart. The headstones are crooked, leaning into the earth like they're trying to lie down for good. Moss and time have all but eaten the names off their faces. Ivy curls upward from the roots, as if it were trying to pull the dead back down.

The air stinks of damp rot and copper, like something freshly unearthed and bleeding. Thunder grumbles above me, not a warning, but a witness.

"Damn it," I mutter, crouching beside the collapsed woman. "Of all the places to drop, you pick your own graveyard. Poetic, I'll give you that."

I have a moment of clarity. A thought whispering that I should complete the job and move on. Clean extraction. Business as usual.

But I don't.

Instead, my hands move on instinct, and I press them against her chest, just over a vertical scar that peeks from the edge of her dress.

Her curls tangle in the mud. Her lips are blue. Her pulse is gone. Her soul is already half out the door, slipping past the threshold.

And I know what I'm supposed to do.

Fate and Time drew up the schedule. The Weavers wove their thread. Big D sent me with full clearance to collect her soul, by force if necessary. I am a reaper—an entity tasked with the collection of souls at their appointed time. But it isn't her time. Not yet.

I've reaped thousands of souls over the centuries, each of them slipping through my fingers like sand. I don't feel them anymore. Not really. Not since I stopped letting myself. But this one? This one I *remember*. The girl from the nursing home. Orange-and-black hair. Combat boots and a du Maurier quote that's been stuck in my head like a splinter.

So, I allow my doctoral instincts to take over and do what this place has told me never to do again. I plant my hands, fingers locked, elbows straight, and I start compressions.

"Come on, sweetheart," I grit out through clenched teeth, finding the gait with practiced ease. "Don't be stubborn."

One hundred beats per minute. A rhythm older than belly dancing. Older than me.

I should walk away. The Weaver Sisters will feel the ripple. Time will scream. Fate will snap. I should care. But I don't. I'm tired of being their blade. A good boy on a chain who jumps and speaks on command. I want to do something *because I want to*. Because I *can*. Because maybe centuries of taking orders is long enough.

I'm going to climb that mountain because it's there. That's why.

Her lips are going paler, and her face goes slack.

Shit.

"No. Not today," I growl, angling her head back.

I press my mouth to hers on instinct, simulating a breath, then another. And another. And then I feel it.

It's not the movie-magic kind of jolt. No dramatic gasp. No spark of divine light.

But *resistance.*

I feel her breath ghost against my lips. I pull back at the sensation, then watch her soul absorb back into her physical form seeing color return from her grey. That's new. Then—her eyes snap open. They are blue-grey storm clouds, unblinking and unnerving.

She stares, not with fear, but curiosity. Like something deep in her *knows* that something changed.

I stand, brushing at the grass stains on my Italian slacks. Grass stains are the least of my worries now. The Sisters are going to metaphorically flay me if I'm lucky. Flay me literally if I'm not.

"Perfect," I mutter. "Resurrect a girl, ruin the tailoring. Is nothing sacred anymore?"

She blinks once, twice, before trying to sit up.

"W-where am I?" she asks, voice thin and frayed.

"Backyard," I say. "Yours, specifically. The cemetery's got great ambiance. Five stars."

She manages to right herself and looks around the graveyard like it might give her answers. Her eyes come back to me, locking with mine in a very unsettling way.

"You're staring," I tell her.

"Who are you?" she asks.

"Dr. Kane Deveraux. Former physician, current reaper. *Enchantée.*"

"Don't see someone like you every day," she says, voice steadier now.

"I hear that a lot," I sigh. "Usually right before the screaming."

She doesn't scream.

"I died," she says slowly. "I felt it. I was *gone.* And now I'm ... not?" Her voice trembles with confusion.

I don't answer right away. Because the truth is I don't

have an explanation. I don't know what happens to a person whose body perishes without a reaper on hand to shepherd the soul. Uncharted territory for both of us. I can't let her know that though.

"Look, Mayday," I mutter, pinching the bridge of my nose so hard that it would bruise if I still had the ability. "Your heart tried to clock out early. We don't do incomplete stories."

"You must be mistaken," she states and I can practically see her mind racing to connect the dots. "I have a heart condition, ARVD. We knew this would happen eventually."

"And it will happen eventually," I reply, probably a little more stoically than necessary. "But this isn't that. Something else stopped your heart just now. A broken heart, I'd guess by all the funereal crying you've been doing."

"That can't be right," she mumbles, blinking.

"Don't interrupt. The reports are never wrong." I sigh through my teeth as I try to construct this. "My bosses have a real flair for drama, but what they *don't* have is patience. They spend eternity spinning everyone's threads into this big cosmic tapestry, and when someone starts pulling on loose threads–well, let's just say things get tangled. Chronology slips. Realities buckle. People start remembering parallel timelines, and it becomes an absolute PR nightmare."

She tilts her head like I just started speaking another language. "Spinning threads. Tapestries. Is this a joke?"

"No, and stop looking at me like that."

"Like what?"

"Like I just sprouted a second head."

She lifts one perfectly judgmental brow. "You're the one who was *on top of me* in a graveyard. Tongue down my throat, no less."

"That was CPR," I deadpan. "And if I recall, it saved your tragically short life, so maybe dial back the outrage."

She crosses her arms and scoffs, "So, how did you even know I was out here?"

"Because," I say slowly, dragging the word out like a lit cigarette, "I was the one assigned to your case."

The look she gives me could curdle blood. "Repeat that."

"I have been assigned to you." I enunciate, as if perhaps the temporary crossover affected her hearing. "As in separate your soul from your body, escort you to the OtherWorld, toss you into the great cosmic filing cabinet. You were dead. The problem is, you weren't *supposed* to be. And that"—I wave a hand at the situation like a magician performing the world's saddest trick—"is a violation."

Her eyes narrow. "Punishable by you?"

"No," I grit, already regretting this conversation. Why didn't I just follow through with proper protocol? "Death is upper management, the final decision maker. I'm a middle-tier executive. Logistics. Paperwork. Corporeal separation and spiritual delivery."

I lean against a headstone and pull out my flask, letting the burn run straight down my throat.

Her stare sharpens. "If you're here to steal my soul—"

"I don't *steal* anything, Mayday," I snap, offended. "I'm not a thief. I'm a courier with a clipboard and a deadline. I escort. I transition. When I'm feeling gentlemanly, I hold the door."

"But you brought me back," she says. And the shift in her tone—gentler now—catches me off guard. There's no bite. No sarcasm. Just confusion. "Why?"

Because I was tired of being a scalpel when I could be a stitch.

What I say instead is a bit of a shifting of the truth. "Because you jumped the queue. And line jumping pisses off the Weaver Sisters. Trust me, you do *not* want them in a bad mood. Fate may start cutting threads."

She swallows. "So, when am I supposed to die?"

"I can't tell you that," I reply automatically, eyes fixed on the rusted cemetery gate like salvation might be hiding behind it. She waits. So, I add, "When mortals know their expiration date, they start acting like every moment is a ticking bomb. They burn too brightly. They try too hard. Or worse, they don't try at all."

"But I want to know," she says softly.

It's not defiant. Not even desperate. It's just ... real. And something about that makes this harder.

I close my eyes for a breath that doesn't quite come. Centuries of this gig, and I still can't find a script for moments like these. No rulebook for the pause between a truth and the ache it will cause.

My voice comes out quiet. "Knowing changes people."

"Tell me anyway," she says, finally standing.

The words are small for the weight they carry.

I look at her. She's not glowing, not fragile, not half draped in angelic light, the way some mortals imagine they'll be after near death. No. She's sharp around the edges. Bright and breakable, but not broken. Her eyes still haven't stopped staring into mine, like they're hunting for something.

I don't want to say it. I shouldn't. No good can come from carrying the weight of that knowledge.

But she asked. Simple as that. And after already breaking the rules, what's one more?

"Nine days," I say, and the words are gravel in my throat. "You've got nine days."

A hard, heavy silence settles in the air around us.

She sways, the color draining from her face, as if someone had just pulled the plug. Her hand shoots back to the nearest headstone, fingers clawing for something solid as the axis of her world tilts beneath her.

"Nine days?" she echoes, and it sounds like a prayer turned inside out. "You brought me back, just to let me die again in nine days?"

I look away, jaw clenched so tight that it aches.

Reckless and selfish—that's the only way to characterize my recent actions. And there is no apology now to make up for the burden my spontaneous outburst has caused her.

I nod. Once. A slow, deliberate confirmation—because lies may spare feelings, but they damn the soul, and I've seen enough damned ones to know better.

"You weren't supposed to go yet," I say. My voice is quieter now.

She stares at the ground like it might open and offer her an easier exit. Her hands tremble. Then curl into fists. Her pulse is back, wild and panicked and painfully human. I can feel it, even from here, like a ticking clock stuffed inside her chest.

I did this. The thread has snapped, and I can't weave it whole again.

I gave her back the seconds she'll now have to spend.

"You're on borrowed time," I murmur, voice stripped of bravado. "Whatever it is you've been waiting to do, don't wait anymore."

She doesn't answer right away, just breathes slowly. And I let her have that moment. Because in nine days, she won't get another.

"If a week of worldly delights doesn't sell you," I say, slipping my flask back out and taking a long pull, "then take the scenic route. Gorge yourself on red meat, guzzle something vintage and ruinously expensive, find someone reckless and flexible and explore the boundaries of tantric sex. Then, on day nine, I'll come knocking and carry you across, gently of course."

Her eyes narrow like a blade being drawn. "You don't know me. You know nothing about me."

"True." I offer a half smile. "But the context clues give away a fair amount here, and I'd say you probably haven't had the most hedonistic journey through life thus far. Just offering you an opportunity here to live a little."

"Presumptuous dick," she mumbles loud enough for me to hear her clearly.

My eyes flash. "Kitten's got claws."

"Keep purring, pretty boy, and I'll have you neutered," she snaps, folding her arms. "So, let me get this straight. I'm alive again, but only for a short while, so you can kill me and drag me back to wherever I was heading, just so your bosses don't get mad?"

"I'm not the executioner," I say, jaw tightening. "I'm just the escort service. Your heart's the traitor, not me."

That lands wrong. Her hands curl into fists, and her face twists in fury. She turns and storms off like she thinks she can walk away from Death itself—which, frankly, I admire.

But then she slips.

The wet grass betrays her, slick and treacherous. I see it unfolding before it happens—her heel skids, her body twists, and her head angles hard toward the sharp granite of her father's headstone.

And without thinking or planning, I move.

I lunge. It's a reflex. Something ancient in my bones that predates protocol. My arms catch her mid-fall, fingers curling around her waist like the most natural thing in the world.

And then everything stops. Because I'm holding her. *I'm holding her.*

I freeze. My hands–dead hands, hands that have touched hundreds of souls and never once a living body–are full of her.

"What the fuck?" I whisper, staring down at the impossibility.

She gazes back, her eyes wide as her breath hitches in her chest. I instantly release her as if I'd been burned, and she drops the last inch to the grass with a thud.

"You have got to be kidding me!" she shouts, smacking the earth in frustration.

But I barely hear her. I'm staring at my hands like they betrayed me.

I shouldn't have been able to touch her.

Reapers can't touch the living. It's rule one. Basic metaphysics. The ironclad law of the OtherWorld. We pass through. We guide. We never touch. We can't.

Except …

My fingers still remember the curve of her hip. The heat of her. The weight.

I reach out without thinking, kneeling beside her, and run my hand gently along her cheek.

Soft. Warm. Real.

It's impossible.

"This can't be happening. There's no w–OW!"

Her fist collides with my jaw before I can finish the thought.

"Don't touch me!"

I stagger back, hand cradling my cheek. She's glaring up at me, radiating fury, and I don't even blame her. I'm too busy panicking. Not the mortal kind–the cosmic, existential kind. The *what does this mean* kind.

She can hit me. I can feel it. I can feel her.

And that means something is *wrong.*

"I–" I start, but my voice is hollow. I inch away from her, walking backwards in a cautious retreat.

"Hey!" she calls. "Where do you think you're going? You can't just leave!"

"I have to check something," I mutter, more to myself than her. "I have to–fuck."

I reach for my Tombstone Phone and press the Home button to initiate an immediate transport out of here. In order to transport between realms, an OtherWorlder needs to be situated in a location on Earth where someone has died or been laid to rest. So my current surroundings are super helpful for this hasty retreat.

I broke something tonight. Not just protocol. Something far worse. I'm just not sure what.

I am fairly certain though that Time and Fate are going to want my head for this.

And Big D?

He's going to want answers for my malfeasance.

Unfortunately for him, I have some questions of my own I want answered first.

Chapter Six

IT'S ABOUT TIME

KANE

WELCOME TO THE OTHER WORLD, WHERE CORPORATE POL-icy and cosmic consequence come to shake hands and stab each other in the back.

The city rises around me like a fever dream etched in stone. Gothic spires claw at the sky like they're trying to drag the stars down to answer for a crime. Streets twist in labyrinthine spirals and coil between monolithic office towers stacked like mausoleums–cathedrals of tedium, humming with fluorescent lights and bad attitudes. The whole aesthetic screams Transylvania chic, swallowed up by Wall Street.

I stand just outside the pulsating heart of this sprawling metropolis, the main corporate headquarters of Death's Door, LLC.

Everywhere you look, buildings and roadways mingle with clouds, mist, and fog in varying shades of greys and purples. Distance and shapes here toy with the eye; the physical laws of Earth stretch just enough to disorient newcomers, like the first draft of a Dali painting. If you've ever dosed hallucinogenic mushrooms in the center of the Old Town in Prague, then you have a good idea of what the OtherWorld looks like.

The massive obsidian double doors ripple like oil at my approach, melting open with a theatrical flourish. Subtle is not in Big D's vocabulary.

I don't hesitate; there's no waiting, no chitchat. I head straight for his office.

The moment I step across the threshold, D's new assistant nearly launches herself over her desk in an attempt to stop me from entering Death's Domain. Yes, he's also labeled the door within the building. He's big on alliteration.

"Oh!" she squeaks, her wide eyes darting between me and the massive set of obsidian doors. "Kane, he's extremely busy right now."

"I'm sure," I grunt, barely acknowledging her as I push past her and shove open the heavy doors.

The office is as ostentatious as ever—massive to the point of silliness, with walls made of black marble and floor-to-ceiling windows that stretch out over the OtherWorld like some kind of dramatic villain's lair. The empty space between the doors and his actual desk feels like a trick of the eye, but it really is just obnoxiously far for no reason. And at the end of the long red carpet—yes, it really does tie the room together—perched behind an absurdly large onyx desk, is the man himself.

Big D.

The nameplate glints gold in the low light, like a joke only he finds funny.

Like a man on a mission, I stalk down the absurdly long runway carpet as Big D spins around in his oversize leather chair like some bored supervillain. He's wearing a look of exaggerated amusement. In his left hand, he confidently wields …

Is that a paddleball?

"Sir?" I ask, arching a brow as he bounces the little red ball against the wooden paddle with expert precision and dexterity.

"You play?" he asks, tilting his head.

I remain standing behind the chair opposite his desk, baffled. "Can't say I've kept up with the … sport, no."

He lets out a dramatic sigh, his disappointment evident. "Shame. It's harder than you may think. It takes a fair amount of concentration, rhythm, and patience. You have to almost become one with the ball and predict its movements. And if there's even the slightest—"

The ball rebounds just a hair wide and smacks him

square in his wrist, causing him to fumble it for the first time since I entered the room. It falls to the floor with a sharp clatter against the stone.

His eyes narrow as he glares down at the toy before slowly lifting his gaze back to me.

"Misstep," he finishes, "it's game over." His voice drops to a sinister pitch.

I think I'm supposed to feel intimidated by this, but I'm too confused by the duel I just witnessed him lose to a child's toy to feel much of anything right now.

"Sir, respectfully, what are you doing with that thing? You're the overlord of the AfterLife, not a six-year-old at a state fair."

"Kane, do you have any idea how long eternity is? It's long, Kane. Really long. I have to find a way to pass the time somehow. You try spending a few millennia doing paperwork and see if you don't start talking to inanimate objects or collecting hobbies."

"Collecting *is* a hobby, sir. You don't collect the hobbies themselves though."

"Potato. Root vegetable. When I took over the head honcho position, I expected excitement, action, maybe even a little danger," he says with a childlike glint in his eye which fades as he finishes his thought. "But instead, it's mostly boooooring."

"Well, as it turns out, I do not have time for this. I have a problem."

"I know," he says with a dramatic yawn.

"You know?" I question, irritation hemorrhaging from my voice.

He shrugs one broad shoulder lazily while leaning back in his seat with a smirk. "Can't call yourself the Big D and not know all the happenings."

"You could actually not call yourself that," I point out dryly.

He snorts, leaning forward to prop his elbows on his desk. "Okay, I'll play along. I do love a good role-play."

"Don't ever say that to me again," I scoff, crossing my arms over my chest.

"What's going on, Kane? What happened?" He smirks, folding to rest his elbows on the desk like we're two colleagues catching up over espresso.

"My most recent case–"

"Rue Chamberlain," he cuts in, the name rolling off his tongue like he's reading it from a grocery list.

The casual dismissal hits harder than I expected, but I press on.

"Yes, the premature heart condition. Well, I …" I hesitate briefly, not entirely sure how to share this part. "I intervened."

"You did?" He feigns surprise in a grossly exaggerated way.

"Please stop that," I growl.

"You're no fun." He pouts.

"So, she's alive," I say through gritted teeth. "Again. But–and here's the part that brought me here so quickly, *Big D*." I make sure I have his complete attention before continuing. "She can still touch me."

"I know."

"You know?"

"I know."

"How is that possible, D? I have assisted in the crossover for so many souls. And never–not once in all this time–has a living human been able to touch me."

Big D leans back, his fingers steepled like he's about to impart some great wisdom upon me. I resist the urge to slap him upside the head with the forgotten paddleball.

I steel myself for the ingratiating tone his voice is inevitably about to take on.

"You see, Kane …" And there he goes, prattling on with a voice that manages to mix boredom with condescension into an aural cocktail that makes me want to kick him square in his thick, veiny neck. "When the order of events is thrown off, Time becomes very mad. And when she's mad–"

There's a shimmer in the air beside him, and the temperature seems to drop. Just like that, they appear. The Weaver Sisters. Time and Fate stare daggers at me, making no indication whatsoever that they just materialized out of thin air. Just another moment of omnipotence.

Neither of them says hello. They don't have to. They're not really here for a casual chat. They're here to find out why I took my leash off and ran in the street. They want to know why I've been a disobedient dog.

In my centuries of service, through plagues and battlefields, I've never been in the presence of these three immortals at once. The potential severity of playing doctor begins to dawn on me as I stare at the trio.

Big D, Time, and her twin sister, Fate.

The air itself goes still, thick as molasses, humming with the weight of power that hasn't had to announce itself in eons. Their presence doesn't just fill the room; it becomes the room.

Time speaks first, her voice curling in the air like cigar smoke in a dimly lit bar–velvet slick, languid, and low. The kind of voice that winds around your spine before you know it's there. "And when she's mad," she says, dragging the words out like the final note of a requiem, "she gets very, very mad."

She slinks behind me, a whisper of silk and shadow, her breath grazing the back of my neck. "And that ... is when Time stands still"–a pause–"for others," she finishes, her smoky murmur descending into a wicked purr, followed by a laugh that uncoils like a serpent. It's not loud, nor is it shrill.

No, it's far worse. It's patient.

"I didn't realize it would cause any harm," I offer in a weak protest. "My old medical instincts kicked in."

"And those instincts," Time hums, swaying like smoke in a storm, "have spoiled my fun." She tilts her head, one long finger trailing lazily along the line of my shoulder. "Now I need to find new fun. Can I have *fun* with you, Kane?" Her voice twists the word *fun* into something more dangerous than flirty.

"I'm not much fun," I mutter. "Ask anyone."

"Ripping you limb from limb and using your extremities as a stopwatch sounds ... delicious." She inches closer, her pupils ticking like clock gears as she scans me top to toe. "I think I could use your body to keep time down to the"–she pauses and rakes her eyes down my body, then darts her gaze sharply back to mine–"microsecond."

I shudder, my stomach turning involuntarily at the mere thought of that particular pain.

I clear my throat, angling toward the only thing that might change the subject. "Why did you jump her crossover date anyway, Time? Her chart was clear. ARVD.

Slow decline. Nine days from now. Why accelerate what is almost done already?"

Fate–draped in her ink-drenched robes and pinched fury–speaks up before her sister can. Her voice is like fire through silk. "Because my insufferable sister enjoys meddling in the storylines she is not supposed to read and most certainly not supposed to write."

"Oh, shut up, little one." Time emphasizes the word *little* with extreme derision.

The bickering commences immediately.

"You're older than me by one minute," Fate snaps, her eyes flashing silver. "One. That's nothing."

"Well, in this case, baby twin, it's everything," Time singsongs while twirling a strand of her blonde braid. "One minute in the universe longer. A lifetime of lording my wisdom and experience over you. A lot can change in a minute, can't it, Kane?" she says hypnotically, her eyes fixed on me.

I can feel her taking over my mind, forcing memories I long buried to the surface. The pain of regret and remembrance pinches my head like a vise.

My brother's betrayal. My wife's screams. Her blood on my hands. My scalpel against my throat.

I stagger, clutching my temples. "Stop that!" I scream, but her attention is drawn to her taunting sister.

"Yet all you have to show for it is the ability to keep a calendar," Fate sneers. "I, on the other hand, weave the tales," she continues, glowing with righteous fury. "You know what it takes to write a mortal life from birth to breathless end?"

Time shrugs. "Not when I choose to intervene. Nothing like a little plot twist to spice up a story."

"How many times do I have to tell you not to mess with my weavings? They are perfect."

"Perfect is boring; spontaneity is fun. Deal with it."

"So, you altered this mortal's timeline, took days away from her physical life–those precious moments we can never appreciate until they're gone–to piss off your sister?" My voice rises to a high pitch at the incredulity of their pettiness.

"That's cruel," I conclude, and Big D sucks air in between his teeth.

"You must be an only child," Time deadpans.

Fate's eyes spark, and she hovers closer to me, quickly coming to her sister's defense. "What is cruel, soul snatcher, is that you, in your infinite stupidity, managed to reveal her official crossover date. Now she's a mortal who knows the unknowable, and that makes her unpredictable, Kane. Her concept of free will has shattered. Now she feels like she has nothing to lose."

"And people with nothing to lose," Time chimes in.

"Are dangerous, Kane," Fate finishes.

"Very dangerous." Time punctuates her sister's sentiment.

Fate continues, "You've told the girl her fate. And you know what people do when they know their ending, Kane?"

Fate stops speaking, and silence fills the cavernous office.

Big D fills in with a long, "Ooh. He thought it was a rhetorical question." He lets out a low whistle as he leans back, eyes glittering.

I clench my jaw. "I do not know. I have never done anything like this in all the centuries I have been a reaper."

"Oh, congratulations!" Fate snipes. "Does the dog want a treat for good behavior? Shut up and listen."

"They try to rewrite it. I am an excellent writer, Kane. And I don't like anyone fucking with my stories!"

"So, change her timeline," I offer. "Make a new painting or weave some new thread–whatever. Just mix it up, and she won't know."

Fate and Time stare at each other for a moment before they both turn back toward me, saying at the same time, "No."

"Why not?"

Fate shrugs. "Because."

"Because what? What kind of answer is because?"

Time flashes me a smile that sends shivers down my spine. "Because we can."

"Because we feel like it," Fate adds.

"She's your problem now, Kane," Big D adds with annoying finality.

"But Time is the one who messed with the story," I protest. "Why can't she fix it?"

"She's family. You're nobody. Family first, Kane," Fate says.

"Thanks, sis," Time chirps with too much enthusiasm.

"Don't start, you meddlesome brat."

"You don't mean that, baby sister," Time coos at her sister.

"You know I do. I never say what I don't mean."

"That is true," D confirms before whispering to me, "She'll calm down. Eventually. It just takes …"

"Time–yeah, I got it," I cut D off, feeling all-around fucked.

"You are a quick study, Kane." Time slaps my shoulder.

"You're gonna do great." Fate pinches my cheek before slapping it.

"We believe in you," they sing in unison.

The Sisters rattle off in quick succession. I take a moment to collect my thoughts, knowing that one false word could bring a swift end to any comfort I've enjoyed in my position in the hierarchy of the AfterLife Processing machine.

Cautiously, I remind the entities in this room of one glaring problem. "I have a full caseload. Souls to shepherd. Spirits to cross over. I cannot babysit some mortal for days on end."

"You can," says Fate.

"And you will," finishes Time.

"Big D can be very flexible …" Fate leaves the last word hanging as she glances lasciviously toward Big D.

He glowers in her direction, his eyes lighting with barely suppressed rage.

Time finishes her sister's thought, but not before the innuendo has been given plenty of room to breathe. "With your schedule."

Big D clears his throat, then speaks. "Yes. You've been taken down to your core workload, key reaps only, and in the interim, you will be tasked with soul supervision of one 'Rue Chamberlain' until such time as her slated crossover commences."

"There you are." Fate smiles.

"Perfect." Time punctuates.

"Now then," Fate continues as her voice pitches down an octave and she gets extremely close to my face, "do not fuck this up, Kane."

"Or do," Time bubbles. "It will be fun for us either way."

Fate laughs so low that I can hardly hear it. "But if your second-chance mortal messes with my tapestry, it won't be fun for you."

"Oh, no, it definitely won't," Time confirms. "But that will still be fun for us. So, good luck, reaper."

On a symphony of cackling laughs, the Sisters' voices reverberate throughout the office, and then they vanish instantly, and the room falls deathly silent.

Big D appraises me, then smiles. "Any questions?"

My mind races and reels until it lands on the one question he still has not answered. The entire reason I came into this office in the first place.

"She can touch me, D. How can she touch me?"

His grin widens slowly. "Ah, yes," he begins, leaning back in his large leather chair. "She is an anomaly now, Kane. A rare return trip. She crossed over for two minutes and forty-nine seconds, if my records are correct."

"They always are," I drone as he speaks over me. "And they always are. Damn it, Kane. I was going to say that. Stop interrupting me."

"Okay. Go on. She was dead for almost three minutes. And?"

"And ... when she returned to the living, she brought her OtherWorld perceptions back with her. She met the Spirit Realm ever so briefly, and, well, it seems she cannot be un-introduced."

"What does that mean?"

"It means she sees and feels the world the way we do now."

"So, she can touch me and see me? Even now? For the rest of her Earth days?"

My mind races back to that last moment on Earth with Rue. I hadn't felt the touch of warm human flesh in centuries. I had buried the strength of the sensation, but it all came rushing back in an instant. A chill drips down my spine at the recent memory.

"She can see all of them. All those lost souls still loitering in the physical realm. Beings too tied to their insignificant earthly lives to begin their transition. All those cases, we—well, you and your fellow reapers anyway—failed to coax to the OtherWorld. She became a spirit, and her connection to our realm fused too tightly. So, now she is both. Vibrating between the realms. Teetering."

None of what D describes sounds good, but surely, a being of his power can do something.

"Okay, so just undo it, yeah? Snap your fingers? Set her straight until her scheduled passing."

He leans forward, resting his chin on his hands, a slow grin spreading across his face. "See, this is why I like you, Kane. You always bring the perfect balance of insubordination and stupidity to my day."

"I do what I can. So, fix this and let's move on. Come on, D. We have history."

Big D chuckles, shaking his head. "I'm afraid I can't do that. You brought her back, Kane. You introduced her to our realm. You gave her our frequency. She tuned in, and now she's riding that wavelength. And that can be a bumpy ride if someone doesn't ensure she's strapped in."

I run a hand over my face. My fingers tugging on my hair momentarily. "Okay. Whatever. She'll be fine then, I guess. I've got her flagged. I'll check in periodically throughout the nine days."

D snorts and shakes his head. "Check in? No. I'm afraid that's not good enough, Kane. You see, Rue was already in a heightened state. Her physical form is fragile right now. Living with ARVD, then struck suddenly by an acute attack of takotsubo."

"Takotsubo," I whisper, the medical clinician in me piqued at the mention of the rare disease. "So, she did die of a broken heart. How did you know that's what—"

He cuts me off, "Kane, please. That's what I do. I know things. I collect hobbies, and I know things. And I also know this: you gave her information that most mortals would not be able to handle."

"I just didn't want to see another life ended from a broken heart," I mumble pathetically.

"The heart betrays them all, Kane. Live long enough, and the heart will break. Metaphorically, perhaps. Literally, quite surely. They all bend to Time in the end."

I do not have a pithy comeback to that.

Big D continues, "And in this particular case, Kane, how do you think her renewed heart will fare? She now carries our infinite energy within her. How do you think she'll handle all of that with her–quote–'pesky' heart condition?"

The reality of the rest of Rue's mortal days slowly begins to dawn on me. The potential to spiral, for her body to give out again. The impulse to do something rash or to do nothing at all. All those possibilities flash before my mind in progressively more depressing images.

"You intervened. Now there is no backing out. You wrote yourself into her story, fool. Now you have to make it to the epilogue. She's your case. You gave her that time; now you get to guard it."

"She's not a case; she's more like a problem," I mutter.

"Call her whatever you want. Just don't call her to the OtherWorld early."

"You have got to be joking," I say more to myself than to the boss.

D leans back, completely unbothered. "Did you hear a *knock, knock* before I said it?"

"No."

"Did anyone walk into a bar?"

"No."

"Did I preface by saying, *Have you heard this one before?*"

"D, in the name of all the spirits in the OtherWorld, I know you weren't joking. It was a figure of speech. How can you have been around for millennia and still be so dense?"

"It's a gift." His deep voice rattles my bones and grates on my nerves in equal measure.

Pinching the bridge of my nose, I feel a very human urge to hyperventilate wash over me. "How? Just how?" I ask weakly.

"Frankly, my Kane, I don't give a single, solitary fuck.

But you've managed to snag the attention of the Sisters, and if you think what I have in store for you is bad–"

"What do you have in store for me?"

"If this mortal affects the natural order of life and death for others? If she manages to sculpt an image outside of Fate's design? Clerical, Kane. You'll be seeing your way to half a millennium in Clerical. So many crossovers. So much paperwork. So little–oh wait, *all the time* in the world." He laughs, the sound pressing on my last nerve. "And that's to say nothing of what the girls have planned. They can be quite"–he pauses, searching his mind for the right word–"creative."

My stomach turns at the alarming infusion of danger and sensuality in his voice.

"What am I supposed to do with her? What am I supposed to do on Earth for nine days?"

D tilts his head, his smirk sharpening. "Knock, knock."

I take a deep breath, preparing to indulge him. "Who's there?"

"Not my fucking problem," he bites and snaps his fingers.

Instantly, I'm ripped through the OtherWorld and dropped back into the damp, moss-smothered silence of Rue's family cemetery.

Of course, it's raining again.

Of course.

Chapter Seven

MY HANDS ARE TIED

RUE

MY HEAD RESTS AGAINST THE COOL, CURVED STONE OF MY father's grave as the breath leaves my lungs in one long, deliberate stream. If you listen closely, I swear you can hear my soul fraying at the seams on the sound. Maybe that's a little dramatic, but frankly, if there's ever been a time to lean into melodrama, it's after you've flatlined in a graveyard and woken up with a reaper's mouth on yours.

I press my palm to my chest, fingers splayed across the aching drum of my ribs, waiting for that steady thump-thump of betrayal to answer me.

You live. For now. I say the words in my head, matching the rhythm of my once-again-beating heart.

This is totally fine. I'm just a bit unraveled. Maybe a touch out of my mind.

But who isn't these days?

I close my eyes and press harder into the granite, like if I push hard enough, I'll fall through time and land in a moment where things still make sense. Or at least where the scariest thing I have to face is Mom trying her hand at social media or a tuna casserole.

"This is just a mental episode," I murmur aloud to the resting soul beneath me. "Like that time I mixed two medications by accident and spent an entire afternoon convinced a spotted sloth was whispering secrets to me."

I exhale a humorless laugh, brushing my hair out of my eyes. "The sloth was so smug about it too."

But that's the thing about my brain: it's never been particularly kind. It bends, breaks, and performs its little circus tricks. Some people daydream. I hallucinate men in black suits with sharp smiles and colder hands who tell me I'm on borrowed time.

I've had worse breakdowns.

I just can't think of any off the top of my head.

It's fine. I'm fine.

I sigh, rubbing my temples.

I focus on my breathing and take stock of what's real to help ground myself.

Beating heart? *Check.*

Air in my lungs? *Check.*

Shaking my head, I run my fingers through my hair. Just another delightful episode of my brain pulling a David Blaine on me.

But if that's the case, why does this one feel different?

My gaze drifts down to the name carved into the cold granite beneath me, and my carefully constructed sarcasm falters.

Dad.

I still feel it—that place, that lonely in-between. I still smell my dad. I feel that warmth. I know what I witnessed. It was no dream.

And then there was *him*. That voice, deep and silk-wrapped, curling around my bones like smoke.

I didn't even catch his name. But his presence is tattooed behind my eyes now—each word he spoke, each touch, each unbearable moment where I should have panicked but didn't, where I should have screamed but stayed silent. I still feel his lips against mine. Warm and certain. What bothers me isn't that I died. It's that when I did, someone was there—and he knew. He'd expected it. He'd caught me. Like it was routine.

Like I was on some schedule.

Nine days.

That's what he said. I have nine days left. My expiration date is stamped on the inside of my chest like I'm nothing more than a carton of milk waiting to sour.

I close my eyes and grip the headstone tighter,

fingers pressing into the carved edges of my father's name. "It's stupid, right?" I whisper. "That I'm sitting here, mourning a man who's been gone for two years while obsessing over a hallucination of a man I met for maybe three minutes."

But even as I say it, I know it's a lie. Because it wasn't three minutes. It was a lifetime. A thousand years in the dark with only the memory of his voice keeping me tethered to something that wasn't madness.

I run a hand down my arm, skin rising with goose bumps that have nothing to do with the cold. My heart flutters, soft and fragile, the same way it always does before something inside me breaks.

I am not the same Rue I was before this. Something has changed–shifted. And no matter how hard I try to shove it into a corner of my mind and label it *Delusion*, it keeps crawling back.

This is real.

He is real.

"Could really use some good fatherly advice right now, old man," I say weakly. "You would've laughed at me, you know. Said I was being silly. Called me kiddo and told me to lay off overthinking before I gave myself an aneurysm."

I squeeze my eyes shut tighter. "I miss your voice. I miss the way you smelled–salt, motor oil, and stale coffee. I miss your ridiculous dad jokes–and, no, I don't mean your clever dad jokes and the way you always ruffled my hair, no matter how many times I told you it was annoying because you somehow knew, deep down, I really liked the gesture anyway." I smile at the memory.

"Hey, Dad, what did you think of my poem? I know we were rudely interrupted, but now that I'm stable, I'd love your feedback."

I take a beat after asking the question, once again giving room for my father to answer. And after the events of the past hour, I am more hopeful than I've ever been that he just might. But it is not Dad's voice that breaks the silence.

"Miss me, *ma chère*?"

"WHAT THE ACTUAL FUCK?!" I scream, clawing at my chest.

He's back again.

Leaning against my favorite tree as if it owed him rent. That insufferable smirk plastered across his too-handsome face. Green eyes glinting like mischief-made flesh.

"Boo," he says flatly, with all the smugness of a cat who just knocked your grandmother's urn off the mantel.

"How long have you been standing there?" I question, suddenly self-conscious.

"Long enough," he answers cryptically.

"No." *This isn't happening.* "I-I don't believe in you!"

"And yet here I am, Mayday. Back to ruin your fragile little reality again." He winks while pushing himself off the tree, stalking over to me.

I continue to shake my head back and forth. This is still the dream. Or the start of a new one. It has to be.

"This isn't real," I snap. "You're not real. You're ... a hallucination." *Albeit a much more pleasing one on the eyes than the sloth, but still.*

He sighs dramatically. "So, we've only reached denial in my absence? Lovely. Let's not linger here—it's terribly boring. At least bargaining offers a little bit of flattery."

"Don't come any closer." I hold up a hand like I've got divine smiting powers. *Spoiler: I do not.*

"Or what?" He chuckles. His voice is pure, unfiltered mockery.

Lunging forward, I try with everything I have to shove him. My hands slam into his very real, very solid chest beneath his expertly pressed suit. He tenses, his eyes going wide for a half-second, like my touch just rewrote a law of physics.

All previous cockiness is gone, replaced with something akin to shock or edginess. As someone who is perpetually nervous, I easily spot this characteristic in others. But why is *he* nervous? I'm the one being haunted by a lithe interloper in my family's cemetery.

He clears his throat and steps back. "Um ..." His lips press into a thin line before he regains his composure. "It would be better if, during our interactions, you could refrain from ... contact."

"Your rule or mine?"

"Mine. Trust me, it's for your benefit." The derision in his tone borders on offensive.

"Wow. You are allergic to sincerity, aren't you?"

He has the audacity to look bored. "Can we move this along? I have another case and would like to get you safely restrained."

"Excuse me?"

"Not like that," he says, already walking toward the house. "Though I do appreciate your enthusiasm."

"Hey!" I yelp as he opens my back door like he owns the place. "I–I didn't invite you in! You don't just walk into someone's home!"

He lets out a comically exaggerated sigh, looking up at the sky, like he's personally requesting divine intervention to deal with me. He mutters something under his breath that I don't catch, but I'm pretty sure it's rude.

I cross my arms. "If you're going to insult me, at least have the backbone to say it loud enough for me to hear."

His grip tightens on my banister before he turns toward me, his eyes nearly flashing.

"Rue," he says slowly, like he's explaining basic math to a toddler, "I am not a fairy, or a vampire, or some whimsical chimera dreamed up by your feeble mortal imagination."

Rude.

"I am your reaper."

"Reaper?" I ask, stomping past him toward the dining room.

"Yes," he answers condescendingly. "And you and I are going to become really close."

"Until I die again in nine days," I say bitterly.

"Correct."

"I don't understand."

"We will have plenty of time to get into all of this because, as I thoughtlessly mentioned in our initial meeting, you have nine days left to live. And now, because of my loose lips and some fine print in my job description, until that time comes, you are under my care."

"I don't need a ghost guide for my final chapter," I insist, crossing my arms across my chest petulantly.

"I am not a ghost, Rue."

"Pale enough to pass for one," I snipe, deciding on

petty insults to lessen the anxiety this conversation is causing me.

"My skin hasn't felt the effects of the sun for centuries. What's your excuse?" he throws back at me.

"I like to read," I reply smugly.

"Ever heard of an Adirondack chair?" The way he draws out the syllables of *Adirondack* makes me wish there were one here that I could throw at him. "Anyway," he continues, "I have a case I have to attend to, and I cannot have you getting into any trouble while I'm away. Any chance you keep a couple of pairs of handcuffs around here?" He eyes me up and down. "Nah, you don't seem like the type."

"Hey!" I shout defensively.

"Oh, I do hope I'm wrong," he purrs, stalking toward me and backing me into a dining room chair.

I fume, "You're disgusting."

"You're not the first to say so. Though most people use slightly more creative adjectives. Now, until I return, you be a good girl and stay. Right. There."

Oh. Oh. He did not. I feel heat rise in my face—not from fear, but from rage.

"Good girl?" I repeat, my fists clenching.

Slowly, methodically, I look down at my mud-caked shoes. Slipping one off, I cock my arm back and toss it directly at his chest. The shoe flies through his body and knocks a vase off the wall behind him. I hear the sound of shattering glass, which feels fitting, as the last thread of my sanity breaks along with it. His eyes travel from his chest directly to my eyes, and if looks could kill, I would be dead for the second time in as many hours.

"Don't have a praise kink either then, I take it?" He chuckles darkly.

"You are insufferable! Get out of my life!"

"I'm afraid I can't do that, Mayday. We all answer to Fate. We all ring Time's brass bell. And the tune she's playing right now is a duet. Best to work on your harmonies rather than trying to rearrange the sheet music. Know what I mean?"

"Do you hear yourself? I have no idea what you're talking about."

He sighs dramatically and rolls his eyes. "Never

mind. I have a work matter I need to attend to. And I need you to sit tight until I return. Can you do that?"

My racing mind begins to slow. As impossible as everything he's told me over the past few minutes is, as unbelievable as the past hour of my–apparently–dwindling life has been, a sliver of acceptance begins to slice its way into me. I look up at the apparition in front of me. He appears as solid and as real as anything else in this room. His sharp and polished sense of style actually fits in quite nicely around all the ornate furnishings of this home.

I take the first steadying breath I've had in what feels like ages. I lock eyes with him and answer his question calmly, "No."

"No? Give me a break. I won't be gone long, and we can have a nice chat about whatever you want to know when I return."

"I'm serious! I'm not spending the rest of my life watching the clock tick down while you lurk in corners like some brooding corpse concierge."

"What do you propose then? A spa day? A wine tasting?"

"I want to go with you."

That stops him cold.

"On the reap?" He blinks, stunned. "Absolutely not."

"Why not?"

"I work alone," he states while stretching his neck.

"Apparently not for the next nine days." I smirk in challenge.

"You're not trained."

"I'll wear a helmet."

"You don't have clearance."

"I only have nine days to live. Remember? Wouldn't want to waste a second of it."

His jaw tightens. "I said no."

"And I said I'm not staying here."

We stare each other down like opponents at high noon. Finally, he groans, scrubbing a hand down his face like I'm the source of all his immortal migraines.

"This is going to end horribly," he mutters.

"Probably, but at least it'll be interesting."

"Look, get comfy. Perhaps read a novel. Order some pizza, and it will be over before you know it."

Moments from my life flash in my mind. Memories and experiences flit through like an old-timey movie. I think about all the things I've done. More achingly, I think of all the things I have not done. And now I know the clock is officially running out. We all know we are going to die; it's life's only inevitability. But who in this world has ever known exactly when they were going to die? If this tall drink of water thinks I'm going to sit on my hands for my final days on this Earth, he's got another think coming.

I smirk. "Oh, so we've reached bargaining?" I muse, causing his face to fall. "I don't think so, reaper. If nine days is all I've got left, then I want adventure."

"I'll bring back some board games," he replies impatiently.

"I can't be trusted not to get myself into all kinds of trouble if I'm left to my own devices here," I answer with a pouty baby voice.

"Then I will have to resort to my earlier suggestion. Where are your cuffs?"

"Come on," I whine. "See if you can take me with you. Maybe if I'm holding on to you."

"Don't touch me." His voice cracks like a whip, sharp and sudden, tinged with something that isn't quite fear, but isn't quite confidence either.

That edge of alarm? It only fuels me.

"Oh, how the mighty panic," I purr, slipping off my other shoe and rising from the chair, slow and deliberate. I stalk toward him with the theatrical menace of a B-grade horror villain, arms raised like claws. "What's the matter, Grim? Afraid of a little affection?"

"I mean it, Rue." He's backing up now, which is satisfying in all the ways that should probably concern a therapist. "Stay back."

But he's out of runway—cornered between the dining table and the curio cabinet. My palms land on his chest like a victory flag. His reaction is not what I expected.

He full-body shudders, as though my touch sends electric voltage coursing through his bones. A soft sound slips past his lips–almost a moan, nearly a curse–and his jaw clenches as his eyes roll back, just for a breath.

"Oh," I whisper. "Interesting."

"Enough." The word hits like a blade.

Before I can blink, he's moved–lightning quick. His hand snaps out, grabbing one of my dad's old ropes off the wall. I barely process what's happening before my wrists are caught, spun, and cinched tight with practiced efficiency. His breath is steady. Mine is not.

"I asked you nicely," he growls, dragging me away from the wall. "But clearly, you're one of those mortals who only learns through escalation."

"You tied me up with nautical rope. You know that's not normal, right?"

He doesn't answer. Just grabs another coil from a hook and gestures toward the hallway. "Bedroom. Now."

"Excuse me?"

"Chair or bed, Rue."

"I swear to–"

"You're about to be tied to the banister if I don't hear a reasonable response in the next three seconds."

I glare at him. Hard. But the truth is, I'm already half bound and out of leverage. So, I choose comfort–grudgingly. "Bed," I mutter.

He guides me in with a hand to my shoulder, surprisingly gentle, then crouches down and starts looping the rope around my ankles. He's meticulous. He does it all without grazing so much as a knee, like this is a task he's done a thousand times.

"Do I offend you that much?" I ask as he ties off the knot.

"In every conceivable way," he replies, standing.

"This seems like an overreaction," I grunt, testing the restraints on my bound limbs.

He looks me over before stepping back.

"You're impulsive, emotionally unstable, and now cosmically radioactive," he says, arms folding as he surveys his handiwork. "This is damage control. Nothing more."

I scoff, testing the binds. They hold.

"Don't worry," he adds, voice going low as he leans in, so close that his breath ghosts over my ear. "It's just until I get back. But if you keep testing me, Mayday ..." His voice dips further, silk wrapped in threat. "You're going to wake up with some very creative rope burns."

He straightens, turns on his heel, and walks out without another word.

The door shuts, leaving me to stare at the ceiling. My wrists bound, my ankles anchored while a reaper paces my hallway.

Well, this isn't a dream, but it's definitely a nightmare.

Chapter Eight

CAPTIVE AUDIENCE

KANE

WHILE DEATH SPENDS HIS FREE TIME ON MINDLESS HOBBIES, I have taken the downtime of my last half of a millennium very seriously. Passion and productivity lead to perfectionist pursuits, and I don't do anything half-cocked.

Upon returning to Rue's bedroom, I admire my craftsmanship. My Shibari training really shines through in the gentle yet effective nature of each of her restraints. She's sleeping when I arrive. I take a moment to write my successful post-case report on my latest crossover before tucking my phone in my pocket and clearing my throat.

Her eyes open with a start, and she sucks in a breath as she sees me. She tugs against her arm restraints. "Oh good, you're back. Untie me now, asshole."

"In a minute. We still have plenty to discuss, and I imagine you'll be easier to converse with when you're a *captive* audience."

"Wow, you come with dad jokes now too? You're the whole package, aren't you?" she quips, her sarcasm cutting through the tension like a well-sharpened blade.

"Drink it in, *ma chère*." I meet her sarcasm in kind. Speaking of drinks, a thought occurs to me. "Would you like a sip of water?"

I can tell from her expression that she doesn't want

me to help her, but given her current state, she smartly weighs her options and reluctantly responds with a, "Yes."

I retreat to the kitchen, bringing back a glass of water, which I help her to drink. Her restraints allow me to sit on the side of the bed without the possibility of much physical contact.

As the first sip dribbles down the side of her face and she coughs, she glares at me. "I appreciate the gesture here, Clara Barton, but do you think you could at least hold my head up?"

Leaving my face an expressionless mask, I run my fingers to the back of her head. The tactile sensations of the warmth of her scalp, mixing with the gentle tickles of her hair running through my fingers, almost overwhelm me. I remain stoic, though inside, I am a volcano. Molten.

She drinks, and then I pull my hand away, her head dropping back onto the pillow awkwardly.

"Owww! Dick."

"Sorry," I concede. "No good deed goes unpunished, I guess."

There is a moment of unnavigable silence before she changes the subject, asking, "How did that 'work matter' go?"

"Quite well. Most souls are content to move past this plane of existence."

"As long as it's their time," she deadpans.

"Time answers to no one. You got it."

"So, where do they go?" she asks, and I can feel her energy shifting from resistance to a desire for understanding. That's a promising development.

I explain the basics, as I've done countless times before. "Your physical form remains here while your spirit essence moves into the OtherWorld. I and many other reapers are tasked with shepherding those souls to that place."

"OtherWorld?"

"Yes, as in not this world. Not the Earth realm, but rather what lies beyond. Not here, but there. Does that make enough sense?"

"Sure," she concedes. "Go on."

"Everyone begins in AfterLife Processing, or ALP.

Every spirit goes through Intake, Instructions, and finally Assignment. That's where souls are given jobs and levels in the bureaucratic hierarchy based on a series of mostly arbitrary factors. Administration in The Nothing is mind-numbing torture. Research and Development in the Vast Library is rather peaceful. You get the idea."

"And what about me, personally? Where am I going?"

The vulnerability behind her eyes undoes something in me. Not interested in dwelling on whatever this feeling is, I take myself off the bed and sit in the chair by her desk. "Above my pay grade, Mayday. Don't know. Don't care."

"That's pretty bleak. Are you really that cold? Did death make you that way?"

"I can't afford to care about every soul's story. Life matters to the living, but cosmically speaking, it's only significant to the individual. We all go in the end, and the closing curtain drops when your story is told for the last time. So, live a life worth talking about. That's all you can do."

I notice Rue pale visibly on the bed. Her voice takes on a defeated edge as she admits, "Too late for me at this point, I'm afraid."

I sigh while contemplating my response to this piteous remark. Finally, I make a decision. I'll be here for eight more days, so we might as well make the most of it. "Why haven't you done more with your life?" I ask.

Rue seems to measure the question as her next words cut right to the heart of the matter.

"I inherited a heart condition from my father called arrhythmogenic right ventricular dysplasia, or ARVD."

"I'm familiar with the disease. You had a fifty-fifty shot of carrying the genetic marker."

"Well, Doctor, my dad one hundred percent gave it to me. I've had heart palpitations and an irregular heartbeat my whole life."

"You'll forgive me, I hope, and I know I don't know you that well, but"–I pause before finishing–"it suits you, Mayday."

"What does?"

"An irregular heartbeat. You strike me as someone

who marches to her own rhythm. Quite literally, it would seem."

"Yeah, well, it's also limited me physically for most of my life, so it's more crawling, less marching." Her voice, though tinged with self-pity, carries a note of resilience that is both inspiring and hopeful.

"Sounds like you inherited an excuse to me, Mayday," I challenge, intrigued by her defiance in the face of adversity.

"An excuse so powerful that it killed me before my time."

"Already told you, that's not what happened," I tell her, then recall my earlier conversation with Big D. "But I did find out what caused that first stoppage."

"Tell me." Her quick reply and firm tone leave no room for discussion.

So, I tell her what D told me. "You had a bout of acute stress cardiomyopathy. Otherwise known as takotsubo or broken-heart disease."

I wait for her response, try to read her reaction in her face, but get nothing. So, I press, "Wanna talk about it?"

"Not with you, my own personal demon."

"Eat your heart out, Depeche Mode."

She giggles. It's not an altogether-unpleasant sound.

"Suit yourself." I get back to the topic at hand. "It's a fascinating physical condition. Your heart literally changes shape. Got its name because it looks surprisingly similar to the misshapen pot used to trap an octopus."

"Why would someone want to trap an octopus?"

"Have you ever eaten fresh octopus?"

"I don't eat anything that can be mistaken for a pig's anus."

"Don't know what you're missing," I reply dryly.

"Meh, we all gotta live by a code, Kane. That's part of mine."

"You really haven't lived." I laugh lightly, though her response indicates she's much tetchier on the subject than I imagined.

"Fuck you."

I cut off my laughter and bring the subject back into focus. "So, what's got your heart so stressed that

a pretty young woman like yourself has had it so broken? Twice?"

"You wouldn't understand," she dismisses.

"Oh, Mayday, I'm an expert on heart trauma."

"I'm sure you are, *Doctor.*" She emphasizes the
occupation.

I correct her without thinking, "That knowledge has
nothing to do with my medical training."

I see the spark of intrigue alight behind her eyes, and
I inwardly curse myself for my repeatedly loose lips.
Before she can pry further into my comment, we are in-
terrupted by a loud crashing sound from down the hall.

"What was that?" I ask, startled.

An intruder would not be an ideal development right
now.

"The house ghost," she answers plainly.

"There's an essence in this house? How do you know
that?"

"They leave cabinets open, knock dishes off counters,
cause low-key, general mischief. After a while, I figured
out it wasn't just the wind."

"Interesting. You've got a lost soul trapped here already." I mutter this more to myself, then glare at the
undead woman tied to her bed. "If I untie you, are you
going to behave?"

"No," she replies candidly.

Well, at least she's honest.

Chapter Nine

FAIR NEVER FACTORS

RUE

THE SOUND OF GLASS BREAKING SHATTERS THE SILENCE, which, given my current state of existential dread, is less than ideal. I smirk as an idea hits me. I eye the man hovering over me with a predatory gleam.

"Why are you looking at me like that?"

"You're a reaper, right? A soul collector."

"A bit more like a soul transporter, but yes. That's my AfterLife Assignment."

"Dude," I say, watching as Kane finishes untying my legs, "get my ghost out of here."

Kane lets out an exasperated sigh, tossing the rope aside like he's doing me some massive favor. "First of all," he starts, straightening his suit jacket, "my name is Kane. I didn't survive the height of the second plague just to have a skinny little waif call me dude. If you're looking for pet names, however, I *am* open to sir, sire, or perhaps even Kane the–"

"My legs are free now, and I am exactly three seconds from kicking you in the face," I interrupt, voice flat.

"Second," he continues, ignoring me entirely. "I don't reap the lost souls. Can't be done."

"And here I thought, I'd finally found a good use for you." My tone drips with disappointment.

"I'm afraid this soul already made its choice.

Something compelling draws that spirit to this place. Which is why it lingers."

"This one lingers quite loudly," I complain as Kane moves to untie my wrists.

For the briefest moment, our hands touch. His grip tightens, and he inhales sharply, fingers flexing before he snaps back, shaking his hand like I burned him.

"Yes, well," he says quickly, clearly unnerved, "I imagine you'd make a bit of noise if your eternal essence was tethered to a place it feels fused to, but you remain impotent to affect any change."

"Am I going to need to keep a thesaurus on hand with you around?"

"You seem to have a robust library as it is. I apologize if my vocabulary threatens you," he snidely retorts.

"Not threatened, just annoyed … *dude*." I pause before continuing, "Can't you just coax it along? Bribe it?"

"Not after the initial crossover window closes. I *can* force a soul through at that time, but my strong preference is not to. It's messy. It's in a soul's best interest to cross over, of course, as there is nothing they can actually *do* over here after the corporeal form fails, but ultimately, some feel tethered too tightly. Once the choice is made, the reapers have to move on. Caseloads being what they are, we simply cannot tarry on one spirit for too long. So, that soul remains tied to where their mortal life ended."

"That's terrible," I whisper while rubbing the tender spots on my wrists.

"They made their choice, Mayday. Just as you will. The last mortal moment for all."

"That's pretty grim." I stand, staring at him in astonishment.

"*C'est la vie, ma chère.* Or I suppose, in this case, it's a bit more, *C'est la mort.*"

"Do you have any compassion? Are all the reapers like you?"

"You mean articulate, good-looking, amusing, and impeccably dressed?" He smirks as we head out of my bedroom.

"I mean overly confident know-it-alls with a superiority complex and an inflated sense of self-worth."

Kane stops mid-step. Turns. And *slowly* looks me up and down. I feel my skin prickle under his gaze.

"That was cute," he purrs. "But are you *sure* you want that to be your response?"

I'm about to respond when I hear more banging in the kitchen.

"Ugh," I growl while storming in there. "I'm not spending the final days of my life listening to this jerk breaking all my family's things. Get it ou–" I stop as a squeak leaves me.

There is a child; he can't be more than ten. He's filthy and crouched on my countertop with a bowl held over his head.

I try to make words, but nothing comes out. The boy looks from me to Kane and back again. We're all silent, no one moving for what feels like forever, before the boy slams my bowl to the floor, causing it to shatter.

I continue to stare in shock. There is a boy in my kitchen. Not just dishes flying everywhere, but an actual boy.

"Can ..." His voice is small with a thick English accent. "Can you see me?"

I nod dumbly, minutely aware that Kane is now beside me.

"So, Big D was right. This certainly ups the stakes," Kane mutters seriously.

"Who can? What now?"

"Never mind about that. Right now, we need to ensure your safety."

"From this little"–I eye the young person standing before me–"boy," I manage weakly. This ... this can't be happening. "No, no, no, no ..." I shake my head back and forth before leaving the kitchen, storming down the hallway and out the front door.

"Mayday! Wait!" Kane calls after me, but I don't listen.

I continue walking down the drive, passing by the gnarly old trees with Spanish moss draped from them.

"Hey!" Kane appears in front of me, blocking my path. "Where are you going?"

"There is a child in my house!" I shout. I don't know why I am unable to control the volume of my voice.

"The soul of a child, but yes. You knew that already. So, again, where are you going?"

"No." I laugh as I begin pacing. "No. No. There was a *ghost* in my house. It didn't have an identity, a face, anything. But now I find out there is a *boy* in there. A boy! A ghost boy! Oh my, I can see ghosts. I can see ghosts; I have a reaper stalking me—"

"That's a bit dramatic—"

"I'm dying in nine days, and now I see dead people!" I bend over at the waist, placing my palms on my knees to try to catch my breath.

Kane stands there, staring at me with a blank expression. "Eight days now, I'm afraid."

"Ya know, now would be a great time to comfort someone. Rub their back, tell them it's all going to be okay—*something* besides standing there like some statue."

"I'm not rubbing you, and you are not okay. Would you rather I lie?"

"YES!" I scream while grabbing a rock off the ground and hurling it at him. It goes straight through his body and bounces off a tree behind him.

"Good throw. How was that lie?" he asks.

I want to yell at him, I want to scream and hit him, I want to run away. But I don't. Instead, my bottom lip—in a betrayal so deep that I may cut it off later for the act—begins to wobble as my eyes start to burn and fill with tears. Before I can stop them, liquid falls from my eyes.

"Fuck," I whimper on a sob.

Kane's eyes grow big, and his expression shifts from smug bastard to full-blown panic. "W-what are you doing?"

"Surely, you've seen someone cry before," I snap as another sob wracks through my body.

"Yes, but why are you crying?! Stop it!"

I glare at him through my watery gaze.

"You don't get to tell me what to do!" I shout out, my voice shaking from the adrenaline. "In a day, I've died and been brought back, only to be told I'm dying again in eight days. I have a reaper following me around and tying me to the bed, and now I can see ghosts?! I can fucking see *ghosts,* Kane! And then I can hit you with my hand, but I throw a rock, and you're like a hologram! None of this makes sense! And it isn't fair! What about what I want? Just once, I want someone to ask me about what I want to achieve in my life—"

"Mayday, what do you want to ach—"

"Shut up!" I scream out. "The man who is about to kill me doesn't get to ask me that."

"Hey!" he barks out while stalking over to me. "We have been over this already. I am *not* killing you. Your heart is doing that. And that is terribly unfortunate. You're young and attractive, and you seem relatively intelligent. Why you have to die while the man across town who lives on fast food and never calls his kids gets to live into his nineties makes no sense. But it's just the way it is, Rue. You will find that in *every* life, fairness never factors."

I shake my head, chest heaving, voice raw. "Fuck you," I spit out. "Don't give me that bullshit line. Do you know how many times I've heard that? I know life isn't fair! But fuck you for not letting me live in ignorant bliss for the remainder of my days! I can see the clock now, every second ticking by, taking my dreams with it."

My breath hitches. Kane pinches the bridge of his nose.

I wipe a tear from my cheek before continuing, "I just—I *wanted* things. I wanted to be someone import-ant. I wanted to help people. I wanted to dance in the moonlight, get lost in a really old library, feel the sting of a tattoo, and lie on the roof in a thunderstorm. I'll never discover the best chocolate cake or soak in one of those fancy tubs."

Kane blinks.

I wipe my face, my hands shaking. "And I don't blame you for that. But I do blame you for stealing the fantasy that I still had time."

There's a long silence between us. Kane stares at me, jaw clenched, green eyes darting back and forth, search-ing for something on my face he'll never find.

"Time is a funny thing, Mayday," he begins.

Rubbing my chest, I start to wheeze as I realize I've done too much. The staccato thumping beneath my ribs tells me to slow down. Now. It feels like a bear squeezing my chest and my lungs are turning to stone.

My voice comes out weak, breathless. "Kane … I can't breathe. My heart. Keeps. Skipping."

"What's wrong?" he asks softly.

I release a tired sob. "I need to lie down."

Kane stiffens as he looks back at the house. "Can you make it back to your room?"

I shake my head weakly. "I don't think so."

He sighs dramatically before taking pity on the wheezing woman doubled over, holding on to the side railing of the front steps. His hands reach out slowly before he jerks them back.

"*Merde*," he mutters to himself.

Then, begrudgingly, he grabs me and lifts me up in his arms. His hold is so stiff and awkward, nothing like the romance books I've read. He moves quickly, eyes straight ahead as he takes us back into the house. As we enter, he eyes the distance to my bedroom and the living room. I can see his mental assessment play out as he opts for the shorter distance. He takes me to the nearest couch and sets me down. Gently, though not altogether gracefully.

"Thanks," I mutter, melting into the cushions.

"Don't mention it. Ever."

And I don't. Not now anyway, as the shock of the past few moments zaps me of all the strength I had left, and though I fight it, I quickly fall asleep.

Chapter Ten

HISTORY & HISTRIONICS

KANE

Rue Chamberlain, whatever am I to do with you?

Sitting here, watching this fragile and momentarily mortal creature resting peacefully on this decadent velour sofa, the thought that keeps resurfacing in my mind irritates me. The idea is so utterly foreign, so uncomfortably human. It took her passing out from exhaustion and curling ever so slightly on the burgundy cushions, but it's pretty clear.

This woman is uniquely gorgeous.

Beautiful in a way that aches. The redness of her mouth is striking against her creamy skin. The curves of her Cupid's bow look painted on. Her gentle breathing and occasional purring are calm. Peaceful.

My mind starts racing back to years long gone, to easy days of gentle love. Of things I had, now lost. Of soft touches in candlelight, of whispered laughter under sheets.

I bring my hand up to scratch my chest, readjusting myself in the uncomfortable chair opposite her sofa, when my reverie is broken by a louder purring. I glance down and see a hideous creature of unimaginable furriness and size, which can only be described as a cat.

I shriek, the banshee-like wail enough to wake Rue instantly and send the hairs on this creature shooting up its back.

"What's going on?" my reluctant patient asks groggily from the couch.

"You tell me," I hiss, pressing myself against the back of the chair. "A spirit is one thing I can tolerate stalking a domicile. But this abomination?" I shudder.

She blinks. "That, dear Kane, is Esther. She's my cat. And don't call her names. She's very sensitive."

"That is not a cat. That is a cryptid."

"She's a Maine Coon." Rue waves dismissively, as if this explains or excuses anything. "Now leave her alone. She's old, and she doesn't like anyone except me."

"I know the feeling," I think to myself, though I must have voiced that thought aloud because Rue responds, "You getting soft on me already?"

She giggles, and the sound hits me in the best and worst way simultaneously. I cannot decide if it's reminiscent of fingernails raking down a chalkboard or down my spine. I shudder again. I need to get myself under control here.

"That thing looks half dead."

"And you look completely dead. Now are you going to help me figure some things out, or are you going to continue being a nuisance? For someone who claims to be invested in my eternal soul, you don't act like it very often."

She sits up fully, stretching, the movement drawing my unwilling attention to the delicate lines of her neck, leading down to the pale skin of her chest and the vertical scar that's etched between what I imagine is a perfect set of–

I look away, scowling. Distraction. I need a distraction.

I take a deep breath, analyzing my current predicament. This is going to be a long week plus, no matter how I approach it. The carrot or the stick? Vinegar or honey? I think about Rue's prickly personality and how to dull her spikes. Her fragile state seems to dominate her energy right now. If I push too hard, she may break. And while I do revel in my acidic side, you know what they say–*kill 'em with kindness.*

"How may I be of assistance to you on this part of your journey, mortal?"

"Don't be glib with me."

"I'm not. This is a lot to take in, and I need you to see it through. So, if I can help, that's what I need to do."

"What do you *want* to do?" She edges.

"Don't push it, Mayday. Ask your questions."

She darts her eyes to the doorway before returning her focus to me. "Why am I able to see him?"

"The whys of the universe are food for philosophers. I am a doctor, Rue. Logistics, processes, and order—these are my areas of expertise. So, I cannot tell you why you see that poor lost soul banging away in your kitchen."

"You are so obtuse."

"Funny. Most people call me a-cute."

"Geometry jokes? Wow," she says with derision, then surprises me with, "What's your angle?"

I try and fail to contain my laughter. "Just here to help you find *proof*."

She side-eyes me.

I get us back on topic. "I can tell you *how*."

She gestures grandly. "By all means, illuminate me."

I clear my throat. "You crossed over, Rue. When the heart stops beating, the soul separates from your physical form."

I watch as her dark brows furrow together in thought.

"So, Dr. MacDougall was right? Twenty-one grams? Our soul has weight?" Rue exclaims while feeling her chest cavity in wonder—a not-altogether-unpleasant image.

I let out a long sigh because, of course, she brought up that hack. "If you're referring to the deeply flawed experiment performed by that quack in 1907, then I would say this: old Duncan managed to come up with the correct conclusion despite his bunk science."

"Even a broken clock tells the time twice a day," Rue quips.

I tilt my head, mildly impressed. "*C'est vrai*, Mayday. This is true. Anyway, your essence began the process of dissociating from this realm, then reintegrated. However, it seems you spent enough time separated— for lack of a better term—that you returned to this form with some of the attributes of OtherWorlders, namely that you can see the lost souls that still roam this plane."

Rue is quiet for a moment, then lifts her chin. "What else can I do?"

I arch a brow, and she shrugs. I don't tell her what I don't want her to know. "We've only got eight days, so we may as well make the most of it."

My mind wanders to the feel of her fingers on my flesh, the impossible memory of physical, human connection. I do not like the feeling this realization gives me, so I decide to distract myself immediately. Now is not the time to explore that dark, dangerous alleyway, so I opt for a redirection.

My gaze slides over to her bookshelf. Her quotidian taste in literature sets my blood boiling.

I stand, striding toward it, plucking a particularly offensive title from the shelf. "So, Mayday, I knew you had questionable taste in people, but now I see you also have questionable taste in books."

Rue's head snaps up. "Excuse me?"

I hold up the book like evidence in a murder trial. "*Collected Works* of Edgar Allan Poe. Oh, of course."

Her gasp is so loud and so full of betrayal that I suspect she may be about to challenge me to a duel.

"Put that down," she hisses, "if you don't plan on treating it with the respect it deserves."

I flip through the pages carelessly. "Poe? Really? You fancy yourself a tragic, brooding figure, so naturally, you latch on to the king of tragic, brooding figures?"

"King is exactly right." She stands, full of righteous indignation. "Poe is one of the greatest writers of all time."

I snort. "Oh, yes, the great Edgar Allan Poe. A drunk, a debt-ridden disaster, a man who had one good poem and coasted on it like a Victorian-era one-hit wonder."

She gasps again, clutching her nonexistent pearls. "You. Take. That. Back."

I smirk. "Make me."

Her eyes narrow, a dangerous glint in them.

And for some strange, inexplicable reason, I think I might actually be enjoying this.

"Oh, please." I chuckle. "His entire shtick was

melodrama. *Oh no, my wife died; let me weep forlornly into my whiskey and write about birds and death!* He's the literary equivalent of an emo band lead singer who won't stop writing songs about his high school ex."

She gasps again, but this time, it's a different kind of gasp–horrified and deeply personal.

"Kane"–her voice is hushed–"I need you to know that I have never wanted to commit actual homicide before this moment."

I smirk, reveling in her distress. "Oh? Am I ruining the fantasy?"

"You are desecrating the sacred." Rue snatches the book from my hands and holds it protectively against her chest. "Poe is the father of gothic literature, the architect of psychological horror. Without him, there is no H.P. Lovecraft, no Shirley Jackson, no Stephen King!"

"Yes, yes, without Poe, we'd have no obsessive freaks writing about ghosts and madness. Truly a loss to society," I say dryly. "Tell me, Rue, do you also keep a quill on hand so you can write wistful odes to your own untimely demise?"

"Not all of us are dead inside, Kane," she fires back.

I tilt my head, intrigued. "Aren't you though?"

She stills, the sharp retort dying on her lips.

For a moment, neither of us speaks. The weight of what I just said settles between us like dust on an old book–quiet but unshakable.

Then Rue does something that surprises me.

She laughs.

A soft, bitter chuckle, as if my words amused in the most tragic way possible.

"You know what's funny?" she muses, sitting back down on the couch, hugging her Poe collection like a security blanket. "You're not wrong. I mean, if you think about it, I have been living like I was already dead. Watching the world move around me. Waiting for the moment when my body finally decided to stop."

I study her carefully.

"You think Poe was melodramatic," she continues, voice softer now, more tired. "But you don't get it. His writing wasn't about death; it was about the fear of it. About the inevitability of loss. How grief wraps around your ribs and squeezes until there's nothing left of you. How it turns you into a ghost long before you die."

She exhales sharply, her fingers tightening around the book. "I get Poe. I am Poe. A person trapped in the waiting room of her own demise."

I open my mouth, then close it. For the first time, I find myself at a loss for words.

Because for the first time, I have nothing clever to say.

Rue watches me for a moment, then sighs and leans back, staring at the ceiling.

"But you know what?" she says, her voice picking up just a hint of its usual edge. "I have eight days left, Kane. And I am not going to waste them debating literature with a philistine."

I snort, repeating her insult. "Philistine?"

She waves a hand. "You heard me," she offers smugly, returning her treasured collection to the shelf.

"You're right, Rue. Eight days is not a lot of time." I begin, then finish with a quote from her precious Poe. "I think I hear the *'bells, bells, bells, bells, bells, bells, bells'* now."

Chapter Eleven

NO TURNING BACK NOW

RUE

FLIPPING THROUGH MY NOTEBOOK, CONTEMPLATING HOW TO live my final days, my reverie is broken by a discordant twang of a cello. Kane reaches into his breast pocket and removes his mobile device. It's the first time I have noticed the design.

"Is your phone shaped like a headstone?"

"Not just any headstone, Mayday. Mine."

"Really?"

"Indeed. All soul shepherds are issued theirs after Processing and Assignment."

"What's written on there?" I ask, trying to read the etchings.

Kane moves farther away from me as he scans the device. "It says I had a good run. Now, back to bed with you."

"What? No way."

"Yes way. My next scheduled case just came due. I still need to handle my essential workload. I won't be long."

"Take me with you," I state emphatically.

"No," he replies just as emphatically.

"You won't even know I'm there."

"You asked before, and the answer has not changed. Now, be a doll and tie yourself up in the bed again. I'll be back *tout suite*."

I don't care what this six-foot-something reaper with

questionable taste in poetry and an unquestionably sharp tongue says; he is not cutting me out of getting the most out of my last days on Earth.

I cross my arms defiantly and state, "I'm coming."

"Absolutely not," Kane snaps for the twelfth time, pacing my living room like a man desperately searching for the nearest escape hatch.

"C'mon," I whine, stalking him like a cat preparing for attack. "How bad could it be? You just show up, escort a soul out of a body, and brood dramatically while looking all domineering in a crisp black suit–"

"Flattery will get you nowhere," he says flatly. "And it's much more complicated than that, Rue. It requires nuance, patience, and precision."

I put my ego aside and lay it on thick. "And I'm sure you're wonderful at it. How lucky I am to be able to learn at the feet of the master."

He raises one eyebrow, unmoved.

"Fine, if fawning fails, there's always bribery." I smirk sadistically.

Kane stops pacing, finally looking at me. "With what exactly? Besides your pretty soul, which already has my name on it, you possess nothing of interest to me."

My smile is slow and devious, causing him to shudder. "Esther."

His entire body goes rigid. "That *thing* is not a bargaining chip."

"You take me with you," I say, my voice sickeningly sweet, "and I'll keep my kitty at bay. You insist on flying solo, and I can't promise that Esther won't 'accidentally' end up using your suit jacket as a bed. Or worse, she loves curling up on chests. Big, broad, dead ones are new for her, but I'm quite sure she'd love to nestle into that cavity and–"

"FINE." Kane's voice is sharp and clipped, the single syllable sounding as though it were forcibly ripped from his throat.

He glares at me with pure, undiluted venom, the kind of look that, in any other circumstance, would make me very concerned for my continued existence. But seeing as I'm on a tight timeline here with zero fucks left to give, I grin like a person with nothing to lose. Because, well ... I don't.

"Pleasure doing business with you," I say brightly as a delighted cackle echoes from the kitchen.

I turn just in time to see the ghost child pop his head out of the wall—never mind the fact that his entire head is phasing through solid matter like this is some low-budget haunted house attraction. I shudder, and my knees go weak. This will take some getting used to. For years, I felt the energy of this spirit, saw and heard the effects of its petulant disturbances, but now, I can see it. *Him.* This is one of the side effects of my brief dance on the other side of life's coin, according to Kane.

"This one here's a pushover." The kid jerks a thumb at Kane.

The gesture is so simple yet so profound, and my mind swirls as I try to make sense of this mystical reality. While I grapple with the mysteries of lost souls, Kane rolls his eyes so hard that I fear they might never return.

"I, for one, find Esther to be a delightful companion," the ghost adds, as though twisting the knife into Kane's side.

The fact that my house spirit has an affinity for my house cat fascinates me enough to swallow my fear and confusion and address the child directly.

"You hang out with Esther?" I ask, more impressed than concerned.

The kid shrugs his skinny shoulders before stepping fully through the wall—a disorienting sight I don't expect to get used to in the next week—and makes his way to my sleeping beast of a cat.

"Before you could see me, it was quite lonely around here," he says matter-of-factly, brushing his fingers near Esther's fur, which—judging by the violent twitching of her tail—is not appreciated. "Especially being trapped in the confines of the house. Esther here was the first to take notice of me."

I take in the seeming realness of this spectral entity. How many times has he been sitting like that? In this house? Next to me. Near me. Beside me. The visual reality of his presence sends chills down my spine, but I push past my anxiety and reach out to the child.

I feel drawn to him and physically raise my arm toward him as I ask, "What's your name?"

Kane clears his throat loudly, forcefully. "This is all very fascinating, really. I haven't been this stimulated since that summer in Barcelona." His tone has a carnal, almost-lustful edge to it as he seems to remember something about Spain.

The sharp pang of jealousy I feel takes me by surprise. I watch as he pulls a flask from the inside of his suit jacket, takes a long, slow drink, then caps the container dramatically.

"But I have a tight schedule," he continues, adjusting his sleeves with practiced indifference. "So, I need to get moving."

"Right," I say, trying not to sound nervous even though I absolutely am. "So, do I order a rideshare or …" I trail off as Kane walks through the kitchen, heading toward the back door like this is some casual neighborhood stroll and not an excursion into the world of literal death.

I wave to the ghost boy before jogging after Kane, my bare feet slapping against the cold floor.

"Where are you going?" I pant, struggling to keep up with his annoyingly long, supernatural strides.

"I told you," he huffs, not even sparing me a glance, "Time waits for no one."

I expect him to head toward the driveway or maybe even the woods, but, no, this asshole heads straight for my father's final resting place.

I bristle immediately.

"Hey!" I snap, shoving him.

Kane stumbles slightly, more out of shock than actual force, before raising his hands in mock surrender, causing me to lose my balance and fall straight to my knees.

I scramble back to my feet, brushing the dirt off my legs with extra aggression. "Get off his grave."

Kane rolls his eyes before adjusting his sleeves again because, apparently, being an insufferable piece of shit requires constant tailoring. "Control yourself."

"You're standing on my father's grave!" I hiss, throwing my arms up. "That's extremely disrespectful."

Kane smirks. "I don't think he can feel anything anymore."

I glare, mustering the strength to kick him square in his smug, statuesque face, but before I get the chance, he takes a deep breath, straightens his lapels, and says, "Relax, Rue. These aren't graves. They're portals. We bury bodies to keep the memory alive. That's fleeting, of course. But the intention is in the right place. And these places become passageways to travel in, around, and through. Now, if you'll excuse me, I have to bend time and space. Be right back."

"What about me?" I demand.

"I thought you said you were getting a car. I can text you the address."

I fold my arms. "I'm going with you."

Kane laughs. Not just any laugh. No, a borderline-hysterical, utterly baffled, full-bodied laugh that makes him look maniacal. Sinister.

Sexy ... I admit to myself very reluctantly.

"You can't," he says, still chuckling. "Mortals can't portal."

I lift my chin. "Seems like there are a lot of things I can do that I shouldn't be able to."

His smirk falters.

"It's not happening. Even if the Reaper Regulations got this wrong, which is highly unlikely, you wouldn't want to. The trip would be too disorienting."

"Awww, is Kane showing concern?" I raise a brow as he grimaces.

"Yeah, concern about having to rearrange your insides or scrape your innards off the floor."

"I'll take the chance. What have I got to lose?" I shoot him a wink.

"No, Mayday," he states firmly. "Not happening. I'm not even sure where to begin explaining the complexities of this to you. There's no–"

"Hold me," I order, causing Kane's entire body to go stiff.

"No," he fires back.

"Yes."

"Never."

"Always." I smirk, watching him visibly shudder.

"Leave." He points toward the house like I'm some misbehaving child. "Go back inside. I command it."

I roll my eyes so hard that I see stars before stalking toward him. Kane backs away, retreating until he's pressed against my father's headstone.

"Shut up and hold me," I say, voice low, challenging.

Kane's green eyes narrow, and for a second, I think he might actually depart without me. I don't give him a chance. Before he knows what's happening, I throw my arms around his neck and jump, wrapping my legs around his waist like a human belt. Kane stiffens violently, hands hovering awkwardly in the air, like he's just been doused in ice water. My pelvis presses into his, our bodies chest to chest, and our eyes lock.

The air shifts, and I can feel Kane's body tense tightly. That instant of discomfort passes powerfully into a moment of pure connection. It's almost as though every point of contact between us sparks an electric charge. I can feel him in a way I've never felt anyone before. Pinpricks of pressure tingle along my forearms, down my chest, and unmistakably between my thighs. His skin heats, literally warms instantly, like that first grip of a freshly poured cup of coffee. And just before he speaks, we breathe each other in, mouths slightly parted, faces inches apart.

"Get. Off." His voice is strained, his whole body rigid with panic.

"Maybe. Later." I grin, squeezing tighter, the innuendo surprising me as much as it does the soul sucker in my grasp.

Kane makes a deep, guttural noise of distress, somewhere between a groan and a growl, and tilts his head toward the sky momentarily before returning his gaze to mine. Something primal lights behind his green gaze, and I feel his entire being shift. His legs and shoulders soften slightly. His arms, which had previously been ramrod straight, bend, and his long fingers press against my skinny back. He confidently presses our bodies ever tighter together, his strength surprising yet reassuring.

"No turning back now, little one."

He closes his eyes, a low rumble begins to grow from the ground, and my entire world gets flipped upside down.

Chapter Twelve

BUT YOU CAN'T STAY HERE

RUE

FREE FALL. I'M NOT SURE WHICH SENSATION IS MORE ALARM-ing—the disorienting weightlessness of moving through unknown dimensions of time and space or the violent surge of power I feel from Kane's protective embrace.

One thing I am sure of: transporting sucks.

Not in the *mild inconvenience* kind of way—like running out of coffee or accidentally liking someone's social media post from six years ago—but in the *full-bodied betrayal of reality* kind of way. It's an existential violation, a cosmic crime, a deeply intimate experience that I would like to never endure again.

One second, I was standing in the morbid comfort of my family cemetery, literally leaping into my new life. The next—

BAM.

I am somewhere else. Somewhere *other*. Talk about an out-of-body experience.

The world jerks violently like it's been yanked out from under me, flipping me in every direction at once in some cosmic blender of suffering. My stomach performs a full gymnastics routine, settling into what I can only describe as pure, unfiltered terror. Everything spins, and I cannot latch on to anything. My heart rate spikes, along with my anxiety. I don't think I'm going to make it through whatever this torturous tunnel has left to give me.

"What is this?" I scream into the dizzying void as we continue to descend, ascend, spin, and finally stop from the fuming tornado of disorientation to total stillness.

My body feels like it's been stretched, frozen, cracked, burned, then reassembled in some haphazard manner. I close my eyes, resist the urge to even think about the growing nausea, and seek solace somewhere.

Immediately, I reach out, my instincts screaming for something stable, something real, something to hold on to before I break into a million fragile pieces.

That something is Kane. He is solid. More than solid.

Kane feels unnervingly real, like something moored deep in the universe itself, an immovable force of cold certainty, wrapped in expensive fabric and disdain.

"Anchor in the infinite," I whisper in the swirling madness.

My fingers dig into his infuriatingly muscular, very well-structured arm, and for a brief, disorienting second, I feel grounded. That moment of comfort does not last, however, as my OtherWorldly benefactor morphs in front of me.

Gone is the man who held me tight through the madness. Returned is the broody reaper who still appears to be repulsed by me. Kane reacts like I set him on fire. His entire body goes rigid, his muscles tensing so violently that for a split second, I think he might actually turn to stone.

In a dramatic display of physical revulsion, he yanks his arm free so fast and so forcefully that I almost crumble. His disgust is as palpable as it is inexplicable.

What is his problem?

He clears his throat twice, like he needs to physically purge the experience from his body.

I watch, confused, as he takes two deliberate steps away, straightens his impeccable cuffs, and smooths down his lapels, like he's trying to reassert his dominance. For someone who literally escorts souls to the afterlife, he is unreasonably bad at human interaction.

"Did you say something a moment ago?" he queries with an intense stare.

"No," I deflect immediately.

His eyes seem to say he doesn't believe me, but he mercifully moves on.

"You asked for this." His voice is flat, bored, and barely masking whatever existential crisis he just had over being touched.

I tilt my head, filing this little reaction away for future torment. Because right now, I am busy processing my own reaction.

If I'm being honest—and I loathe being honest with myself—touching him wasn't terrible.

I mean, sure, I'm dying, so maybe my standards are dangerously low, but Kane is warm, which is the opposite of what I expected. He isn't cold or lifeless, as I imagined a reaper would be. His body isn't hollow. It isn't spectral. It's strong and not all that terrible to hold on to when your entire sense of self is spiraling through time and space.

I pretend I don't miss his nearness since he pulled away.

"Where are we?" I pull myself back to the present and become aware that I have no idea where we have emerged. "Is this ... someone's bedroom?"

"Do me a favor, Mayday. Make like a piece of leather and hide. We cannot have the living see you in here."

I take a deep breath, level my nausea from the trip and his terrible pun, flip him off in slow, deliberate retaliation, and begin to take in my surroundings. I see floor-length window curtains and move behind them. Then I peer around them and continue to survey the room.

We are in a bedroom inside someone's home. Dated floral wallpaper peels from the corners and is covered by pictures, showing a couple in a nearly identical pose in each shot. The only difference is the background, a reminder of a place explored and memories made. The desk and end tables are cluttered with knickknacks and even more photos. A life reflected in things, a story told by stuff.

The air smells stale and feels heavy somehow.

My eyes travel to the bed in the center of the room, where tubes and wires connect the body to various machines. Her eyes are closed. She looks peaceful. The elderly man holding her hand does not. He looks dev-astated, broken. The Greeks would have made a statue of such a scene–painful and powerful in its simplicity and inevitability.

My ears catch up to my eyes as my body settles into this strange yet familiar place, and I hear his quiet, hopeless sobs. The symphony of his heartbreak pricks a staccato rhythm against my skin. I can feel–physi-cally feel–his loss. The flatline hums through the room like the final note of a song that was never long enough. And then she separates.

A small cloud pools just above her chest, swirling and grey. The woman's soul drifts weightlessly like the lingering warmth of a fading candle. The cloud takes a translucent shape above her physical form, mirroring her body.

Kane sighs. I gasp. The man continues to cry.

The dead woman blinks, confused at first, then looks down at herself–at the frail, lifeless version of the body she just left behind.

And then to him, her husband. Still holding her hand, his thumb brushing gently over her knuckles, his body curled toward her like she was still here, like he could keep her close by sheer will alone. His eyes are wet and unfocused, his breath uneven, like he's lost in a forest and all the trees look the same.

She exhales deeply, a sound full of both sorrow and love, before turning to Kane.

"I have a little more time, don't I?" she asks meekly.

Kane nods, expression unreadable.

She moves closer, pressing ghostly fingers to the side of her husband's face, though he doesn't react–un-able to feel her anymore. But she touches him anyway, smoothing back the stray silver strands of his hair, like she's done a thousand times before, as if muscle mem-ory alone could make the world feel normal.

"My love," she murmurs, kneeling beside him, "you were the greatest gift I was ever given."

His breath hitches, like some part of him knows she's still there.

"You were my home," she continues, her voice ten-der, steady, even as the weight of finality settles around her. "And I know you think you'll never be whole without me, but you will be. Not today, not tomorrow … but someday. And I will be so proud of you when you do."

A single tear slips down his face, and she smiles, attempting to brush it away, but her fingers turn to wisps against his unaltered cheek. He does not move, nor does he stop his soft sobbing.

"Thank you for loving me," she whispers. "For all the days we were given. For making me laugh when I didn't think I could. For keeping your promises, even the little ones."

She exhales weakly, then presses a featherlight kiss to his forehead. Her lips dissipate against his flesh and retake their shape again when she pulls away from him.

His shoulders shake.

She closes her eyes for a moment, committing this last look to memory, then pulls back, looking at Kane.

"I'm ready," she says, her voice quiet but sure.

Kane nods once, then raises a hand. And just like that, she is gone.

The man at the bedside lets out a shaky breath, one that sounds like loss and love, wrapped into one. His hand remains on hers, though she isn't there anymore.

I swallow hard, willing myself to feel nothing.

Chapter Thirteen

NOT NOTHING

KANE

Upon returning to Rue's home through the family plot portal, I set the woman down, only to watch her knees buckle and her already-pale face go grey. She falls to the ground as her breathing becomes labored. Naturally, I sigh loudly for no one's benefit but my own. Bending down, I pick her up and carry her through the yard and return her to her spot on the living room couch.

"Precisely why you should've stayed," I mutter as she lolls her head against my shoulder, falling into unconsciousness. "Transport is not meant to be a luxurious ride. You have one foot through to the other side and decide you're wanting to try out the supernatural transit system? Foolish."

I stand behind the chair facing the couch to wait for her to wake up. Deciding I need a distraction, I focus on my mobile and make notes. The cold, clinical task of filling out the case report grounds me in what I laughingly refer to as my reality. I log the details: *Peaceful departure, minimal resistance. No haunting probability. Standard grief levels in the next of kin.* It's a textbook case, and I should be satisfied. But I'm not. Something rankles.

I'm about to send off a status report to Big D when a drowsy, purring sound from the couch pulls my attention. It's not the dreaded cat, but rather a creature I'm finding may be far more dangerous.

Rue Chamberlain.

Her blue-grey eyes flutter open, tired, confused—yet somehow still radiating a light that's so damn impossible to ignore. She rises, slowly pulling herself up, hair mussed, lips parted, breathing deep. I've witnessed thousands of humans wake. But none have affected me quite like this.

There's a grace and fluidity to her movements that weren't there before, or perhaps I didn't notice them. Either way, I cannot deny the growing pull this frustrating human has on my thoughts. I loathe it. *I think.*

"Welcome back," I droll, attempting to sound aloof.

"Is it over?" Her voice is hoarse, raspy, like gravel over silk.

"For Olivia in this life? Yes."

"Her name was Olivia," Rue repeats, her gaze softening as she voices the name—that reverence in her voice makes my chest ache in ways I don't care to admit.

"Yes, well ..." I clip, brushing past the raw emotion that is starting to linger like smoke in the air. "You should go get yourself some water. You sound hoarse."

I avert my gaze, but the truth is, I don't care about the damn water. I care about the way she looks, sitting there, the way her eyes flicker with something almost hopeful despite it all.

"How do you do it?" she blurts, uncharacteristically raw, her words slipping out like the breath she's been holding since we stepped into this strange, uncharted territory together.

"Do what?"

"All of it. Any of it. It's so ..." She pauses—searching for the right word, I imagine. "Sad," she eventually finishes.

The word sits heavy between us.

Sad.

Such a small, woefully inadequate word for what it really is.

I stare daggers back at Rue as my jaw tightens. Hundreds of years of practice, of repression, of keeping my spine straight, heart closed, and duties cleanly executed–and this little flame of a woman dares to see through the cracks.

I sigh, unable to wholly ignore her empathetic energy. "I wish I could say it gets easier, but it doesn't," I admit. My voice is lower. "It's just different."

"But they don't really die, do they? Not forever? There's something else. It's not the end," she presses, the hope of something more, something bigger still clinging to her.

"No, it's not the end," I reply solemnly, my voice dragging, careful not to break the illusion she's clinging to. "But it's not the same. You lose control. You go where Fate decides. You're part of a system that forces you to give up any autonomy, any free will you might have had–and probably took for granted for too long."

My mind flashes briefly back to my mortal days–simple memories of the ocean air tickling my cheeks or a warm blanket enveloping me and–

"But surely, there are moments of joy in the OtherWorld?" Rue breaks my reverie. "Experiences worth living for, for lack of a better phrase?" Her voice is hopeful yet tinged with something, as if she can sense the quiet, buried sorrow in me that I try so desperately to ignore.

I hesitate. I should shut this down, but instead, I find myself responding. "Indeed, but don't underestimate the power of feeling," I say in a rare, unguarded moment. The look in Rue's hopeful eyes pulls more words from me. "And I don't just mean emotionally because that does stay–oh, believe me, that does stay. But physically too. Feeling. The power of touch is everything. It's singular and the heartbeat of mortal living. And it is strong."

"She tried to kiss him."

"What?" I ask, missing Rue's transition.

"Before we left. The reap. Before she moved on to Processing or whatever you call it."

"AfterLife Processing. ALP. Yes. Go on."

"Yeah. She tried to wipe a tear and kiss his forehead. But the tear didn't move, and he didn't respond."

"That's right, and that's because she couldn't. Not anymore. But her first impulse–many souls' first impulse as they begin to pass over—is to stay connected to this world through physical touch."

I think about all the final touches I was witness to, all the desperate moments of desperate souls clinging to metaphorical lifesavers, unaware that drowning is inevitable. Better simply to give in, to give over, rather than be stranded in the middle of the unforgiving sea.

"But I can." Rue's gentle voice breaks my melancholic meandering yet again.

"Yes, you can," I assure her. "You still have some time left to feel the full experience of this world in every tactile, emotional, and sensory way you possibly can. And you should. I want that for you."

"No, that's not what I mean." She shakes her head and waves her hand dismissively.

"I take it back then." I undercut, but she ignores me.

"I can touch *you*," she says, realization dawning in her eyes.

Rue scoots herself to the edge of the couch, her hands clinging to the lip of the wooden frame.

"No, you can't," I insist pointlessly. I can see the wheels turning in her mind.

"Yes, I can. I've done it. Before you tied me up. Then you carried me. And in the portal, when I grabbed you. You were solid. To me, you felt real."

The passion in her voice grows with each word she utters, ignorant to the fact that they cut like razor blades against my undead flesh.

"Never mind about that."

"No, it's important. That woman's lips faded when they reached her husband's forehead. I've thrown objects *through* you, Kane. But *I* can touch you. Why? How?" she says, rising from the couch and walking toward me.

An eerie sense of déjà vu plagues me as I replay our previous interaction, this maddening dance playing on a loop. I decide the only way to break the cycle is to let her in. Give her the rest of this part of the story.

"It's another one of the side effects of your having begun the process of crossing over. I didn't tell you before because I do not want you to do that."

She continues her slow pursuit. "So, I can touch you."

"Yes, you can. But are you permitted? No."

"You can be touched again." She marvels, completely ignoring me.

"But please don't."

"Have you felt physical touch since …" She leaves the sentence unfinished, and the silence hangs between us, momentarily stopping her approach.

"No," I admit. "And I'd prefer to keep it that way."

"Centuries," she says, her rich voice carrying a sense of awe.

"And I aim to continue the streak."

"Why?" she asks simply.

Because I cannot be hurt again if I do not open myself up. Because the poets and romantics got it wrong. It is better to have never loved at all. Because without feeling, there is no pain, and a world without pain works pretty fucking well for me. I think all of that and say none of it. Rue fills the silence as she closes the space between us.

"Everyone deserves to be touched, Kane. Everyone deserves to feel."

The words hit my ears with a deafening clang.

Rue inches closer as I retreat from the safety of the chair and find myself pressed against the far wall. Only, unlike last time, there's no rope nearby to come to my rescue.

Rue presses in, her thin hips swaying rhythmically. She's become a panther, and I am being stalked. She takes a final step and stands directly in front of me, looking up eagerly as I lean down at her. She closes her eyes, and I am pretty sure her next move will be to crane her neck and kiss me.

I am frozen. Physically incapable of movement and unsure whether I want to or not. But instead of her bringing her lips to mine, with my eyes and attention fixated firmly on her face, I feel it suddenly.

She locks her skinny fingers with my long ones, interlocking our hands at our sides, and she hums. The connection electrifies the room and burns into the center of me. Her hands are cold, but her touch is scintillating. I expect an onslaught of previous memories. I prepare my mind for a barrage of past moments, but none appear. No old nightmares surface. Just this. The power of the present radiates in this infuriatingly gorgeous creature.

The confidence and brashness with which she has demanded this connection unlock something I thought I had thrown the key away to long ago.

Well, I might not have rope, but I do have strength. In one swift motion, I dig my hands more firmly into hers, press into my heels, and spin her around. Before she can open her eyes, I have her hands above her head, her back pressed to the wall. She crashes against the wood with a thud and a small gasp.

With a predatory gleam in my eyes, I ask, "Did I hurt you?" My voice is low, ragged, and foreign to me.

"No," she whispers in reply, her chest rising and falling with her increased breaths.

"Good. Please do me the honor of returning that favor," I beg.

Crashing my mouth to hers, I take Rue in a kiss that could only happen when the elements of hundreds of years of repression ignite with a single lifetime of longing and passion that has yet to find its release.

Combustion.

Our mouths move desperately between us. Decorum is set aside for desperation, risk over rationality. Time stands still, and I realize I could gladly stay here for the next several centuries.

Using my free hand, I hold the side of her face, tilting her to deepen the kiss. Her tongue is so soft against mine, and the needy whimper that I consume from her—if I had any resolve left, that noise stole it.

I'm about to lift her up to wrap her around my waist—desperately missing the feel of her in my arms from back at the plot. But our connection is severed by a tiny voice that pulls us from this moment of reckless passion. His high-pitched gasp rips Rue and me away from each other and has us staring directly into the eyes of the house ghost.

He looks at us and exclaims, "The plot thickens."

Chapter Fourteen

WHAT'S IN A NAME

RUE

"Hello." The house ghost continues speaking as he waves innocently at the two of us.

I flinch so hard that I nearly fall backward into Kane's very solid, very annoyingly silent form. My hand shoots out on instinct, grabbing his arm for balance. Evidently, that is a mistake because the moment I touch him, the warmth returns. Not the gentle, *oh, he's wearing cashmere* warmth, but the kind that seeps under the skin, coils around my ribs, and whispers, *Stay.*

He tenses immediately–as if I were fire and he were dry tinder.

He pulls away from me so fast that you'd think I'd slapped him. His face is blank, but his green eyes flicker just for a second.

I bite the inside of my cheek, keeping the rush of disappointment from leaking out.

"I don't think I'll ever get used to this," I mutter, mostly to myself. My heart's still skipping around like I forgot to take my medication. I tell myself it's because of the pint-sized ghost, but my body knows better.

"Um ..." Kane stammers like a man who just woke from a dream and hasn't decided if it was a nightmare or a fantasy. Probably the former. He clears his throat. "Well, lucky for you, you only have days left, so getting used to anything is frivolous at this point."

What a romantic.

"You are such an asshole," I snap, brushing past him. My shoulder hits his as I go, and, damn it, there it is again—that low flicker of heat curling in my gut. I hate that it's there almost as much as I hate that I like it.

And I really hate that he pulled away as if he felt it, too, and didn't want it.

"Do you two not like each other?" the spirit asks a little too brightly.

"We're growing on each other," Kane says suggestively.

"Like bacteria," I bite back immediately.

"The petri dish was invented in 1887 at Berlin University by an assistant to Dr. Robert Koch," the diminutive spirit spouts out.

I blink. He's standing in the kitchen doorway, hair messy, soot-smudged cheeks.

"Okay …" I draw the word out to fill the silence. I'm unsure how else to respond to that random comment.

"And how would you know that?" Kane asks.

The boy shrugs his small shoulders. "They have this invention called a tel-e-vision. Be surprised what facts you pick up on when it's running."

Despite myself, my heart clenches. This child has been terrorizing this home for as long as my family has lived here. Flashbacks of terrified moments and pulse-pounding scares race through my mind. Those adrenaline spikes aren't ideal for me. I rub at my chest mindlessly. I've spent countless hours over the past years cursing this specter that I can now see clear as day. His pale skin peeks out from behind his charcoaled face, which also makes his innocent blue eyes pop even more brightly.

He can't be more than ten, I think to myself, lost in the absurdity of this moment that feels so real.

That's because it is real, Rue, I remind myself. *This is your life now. Such as it is.*

The fire from my previous exchange with Kane mixes with the confusion of facing the ghost who has haunted this house for generations, and my mind begins to spiral. I take a steadying breath, reminding myself that I don't need to fix everything at once. Start small.

"What's your name?" I ask the wide-eyed, hollowed-cheek boy on the opposite end of the living room.

"Haven't got a name," he replies matter-of-factly.

Well, this is off to a great start.

I glance over at Kane.

"Don't look at me," he says. "I just work here."

"What do you mean, you don't have a name? Everyone has a name. Mine is Rue."

"That's a lovely name," he whispers. "Can I have that one?"

"What? No. You cannot have my name. What did your parents call you?"

"Haven't got those either."

"Everyone has parents, child," Kane says only slightly dismissively. "It's a bit of a biological necessity."

"I never knew mine. Raised in an orphanage, I was. Managed to get meself on a ship headed to the 'New World,' they called it. The boat landed here, and I saw all these beautiful homes with these incredible chimneys. Thought to meself, *Self, you're small. I'll bet you could make a bit of coin cleaning those chimneys. Provide a useful service on top.*"

"How old were you? How old *are* you?" I ask, fascinated.

"They didn't take great care with birthdays or recordkeeping at St. Stevens, so I don't quite know how old I am. I think I mighta been nine when I came over and couldn't have worked the homes more than a year before I met my end. Which turned out not to be much of an end in the end."

"So, your age is unclear too. Wow."

I think for a moment before the ghost boy interjects with more of his tale.

"Got stuck in the chimney I did. Got proper scared, but told meself it was just a little game of hide-and-seek and someone would come looking for me any minute. That helped with the fear, but didn't change the outcome."

"So, what are you still doing here? Why didn't you cross over? And what is the deal with all the cabinets opening and plate throwing?"

"Oh yeah. I stayed because I'd never belonged anywhere before. Never had a home. It felt nice to feel like I was a part of something, tied to somewhere after a short life of wandering nowhere. Now I'm just a bit bored, I guess."

"Shine wears off after a couple hundred years," Kane mutters.

"I still feel a deep connection to the house that I can't seem to shake, but I remember what it was like to disappear in that darkness, no one even bothering to look for me. I've been trying to get someone's attention ever since. Been trying to play hide-and-seek for ages, and no one ever tries to find me. So, I make a bit of noise to make it easier for them."

"Aside from being invisible to me until recently, you haven't been that hard to miss," I say, a bit awestruck at all of this.

"You two sure weren't easy to miss with all the noises you were just making in here."

I blush at the memory, and then my mind catches up with my mouth as I try to wrap my head around this specter's sad story. "You never knew your parents. You never had a birthday. And you don't even have a name. That's awful."

I look at Kane, who stares on, nonplussed. "Do something."

"We all play the cards we were dealt, Mayday. Not everyone's story belongs to the annals of time. Most don't, in fact. Most do the best they can with what little time they have and are forgotten faster than their bodies can cool. If they're even ever truly known in the first place. Which, it sounds like, this poor chap wasn't."

"That's grim," I reply. My feelings of pity and hopelessness overwhelming me.

"That's life."

"Or in this case, afterlife," I mumble.

"Don't shoot the messenger." He speaks over me.

"Or in this case, the reaper." My ire for Kane bubbles back to the surface.

"Grim. Reaper," the young ghost coos on a light laugh, seemingly unfazed by his own doomed lot in life. "The concept of a scythe-wielding skeleton of death originated during the Black Death in Europe, when robed figures began appearing in art meant to depict the savage destruction of a third of the population."

"Weren't you alive during the Black Death?"

"No. My story begins many years later, during a second epidemic in France in the 1600s. I'm not *that* old!"

"Well, either way, I think that's a fitting name for your melancholic moodiness, *Grim*."

"We're not doling out nicknames when this poor child hasn't even been given the honor of *one* name. Really, Rue. How very rude," Kane deflects sardonically, but there's a sliver of truth to his jab that hits me right in the solar plexus.

As I think back on all the things I've said to this faceless entity over the years, I blanch. I am mortified that I spoke so hostilely to a mere child. I never stopped to think about his circumstances. It never occurred to me he could be anything more than a nuisance to me. I used words that cut and wounded because I had no sense of who was causing this trouble. He had no face. So, I treated him as if he didn't have a heart either. And now that I can see the warm gaze and friendly demeanor of this apparition, I feel terrible for the way I mistreated him in the past. We are so quick to show unkindness to that which we do not know.

Determined to do right by the family ghost, I decide to make up for past faults. "You're right," I say begrudgingly to Kane, then turn my attention back to the boy. "And you. I am very sorry that I've been so mean to you over the years. The way I've spoken to you is unacceptable. I never stopped to think of what you might be going through."

"It's okay. How could you have known?"

"Well, I won't let it happen again. We need to give you a name." I think back to his tale for clues about a proper name. "What about Steven? In honor of the first place you remember living."

"Don't much care to remember that place. Bad memories there, to be certain."

"Of course. That makes sense." Then it hits me. "Since you don't have to hide anymore, little guy, it's your turn to explore. What about Seek?"

"I like that," the child says, his ash-stained face alight. "Call me Seek." He beams with pride.

"And now you've been found," Kane grumbles to my left, taking in the exchange between me and the child with something unfamiliar behind his eyes.

My eyes stay locked on Kane, who has gone eerily still, his jaw clenched so tight that I can see the muscles twitching. His hands are fisted at his sides, but it's not anger I see–I don't know what it is.

Is he mad at me? Is he upset over the kiss?

I swallow hard and turn away. "I'm gonna make some tea. Wanna help pick out the cups, Seek?"

"I'd love to!"

"The selection is limited on account of a certain ash-faced adolescent using the china for gravity experiments, but I'm sure we'll find something." I smile at Seek as we walk to the kitchen.

My fingers tremble as I reach for the kettle. I need to ground myself, focus on something real. Boiling water, tea leaves. My mind wanders where it shouldn't. To Kane's lips.

Those lips.

I lean against the counter and shut my eyes, trying to block it out–but it's there, vivid as ever.

The way his mouth claimed mine. The press of his body. The sound he made–somewhere between a growl and a sigh.

He kissed me like he was dying. Or like I was. And now? He won't even look at me.

I stare down at my hands. They're still shaking. From the grief, from the boy's story. From Kane.

I don't know what he's thinking. I don't know if he regrets it. But I do know this: I've never been kissed like that before.

Like I mattered. Like I was something to be treasured. I don't think I'll ever forget it. Even if he already has.

Chapter Fifteen

I SCREAM, YOU SCREAM

KANE

RUE SPENT THE EVENING SLEEPING—THE FIRST SMART DECISION she'd made since I arrived. I could not sleep. Though I do not need the same amount of rest as a mortal might, my energy levels still require regular resetting. But that quiet has been hard to come by since that kiss. My mind was consumed. The gentle pressure of Rue's lips against mine lingered. The honeysuckle taste on her tongue haunted. The warmth of her touch radiated.

It's been hours since Rue and I had crossed over into a territory far more dangerous than anything I've experienced since my own crossing over, and I was having a hard time concentrating on anything else. As Rue rested, I read. My mind flitting between the pages of her well-worn library in between fits of distraction as our kiss played in a loop in my mind. Not even the haunting prose of Brontë could keep my thoughts off Rue.

"Now what?" Rue blurts from her spot on the couch. She sits in the lotus pose, her back straight, her eyes peering straight ahead.

When she entered the room, I have no idea. How long she's been there, I could not say. For a being with an actual body, she is quiet. And I must be even more distracted than I thought. I need to pull it together.

I glance out the window and see the sun pouring through the curtains. "Good morning to you too."

"Let's go somewhere."

"Before breakfast?" I deadpan.

"I don't have time for breakfast, Kane. I need to do stuff," Rue huffs, her frustration coloring her cheeks crimson in an infuriatingly adorable way.

"You should always make time for breakfast, Mayday. A perfectly brewed cup of coffee, accompanied by a freshly baked croissant, enjoyed leisurely on a balcony overlooking the Seine? I can almost smell the beans and taste the folded layers of butter now. Divine." I briefly close my eyes and take an exaggerated inhale. "If you haven't done that, can you even say you've lived?"

Rue stares daggers at me from across the room. I wish she'd point those peepers down at the table between us, where that mini mountain of a cat lies like a crumpled afghan. The tension in her forehead softens.

"Fine," she says calmly. "Let's do that then."

"No can do, Mayday. This isn't Disney, and I ain't a genie." I pause for a fraction of a second. "But you're welcome to rub me if you want to be totally sure."

She ignores this crass comment, staying on topic.

"I'm serious, Grim. Let's go. Portal to Paris, please."

"*Ce n'est pas possible, ma chère.*"

"Why isn't it possible? We took that portal before. Let's take another one."

"The portals are reserved for business use only. Death's Door, LLC runs a tight ship. *Company property is to be used for company business only.*" I recite the passage from *Reaper Regulations* from rote memory. "I can use them to return to the OtherWorld. We can use them to attend to a soul departing, but they're not available for personal use."

"So, I guess I can cross Everest off the bucket list," Rue jokes.

"Yeah, my leadership doesn't sanction a lot of vacation time, probably because time doesn't belong to us anymore after we cross over." Not much of anything belongs to us anymore over there, but I don't share those bleak thoughts with Rue. She doesn't need to know about the crushing mundanity and loneliness that most endure.

Moments of my mortal life that mattered pierce the veil of memory. I shake them off. "Anyway, I'm afraid there's no private passage to reserve."

"Bummer. High altitude isn't really my thing anyway." She pauses for a beat, then smiles. "You know what airline travels to the OtherWorld?"

I stare at her blankly.

"Spirit."

"Wow."

"Oh, come on! That was good."

"It wasn't bad. More entertaining than ALP's *Soul, You Made It to the AfterLife. Now What?* welcome video."

Her face falls. "Are you serious? There's a welcome video?"

"Sure, it's all very corporate. The world is overpopulated as is, lots of deaths every second of every day and we have to get each one to processing. It's just easier to have you all watch the welcome video that answers the same questions you all have so we can continue with our jobs."

"Will I live in the OtherWorld when I die?" My spine straightens at her question.

"Doubtful. Not every soul lives there. The OtherWorld is Big D's territory so most who live there work for him. There are other sectors that some go to if they're chosen for placement, and then some choose bliss."

"Bliss?"

"Uh, yeah." I scratch the back of my head. "It's better explained in the video during the 'Which Soul Are You?' quiz."

Rue chuckles softly and I can't help but note how nice it sounds. "I would rather hear it from you."

"Fine," I relent. "The Bliss is where the majority of crossovers end up. Your own little peace of happiness. For you I would imagine it would be a library of endless books. Some will have an endless rock concert. Others, a fishing trip that never ends. It's very personalized."

"Wow, that sounds amazing," She pauses and I see the question forming before she asks. "Why would you choose reaping over that?"

"Nothing is given for free, Mayday. Bliss has a heavy cost."

"What's the cost?"

"You forget," I manage while walking toward the window and looking outside at the greying skies.

"Forget what?" She asks.

"Everything," I turn back to look at her. "Family, friends, loved ones–anything that makes you, you is erased. Some souls are given the option to work, to–for a lack of a better term, 'live', in the world they are assigned to. Or they can forget."

"Wow, I don't know which is worse, forgetting everything, or remembering and being unable to see your loved ones again."

"It's not as bad as you think. You learn fast to remember what you need to in order to do your job and keep your sanity while tucking the rest away."

"Why?"

I find myself growing tired of her questions.

"Because remembering too much gets you in trouble, and that's the final question." I point my finger at her as she opens her mouth to ask another question.

"Fine," Rue uncrosses her legs, stands gingerly from the couch and heads to the kitchen. "Esther," she yells over her shoulder and the cat instantly pops its head up, peers toward Rue and saunters after her, but not before glaring back at me with a vicious amount of side-eye.

"Feeling's mutual, furball, I assure you."

Rue returns moments later, a new look of determination in her eyes. "Get your coat," she says.

"I don't have a coat. Just this suit. I'm impervious to temperature on Earth."

"Well, that was anticlimactic."

"Sorry to disappoint. I'm normally quite climactic."

"Has that line ever worked?" she asks dryly.

"More times than I can count." I smirk.

"Because you're so terrible at math?" Rue fires back.

"Exactly." I give her the verbal-sparring victory and change the subject.

"Where are we off to?"

"I want ice cream."

I stare at her, brow cocked. "Ice cream?"

"Yes. Ice cream."

There's a beat of silence while I try to figure out if she's being serious.

"That's what's keeping you from spiraling into despair? Frozen dairy?"

"That and spite," she says brightly, grabbing her bag. "You coming or what?"

Someone save me.

"Going out in your condition is ill-advised."

"Trying to stop me is also ill-advised. Do you really want to find out who's going to win this argument?"

Even though I know this is a terrible idea, I stand and button my jacket. Rue grins victoriously.

She's dressed like the lead singer of a band that performs in catacombs—black combat boots, ripped fishnets, a short black dress, and a jacket with more silver hardware than seems strictly necessary. Her hair is thrown up in a half-messy bun with bright orange streaks peeking out, and her eyeliner looks like it could cut someone.

She looks absurd.

And I hate to admit that I like it.

Also, Catacombs would make a great name for a band, but I digress.

She looks like a gothic fever dream—defiant yet delicate, like something that shouldn't belong in the sunlight but roots itself there anyway.

We head into town. She insists on walking instead of getting a ride. I once again advise against it. She reminds me that this may be her last chance to walk to town, and I have no comeback for that, so I fold.

As we walk, I ask about the cat. "Why Esther?"

"What?" Rue asks at the question I volleyed without a preamble.

"The cat. Loathsome little thing. Why did you name it Esther?"

"Oh. Why? Is she growing on you?"

"Absolutely not. I was simply making conversation. Which I am happy to unmake. Forget I asked."

"I named her after Esther Greenwood. The protagonist of—"

"Sylvia Plath's *The Bell Jar.* Yes, I know. I've been around for centuries. I read. A lot."

"Yes, well, she's one of my favorite characters from literature, so I named my favorite creature after my literary heroine."

"Esther's road was rather bleak. Alienated, isolated, suicidal. And you say I'm the grim one."

"She was passionate about learning, felt outcast from her peers, and was terrified of what lay ahead in her life. So, yeah, she resonates with me."

"Maudlin, party of one," I growl, low in my throat.

"Pompous, party of *fuck you*," she fires back, much to my satisfaction.

I do seem to love getting a rise out of her.

I snicker softly, which she harmonizes with a grumble. Then we walk for a while in decidedly comfortable silence.

This part of town is small with a historic air. The bricks hold the stories that the old people in rocking chairs no longer tell. Humidity adds a stifling weight to every measured step we take. Rue stands out like a single storm cloud on a clear day. People stare. She doesn't notice—or pretends not to.

When we arrive at the ice cream shop, she practically vibrates with joy.

"Aha!" she crows. "I can smell the sugar from here."

"It amazes me you actually consume this willingly," I mutter, eyeing the pastel-colored chalkboard menu with deep suspicion. "It smells like melted feelings and burned marshmallows in here."

I take in the vibrant walls decorated with cartoonish representations of medieval battlements and then spy a list of nonsensical flavors. I shudder.

"Kane," she says solemnly, turning to me as she points at the glass case, "that is strawberry funnel cake. It's everything you love about the state fair in dairy form. Don't disrespect it."

"What's a state fair?"

"How old are you?"

"Very. Also, not from around here, so ..." I leave the vowel sound hanging between us as an eager youngster comes to greet us.

"Welcome to Dairy Castle. I'm Jake, your court scoopster. Care to try any of our regal flavors, milady?" the poor kid intones with as much enthusiasm as he could possibly muster for such an asinine job.

Believe me, kid, I get it. And I wish I could say it gets better. But it doesn't.

I look at Rue, whose face is alight.

"Can I try the Damsel's Double Chocolate and the Moat-cha Mint?"

"Moat-cha? Are you serious? This place doesn't just have regular ice cream?" I ask, shocked at the inanity of this place.

"Shut up," she responds. "What flavor do you want?"

"I do not want."

"No way. I'm getting you something."

Jake hands over two tiny spoons of semi-hard cow's milk, and I work feverishly not to vomit.

"Oh, these are both delicious," Rue moans after the bite.

The sound sends undeniable daggers to the base of my spine. That's definitely a noise I'd love to produce from her. Which is a thought I try to suppress, followed immediately by another annoying epiphany. *Am I jealous of ice cream?*

Rue's response to Jake brings me back.

"I will take a scoop of each in a bowl. And he will have …" Rue looks from me to the case and back again.

I indicate nothing.

"Let me get one scoop of A Court of Thyme and Rosewater."

The nausea returns. "Whatever happened to plain old vanilla?"

"You snooze, you lose," Rue singsongs.

I can't help but notice the befuddled look on Jake's face. I do everything I can to repress the laughter threatening to bubble over.

I manage to control my amusement while Jake doles out a few scoops. Rue pays, and we make our way back outside.

Rue's continued exuberance makes it almost difficult to brood. Almost.

I sigh heavily. "I'm not eating the ice cream."

"Oh, yes, you are."

"I'm a denizen of the OtherWorld. I don't need food."

"You have no problem downing the booze in your pocket," she says under her breath while poking the spot where my flask resides. "Therefore, you can consume this."

"I *can* eat. I just don't need to. Can't say the same for the delicious burn and sweet relief of a drop of grappa."

We sit on a bench outside, the sun filtering through the trees in soft gold. Rue takes a bite of her ice cream and makes that delicious sound again. The ice cream I could take or leave, but that moan I would gladly devour.

"You're going to stare at me the entire time like a judgmental statue, aren't you?"

"I don't judge."

"You're literally judging me right now. I can practically see the gavel growing out of your ass."

"I'm observing. Professionally."

"Whatever. Do you," she says and takes another huge helping to her face. After she swallows, she looks at me. "Is it just me, or was Jake looking at me kinda funny? I mean, most people in this town look at me like I have a third head, but I don't know. There was something off about the whole vibe."

I think about whether or not I want to fill Rue in or if this is one of those post-mortal realizations that one must come to on their own terms. She's got a lot to digest, I decide, not the least of which is mounds of lactose, so I'll get her up to speed.

"Well, Jake couldn't see me, so perhaps he found it odd, watching you yell at thin air and order ice cream for your invisible friend."

"What do you mean?"

"We've been over this, mortal. I am not from around here. I come when needed–which is usually a coronary episode. Those I come for can see me. Those who will live on get to carry on in blissful ignorance."

"So, that kid watched me have a full-blown dialogue with what?"

"Nothing, I imagine. Must have looked pretty weird. Even for you, Rue."

Her lips purse in irritation. "I'd tell you off, but I doubt it would land."

"Probably should save that precious breath then." I wink as she rolls her eyes.

"You're impossible."

"You've mentioned that a time or three. You're running out of material, Mayday."

She ignores me while scooping another bite and shoving it toward my face.

I blink. "You can't be serious."

"Live a little, Kane."

"I did–centuries ago. Overrated, in all honesty."

Her face drops into an annoyed scowl as she wiggles the spoon.

I roll my eyes. "You want me to eat a spoonful of sugar paste from your bowl like some pathetic romantic-comedy side character?"

"Yes. Precisely."

I give her a long look. She doesn't blink.

With an exaggerated sigh, I lean forward and take a bite. The flavor hits like it's settling a score.

"Well?"

"It's not awful," I state plainly. "Possibly the least offensive mortal invention I've tasted this century."

She beams before reaching over and running her thumb over my bottom lip. I freeze, unable to think as she pulls away and brings her thumb to her mouth, sucking off the ice cream.

Well, that's going to be an image that will haunt me this evening.

She seems happy and peaceful for a moment longer, and then something dawns on her. Her entire countenance shifts.

"Wait," she says. "If Jake can't see you, if people can't see you, then how are we going to spend the next several days together?"

"Do you want to spend the next several days together?" I ask with a small level of surprise in my voice.

"Well ..." she hedges.

"Not that I was complaining," I clarify.

"I just mean, how can I do earthbound activities with someone who is invisible to all but the undead?"

"No, I got it."

"I'll look like a crazy person, talking to myself."

"That does seem to be a potential side effect," I admit.

A light bulb goes off behind Rue's eyes. "I have an idea."

"What?" I ask, intrigued.

"I'll put my earbuds in. People walk around all day long, looking like they're talking to themselves. No one will blink twice."

"Okay, there's one crisis averted. Now to figure out how to actually spend that time ..." I offer, and there is that light-bulb moment again. She's like the Christmas tree in Rockefeller Center.

"Come on," she says, her voice soft. "Let's go sit under the tree."

I look from her outstretched hand to the large tree across the street. "There's no bench, and I'm not holding your hand." I can't, not when the memory of her lips and tongue against mine is on replay in my brain.

"You sit on the ground–"

"HA!" I snort, shaking my head. "I already had to return home once because you ruined a good suit. I refuse to allow you to mess up another."

She rolls her too-pretty eyes at me.

"So, stop wearing a suit! Put on some jeans, unbutton that top button."

I swat her hand away as it goes to my collar. I'm not ready to answer those questions. My hope is she'll be gone before the topic can be broached.

Rue acquiesces as she holds out her delicate pinkie. "Fine, one finger?"

I eye her warily while standing up. "Some might say you enjoy touching me, Mayday."

She shrugs, trying to act nonchalant, but her cheeks flush a pretty pink that is undeniable. Since I'm in such a giving mood, I relent.

I wrap my long finger around hers while pulling her across the street. There it is–the feeling I hate and love. The heat I feel from our connection–it's more addictive than anything has a right to be. I'm beginning to crave her touch. But I can't. I won't allow myself to become attached to her.

Here I am, a centuries-old reaper with a dark past, lounging under the shade of an elm tree, watching Rue shovel bits of medieval-themed ice cream past her decadent lips.

"What's your favorite color?" she asks out of nowhere.

It's such a human question. The unexpectedness of it catches me off guard.

I could ask her why she cares. I could ignore the question altogether.

Instead, I repeat back, "Favorite color?" like the concept itself is foreign. Which it is actually. What a pointless thing to ask a reaper.

I glance down at my ever-present black suit, then think of my home in the OtherWorld—a place of countless greys and shadowed light.

Is brown an acceptable favorite color? Would she laugh at me if I said it?

"Purple," she says suddenly, nodding like she's just come to a great realization.

I frown. "What about it?"

"I think purple is your favorite color," she says simply.

I blink at her. "You asked me a question and then proceeded to answer it yourself?"

"Well, you were taking too long," she teases, licking a stray drop of ice cream from her spoon.

I feel something tighten in my chest and in my pants. Fucking perfect.

I arch a brow. "What makes you think my favorite color would be purple?"

She tilts her head, considering. "Not like standard-crayon-box purple," she clarifies. "You're far too sophisticated for that, Grim—I know that."

I narrow my eyes. "Are you mocking me?"

She grins. "A little."

I exhale through my nose, already regretting sitting

down. "Go on then," I say dryly. "Enlighten me. What kind of purple am I exactly?"

She hums, tapping her spoon against her chin. "I see you as a deep, dark purple," she declares. "Not the kind with red undertones–no, that would be too passionate. Yours would have blue undertones. Something cool, controlled, balanced. A color that holds weight, but doesn't demand attention."

"That was oddly specific," I murmur.

"Well, you are oddly specific, Kane," she counters, stretching out on the grass and looking up at me through thick, dark lashes.

I should look away. Really, I should. I've never been good at doing what I should though.

"You're a man who's seen every color the world has to offer," she continues. "For something to be your favorite, it would have to stand out. It would have to be memorable, different."

She lets the words linger, something unspoken hovering between us.

Something I refuse to name. For a while, I don't say anything.

Because the truth is, I don't think she's wrong.

Purple–deep, cool, regal–is a color that has always drawn my eye. It's rich without being garish, elegant without demanding.

I clear my throat, tamping down the lingering sensation her words leave behind. "You're dangerously perceptive," I say at last.

"It's a gift." Her smirk is infuriating.

I shift my focus to her instead, deciding it's only fair to turn the question back on her.

"So," I say, leaning in slightly, letting my voice drop into something low and deliberate, "what's your favorite color, Mayday?"

For the first time since I met her, Rue pauses. Her pupils dilate, and her plush lips part ever so slightly. Does she feel something?

Before I can think too much about it, Rue blinks and clears her throat to answer; her voice is quieter than before.

"The color of the sky before a storm," she murmurs,

watching the clouds roll overhead. "When it's almost black but still blue. When it looks like it's holding something wild inside it, something waiting to break loose."

I stare at her for a long, long moment. Because that is precisely what she looks like to me. Something on the verge of breaking loose. Something beautiful and fleeting and impossible to hold.

Rue turns her head toward me, brows raised slightly.

"You look like there's a battle being waged behind your eyes," she observes.

"That's because there is." No sense in denying it.

She snickers, tossing her spoon into the now-empty cup. "Good. You deserve some internal struggle."

I shake my head, exhaling through my nose, hoping this sensation will leave through my nostrils with the effort. But it doesn't. And as I stand to my full height and brush the earth off my spectral vestments, I cannot help returning to a single, nagging thought– *This was nice.*

Chapter Sixteen

A SMALL STAIN

RUE

I'M HALFWAY THROUGH A BOWL OF REHEATED SPAGHETTI MY mother left me before she went back home. It's the only meal she knows how to make and a skill—or lack thereof—that she's passed down to me. In Chez Chamberlain, it's the microwave or delivery. Looking around the quiet living room, I wonder briefly if Kane has decided to take his dark brooding elsewhere when the air suddenly feels thicker.

A chill races down my spine, dragging tiny claws over my skin. I freeze, fork halfway to my mouth as an eerie, almost-electric tension hums through the room.

"Fuck." Kane's voice sends icicles shooting through the humid air.

I jump when I spot him. He's standing by the window, stiff as a statue, jaw clenched tight enough to shatter marble. His cemetery-inspired phone glows dimly in his hand.

"What's wrong?" I ask, lowering my fork into my bowl.

"Nothing that concerns you," he dismisses in a clipped voice walking toward me at the table.

Rude.

"Okay, Grim, I was trying to be nice since we had a moment earlier with the ice cream. Never mind."

"That was dessert, not destiny, Rue. Don't start seeing things that aren't there."

Kane stares at me, eyes wide as I run my hand under his suit jacket, grab the peak of his left nipple, and twist. Hard. He releases a sound somewhere between a cry and a moan as he winces slightly, though I admit he manages to maintain more composure than I expected.

He stares daggers at me before peeling his jacket open and looking down at his rumpled shirt. We both eye the small red stain above his pectoral.

"Don't patronize me with your presence. Got it, Grim?" I say with steely conviction.

"Did you just get spaghetti sauce on my white Brunello Cucinelli dress shirt?" he asks with deliberate slowness.

"Maybe it was destiny. How about that?"

"How about you learn to make proper pasta? Some All Purpose flour, some water, an egg." He begins to mime the process of kneading the dough like a culinary conductor.

"How about you eat me?" I blurt out petulantly.

He ends his spaghetti symphony and stares into my eyes. "Now, that is a meal I would ki–"

"Don't you dare finish that sentence, Kane!" I cut him off. That does not stop an alluring image from forming in my mind, which I physically attempt to shake loose with a twist of my neck.

The headstone phone chimes again, pulling him away from whatever this moment is. He doesn't move. Doesn't speak. But I can see it–the barely contained storm swirling in those dark green eyes. His fingers twitch around the phone, knuckles white as bone.

"It's a Code CAT," he mutters, lost in his device.

I've never seen this look on his face before. He looks troubled, and it does not instill confidence in me. I knit my brows.

"Code CAT? What's that? I thought you hated cats."

He doesn't look at me as he continues, "Code CAT is short for catastrophe–from the Greek word *kata,* meaning down, and *strophé,* meaning turn. It's a mass casualty event." Any emotion has been sucked out of his voice, but does nothing to lessen the impact of his words. "Bus accident. No survivors," he concludes somberly.

My heart stumbles, skipping like a broken record. The weight of those words sinks into my bones, pressing down, making it hard to breathe.

"How bad?" I ask softly, my snark evaporating.

"Bad enough that Big D is sending me as backup." Kane's jaw tics, his voice dripping with disdain.

"Backup?"

"Yes, Asher"–the way he says the name makes me blink; he practically spits it out, like it tastes rancid on his tongue–"is apparently unable to handle the large influx alone."

"Asher?" I echo. "Friend of yours?"

"Hardly." Kane's lips press into a tight line, his posture somehow going even more rigid. "He's another reaper. Smug and insufferable."

"Wow. He sounds terrible." I smirk. "Why don't you like him? He steal your scythe or something?"

Kane's jaw tightens so hard that I swear I hear it crack before he turns around and glares at me.

"Some folks just don't get along, Mayday. Not meant to be. Asher and I are like oil and water–as in I'd love to burn him in oil and drown him in water."

The look on Kane's face is enough to halt this line of questioning. If he wants to tell me more, he can, but I'm not going to pry. I shake my head while eyeing his shirt, which he keeps glancing down and picking at.

"I might have one of my dad's shirts upstairs if you want it."

"This is a custom-tailored–"

"Shirt with a stain. Wouldn't matter if it was Versace at this point. Better to have something that's at least one uniform color. Now come on. Let me help," I say, stepping closer to him and grabbing the shirt by the collar and beginning to open it at the neck. I notice briefly what looks to be scar tissue just above his collarbone before Kane swats my hands away like they are a pair of houseflies. "What is that?" I ask of his discolored and raised skin.

He ignores me and attempts a joke. "Mayday, while

I can understand your primal urges, I must insist you control yourself."

I stare at him, mouth agape. "Excuse me?"

He looks me over before nodding. "You're excused. Now, if you don't mind, I have thirty-some-odd souls that need to be cleaved unwillingly from their mortal sacks to begin the journey to the OtherWorld. I believe the phrase you use is *BRB*," he says, condescension oozing off each letter.

"Fine," I huff, letting the subject go for now. "But I'm coming with you."

He scoffs while walking out the door toward my cemetery. "Absolutely not."

"Absolutely, yes." I stomp after him as he exits the house at breakneck speed, refusing to lose this battle. "We've been over this, Kane. I'm not sitting around while the clock's ticking on my final days. I want them full. And if that means tagging along while you reap a bunch of unfortunate souls, so be it."

We stop at the first headstone, and he looks back at me, his lips pursed in irritation.

"You have no idea what you're asking for, Rue." His voice is low and dangerous, but I see it. The flicker of uncertainty in his eyes.

"I don't care," I whisper, my voice softer now. "I'm not wasting another second. Please, Kane."

He closes his eyes like he's fighting an internal war. When they snap open again, they're darker. Sharper.

"Fine." He exhales like he's regretting this already. "But you stay out of the way. No talking to the souls. No touching anything. No–"

"Got it, Grim. I'll be a good little shadow."

His eyes narrow. "Somehow, I doubt that," he mutters while holding his hand out for me to grab.

"What? No hugs this time?" I tease before releasing a squeak as he tugs me flush with his body. My hand hits his hard chest, and it takes me by surprise, not feeling a heartbeat.

"Hold on," he breathes in my ear, causing goose bumps to erupt all over my body.

"I'm obviously already–"

And before I can finish the sentence, the world swirls.

I swear, transporting gets worse every damn time. I feel like I've been stuffed into a blender set to liquefy and then spit out into a new dimension. My stomach flips violently, threatening to stage a full-scale rebellion.

Kane's arm is the only thing keeping me from face-planting into the pavement as we appear by a road marker with ribbons wrapped around it.

"We need to work on your landings, Grim," I mutter, blinking away the dizziness. "Ugh, I'm going to hurl that spaghetti."

"Stop talking."

"Charming as ever," I mutter, just loud enough to be heard as I shift my focus forward—and immediately wish I hadn't.

The scene before me is something out of a nightmare.

Twisted metal, scorched rubber, and the skeletal remains of a bus lying in a tangled heap off the highway. The sky is choked with smoke that rises in thick tar-black plumes. Emergency vehicles swarm the site, their flashing red and blue lights strobing across the broken landscape. Sirens continue to scream, the sound shrill and endless, but even still, they're not enough to drown out the other sounds, the ones that come from the wreckage itself. The cries, the ragged sobs and wails of the dying.

I blink hard. My brain is trying to shield me, to soften the edges of what I'm witnessing, but it can't. There are too many bodies. Too much blood. Too many limbs bent in ways they shouldn't. Old, young, male, and female. There's no discrimination, no mercy. Just absolute devastation. My lungs seize in my chest, and for a moment, I am unable to draw in a breath.

"Rue?" Kane's voice is different now. It's not curt or clipped, but softer. Hesitant and almost concerned.

"I'm fine," I say, though I'm anything but.

The weight of this place is clinging to me in the most suffocating way. The grief, pain, and confusion are not just being witnessed. They are consuming me. "Their cries are just haunting. Can't you save them?"

"Rue, there are no survivors. What you hear are the

caterwauls of souls not prepared to cross." I tear my eyes away from a delicate, lifeless hand tangled in a seatbelt and look toward the side of the road. I need something–anything–less unbearable.

My gaze lands on a male figure, casually leaning against the crumpled guardrail. He's tall with long, thick limbs and powerful muscles under a rich black suit that somehow manages to look both expensive and recklessly undone. His dark hair is slicked back, his tie is perfectly loosened with the dress shirt's top button left open. He's not trying too hard, but he doesn't have to. And his smile? Holy shit.

"Well," he murmurs, his voice low, "hello there, gorgeous."

Heat crawls up my neck, spreading across my cheeks like wildfire. His voice is rich and rough, kissed by a British accent and smooth as the grin playing on his lips. I blink. Kane steps in front of me so abruptly that I nearly trip. His back acts as a wall between me and the stranger.

"Rue," he growls in a low warning.

"Ah." The man–Asher, I am assuming–straightens, his smile widening while peering over Kane's shoulder and sweeping his dark eyes over me like he's memorizing every detail. "This must be the special case Big D was going on about with Fate."

"Don't." Kane's voice is pure venom, but Asher just raises a perfectly arched brow.

"Relax, old friend." Asher's grin is lazy, dripping with charm. "I'm just introducing myself; after all, what kind of gentleman would I be if I didn't?"

Kane's jaw clenches so hard that I'm surprised his teeth don't shatter.

"Rue, was it?" The man's gaze locks on to mine, and there's something in his eyes–something warm and inviting, like stepping into the sunlight after a long, cold night. "I'm Asher. A pleasure."

"Uh ... hi." I blink, trying to remember how to function.

Asher's grin deepens. "Charming and beautiful. Kane's been holding out on me." Asher goes to grab the hand unoccupied by Kane's tightening grip.

Kane barks, "Off limits," while pulling me back.

Asher's smile never falters as he steps back. "Just wanted to see if it was true, is all. Not a worry, Doc."

"Doc?" I snicker, causing Kane's eyes to dart my way. "And you hate Grim as a nickname? Doc?"

"All right, Asher." Kane's voice is like ice, his body tense as he ignores me. "Let's get this over with."

"Of course, *Grim*." Asher winks at me before turning back to the wreckage. "But you might want to keep an eye on your girl. I'm waiting for the Sisters to arrive. Once they make their grand entrance, we'll get this party started."

I blink. What does that mean–Sisters?

Kane must sense my question, but doesn't allow me to voice it. He just grabs my arm and steers me toward the wreckage, his grip a little tighter than necessary.

"What's his deal?" I ask, casting a glance over my shoulder at Asher.

"Don't." Kane's voice is low, dangerous.

"Don't what?"

"Don't encourage him."

"Who said I was encouraging anything?"

"You looked at him like you would have given him a kidney."

"Didn't look like he needed a kidney," I mutter under my breath.

"What did you say?" Kane grates out.

I blink, surprised by the edge in Kane's voice.

"Are you …" I trail off, a slow grin tugging at my lips. "Are you jealous?"

Kane's jaw tightens. "No."

"You're a terrible liar."

"I'm not terrible at anything."

I look at the dead body next to me, and suddenly, I'm filled with shame. I forgot for a moment what they're here to do. They act so casual that it's easy to lose sight of the enormity of their assigned task.

"Stop looking at him," he mutters.

"Why?" I manage out weakly as I look at the shocked look frozen on the man's bloodied face.

"His fundamental essence is still trapped inside that body. You looking at him is only going to scare him more.

The more scared they are, the harder they are to reap."
Kane pulls an obsidian handle from his breast pocket.

Where did that come from?

I note the small silver nub on the side and realize
it's a switchblade. He deploys and retracts the long silver knife's edge several times before returning it to his
pocket. I whip my head up to him in shock.

"His soul is in there, crying out for help?"

Kane winces as he nods. "Yes, they're all very loud."

"So, help him!" I say frantically while trying to pry
myself from Kane's firm grasp.

He jerks me back to him and pulls me around the
bus, where there is no one standing. "I can't let go of you.
Stop trying to remove your fucking hand from mine,"
he growls out.

I look at him and raise my brow. "Why?"

"Because you're alive, remember? When we are
physically connected, I can pass my spectral energy to
you, rendering you invisible to the other living souls in
a space. You let go, they will see you, and you will be
told to leave. Actually, that might not be the worst idea."

"Shut up." I shove his chest. "Help them, Kane! You
can't let them suffer like this."

"Mayday, you think I enjoy this? I'm a reaper, not a
monster. I want these souls to cross over. I do not get
off on pain."

I side-eye him, remembering the way he absorbed
the impact of my firm pinching of his flesh at the house
earlier.

"Not all the time anyway," he amends before continuing, "But if The Sisters are coming, we can't."

"The Sisters?"

"Time and Fate. One controls the *when*, the other the
how. They show up during instances like this to make
sure all souls are properly accounted for."

"Really?"

"Yes, it happens often. So many stories having their
endings written at once requires direct supervision.
Fate's loom moves down to create a new tapestry every
so often and the results are–"

I cut Kane off, "Catastrophic. *Kata, strophé.* A down-
turning." I mime the twisting of the wheel.

"Very good, Rue. So, you do know how to listen. There may be hope for you yet," Kane praises, and while I'm surrounded by this carnage, it shouldn't send a dopamine rush, but it does.

"But these events can be a logistical nightmare," Kane continues. "So many souls to process and cross in such a short amount of time. One slip from a reaper, one miscut of the soul from the body before going to the OtherWorld can ripple and alter pivotal moments in the future of both realms. So, we wait so they can oversee the reaping."

"So, these Sisters, they make the rules then? Did they tell you to bring me back?"

"No. Actually ..."

I jump at the strong female voice and look to see a powerful woman standing next to us. Her long flaxen hair travels past her large breasts. Her skin is bronzed, and her dark eyes look at me in a way that makes me wish I could be invisible from her too.

"Time," Kane mutters, and I watch her lip curl.

"Dr. Kane Deveraux. My, my, my, it's been far too long."

"Funny. I was thinking it hadn't been nearly long enough." Kane's tone is clipped, a blend of defiance and fear.

Time doesn't move. She flows. Everything about her is smooth, graceful, and deliberate. She stands with a kind of poise that makes me feel like I'm a clumsy kid tracking mud across a marble floor.

Her iridescent gown is a shimmering gold that moves like liquid sunlight, swirling around her generous curves, as if it were a living thing. Her skin is flawless, kissed by a thousand sunsets, and her dark eyes stare straight into me.

"Ah." Time tilts her head, eyes narrowing. "So, this is the one who shouldn't be."

I feel my spine straighten, instinctively defensive under her scrutiny. "Excuse me?"

"Rue Chamberlain." Her lips curl into a slow, knowing smile. "You've caused quite the disruption to my symphony, my dear."

I glance at Kane before looking back toward her.

"What's that supposed to mean?" I ask, forcing my voice to stay steady.

"She means," another voice purrs, silky and venomous, "that your thread was severed, your fate sealed. And yet here you are. *Alive.*"

The temperature drops.

"But I thought you just mentioned music," I state shakily.

"That"–she clips the ending *T* sound with powerful effectiveness–"is Time. She is the poet, and I, Fate, am the painter. While she conducts, I weave; while she performs, I sculpt."

Fate towers over me, cold and unyielding. Time amplifies her sister's energy.

Fate's presence is razor-sharp. Her dress is midnight blue, threaded with silver, as though the fabric itself were woven from the night sky. Her jet-black hair falls in thick waves over her shoulders. Her lips are painted a deep, rich red, the color of crushed roses. Her icy eyes, filled with menacing rage, pin me in place.

"Fate," Kane murmurs, his voice a low warning.

"Kane," Fate replies, her tone dripping with disdain. "A mess still follows everywhere you go, I see."

I don't like her.

Not one bit.

"Mess?" I echo, my voice sharper than I intended. "Is that what I am to you?"

Her gaze locks on to mine, and I swear I feel the air around us tighten.

"Don't flatter yourself, mortal." The word is spit like an insult. "You're not special. You're a glitch. A mistake."

My stomach drops.

"Fate." Time's voice is softer, but there's an edge to it. A warning.

"Don't," Kane growls, stepping closer to me–between me and Fate. "I didn't have a choice."

"Didn't you?" Fate's smile is lethal.

"Enough." Time's tone cuts through the tension like a knife. "We're not here to litigate Kane's actions." She turns her gaze toward the wreckage. "We have a job to do."

Fate does not heed her sister's recrimination though.

Her gaze remains fixed on me. "I should cut your thread right here." Her voice is tight, taut with anger. "She altered the tapestry. *My* vision," Fate roars to all who can hear.

"She didn't do it." Kane's grip on my hand tightens. "I did."

"She doesn't belong," Fate snarls.

I can't breathe. Is Fate doing that, or am I just nearing my physical breaking point?

"Enough." Kane's voice is lethal.

His body tenses beside me, and for a moment, I swear the air crackles.

"You may weave the tapestry, but you still need the threads. You cannot sculpt without a chisel, nor can you paint without a brush." Kane's voice rises with commanding authority on each line. He glares at her hovering form. "You still need me, Fate. The higher-ups still need the reapers. Is this a war you're willing to start?"

There is a long silence before Fate sighs, relenting.

"You're right, Kane." Fate's lips curl into a cold smile. "I do need you. For my dirty work. So, I suppose I'll keep you for now. But the thread is fraying, *Doctor*. And when it snaps ..."

Fate glares at Kane for a moment longer before finally shifting her attention to the scene before us.

"Let's get this over with," she mutters, her voice like frost on glass. "Time," she calls affectionately to her sister as they lock eyes and smile mischievously. It's the closest they've looked to twins.

The air ripples like a pebble dropped into a still pond. Time raises her hands, and the world around us seems to slow. The flashing lights, the chaos, the movement–it all becomes muted.

And then the fallen bodies glow. Dozens of them. Men. Women. Children. Writhing and moaning in a sea of fire, blood, and gore, the poor humans glow bright as Fate and Time move through the scene like snakes through sand. Their ethereal forms bend and twist around the mass of agony. I can see the power and pressure that Fate's form elicits from the bodies as Time begins to sing the sweetest, most haunting melody. Time's song is overtaken, however, by the souls, now screaming in their mutilated bodies, begging for help. I grip my chest, my heart beating wildly out of control as a small girl's voice comes from somewhere in the chaos, screaming for her daddy.

"Shit," I whisper, my throat thick with emotion.

"Hey. Hey, look at me." Kane's voice is soft, but there's steel beneath it. "Mayday, breathe and stay here. No one can see you while time stands still."

He releases my hand, and I nearly sob at the loss.

"K-Kane!"

"Rue." His eyes meet mine, and for once, there's no sarcasm. No teasing. Just earnestness. "Please, let me do this. Don't acknowledge the souls. Just soften your focus. This will all be over soon, and then I will get you home."

I nod, swallowing hard as I step back.

Many of the spirits begin to separate from the bodies, their essences hovering in much the way the old woman did on Kane's previous reap. It's simple and haunting and oddly beautiful. But others do not seem to be bending to the pressure of Fate's swirling energy and Time's lyrical tune.

Their bodies convulse, and the sounds that pour forth are not of this world.

"What's happening to them?"

When Kane answers, I realize I asked the question aloud. "They are hesitant. They don't want to cross over. Sometimes, souls don't want to let go. Or they don't know how. Fear. Regret. Love. It anchors them here."

"Can't we help them?" I ask desperately.

Asher chimes in, having made his way back to us as Fate and Time perform their opening act, "Some souls may choose to wander, but that option is not on the table for those whose earthly stories end in catastrophe. All of those must be reaped and rent from their mortal casings and crossed over. No alternatives. No exceptions."

"And if they don't go willingly?"

I immediately regret asking. Asher's face takes on a demonic edge, and Kane's face is painted with a mixture of madness and sadness.

Asher answers with steely resolve, "Then we make them."

Kane and Asher share a glance, then each draw a hand to their breast pockets. Kane pulls the shiny black-and-silver switchblade from before, immediately drawing the sharp edge out through the top of the handle. Asher brings a large hunting knife out of his, the teeth of its serrated edge adding a layer of menace to the already-terrifying instrument.

"Boys," Fate thunders from above, the noise cracking all around us.

Her sister chimes in, "It's time."

They both laugh, causing the air around them to burst into violent fits of thunder and lightning. Rain begins to pour as the Sisters cackle.

Kane slowly removes his jacket, handing it to me, all expression, all feeling gone from his face. "Hold this for me, please. This will only take a minute."

I take his jacket, noting how much broader his shoulders are than I thought. He rolls his sleeves up, one at a time, the blade glistening in his firm grip as the veins in his forearms throb.

My eyes trail up his arms to the single spot of red I put there what now feels like ages ago. And perhaps in many ways, it was.

"Be careful," I find myself saying, suddenly very concerned for Kane's well-being. "Wouldn't want to mess up your fancy Italian shirt," I joke to break the unbreakable tension in the air between us.

"If you can," Kane says gravely, his eyes boring into mine, "look away. If you can't"–he pauses–"try to remember this is not who I am."

"Not all of you anyway," Asher says as he slaps Kane on the shoulder and smirks his devious grin. "Shall we?" he asks, and the two turn toward the catastrophe.

And then there is carnage. Pain and depravity, the likes of which I have never seen. No one has, not living anyway. It's unthinkable. Asher and Kane stalk through the wreckage and the dead bodies. They deftly move from one wispy form to another, using their blades with stone-cold precision. But their knives don't pierce the flesh, nor do they draw blood. They're severing tendrils that tether the soul to the body. Grey and black wisps that wrap around the smoky souls like veins or vines.

The reapers don't speak. They move with practiced ease. Asher steps up to a body, lifts his curved steel, and makes a clean movement just about the chest. There is a small jolt, the inky tethers separate from the essence, and the soul detaches before rising.

Kane mirrors the motion a few feet away. He doesn't look at the faces of the dead. His focus is on the exact placement of the blade, the timing of the release. He completes the task without hesitation.

Every time a thread is severed, Fate intones the word: "thread" in a deep, sonorous voice. Immediately after, Time responds with a sharp, high-pitched sound.

The process is surgical. Clinical. The bodies remain untouched beyond the final stillness. Nothing is left behind except silence and order.

I try to look away, but I cannot. I am transfixed by the magic and the mayhem of it. Then it happens.

Kane moves to a body whose spirit won't separate. The smoke remains tethered to the chest. He steals a glance my way, and I watch as his face drops at the realization that I have not followed his simple instructions.

He mouths again, *Look away.*

The rain continues to pound, sending diamonds of light popping off his silver switchblade. I do not avert my gaze. He looks skyward, only to see Fate and Time glaring down at him. He sighs and returns to the stubborn soul. He raises his powerful arm up in the air and plunges it into the chest cavity of the young man beneath him. And then again. And again. Stroke after stroke, Kane destroys this being with an animalistic fury that takes my breath away.

Blood spurts and splashes everywhere, covering his already-soaked shirt in pools of crimson and pink. He looks completely unhinged. There can be no denying his raw ruthlessness. Kane continues to brutalize the body below him as small wisps of smoke plume from each new slice. Despite the brutality of this scene before me, Kane's power is undeniable.

Then I look up and see the two Sisters singing and laughing, conducting and weaving. And I realize with my next breath how utterly powerless Kane truly is. His physical strength juxtaposes with his captivity, and it is impossible not to see a new side to my Grim Reaper—a chained animal, capable of unthinkable destruction.

As Kane effortlessly slashes away and the man's spirit finally cleaves wholly from his mortal form, I remember what Kane said just moments ago.

"I'm a reaper, not a monster."

Thoughts race through my head, ramping up my anxiety as I pore through a series of unimaginable scenarios.

He may be a reaper, a cog in this system of beings in the OtherWorld I cannot begin to comprehend, but there can be no denying that this ferocity belongs to a monster.

My mind begins to quiet, and my body stills as one singular thought takes hold. *My monster.*

Chapter Seventeen

ONE DAY I WILL WAKE UP

RUE

THAT MUST HAVE BEEN A DREAM. THERE'S NO WAY THAT wasn't a nightmare. What just happened could not have happened. Not in this reality. Not in any reality.

I blink my eyes closed, physically scrunching my face to push these haunting images out of my brain. In the dark behind my eyelids, Kane's mayhem plays on a loop, accompanied by the sounds of innocent suffering.

I open my eyes again slowly. Hoping to be reborn into a new world. One that does not contain the horrors of catastrophe.

But of course, I do not. I rouse into this cold one.

I don't remember how we got back. One second, I was surrounded by smoke and chaos and death; the next, I'm home.

I sit up from the couch, my body heavy with exhaustion. The weight of what I saw and felt sinks into me, dragging me down like quicksand.

I don't even realize I'm shaking until Kane crouches in front of me, his green eyes softer than I've ever seen them.

"Rue." My name is a whisper, an olive branch.

"I ..." My voice breaks. "That was ... I ..." I can't form words.

"I know, *ma chère.*"

And he does. I know he does. This man has seen, felt, and heard all those cries for centuries, been party to limitless pain, absorbed infinite sadness. He's been forced to play a wicked part in Time's cruel play. He has the skills to help Fate mold and paint the most surrealistic of horrors. He is Death's spawn. And he has burrowed dangerously deep under my skin.

I look up at him, my eyes burning with unshed tears.

"Your shirt is clean," I say, noticing how crisp, white, and dry his button-down is. And looking for any way to divert the conversation from where my mind and heart think they want to take it.

"Well, you've been asleep for a few hours, so I had time to change."

"What?!" I say frantically. "I've lost so much time!"

"That was a lot," he states calmly. "Your body needed time to recharge."

"But it felt like only moments ago. The memories are so fresh."

"Those won't ever go away, I'm afraid. And they won't get any easier to cope with." I can hear the knowledge in his voice.

"Kane." My throat is tight.

"Talk to me. I'm here." He reaches for me, placing his firm hands on the tops of my thighs, and I flinch at the contact. He looks down, then back to me. He does not release his grip; instead, he digs his deadly hands more firmly into my flesh. "That is not me, Rue. I have no choice."

"Not all of you anyway," I parrot Asher's line meekly.

"What I am capable of does not define who I am." The silence lingers. "And I will never hurt you."

The look I give him must make him see the doubt because he repeats himself earnestly.

"Ever."

"No one can promise that," I whisper, thinking of the many ways Kane could do just that. Now that he's found his way under my skin and into my heart.

I take a steadying breath. His statuesque form frozen below me, arms still atop my thighs, face locked on mine.

Then I surprise myself by smiling. I place my hands momentarily over Kane's, then run my fingers along the length of his outer arms. I drink in the muscle and corded tension as I wend my way up his biceps to his shoulders. My hands trail over the crease of his neck, and I finally place my palms as firmly on his cheeks as his are on my thighs. Without words, with something more than words, I speak to Kane as I move my face closer to his and pull his nearer mine. He willingly gives me the lead as I give myself over to this sometimes man, sometimes monster, sometimes *mine.*

Except he isn't a man. He isn't a monster. And he isn't mine.

But before I can let those thoughts cloud my judgment or falter my resolve, I pull his face to mine and kiss him. I tell him with my assertive action that I see all of him and I want in. I dive my tongue into his warm mouth and beg him silently to ravage me. He digs his fingers even more firmly into my thighs. I can feel his strength, and it sends warmth instantly up my legs. His fingers dig into my bare flesh. I can feel the marks he's leaving, and all I can think is, *More.*

I want him to mark me everywhere. I want him to claim me. To consume me.

My tongue works feverishly to encourage him to pursue me and push further, harder. I feel myself coming unglued, giving over to temptation and lust in ways I've never known in all my days.

And in an instant, Kane takes the lead in this dance in the most unexpected way. He trails his hands up my sides, mirroring mine from moments before. He brings them to my cheeks. His hands dig into the space behind my jaw, his nails clawing my flesh. And I love it.

And then he presses his forehead against mine and pulls our lips apart. We both breathe heavily, my heart pounding. He peppers kisses against my mouth, alternately swiping his tongue along my chin and lips, as though I was the first meal he'd had in ages.

He slows, wrapping his hand around the back of my head, his fingers splayed between the strands of my hair.

He hums against my lips in a final chaste kiss and then pulls his face away from mine so he can look me in the eyes.

His right hand slides forward again to cup my left

cheek. He does not need to say anything. But he speaks anyway. "Thank you."

I smile in response as a single tear escapes from my eye, wetting his thumb with my unsaid response.

My thoughts trail from Kane's fractured centuries to this moment of pure bliss. I sigh. I try to take it all in. It feels wonderfully impossible. Like the world is always a little bigger than we are, and that's exactly the way it's supposed to be.

Then my mind drifts to my now, and I voice a question that I'm not sure Kane wants to answer. I have to ask it anyway. "When it's my time"–I swallow hard, my voice barely a whisper–"am I ... am I going to be scared like them?"

His expression softens. And for a moment, the guarded walls he always keeps up–those impenetrable shields–crack.

"No," he says, voice gentler than I've ever heard it. "You won't be."

My chest tightens.

"Will I ..." My voice breaks. "Will I be trapped? In my body? Screaming for help, but no one can hear me?"

His jaw clenches, and something dark flashes behind his eyes.

"I won't let that happen." His voice belies his resolve at this promise. "I swear it, Rue." His voice is steady again as he grips my hand firmly, bringing it up to his lips. "When it's time," he whispers against my knuckles while closing his eyes, "I'll be there. I'll make sure you are not alone."

My vision blurs as all the tears finally fall.

"Thank you," I whisper, my voice barely audible.

Without thinking, without hesitating, I fall into him, wrapping my arms around his neck and holding on like he's the only thing keeping me from crashing against the rocky shore. My lighthouse in the dizzying fog. For a moment, he's still. Rigid, like I've come to expect from him. Like he doesn't know what to do.

But he doesn't pull away. "Mayday," he whispers into my hair as his arms come around me, holding me tight. He says it not like it's my name, but rather like he's the one that might be desperately lost at sea.

I cling tighter to him, marveling at his warmth and solidity. And for the first time since this nightmare began, I let myself breathe.

Because, in this moment …

I'm not alone.

Not anymore.

At least not for now.

Chapter Eighteen

PAGES UNFOLDING

KANE

THE HERMLE GRANDFATHER CLOCK IN THE HALL OF RUE'S family home announces the evening hour in eight steady notes. Each gong marks the passage of a second. They seem so insignificant when taken in this way–seconds, one at a time. The setting of the sun feels like a more tangible reminder that time is fleeting. In this realm anyway. Perhaps seeing the change take place helps our comprehension. Another sense to help us wrap our minds around the inexplicable.

At any rate, it's now the evening of the day following our kiss, and Rue is laughing. Not just smiling. Not the sarcastic snorts she seems to enjoy tossing my way when I'm being *intolerable*. No, this is a real laugh–light, full-bodied, spilling out of her like sunlight through stained glass.

She's sprawled across the rug in the living room, a halo of tangled hair fanned around her head, teasing Seek with a feathered cat toy that Esther keeps trying to murder. Seek shrieks with delight, flipping through the air like gravity is more of a suggestion than a rule.

It should be funny. They are amused. I can decipher from social cues that I, too, should be amused. But all I can do is watch her and see the shadows growing deeper under her eyes. The way her chest rises and falls just a little too heavily after a good laugh.

She's fading.

Not all at once. Not in a way she'll admit. Perhaps not even in a way she is wholly aware of. Toss a frog into a pot of boiling water, and it'll jump right back out. However, place it in a warm bath and bring the water to a boil, and you'll have frog legs for dinner.

We often fail to notice the significant changes that occur gradually over time. Humans miss the cues until the writing is painted on the walls in neon blood. People never seem to know until it's too late.

But I know because I know what to look for. I can read the signs.

I've seen death up close for centuries. But watching it wear away at her day by day, like the tide carving out a shoreline, is unbearable. It's frustrating, baffling. I've seen the worst this world has to offer both in my living and nonliving professions. I would suffer through the height of the plague a thousand times over if it meant not witnessing her drift any further.

And that thought? Fucking terrifying. Why? Why now? Why her? Why can't I detach? Why must this infuriating creature continue to wiggle her way under my skin?

Rue does not notice me watching. Or if she does, she does not care. I turn and spy her coveted notebook abandoned on the coffee table, pages flipped open and carefully marked by a raven feather bookmark.

I glance down. Just a glance. But it's enough. I see the title she's written in thick letters across the top—*I Know the When.*

I look away briefly, but my curiosity consumes me. These are Rue's private writings. If she wanted me to read them, she would share them. It's not for me to pry. Even as I think this, I feel my eyes roaming back over the stanzas below the title, moving almost of their own volition.

My hand reaches out to grasp the book, and I take in the entirety of the page.

I KNOW THE WHEN

The steady pulsing of a beating heart
Reminds us of the finitude of time.
Each of us bound to a specific part.

Set number of days with only one rhyme.
My silver ticker beats out of rhythm.
Not the metaphor I hoped. Such a shame.
My disease creates a literal schism,
Though Fate and her rules apply just the same.
The difference, however: I know the when.
My story's secrets revealed- a mistake.
Open my inkwell, pour forth from this pen.
What care I now for banal mortal's ache?
What of my life will people remember?
Cold legacy will end this December.

My heart left me centuries ago, yet as I look over her words again, I feel the remnants of it cracking. Rue's pain and resiliency mingle beautifully in her words, and I am overcome by a feeling I've worked tirelessly to suppress–shame.

I did this to her. I intervened in ways that I should not have, and the effects now fall squarely on Rue's slender shoulders. I meddled in someone else's timeline. *Again.* The results of my previous intervention cloud my mind and threaten to pull me under. I shake off the haunting memories for a moment and return to the sad present.

It's not fair.

It is as simple as that, yet as complicated as it gets. She's trying so hard to live in the seconds between the countdown. To leave something behind that isn't just an echo. And all I can do is watch her tick away like an hourglass I can't flip.

I clouded the end of her story. I misspoke and revealed her end date. I saddled her with impossible knowledge. Every soul knows they are destined to die. It's the one certainty in life. But to be burdened with the exact date? The when and the how. That's unthinkable, unfaceable. And I carelessly yoked her with that burdensome wisdom.

Amazingly, she continues to fight still. She continues to be brave and find ways to create meaning in the mundanity.

Despite her weakened physical state, Rue is so much stronger than–

My thought is cut off by her shriek.

"What the fuck, Kane?"

I turn to see her standing in the archway, her stormy eyes burning holes through my hands that still firmly clutch her notebook. I clock the anger and disappointment etched on her face–but it's more than that. Anger and disappointment I can handle–I might not like it, but I can get over it. No, it's the betrayal, the embarrassment written all over her pretty face, that guts me.

"Rue," I say slowly but am immediately cut off.

"How dare you?" she says, her voice now low and sharp.

I flinch while muttering a curse. I do not speak, but my eyes stay locked with hers as they swirl with a cocktail of hurt.

"That belongs to me," she growls.

"It's beautiful–" I try, but she refuses to hear me.

"Your actions are anything but," she spits.

"It should be shared with the world."

"Yeah, well, that should be *my* decision to make. Not yours. You took my choice away and couldn't respect my privacy, could you, Kane?" Her short laugh is cold. "Then again, you've already meddled in my life in unthinkable ways. Why stop now? Right?"

"Rue–"

She grabs the notebook and slams it shut, pressing it to her chest like a wound.

"It wasn't intentional." It's a weak excuse, but I can't find any other words. I should be able to shrug, say something dismissive or demure. And yet I can't bring myself to feign disinterest.

"Oh, so you didn't mean to sit down and read my naked soul scribbled out on paper?" Her voice cracks, and shame crawls back over me.

My throat tightens. "I just ... it was open, and I saw the title–"

Her eyes gleam. "And what, Grim? Privacy means nothing to you? I'm dying, so the rules don't apply to me? In a few days, I'll be rotting on the floor somewhere, and you'll have your soul to shove into AfterLife Processing or whatever, so what does it matter about my silly little poems or my sad little dreams?" She shoves past me, grabbing her coat off the hook by the door.

"I'm sorry." I finally say what I should have said right away.

She pauses, but her resolve does not waver. "I'm leaving."

I step in front of her. "No, you're not, Rue. I'm responsible for you and–"

"Oh! Yet another thing I didn't ask for. Now. Get. Out. Of. My. Way."

"No." There is no malice behind the word, no threat.

"You don't own me, Kane."

"I do actually," I say quietly. "Your soul is mine until you cross over. And I'm not letting what's mine walk out of this house overly emotional and under protected. Now calm down and talk to me. Please." I should've come up with a better line. Something softer, something that doesn't make her sound like a *thing*.

She turns to leave, taking all my thoughts with her.

All save for one: *What if something were to happen to her?*

Perhaps sensing the intensity of my thoughts, she turns back around. Her jaw works as she glares at me. Her nails dig tightly into the cover of her leather notebook. "UGH!" she shouts, her small body shaking with rage. "You are not a good man, Kane. You're not even a man. I am starting to doubt that you ever were."

She hits my chest with her notebook and balled-up fist, then goes limp. I can see the last of her energy leaving her body.

I'm not sure which hurts worse–the sting of her words or the powerlessness of seeing her weak. They both cut deeper than the sharpest scalpel. My neck throbs, a phantom pain, as Rue storms out into the glowing moonlight. I scratch at the scarred ridge on my neck, then follow her despite her protestations.

"Stop following me," she says over her shoulder as she makes her way to her father's plot.

"I'm afraid I can't do that."

"You managed to exert some free will when you went and rifled through my private writings," she mumbles through her breaths as she comes to a stop.

"I wasn't rifling through the pages. It was open to that page. I only read what was in front of me. And any amount of free will is reserved only for the living. Enjoy it while it lasts." I mumble the last sentence, though perhaps I shouldn't have.

"Oh, don't split hairs with me, Kane. Those are my words, and you stole them. You took my broken heart and my shattered soul as your own, with no regard for how I would feel. And why? To satisfy your curiosity? You took everything else from the dying girl, so why not this too?"

"Enough." I take a deep breath.

One of the reasons I didn't have many friends in my mortal life or in the OtherWorld is that it's easier to avoid disappointment. If no one relies on me, then I can't let anyone down.

The fourth rule of the *Reaper Regulations* states clearly: '*Limit personal interaction with assigned souls. Crossovers are cases, not companions. Complete the task and proceed to the next assignment.*'

Safe to say that ship has sailed where Rue is concerned. At the very least, I owe her candor now.

"I'm sorry." I repeat my plea from before in even more earnest. "I'm not trying to defend myself. I'm simply trying to provide context. The book was out. It was on the table. I did not go searching for it or even turn a page."

She glares at me, but does not yell, which I take as a good sign, so I continue, attempting to insert some levity, "I wouldn't have read it if I didn't think it was good. So, really, it's your fault I read the whole thing. If it was garbage, I would have already set it down."

"What part of me looks like I am seeking your approval?" she snips, but I notice the softening in her eyes and the slightest blush in her cheeks.

Her hips sway softly, causing her purple plaid skirt to move. I cannot help my momentary scan of her exposed thighs.

"You really liked it?"

Her question snaps my attention back.

"You have a real gift. Shakespeare would have been happy to share his sonnet structure with your words."

"You recognized the style?" she asks, her ire subsiding and her confidence growing. It looks good on her.

"I've been around for a long while, Mayday. Plenty of time to study up on all sorts of things."

She hums curiously. "You don't strike me as the poetry type."

"There's plenty you don't know about me, Rue," I state cryptically, which gives Rue pause.

I absentmindedly rub at my throat as she eyes me.

"Even in the face of having learned what comes after life, I still contend there is nothing quite so magical as a book. Nothing as powerful as a story."

Rue inches near, a softness and a hunger replacing the fire behind her eyes.

"So," I venture, "in this story, am I forgiven for reading your poem without permission?"

"I'm considering it," she muses, her entire demeanor taking on a new edge.

I am intrigued by this side of Rue.

"Anything else I can do to pay penance?"

She thinks, smirks, and speaks softly as she steps even closer to me. "Tell me something, Kane. Tell me a part of your story. You've seen me naked. Maybe it's time to show me the goods."

I laugh softly to distract from the uncomfortable feeling beginning to surface.

"There's not much to tell," I deflect.

This is too much; I can't play quid pro quo with her. Am I full of regret and shame for peering into her personal thoughts? Yes. But I will not allow her to find a way to break the seal on my box. I refuse to release those demons.

Rue's gaze cuts from my eyes to the place on my throat I was just rubbing. Her hand moves to that same spot as she asks, "where did you get this scar?"

A tsunami of memory rushes forth at the gentle coaxing of her soft question.

I swallow back the lump forming and stare icily at her. The second her fingers make contact with my flesh, a searing heat courses through me. I can almost physically feel the armor wrapping itself around me. I grab her hand and remove it from my neck in one swift motion.

"My past is buried, Rue. Don't go looking for shovels," I growl low in my throat.

Rue cowers and takes a small step back. The distance feels like a chasm, and I want to erase it while I feel the need to run as far away from her, from this, as I can.

"Sorry, Rue. I didn't mean to snap."

"You don't have to be afraid of me, Kane." Her eyes match the pleading tone of her voice.

"You have no idea how wrong you are." I swallow the space between us, taking the lead in this dance.

"I just want to know you, Grim."

"No, you don't, Mayday. I promise." I take her hand back in mine and place it back on the tender flesh of my neck—an apology without words.

"What happened?" she asks in supplication.

"The unspeakable." I give language to that heinous act of so long ago for the first time since the deed itself was committed. If only Rue knew what a mountain of shame I have had to climb to offer even that much. I say her name achingly. "Rue." It's a shocked breath as her fingertips brush over the line, so gently that I almost don't feel it.

Almost. But I do. Every nerve in my body goes taut. Her touch burns. Not in pain. In feeling.

She presses her lips to my scar, and something inside me snaps.

Her tender lips on my callous flesh feel like unspoken absolution. Like Rue doesn't need the details of that sordid, sad story. Like she accepts me regardless of the depth and darkness of my flaws.

I lurch forward. My mouth crashing into hers, wild and claiming. I swallow her gasp as I wrap my arms around her, pulling her flush to my chest.

Her hands fist into my shirt, dragging me closer, deeper.

This kiss isn't sweet. It's desperate and vital.

She tastes like rain on scorched earth, and I long for her liquid cool.

She bites my lower lip while pulling us to the ground.

"Fuck," I groan, one hand trailing down her spine to anchor her against me as she climbs into my lap without hesitation, legs straddling me, her skirt bunching between us, heat radiating from every inch of her.

Her lips trail from my mouth to my jaw, down the side of my neck—over the scar again. She tongues the marred flesh, gently kissing that one spot. Rue's impassioned strokes cleanse my shame.

"Rue," I reluctantly pull her back from my neck—the separation a most acute torture—and look her in the eyes, "I was overcome. I had lost everything. I did an unimaginable—"

She places her finger over my mouth, shushing me. "I don't need to know, Kane."

She keeps her eyes locked on mine as she returns to the same spot as before. She sucks on my scarred flesh again, purifying my pain. Rue takes away centuries of guilt and regret with her unconditional forgiveness of my deepest hurt.

"Mayday," I whisper, broken. How do I tell her to stop and to keep going at the same time?

She grinds herself against me, and I roll my eyes at the feeling as my hand grips her thigh.

"I need you," she breathes. "Please."

I should be the one to stop this, but I don't. I let myself feel everything. The pain, the lust. The ages of hunger and loneliness and restraint—all of it unraveling under her small hands, delicate mouth, and soft body pressed against mine in a cemetery filled with ghosts.

I don't because, for the first time in many years, I feel again.

Because of her. And I would trade every agonizing ounce of immortality for one more strike of the clock in this moment. Even if it's the last one we ever have.

Her body ignites against mine. Not just heat. Not just skin. But something elemental. Something divine.

Rue clings to me like I'm the last solid thing in a crumbling world, and I don't deserve to be held that way. Not by her. Not by anyone. But, fuck me, I take it. Her lips are still on my neck, pouring reverent kisses along the scar that marked the end of my life. Her touch makes it feel like the beginning of something new now.

Doubt creeps into my thoughts, and I try to silence the noise. This is the beginning of something I cannot have. These feelings do not belong in our story. They can't. They are impossible. Every time she touches me, it's like she rewrites history. Like the centuries of cold, the years of silence, the burden of duty—all of it burns away under the brush of her hands. I will those thoughts out of my head.

I pull her back just enough to look at me. Her eyes are wide and glassy, her chest heaving like she's been running for miles. I don't think I've ever seen anything so heartbreakingly alive.

"I don't know how to do this," she whispers. "I don't know what I'm allowed to want anymore."

I reach up, tucking a strand of hair behind her ear, my hand trembling. "You can want anything, Rue. Anything."

Her eyes flick to my mouth. "Even you?"

Tout sauf ça. Anything but that.

I lose the last thread of control.

I grip the back of her neck and pull her into me, kissing her like I'll never get the chance again. Because maybe I won't.

There is nothing restrained about this. This is not the practiced hand of a centuries-old immortal. This is need—raw and frantic and terrified.

She moans into my mouth, and the sound tears straight through me. My hands move down, gripping her hips, guiding her down until her core grinds against mine, and I swear I see the entire span of a star's life play out in a second. And Rue, like a powerful black hole, sucks me all the way into her orbit.

She rocks against me, slow at first, searching, then more. She's insistent. *Desperate.* The friction is unbearable in the best possible way.

Her skirt is riding up her thighs. My hands slide beneath the fabric, finding bare skin.

Rue whimpers when I touch her. When my fingers trace deliberate lines along the inside of her thighs. Her head drops to my shoulder, and she gasps, the sound of her need pressed right against my skin. I want to taste her. I want to lay her down beneath the shadow of her family tree and make her forget what pain is.

I want to give her the antidote to loss. I want to make her feel pleasure unbound.

"Kane," she breathes, her voice broken and shaking.

My name moaned from her lips must dilate my pupils because moonlight floods into my eyes.

I grip her tighter, my resolve, my restraint leaving me. "Say that again." It's a near beg.

"What?" she asks, the confusion in her voice adorable.

"My name," I demand with a predatory growl. "Say it again."

She pulls back, her forehead pressed to mine. "Kane ..."

I shift her in my lap until she's straddling my thigh. My mouth moves from her lips to her throat, nipping, sucking—marking her. Her skin tastes like salt and magic and some forgotten thing I buried long ago.

"Tell me to stop," I murmur, my lips brushing the shell of her ear. "Please, Mayday, tell me to stop."

She shakes her head. "Not a chance, Grim."

I press her down, grinding her hips against mine, and her moan splits the quiet night like thunder.

I kiss her again, taking my time. Because this is more than want. More than lust. This is the intermingling of souls made flesh. This is the physical manifestation of all that is felt and can never be named. And underneath it lies the aching fear of loss, curling its claws around the space between us. But I do not pull away.

I cannot. I close the distance as much as possible. Press myself harder against her.

Because Rue feels like the last page of a book I never want to finish.

And if she's going to leave this world, then I want to be the one to help her write an epic final chapter.

Her fingers are in my hair. That's the first thing I register. Tangled tight, urgent, trembling. Like if she lets go, she'll lose her grip on reality.

Maybe I will too.

I press her back against the grass—soft, damp, and littered with the petals of dying flowers. The family plot. There's irony in that. *Or poetry.* I can't tell anymore.

Rue's skirt is hiked around her waist, her legs parted

for me like she's offering something sacred. And that is an altar I am only too happy to kneel before.

I drag my hands up the backs of her thighs, feeling the goose bumps rise under my touch. I slide her underwear down her legs, tucking them in the pocket of my trousers, leaving her bare–no barrier. Just open and waiting.

I part her slit with my fingers. "You just licked away my darkest pains. Now let me lick you into unimaginable pleasure," I murmur reverently.

I press my mouth to her already-slick center. She cries out, hips jolting up, fingers clenching in my hair. I groan against her–guttural and broken–and the vibration makes her whimper. I lap at her slowly at first, tasting her, exploring her, savoring her. She's warm and wet and sweet, her taste addictive, heady. She gasps my name, her breath catching on every flick of my tongue, and I swear I could die like this.

My cock is already painfully hard, pressed against the inside of my trousers, aching with each sound she makes. The heat from her seeps into me, tightening every muscle in my body, every needy, hungry stroke of my tongue only stoking the fire.

I shift slightly, gripping her thighs and dragging her closer.

She's shaking now–tiny tremors running through her legs, her abdomen, even her hands as they twist tighter in my hair.

Her back arches, and her hips start moving–small, needy rolls that grind against my mouth. I let her. I want her to use me. I groan again, louder this time, and I feel her body react–feel her clench around nothing, feel her breathing stutter.

I suck her clit gently, before circling it with the flat of my tongue, again and again, until she's gasping like she's drowning.

The sounds she makes–soft and sharp and frantic–pull at every thread inside me. I can feel my cock begging for release, straining against the fabric.

Every part of me is consumed by her. Her taste. Her scent. Her sounds. Her full-throated need. It's unraveling me. I'm losing rhythm. Losing sense. Losing control.

I grind my hips down into the ground, desperate for any kind of relief, my breath coming harder now, almost in time with hers.

"Please," she gasps, her voice cracking. "Kane, please don't stop."

I won't. Not until I feel her fall apart. Not until I have used my tongue to praise her for her beautiful absolution. I will defile her with the same instrument she just used to purify me.

Then I remember—*her heart.* Can she handle this? I am on a mission here.

But I have a much more important one now, I think to myself as I slide my hands up her thighs, spreading her further for me. I dig my fingers into her inner thighs, palpating her femoral artery.

At the pressure, she gasps, "What are you—"

But the question is cut off as I apply long licks with my tongue to her wet cunt while I count the beating of her heart by the thrumming of her blood.

Elevated but manageable, I deduce after several focused seconds.

Time to put these fingers to another use.

I slide two fingers into her, deep, curling them up until she chokes on a cry. She clamps around me, already so close.

"Come for me," I say against her center, my voice low and raw. "I want to feel you lose it."

She lets out a needy whine that nearly takes me out. I continue to lick and suck while my fingers move inside her.

"Come on, *ma chère.* Let go."

I feel her walls tense around my fingers as her back arches, and she releases a delicious cry.

"I knew you were a good listener," I hum into her cunt as she comes undone. "Such a good girl."

Her whole body seizes, a sob tearing from her throat as she clutches at me like I'm the only thing tethering her to this plane.

I do not stop. I lick her through the spasms, slower now, softer, catching every last tremble, every last quake of her release until she finally collapses back into the grass, spent and trembling.

I press my left hand into her femoral again while sliding my other fingers out of her pulsing pussy to ensure her heart rate is still at a safe level. When I note that it is, I pull back, breathless and aching.

Her thighs are still twitching. Her chest heaves. Her eyes are wide and glassy as she looks down at me.

"You …" Her voice is shaky. "That was …"

"I know," I whisper, wiping my mouth with the back of my hand, though I can still taste her, feel her. *Crave her.*

She looks wrecked. And beautiful.

I adjust slightly, trying to ease the pressure of my painfully hard cock, still untouched, still pulsing with the need I haven't allowed myself to act on.

Her eyes drop to the movement, and for a beat, we just stare at each other–caught between restraint and ruin.

But I don't move toward her. Not yet.

I need a moment and some distance to absorb the magnitude of what we just shared, of what we just started.

We have begun something terrifying, dangerous, and possibly forbidden. But nothing that anyone says or does now can undo the bond we created in this moment. There is no going back now. Only forward–together.

In the distance, from inside the house, I hear the faint sound of the grandfather clock beginning to strike the top of another hour.

Chapter Nineteen

THAT'S NOT HOW THAT WORKS

RUE

"I CAN DO THIS ALONE. JUST STAY HERE." KANE'S VOICE IS low, steady, the kind of voice one would use when trying to shut a door quietly instead of slamming it. But the door is being shut all the same.

His eyes won't meet mine. They haven't since the cemetery. Like if he doesn't look at me, nothing actually happened. Or if he closes his eyes tight enough, he can pretend I wasn't trembling beneath his touch, begging him for more. Well, he can pretend all he wants; I'm not spending my final days in an awkward silence with this man.

"No," I say sweetly, grabbing my boots. "We make a great team."

I follow him out of the house as he lets out an annoyed huff.

"We're not a team. I work alone."

"Oh, c'mon, Grim. Don't make me do something rash."

His eyes narrow as he continues to glare at the Tombstone Phone. "Like what?"

I tap my chin thoughtfully. "Well, since my days are numbered, I suppose I'll just head on down to the local news station and share my thoughts on Death and Fate and Time. Maybe toss in a little exposé on reapers and portals."

He doesn't flinch, but I see the flicker in his jaw. A tic. A twitch. I'm counting that as a win.

"Hop on," he mutters, and deciding it's now or never, I leap onto his back, wrapping my legs and arms around him. "I wasn't being literal," he grunts.

I try not to read too much into his tension or the way it feels like he's holding me like he never wants to let go. Maybe that's wishful thinking on my part. It's possible that he only did what he did out of pity. One last ride for the dying girl? I mean, he seemed to be enjoying it, but what if it was an act? When his phone chimed with news of a new case, Kane leapt at the opportunity to switch to work mode. I've never seen anyone so excited over a death before. I'm trying my best not to take offense to it. I'd be lying if I didn't say it stung though.

"Hold on," he mutters after placing his phone in his pants pocket before we take off.

We land hard. The sky is grey. We arrive in front of a small shotgun-style house, tucked into a quiet corner of town, overgrown ivy climbing the white siding and cracked concrete steps leading to a door with peeling paint. Kane holds my hand as we walk in.

"This should be an in and out," Kane mutters. "Old man, natural causes, no partner, no next of kin."

My steps falter at the coldness of his words. You would think he was talking about the weather.

"No one to miss him?" I say softly while looking around the dated living room.

The air inside is still. Faded wallpaper curls at the edges in every room. A threadbare recliner sits near a dusty bookshelf, stacked with yellow paperbacks. I see one on the coffee tray by the chair, and the hair on the back of my neck stands on end. I walk to the worn book and nearly sob at the words written inside on the first page—in my handwriting.

Seul l'impossible peut faire l'impossible.

"No," I breathe out, looking at *my* copy of *Interview with a Vampire*, the copy I lent to GG.

"No one to tie him here" Kane snaps, pulling me out of my thoughts. "And stop touching his belongings. This isn't an estate sale."

"You think no one will remember him? Will miss him? Mourn him?" I insist while stepping in front of the large man. "You know, sometimes, I forget you don't have the capacity to feel compassion," I spit out.

Then my eyes travel to the window, and I see the little tray he has set up with a chessboard, two moves in. This was the last game he and I played. I had to cut it short because I wasn't feeling well and Mom was going back to Chicago. He brought the board home and set it up to study for our eventual finish.

"What is the matter with you?" Kane asks, making eye contact.

"At least you can still look me in the eyes," I state while crossing my arms over my chest.

Kane gives me a forced smirk. "Right now, I have a soul to collect. If it were up to me, I would do nothing more than stare into your eyes. For eternity. But it is not, so do me a favor, and let's try to keep things professional."

I gape as Kane walks around me to move down the hall. I realize he didn't bother taking my hand again. Though I guess he doesn't need to if we are the only ones here.

I follow Kane, making my way into the bedroom, only to stop in my tracks.

"Oh, GG," I squeak out at the motionless body in the bed.

Kane's head whips around as he stares at me. "You know my client?"

My lip wobbles as a burning sensation tingles my nose and pricks my eyes.

"Yes," my voice is so small as I try to make sense of what's happening. "I...he...we just played chess a few days ago at the center."

"The community center?" he asks, and my gaze meets his.

"How did you know that?"

"I saw you," he says softly. "I was cleaning up a reap from a subordinate and saw you talking about a book. Rebecca."

"Yes," I breathe, his words stunning me. He saw me there? He remembers what I was talking about? "I volunteer twice a month at the community center in town. I read, play chess…Oh, Kane, he is such a nice man." I whimper as a tear falls from my eye. "Surely there's a mistake."

Kane exhales sharply, glancing toward the bed. "Nice people die too, Rue. If it's any consolation, he went peacefully."

I shake my head, not willing to accept this. "Small comfort."

Kane touches Mr. Guidry's arm, and his scowl deepens.

"What's wrong?" I ask. "Where is his spirit?"

"Still inside him," Kane says like a curse as his grip on the body tightens.

"Can he hear us?"

"Obviously," Kane grits out.

"Then talk to him."

Kane whirls his head around and raises his brow. "I'm sorry, who is the experienced reaper here? Not you, correct?"

Kane leans over Mr. Guidry. "Come on. It's time. I know you're scared, but there's nothing on the other side to fear." There is only silence, and Kane growls in frustration.

He looks at me and sighs. "He's holding on, says he can't leave."

I inch closer. The silence is thick, and Kane's shoulders tighten with each passing second.

"Why are you so tense?" I ask softly.

"Because nothing is easy anymore," he mutters, staring at his phone. "Can't even process a single, simple crossover."

"Hey, that's my friend, asshole."

"My apologies. I just want something to go smoothly this week. Anything."

"Okay, so if you're in such a rush, why don't you just use your knife thing?" I whisper.

"You mean *Baiulus*?" he questions.

"Is that the thing I saw you use during the–"

"Yes," he cuts me off.

"You named your knife?"

"All reapers have a cleaving tool and all have a name. They allow us to sever the thickest threads that bind souls to their physical hosts. Those final pieces of connection are always the hardest to break."

"And *Baiulus* is yours?"

"Correct."

"What does it mean?"

Kane sighs. "So many questions. It's Latin. It means pallbearer, or one who carries a burden."

"Fitting," I mumble softly. Then I remember something and ask, "What did Asher name his blade?"

Kane bristles at the mention of his fellow reaper, but he answers, "I don't know what it's called, but he didn't name it. When one becomes a reaper, you are assigned your tool. There's a ceremony. The weapon is presented, and when you first grasp it, the name etches itself into the handle. And it becomes tied to the user. Irrevocably. For eternity."

"That's intense."

"The higher-ups are nothing if not dramatic. Nothing like a bit of pageantry to raise the stakes of eternal mundanity."

"Okay, well … yeah. That. Why don't you use that and get Mr. Guidry moving?"

"That's complicated." Kane eyes me.

"Try me."

"Well, for starters, using my blade takes energy. It's also violent and messy and a bit barbaric, and as I said, that's not me."

"Not all of you," I mumble back, remembering Asher's words from before.

"I heard that," he responds sharply.

"Good," I fire back. "What other excuse do you have? Souls shouldn't be here, right? It's better if they cross over?"

"It is," Kane says steely. "Decidedly better. Because when spirits stay here, they rot." His green eyes flick to mine, sharp and burning. "They have no purpose and no power. And that which is powerless atrophies in time. They see and feel all that they remember, but they have no way to engage with it. They are no longer a part of the world, simply trapped in it."

He steps closer to me, and his presence is a shadow, wrapping tight around my body. "Eventually, they forget who they were, Rue. They forget why they mattered, what mattered. Or even if anything ever mattered. They're no longer the complete soul you see before you. They become a distillation of their grief. A haunting echo of their worst memories. At best, they become a nuisance. At worst, they become dangerous."

I shudder, something cold and foreign curling beneath my skin.

It steals my breath.

"But," he continues, his tone shifting, "this choice, this moment of resistance, it's the last act of human will he'll ever have. After this, it's over. There's no more deciding. No more agency. Everything that follows is assigned. Processed. Ordered." He steadies himself while shaking his head. "And I don't want to take that final act of will from any soul. Not if I can help it."

The air grows heavier, and I feel a tingle run up my spine.

"Obviously, there is something here that makes him want to hold on. Something your notes didn't cover."

"Rue, he's alone," Kane continues, and I can tell he's done humoring me. "No family, no legacy. Just that weathered body and a worn-down mattress in a house that smells of dust and mold."

"You really are something, you know that?" I snap, shaking my head. "Thinking everything human can be put down on paper and explained away. Insistent that everything has a reason and a way." He looks at me like he doesn't know what to say, and I roll my eyes before continuing, "Life is messy, Kane. And complicated and scary and so many other things. So, maybe you should be doing more than keeping your knife sheathed. Maybe you should be listening, guiding, and leading with love."

My outburst is cut short by a dark grey cloud that floats out of the center of GG's chest. It steals my entire focus as his physical form takes a smoky shape.

This grey version of him looks at me and smiles. "Looks like we won't be finishing that game after all."

I give him a short laugh. "Maybe someday, GG. You never know."

Mr. Guidry's face softens.

"You've run out of time," Kane interrupts. "I'll mark you as unwilling to move on, a lost soul. Enjoy your eternity here."

"Kane!" I go to grab his arm, but he moves it away.

"I can't leave!" Mr. Guidry barks out. "Winston needs me."

"Winston?" Kane questions, and it hits me.

"His dog," I say, looking around before going to the bed and lifting the blankets to find the cocker spaniel tucked up against the body like a small, grieving shadow.

"You chose to stay," Kane says slowly, like he's trying to make sense of the madness, "for a dog?"

"For the one creature who loved me without asking me to earn it? Yes. For the being that taught me the meaning of unconditional love? Yes."

Kane huffs out a cold laugh before shaking his head. "Fine, it's too late anyway. Come on, Mayday," he says, brushing past me. "Let's go."

But I don't move.

"Hang on a second."

"Rue–"

"Love is love, Kane. The object of that desire does not make the feeling any less powerful or any less real," I insist. "This beautiful old man clings to love. Can you blame him? Have you never known lo–"

"Do not finish that sentence, Rue." The threat and the warning are very clear in his tone.

I change tack.

"Let me"–I hesitate–"talk to him," I finish unsurely.

Kane sighs and looks at his Tombstone Phone. "Fine," he relents. "I don't see the harm. You want to waste your time talking to the ghost? Go for it. His window for crossover is rapidly closing, and once that portal is shut, this is where Mr. G's soul shall remain."

I eye Kane as a resolve takes over. I feel my spine stiffen, and I make my way toward the spectral energy hovering above, though still attached to, Glen's physical form. I am not sure I can help him, but I know I can speak to him. And even when faced with the impossible, it's easier to brave it when we aren't alone.

I kneel beside the shimmering remnants of Glen Guidry and give him a soft smile. "Tell me about Winston, GG."

His translucent smile tugs at my heart. "He's my heartbeat. He knows when I'm tired, sad, hurting. He's been the rhythm of my days since Agnes died. He sleeps at the foot of my bed. Nudges his bowl for breakfast and dinner at the exact same time every day. He's my own lovable alarm clock. I could measure the whole day by his needs. He would even remind me to take my pills at night."

"How'd he do that, GG?" I ask warmly.

"He'd look up at my nightstand, yip once, and then spin counterclockwise. Eight thirty-five every night. If I didn't reach over and grab my dispenser, he wouldn't stop." He pauses, sighs, and smiles. His smoky form wavers slightly in the air. "He loves me, you know? Maybe that sounds silly to you because he's just a small dog, but he does. He loves me. I don't know how to leave him behind."

"You don't have to," I whisper. "He'll carry you with him. Every day. In every bark and dream and stubborn spin around the kitchen floor. That bond doesn't just end. It can only shift."

I reach out, and to my surprise, my hand finds the edge of his soul, and like with Kane, it's solid.

"You loved him well, GG. That's what matters. That love? That's not ending. That's eternal."

His eyes go glassy. "You think he'll be okay?"

"I know he will. Because he had you, and I will make sure he's well looked after."

"Thank you, Rue," he says, voice trembling.

The edges of the cloud of him begin to separate and disappear like cotton candy in the rain. Winston whimpers. He sighs in response to the sound, then releases a second resigned exhale.

"I'm ready to go now."

"Checkmate," I say to GG wistfully.

He smiles. "But what a game!"

We share a final moment as he begins to laugh lightly. The sound fades as the last smoky wisps of his apparition does as well.

And then he's gone.

"Did he ..."

"Yeah," Kane says, voice low and unreadable. "He moved on."

"I did that?" I whisper, staring at my palms.

"It would seem so," he breathes. "And mere moments before his portal closed at that."

I give him a nervous smile before shrugging, "Beginner's luck?"

Chapter Twenty

REPRIMANDS AND RSVPS

KANE

The Other World

As I step through the OtherWorld into Death's Door, LLC, the scent hits me like it always does—a punch of ozone and burned offerings. The sights and sounds of this place always feel heightened. But today feels especially oversaturated.

I head for Big D's spa, my shoes echoing across the onyx floor. Crimson light beats beneath my steps in a telltale thrumming, as though the OtherWorld itself has a pulse, even though its denizens do not.

He's waiting in his private atrium—if one could call a gold-and-black pearl bathhouse surrounded by floating skulls and cascading water fountains an atrium. Big D reclines on a skeletal chaise lounge half submerged in black water, wearing a blinding lamé Speedo and a silk robe open down to his navel. Twizzlers trail down his chest like candy leis, and he's sipping something electric blue from a chalice shaped like a spinal column while using a Twizzler as a makeshift straw.

"Kane!" he shouts, arms wide. "To what do I owe the pleasure? Let me guess. The girl died before her time *again*, and you tried to mess with time *again*."

"She assisted on a reap," I say flatly, stepping onto the marble platform circling the pool.

Big D sits up so fast that the water sloshes over the

rim. "She did what?" Big D's voice booms, rattling the walls of his bathhouse. The sound would probably have me shaking in my Stefano Ricci shoes, if I was wearing them. D's bath house rules: *'Shoes kill the vibe'.*

"She assisted on a reap," I repeat, not responding to his theatrics. "She helped a soul cross," I say. "Willingly. There was peace. She talked to him, calmed him. Listened."

"Why was she even there?" he growls, his candy falling into the dark water around him. "You're supposed to be babysitting the body, not holding reaper orientation week."

Choosing to ignore him referencing Rue as *the body*, I stretch my neck before speaking. "Well, she's my responsibility until her official crossover date. That was the arrangement. You and the Sisters were pretty clear on that."

He stands, and water steams off his skin. *Subtlety, thy name is Daryl.*

"Yes, she is your responsibility because you told her everything. Kane, you handed her AfterLife information without waiting until she was in the actual fucking AfterLife."

"You don't need to yell. I am aware of the situation."

"There can be no *slips* in this, and yet here we are, on our back with a banana peel on our face. You gifted that mortal unknowable knowledge and forgot to hang on to the receipt."

"I didn't mean to! I already apologized. What else do you want me to do?"

"I can tell you what you should *not* do, and that's take a mortal on your assignments like she's on a school field trip to the zoo."

"She's twenty-six, D. She can just go to the zoo if she wants."

"That's not what I'm talking about," Big D fumes, and I can literally see smoke come out of his ears as he paces. He reaches down, yanking a Twizzler from the bubbling water, and takes a bite off one end before pointing it at me like a sword. "This isn't a buddy-cop comedy, Kane. She's not your sidekick. She's your burden. You supervise her. Until she crosses. Got it?"

I bristle internally. Big D always grates on my nerves, but his flippant tone and dismissive attitude where Rue and her last days are concerned twist a particularly sensitive spot inside me.

"I cannot tie her up every time I have to leave her side, D. That's ridiculous."

"Of course you can. And you will. This is a run out the clock situation, Kane. Make sure she doesn't play any tricks on Fate and Time. You don't want to piss them off any more than you already have."

"Got it, boss," I say in a clipped tone.

"You've reaped thousands, maybe tens of thousands of souls, Kane. She's just one more."

The second he utters the glib remark, I cannot stop the thought from forming. Rue is so much more than just another soul to me. Her spirit brims with untapped energy and shines with an earnestness I've never seen before. She deserves so much more than she's gotten out of life, and she will get as much as she can from her last days, even if it means sacrificing my own soul in the process to make that happen.

"Watch your tone, D." I speak in a low growl, the words coming unbidden.

Now the center of his dark black eyes sparks with flame.

I've done it again. Why can't I keep my mouth shut?

Big D's mouth breaks open in a huge grin. "She is just another soul, right?"

My spine straightens. "Sure," I say quietly, unable to say anything else. Apparently, that works, too, because my silence is speaking volumes to him.

He claps his hands once with thunderous effect. "Oh Kane, don't tell me you're getting sweet on her." At my blank response, he laughs—a deep, resonant sound that physically moves the air around us. "This is too good. You're growing feelings for the mortal whose timeline you distorted, and now you're dancing very close to the realm of Fate's tapestry. I can't imagine she's got enough thread to weave you into Rue's picture. Oh, I cannot wait to see how all this plays out." He brings his hands in front of his mouth and claps obnoxiously before dancing his fingertips against each other like a cartoon villain.

"She's kind," I murmur, jaw tight. "Kind in a way I haven't seen in centuries. She listens, even when she's scared. She believes in people, even when she shouldn't. She stayed to comfort an old man who had nothing left in the world but a dog."

Big D quiets. Just for a second. His smirk falters. "So, you're willing to put your position of privilege in my very regimented society on the line because she had a chat with a doddering old man?"

"I'm willing to make sure her last days matter."

His black eyes spark gold, then red. "You're getting reckless, Kane. This is exactly what Fate warned about."

"She's not hurting anyone."

"*Not yet.*" He throws up his hands and spins toward the bar cart. He stops abruptly, his right hand flying to the top of the cart.

D presses an intercom button, and a squeaky voice immediately speaks. "Yes, sir? What is it, sir?"

"April, make me one of those free-standing popcorn machines. With the good butter."

"Whatever you wish, sir," April, his receptionist, responds, no hint of confusion or surprise in her voice. She must field ludicrous requests from him on a regular basis.

"She's not a source of entertainment," I say through gritted teeth.

"Oh, but she is," Big D hums, pouring a drink. "And it sounds like you might be the leading man in the tragedy to come."

"I'm not developing feelings, D. Unless you consider *pain in my ass* to be a feeling."

"Methinks the reaper doth protest too much." D smirks.

There is a moment of silence that stretches. Big D simply stops talking. His eyes take on a vacant stare.

Finally, his attention returns to the present. "Oh, you're still here. You're free to go."

I turn to leave.

"Wait. No, there was something else I needed to discuss with you. Shit, it was very important."

I turn back to face him.

He snaps his fingers, and I can almost see the light bulb above his head going off.

"That's right! Big D's Devilishly Deviant Dress-Up Dance is in two days. I haven't received your RSVP yet."

"That's a lot of Ds."

"That's what the nymph said at her first orgy." He laughs heartily at his awful joke.

I cut off his wailing. "Why don't you just call it a masquerade ball?"

Big D's face turns extremely serious. "Because I love alliterations, Kane."

"Same," I concede.

"Everyone does. Almost as much as the nymph loved her first orgy."

"Okay, D. I will be there. Consider this my RSVP."

"Good, because attendance is mandatory."

"Then why did you need my RS—you know what? Never mind. Thanks for the chat, boss. See you in a couple days."

"Not if I see you first." He giggles again. "Seriously though Kane, do not do anything to further upset the Sisters. Your attendance at that catastrophe was no mistake. And if you misstep, overstep, or even Texas two-step with this Rue person any further, I do not want to know what tortures those two might have in store for you."

"Yeah, okay. Thanks for the heads-up."

I turn to leave, but just before I reach my hand out to open the door, Big D's voice carries down the length of this humid room and stops me in my tracks.

"Oh, and Kane, in light of your recent *situation*"–he emphasizes the last word to great euphemistic effect–"I will go ahead and put you down for a plus-one. Since it's so hard to find a sitter on such short notice." His laugh follows me down the corridor.

Chapter Twenty-One

STORM. COMING.

RUE

I TRAIL MY FINGERS ACROSS THE SPINES OF THE BOOKS LINING my home's built-in bookshelves, the whisper of leather and paper grounding me in a way my body no longer can. Two tall columns flank the doorway, the top shelf stretching across like a crown above the entry. Sometimes, I take as much solace in the spines as I do the stories contained therein. I don't just love reading books; I love looking at them, almost as if the titles etched down the sides contain the full knowledge of the pages bound within. It's as though I can absorb the full dramatic weight and entirety of the exploration of the human condition within each of these books simply by reading the title. Even the books I have yet to read fill me with a power and a wonder by the mere fact of their existence. There's something sacred about unread books. The promise of them, the reminder that there is always another story out there, waiting to be shared.

And I need that comfort right now. My mind races, and I feel myself beginning to spiral again. The thoughts begin to hit, subtle as a pinprick and just as sharp. My heart stutters. A dull, familiar ache flares beneath my ribs, a reminder that I'm a ticking clock, wound too tight and worn too long.

What about my story? Mere days remain, and I feel the staggering weight of that knowledge pressing down so relentlessly that it steals my breath. Death is a certainty. Fate comes for us all. But the *when* remains a mystery so we can live free in our moments without fear or foreboding. Kane might have saved me, but he doomed me in the same breath. Gave me back time in such an exacting way that it makes enjoying the seconds of it nearly unthinkable.

"Nearly," I repeat to myself, voicing the weak affirmation out loud.

I don't remember walking, but I've somehow drifted to my couch like I'm already a ghost in my home. My body moves without command now, like it's trying to conserve what little energy I have left for the things that matter.

I crack open the spine of my leather-bound notebook, my private collection of musings and poems, opening to a fresh page. Is there anything as daunting as staring at a blank page? Death perhaps.

Only one thing for it: time for me to make the most of all the words that come before *The End*.

I grab my pen and begin to furiously scribble out a new sonnet. Measured rhymes and structured meter give a shape to my imaginings and form to my dreams. The stressed/unstressed rhythm of the syllables of each line celebrates the constancy of a beating heart. The imagery and metaphor celebrate the truths found all around us.

The words pour forth, surrounded by a sea of asides, crossed-out attempts at brilliance, and naked stabs at saying something worth saying. The stanzas begin to take shape on the page as a slowly lumbering Esther makes her way toward the couch. I pause to watch her eye the distance from the floor to the couch, steel her constitution, and make the graceful, if labored, effort in a split second. Her back curls as she preens in satisfaction at having made her mark, even with all her mass. She promptly walks from the cushion to my lap, tickles my thighs with her protracted nails, curls up, and lies down. Within seconds, she is asleep.

I smile wanly at her gently pulsing belly as she breathes steadily. Her sleeping form brings me great comfort. The way her body gently vibrates as she snores calms me. The finitude of my time, the erratic beating of my

broken heart, the impossibility of it all melts away when
this loyal feline perches on top of my thighs and rests.

I jot down a closing couplet in my notebook. My vision
softens as I feel fatigue overtake me while reviewing my
words. I haven't been awake long enough to already be
tired. I close the worn book, wrapping the string around
the catch while letting out a yawn. My head slumps back
against the cushion as my pen slips from my fingers. My
eyes close of their own volition, and I feel myself fall.

The atmosphere hums like static against my skin—warm,
electric. I'm standing in pitch darkness, jagged earth beneath my feet. The air filling my lungs feels thin and cold
here. I look up, or what feels like up to me in this dark
place, and see no light source in the sky. No sun. No moon.

I try to move, but I cannot feel the ground underfoot
in any direction. I feel trapped, and my pulse quickens.

Just then, a pinprick of light appears before my eyes.
It swims and swirls in tiny arcs around me, and I follow
it closely. It lands on a figure standing in the distance.
Her curvaceous outline speaks of a soft femininity. Her
auburn hair pours in waves over her shoulders. The small
light dances in front of and around the unknown figure who looks statuesque in her stillness and her grace.

"Lead with love," she whispers, and the light races
away from her, casting her back into the pitch black.

I follow the light source as it travels in front of me
and lands on another figure. This form is hard, sharper,
and angled. The broad shoulders and trim waist could
belong to only one man.

Kane.

I know it's a dream. But I don't care.

He stands an unknown distance away, the light bouncing off him in stark relief. His hooded eyes stare at me
hungrily. Not the usual dark resignation he wears like
armor. This is something rawer. Looser. Dangerous in
a way that makes my knees tremble.

The small, floating light zips toward me, resting near my feet and lighting a path to tread toward Kane. I move cautiously and intentionally closer. When the light pulls us within inches of each other, I look up at him.

"You shouldn't be here," he says, voice hoarse. "This isn't safe."

"Then why are you?" I counter, barely above a whisper.

His jaw tics. "Because I can't stay away."

My pulse stutters.

He moves toward me fractionally, and that's all it takes. I'm in his arms in a rush of breath and reckless motion, fists curled in his shirt, mouth crashing into his. His kiss is fire. Heat, chaos wrapped in reverence. He drinks me in like he's been dying of thirst and I'm the last drop of water left in the world.

His hands roam–slow at first, almost worshipful, then more desperate. One slides up to cup my jaw, and the other presses low against my back, pulling me flush against the hard line of his body. I can feel him–every inch of him. And it's not enough.

"I dream of this," he groans against my mouth. "Of you."

My fingers tangle in his hair. "Then stop holding back."

"Rue," he growls–an actual, low sound in his throat– and his lips trail to my neck, my collarbone.

His teeth graze skin, and my knees nearly buckle. I feel him smile there, unrepentant and wicked. Like he knows exactly what he's doing to me.

His mouth moves lower, dragging the strap of my dress down with agonizing patience, exposing my shoulder. He kisses the spot reverently, his breath hot. "This isn't real."

"I know," I say on a pant. "But let me feel something while I can."

My words break him. He lifts me like I weigh nothing, my legs instinctively wrapping around his waist. The friction between us draws a soft, involuntary moan from my throat, and his gaze darkens. His mouth is back on mine–rougher now, urgent. One hand grips my thigh;

the other cradles my skull like I'm breakable. And maybe I am.

"You haunt me, Mayday," he murmurs, his mouth against the shell of my ear. "Every fucking second."

And then he's gone.

I choke on a broken exhale as my eyes come into focus on the space around me. The room has not changed since my eyes closed, save for the outline of a small child sitting–or rather, sort of floating–in the chair opposite the couch, his legs swinging lackadaisically.

" 'Ello," Seek sings in his soft Cockney accent.

"Hi, friend," I rasp, my throat feeling dry. "What are you doing?"

"Watching you. Kane's orders. No mischief, he said."

I laugh humorlessly. "That figures. Wondered why I wasn't chained to the refrigerator or something."

"He said I'm your responsibility until he gets back from seeing his boss. Wait, no, said that backward. You're *my* responsibility until he gets back."

"You probably weren't supposed to say anything at all, Seek. But I appreciate your honesty."

"Oh, well, I hope I'm not in trouble then."

"Don't worry. I won't tell the Big Bad Reaper you told me. And I won't get into any 'mischief,' " I say with air quotes, "while he's gone."

"Great. What do you want to do until he returns then?"

I smile softly at his excitement.

"I was writing before I dozed off, but I'm not feeling particularly inspired right now. How about we do some reading?" I suggest while gesturing to my bookshelves.

His brows pinch together as his head falls to one side. "I don't know how to read."

"What?" I ask with more incredulity in my voice than I intended.

I hope I didn't sound hurtful. By the look on Seek's young face, I might have.

"Never learned," he says simply. "Not much use for an orphaned chimney sweep to learn how to read. Who would have taught me anyway?"

Pursing my lips, I shake my head. "I don't care for that one bit. Would you like it if I read to you?"

Seek's face lights up as if I gave him a gift. "I would love that!"

"Can you pick the book? Esther has me rooted to the spot here, I'm afraid." I motion to the still-slumbering cat on my lap.

"Of course." Seek bounds over to the bookcase behind me. "But which one? I can't read the words on the sides of any of these."

I close my eyes and visualize the shelves I've spent countless hours perusing, combing, and simply gazing at. I hum to Seek, "On the right side of the third shelf from the bottom, about a third of the way from the right, there should be a blue book with swirly gold letters on it. It's a bit thinner than the books on either side of it. Do you see it?"

"Yes!" Seek exclaims, then returns to the couch with the book in question.

I smile as he hands me the thin volume, then inches closer to me on the couch. I open to the prologue and begin reading aloud.

"*Alice was beginning to get very tired of sitting by her sister on the bank, and of having nothing to do.*"

Seek slides even closer to me, resting his small head on the outside of my arm. With the young boy nestled in the crook of my arm and my oversize cat sound asleep, I continue blissfully down the rabbit hole.

The back door creaks open, followed by the soft, familiar sound of Kane's shoes on the hardwood.

I glance up from where I sit cross-legged on the floor with Seek, who's currently draping a crocheted blanket over Esther. Kane doesn't speak; he watches.

He looks at me as though his gaze alone could break me. It's both comforting and patronizing at the same time. His hands twitch at his sides before he clenches them into fists and swallows whatever words threaten to escape.

"How was Big D?" I ask too casually.

His jaw shifts as he glares at Seek, knowing the child told me where he went. "Much the same."

He doesn't offer anything else, and I don't push. Whatever Big D said has his hackles raised and the shadows under his eyes deeper than usual.

Clearing my throat, I gesture toward the window. "What do you want to do tonight?"

There's a pause. He knits his brows, considering me like I'm a question he hasn't yet figured out how to answer.

Seeing as he's choosing not to answer, I do it for him. "I was hoping," I murmur, "we could take a boat ride through the harbor."

His eyes flicker in surprise.

"My dad ..." I continue, looking past him to the rain-spattered glass. "He loved getting lost on the water. Said the ocean was the only place big enough to hold all the things he couldn't say out loud."

Kane opens his mouth, but before he can reply, thunder cracks across the sky like a whip. The windows flash with white light, then dim into a sudden, torrential downpour.

"On second thought ..." I exhale, rubbing at my arms. "Maybe not."

We fill the next hour with a board game. Well, Seek and I do. Kane sits broodily, staring out the window, soaking in the grey. The object of the game is to spell words for points, but I decided we could use the pieces and playing board as tools to help Seek understand reading. He does great.

Can I teach him how to read in the time I have left? No.

Should that prevent me from filling our time with meaningful activities, like learning and laughing together? Also no!

The rigor of the activity seems to have a draining effect on the little spirit's energy though, and eventually, Seek excuses himself. That leaves me alone with Kane, who continues to gaze menacingly out the window.

"Okay. Enough is enough. We're not letting a little rain stop us from having fun." I break the silence in the room.

He humors me with a laconic reply. "What did you have in mind?"

"I don't know. We can talk. We can cook something. We can read."

"You and I might have very different definitions of *fun*."

His dismissal frustrates me to no end. I cannot believe some rain is ruining one of my last nights on Earth.

"Fine. I'm going back to my writing then."

I pull my notebook out from beside me on the couch and flip to a new page. That nausea that comes from staring into the abyss of a blank page returns, and instead of words, I begin to doodle furiously. I need this page to have something on it immediately.

"What are you doing?" Kane asks after watching me work.

"Doodling. I usually work on my poetry in here, but someone is staring at me, and I can't concentrate."

"Read me something." His eyebrows lift.

"No way." I do not hesitate.

"Read me something."

"A compelling counterargument."

"Read me something," he repeats like a stubborn child being denied dessert, and like a tired parent, I relent.

"Ugh, fine. I wrote this one the other day. After some pompous know-it-all informed me of the exact moment my living days would cease to be."

"Sounds like a real charmer."

"He's not," I deadpan.

I glance down at the page I have held open. A sonnet I

wrote, inspired by this moment in my life, stares back at me. I take a deep breath and throw caution to the wind. Then, I begin to read aloud.

Before I Go

When you know that your days are quite numbered
And you can count them on just one frail hand.
A lifetime full of dreams now encumbered
By days much too short for hope still to stand.
When will I ever swim under the moon?
The celestial power purifying.
To know love's fall, then it must happen soon
As, like Addie Bundren, I lay dying.
How can I expect to feel something more
When my deadline's a whispered reminder?
Haunting, infecting, seeped into my pores.
Lost in a library, come and find her.
So much I had hoped to do with my life.
Now I have knowledge that cuts like a knife.

I finish reading the words, but keep my face buried between the pages. There is nothing left to read there. The only thing left to read is the expression on Kane's face, but this moment of vulnerability, coupled with the potential of his disappointment, keeps my neck down for several additional beats.

Kane clears his throat, coaxing my gaze upward like a snake charmer's flute. When my eyes lock with his, I know before he speaks. And I exhale.

His words confirm what his eyes have already told me. "That was beautiful, Rue. Simply divine."

"It's nothing," I deflect, my default reaction to a compliment.

"Don't do that," Kane states with an edge. "Don't minimize what you've done."

"It's just a poem."

"It's your soul on a page. It's enduring, and it shines, Rue."

His insistence is convincing, and I take a breath to receive his words.

"Thank you," I state simply.

"Good girl." He smirks in reply, and the sensation that awakens in me is undeniable.

Lightning crashes, sending brightness pouring momentarily through the windows, and I can see Kane's mind spark with something undecipherable.

Thunder follows, then Kane's voice chases after the boom. "Come with me."

"Where are we going?" I ask, not one to trust this man with spontaneous decisions.

He begins to move but turns to see I'm still rooted to my spot.

"Fine," he sighs. "We're going to the roof."

"To the roof? Are you mad? It's raining and storming and–"

I close my mouth when I run out of excuses.

"And?" he repeats.

When I stay silent and still, his expression softens, and he extends his hand. I take it as he guides me up a ladder.

We climb through the attic and onto the roof like we're kids sneaking into forbidden places. Kane helps me balance as we step onto the old slate tiles, slick with rain and gleaming like black agate under the moonlight.

The storm hasn't stopped, but it's slowed. The thunder rolls lazily, lightning streaking purple and gold across the sky like celestial graffiti.

"This," he says, turning to me, "might be as close to swimming under the moon as you're going to get."

The rain plasters my dress to my skin. I laugh, breathless from the climb, from the view, from him.

"That's very sweet," I acknowledge.

"A bit out of character, I know, but gotta keep you on your toes," he answers sardonically.

"Why are you really doing all this?" I ask, suddenly quiet.

He eyes me and sighs heavily through the drizzle. "Because time is cruel. And you've had less of it than most."

We stand side by side. He doesn't touch me, but his presence hums warm and steady beside me, like a promise he hasn't made yet.

"You talk about your father," he says, "but not your mother."

I sigh, rain trailing down my cheek, like it's doing the crying for me. "I've always been closer to my dad than Mom. You wouldn't think that would be the case with her being an artist, but—"

I shift and nearly slip. Kane instinctively reaches out and grabs me, pulling me flush to his soaked form. I've forgotten what I was saying. All I can think about is my dream and how this feels so much better than my brain envisioned.

"But what?" His voice is too husky, and I feel my thighs clenching together.

"B-ut … her art isn't mine. I love her. She's always been as caring as she could. But she's a rolling stone. She wasn't the *stay home and bake cookies* type of mom. She's an artist. My dad was the one who got me into books. They divorced when I was young, and I spent most of my time with her in Chicago, unless Dad was here. So, we planned books to read while he was working. That way, it never truly felt like we were apart for long."

"Wow," he murmurs.

I notice the distant look in his eyes and see if I can bring him back to this moment. "What were your parents like?"

"Surprisingly similar. My mother was sharp and whip-smart. She hosted artists at our estate for monthly celebrations. The rooms would be abuzz with music and poetry and conversation. She was instrumental in helping many young authors find funding and support for publishing their work. She, perhaps, did a better job of instilling a love of the arts in me than she did of simply loving me, but I was always provided for." Kane runs his fingers through his hair before continuing.

"My father, Ambroise, was a busy man. He was a doctor before me, especially accomplished in tending to the fallen in battle. I played with his surgical instruments more than I played with him."

I give him a dry smile. "And yet you turned out so emotionally available."

He snorts. "I made a damn good doctor and a fine lover … of the arts."

The soft smirk he offers suggests that the pause in that sentence was intentional. He thinks he's being cute, but I know he's simply trying to deflect before this conversation gets any more personal. I relent and give in to the quietness of the wind and the rain.

The roof is slick beneath my bare feet, rain falling in sheets that glitter beneath the almost-full moon. Lightning shreds the sky, illuminating Kane's silhouette as he stands next to me, his arms still supporting mine. His clothes are completely soaked through, his white shirt clinging to every plane of muscle like a second skin.

This might be the closest I ever get to swimming under the moonlight.

"You're going to catch a cold," he cuts in, his voice rough and reverent.

"I think I can risk a little pneumonia." I slide down slightly on the graded rooftop, peering below.

His jaw clenches, lightning catching in his eyes. "Don't do that," he snaps.

"Do what?" I ask, raising my face toward him.

"Come back up here. I don't want you to fall off the edge."

"Why not?" I half joke.

The thunder rolls long and deep behind us, and the rain falls harder. He bunches his hand around the back of my dress and pulls me back forcibly. When we are side by side again, he takes that same hand and brushes a strand of wet hair off my cheek. His warm palm lingers, steadily cupping my jaw.

"Believe me," he says so quietly that it could be mistaken for wind, "it's very dangerous to fall."

"Good thing you stopped me before it's too la–"

He cuts me off with a brutal kiss. His mouth crashes to mine like a storm all its own. There's no hesitation this time—no lingering touches or half-breathed apologies. Kane devours me. Rain slips between our lips as his hands find my hips, lifting me to his waist like I weigh nothing. I wrap my legs around him. He pulls away long enough to move us to a flat plane in the center of the rooftop.

He lays me down on the wet slate, his body hovering above mine, drenched and desperate. His mouth is everywhere—on my neck, my collarbone, down my breasts, and over my scar. Fingers trail up my thighs beneath the thin fabric, reverent and aching, until I gasp his name.

"Oh, Grim."

At the sound of my voice, he pulls back, a new look behind his eyes. Tension crawls up his spine as he goes stiff. "We can't do this," he rasps, thunder cracking behind the words. "*Putain*, Rue. This isn't just wrong; it's impossible." His voice is frayed, unraveling at the edges. Not a demand, not even a plea–something more desperate than either. Like this moment could break him in a way nothing else ever has.

I fist the front of his soaked shirt, dragging him down until our lips nearly touch. "I want you," I breathe. "I want this. You. Now. Before time runs out."

"There will never be enough time," he rushes out. "Your touch, your skin, your fire," he intones, kissing and breathing me in between each phrase. "This is too good to be real. You are too good to be real."

I dig my nails deeper into the flesh beneath his shirt as I grit out, "Feels pretty real to me." My eyes lock with his, a silent entreaty shared between us.

"This isn't a part of your story, Rue. It can't be."

"Then I guess it's time to write a new one." The conviction and power in my voice would surprise the old me, but the Rue in this moment has never been more certain of anything.

The sound he makes is somewhere between a groan and a growl, pure devastation and hunger bleeding into one.

"Fuck Fate," he utters so low in his chest that it's more of a vibration than words.

Fireworks of lightning dot the night sky, and thunder booms.

And then his mouth crashes against mine with finality. His kiss is punishing and deliberate, brutal and breathtaking. His hands move like he's memorizing every inch of my flesh before I disappear–leaving trails of fire over my rain-slicked skin. He cups my face, grips my waist, and slides his hands over the curve of my ass, like he was born knowing my body.

There's nothing delicate in the way he cages me under his form–nothing soft or gentle in the way our hips align like puzzle pieces that have waited lifetimes to click into place.

The rain is cold, but I'm burning alive. His teeth graze the skin above my breast like he's considering whether or not to devour me whole. My back arches against the hard stone shingles beneath us, but I don't care. I want him to mark me. I want to remember this night in the storm.

Actually, *fuck that*, I want the storm to remember us.

His breath is ragged as his body grinds against mine in a most maddening rhythm. His thigh wedges between mine, and I moan shamelessly, the pressure just enough to make me shudder.

"I'm not"–he breaks off, voice rough–"going to be gentle."

"Good." I pant, curling my arms around his shoulders as lightning explodes overhead. "Make me feel, Grim."

He presses his forehead to mine, and we get lost in a moment between a heartbeat and a breath.

"That name is growing on me."

I slide my hands down, unbuckling his belt with trembling fingers. The metal clinks under the storm's roar as I unzip his pants, my hand slipping inside, finding him. He's hard and heavy. And when I wrap my fingers around him, he lets out a broken, tortured sound that rockets straight to the center of me.

"Looks like you're growing on me too."

"Rue," he groans, voice cracking on my name like it physically hurts him to say it, "watch your fucking mouth."

I stroke him once, slow, then again, tighter, and his hips jerk into my palm as he claws the tiles on either side of my head.

"Fill me." I whisper the command into his mouth, and like a skeleton key, it unlocks every door.

His whole being moves with measured desperation now, dragging my underwear down my legs, then casting them aside. His fingers slide between my thighs, finding me wet and wanting, and he curses under his breath.

"Fuck, Rue," he growls. "You're soaked."

"It's raining, Grim," I bite out, breathless.

"Not the rain," he says, and the heat in his voice nearly undoes me.

I pull his stunned face to mine as needy whimpers escape me, my thighs trembling around his hips as he pumps his fingers into me. Each thrust is a pulse of need, a spark across raw nerves. I shudder beneath him, voice caught somewhere between a gasp and a sob.

"Please," I whisper, dragging my nails down his rain-slick shoulders, "let me feel you."

"All of me," he breathes, like a promise and a threat.

His mouth fuses to mine, our tongues tangling. He hikes my dress up with shaking hands, groaning as the head of his cock brushes against my aching center.

"Kane," I whimper, rolling my hips toward him.

I can feel how hard he is, feel the tension rippling through him as he hesitates.

His eyes lock with mine, stormy and deadly. "Rue–"

"Don't," I cut in, breathless. "Stop." I drag my tongue along his bottom lip, tasting him, claiming him. "Not now."

"I couldn't even if I tried," he grits out, one hand braced next to my head, the other sliding around my throat.

I gasp at the expected pressure. I am struggling to breathe anyway, and the animal inside Kane seems ready to consume me. His eyes have literally changed color, and his beautiful smile holds a predatory gleam.

If this is how I go out, I am ready to embrace it.

But the pressure never comes. Kane grinds his thick length up and down my throbbing center as his index and middle finger slide under my jawbone. I am powerless in this position. He has me physically and emotionally overwhelmed, but he's–

"You're checking my pulse," I say softly as I realize what he's doing.

He holds himself in place. "I want to destroy your cunt, Rue. Not your heart."

"Then may I offer some friendly advice?" I ask dryly. "Stop focusing on my heart and start focusing on my pussy."

His laugh twists the tension like a vise. It's dark, primal, and full of the kind of ache that says he'd do anything to keep me.

"Then you'd better spread those legs a little wider," he mutters, the words gritted as he shifts, lining himself up.

I splay my knees and feel his girth begin to penetrate

my tight heat. The first stretch is slow, torturous. My breath leaves me in a gasp as he pushes in, inch by inch, the thick swell of him opening me like I was made to take him.

"Kane—" My voice breaks on his name as my nails dig into his rain-drenched back.

"That's it," he groans, forehead resting against mine. "Relax, baby. You take me so well. You feel that?"

Pleasure courses through me at the surprise in his voice. And I do feel that. The way his cock fills and penetrates every place that was empty inside me. It's not just pleasure. It's a detonation. His body moves like he's searching for salvation inside me. Like if he gets deep enough, he'll find it.

He pulls back and thrusts—hard—and we both cry out. It's instinct now. A rhythm set by the unbound thrumming of raw need. And it is a dance we fall into seamlessly, like our bodies have been waiting for us to find this moment forever. The rain pelts down, soaking our skin, drenching the rooftop. I arch into him, legs locking around his waist, pulling him deeper. He drives in again and again, faster now, rougher. The kind of punishing pace that might leave bruises on my pelvis and his branding on my soul.

"Mayday," he pants against my neck, every thrust a broken whisper of my name. "Mayday. May—"

"I'm here," I cut him off. "Right here, Kane. Please ..."

His hand pounds the wet slate next to my head as his hips snap harder. "Please what?" he grits. "Use your words to voice what my soul already knows." He punctuates his words with a quick thrust. Hard.

"Fuck, right there, yes—Kane," I cry out as he hits something deep that makes the world flicker behind my eyes. "You're so deep—don't stop—please, don't stop—"

"That's better, Rue. I love to hear you beg," he growls, voice wrecked.

I look up at this ghost of a man who has morphed into an apex predator right before my eyes. His voice is barely recognizable, but our connection has never felt more complete. I moan—that's all I have left now. Just sounds.

"So tight, so fucking warm–shit, Rue," he praises as he pounds into me.

We're soaked and shaking, lightning splitting the sky above us as he buries himself deeper, until we're nothing but heat and breath and the animalistic sound of skin on skin.

"I'm gonna–" he gasps, hand finding my face like he needs to anchor himself. "Rue ... look at me. Look at me."

My eyes snap open and meet his, just as the tension coiled in my belly explodes.

"Kane!" I cry, finding the only word in the universe that matters in this moment. Body locking, legs trembling, I shatter around him.

"Fuck–Rue–" he growls, kissing me as he follows me into oblivion, thrusting deep one last time before he comes deep inside me.

His hips jerk, his mouth crashes to mine, and we fall together–shaking and so potently alive.

He holds me through it, chest pressing to mine, my heart racing fast and hard enough for the both of us. We lie there beneath the storm, bodies tangled, my breathing ragged, and my heart still trying to catch up.

He uses his free hand to wipe the rain from my face–from my forehead to my chin. His touch has a primal edge to it, a roughness that disappears when his hand continues its descent from my chin to my throat, where he delicately checks my pulse again.

"That ..." I whisper breathlessly. "That was worth every second I have left."

He flinches like the words cut bone deep. But he doesn't pull away. Instead, he kisses me again.

His voice is thick when he murmurs, "*Absolument.* Absolutely."

In this moment, I don't feel like I'm dying. I feel somehow more than alive. Like time itself does not exist, but I do. We do. And together, we are infinite.

Chapter Twenty-Two

SLIPPER WEATHER

KANE

THE RAIN HASN'T STOPPED, AND NEITHER OF US SEEMS TO care. We just lie there, limbs tangled, the storm crackling above us like it's bearing witness.

Rue is half draped over me, her lips still parted, eyes closed, hair soaked and wild against my chest. Her body is warm despite the chill, but I can feel the edges of her shaking–small, barely there tremors from exhaustion or cold or maybe just the unraveling of whatever she's been holding on to.

I tuck her tighter against me, shielding her from the wind. I wonder if my body provides any warmth to her. At least it can provide shelter.

My palm rests on her chest, her heart beats soft flutters now beneath my fingers. I count silently, clocking her pulse.

It's slow, and the beats are faint.

The cold clinician in me quiets as another voice in me rises in volume. Panic whispers through me before I can stop it. Quiet, soul-deep dread that seeps into my very marrow.

She shivers again, and it pulls me back to the present. She's too cold. I don't hesitate, scooping her up, soaked dress and all, and carry her down from the rooftop. My arms begin to shake in ways they never have before. It's not from the weight of her. I'm a reaper. I can lift vehicles without much effort. No, this is from the thought of what's to come. What I'll do when I no longer have the option to carry her.

Inside, I move on autopilot as I lay her on her bed. I grab a towel and fresh clothes from her dresser, and I begin to strip her out of her soaked garments. My hands move gently but efficiently.

She's barely awake, murmuring something I can't quite make out as I dress her in a baggy black T-shirt. It swallows her whole, hanging off her frame like a shroud.

Her eyes flutter open once, bleary and heavy-lidded.

"Hi," she whispers.

"Hey," I reply, brushing damp hair from her temple. "Sleep. I've got you."

Her lashes lower again, and she sighs softly, curling into the blanket like a child seeking shelter. I kneel beside her bed, hand still on her hair, watching the rise and fall of her chest.

I press a kiss to her forehead and smooth back her hair.

"*Somnus mortis frater est,*" I whisper darkly to the sleeping Rue, voice raw and hollow. "Sleep is Death's brother. Might as well get some practice."

Her fingers twitch, but she makes no offer of reply, just continues life's metronome in even, slowing breaths.

I watch her sleep, hoping to absorb her quiet, but my growing feelings are yelling too loud. The ache in my hollow chest pinches, a physical sensation I've not known in centuries.

I sigh, the sound voicing the only thought in my head. *This is going to be fucking devastating.*

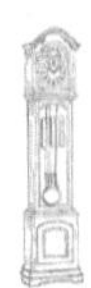

She's humming this morning. *Humming.* Sunlight filters in through the sheer curtains, casting long, sleepy rays across the kitchen floor, and there she is–padding across the tiles, singing off-key like a broken siren.

As I take in the scene before me, my eyes travel down

the length of Rue's body to the slippers on her feet. What looks like a pair of enormous clouds consumes her small ankles. Her feet sit inside the puffy masses of cotton that appear to be swallowing her legs slowly. As she turns to face me, I notice the slippers are not clouds. I am staring back at the face of two identical bunny rabbits.

"What are those?" I ask, the derision evident in my tone.

"These?" She wiggles her feet obnoxiously.

"Yes."

"These are my hippity-hoppity flippity-floppities."

I do not respond.

"Do you like them?"

"No."

"I have another pair that might fit you. If you want to try them on. They're surprisingly comfortable. Like walking on air."

"I can do that without wearing those abominations."

"They're not abominations. They're slippers, Kane."

"Slippers," I scoff.

"And not just any kind of indoor footwear. No, no. This is Bunny," she says and holds up her left foot. "And Cher." Then she shakes her right foot.

"You did not name your slippers."

"My hippity-hoppity flippity-floppities, you mean? Yes, I did. I named them Bunny and Cher."

Having no idea how to respond to this childish inanity, I opt for silence. Eventually, she turns back around and continues her task.

I stand in the doorway, watching as she cracks eggs into a bowl with an absent smile on her face, her hair messy and her cheeks still rosy from sleep.

"Something wrong, Grim?" she asks without looking up, her voice light, teasing. "You look like a man staring into the abyss. Again."

"Just concerned about Fate," I murmur absently.

She glances back at me, one brow arched. "Mine?"

I shake off my darker thoughts and return to the present. "Of those eggs actually." I shrug, dragging a hand through my hair.

She rolls her eyes and goes back to whisking. "I make excellent eggs."

"Everyone says that, and most people don't."

She glares at me suspiciously. "It's basically impossible to ruin scrambled eggs."

I meet her gaze defiantly. "You seem to be well on your way."

"Oh, really? And what exactly am I doing wrong? Eggs. Bowl. Beating. Seems pretty cut and dry to me."

I sigh, debating if this is worth my time. If it's worth her time. Deciding it's never too late to learn something new, I move from the archway of the kitchen toward her as I begin to instruct, "Set the bowl down. Turn that burner off and get a new pan."

"What? Why? This one is preheated."

"Yes, I can see that. And you will burn the flavor right out of the yolks. Now, are you going to listen and do as you're told? Or am I wasting my time?"

The command in my tone makes her pupils dilate, matching the black in her oversize T-shirt.

"I'm listening," she concedes. Then she proceeds to turn off the burner, removes the first pan, and grabs another from a drawer.

"Good. Now, set the burner on the lowest heat possible. Grab some butter and place it in the center of the pan."

She does so, and I relish watching her flit about the kitchen, enjoying the obedient little sprite side of Rue. Once she's done that, she looks to me for further instruction, though she can't hide the glint in her eyes.

"Now what, Chef?" she asks with deviant emphasis on the final word.

"While we wait for the pan to gently warm, we will properly whisk those eggs. Timing is critical now. Take the bowl and the fork. Press the tines to the bottom of the bowl and circle your wrist in a tight clockwise motion."

She begins as the butter begins to soften in the pan next to her. I move behind her as she works.

"Faster, Rue. The second that butter coats the entirety of that pan, you need to pour those freshly beaten eggs into the low heat."

Her pace picks up as the eggs begin to turn a uniform yellow color.

"Good," I praise as she continues working, the bowl hovering over the pan while I hover over Rue.

"Like this?"

"Exactly." The second the final solid bit of butter glistens against the pan, I command, "Keep whisking while you pour them into the pan. Now."

The eggs make a soft sizzling sound as they come in contact with the warm metal and begin to mix with the butter and spread across the surface.

"Take that spatula and stir."

"Stir?"

"Yes, Rue. Stir the liquid in the pan and do not stop until I say so."

"Didn't realize making eggs would be such a physical activity," Rue mumbles under her breath.

"Doing things right often takes more energy than most are willing to give. Now keep stirring." I soften my voice on my last direction, seeing some frustration begin to surface.

Rue's shoulders relax, and she finds her rhythm with the spatula.

"That's it. You don't need to work hard, just don't stop. Slow and steady."

She continues for a minute and then admits, "This is nice actually. Kind of calming."

"Good. Just don't lose your focus because the timing is key now."

"It's all still liquid, Kane," Rue points out.

"Good things come to those who wait, *ma chère*."

Rue purrs at the pet name and shifts her focus from me back to the pan.

"Seek," I call out to the room, "we need a plate here, friend."

Out of the wall immediately appears our little friend, who heads straight to the cabinet. "Here you go," he says with a noticeable hint of pride in his young voice.

"A fork too, please."

He complies instantly. "One fork."

"Thank you, Seek. You may go."

"With pleasure." He smiles and disappears back into the wall.

"It's happening," Rue announces with glee.

"Good. Keep stirring. You're almost there."

The eggs begin to solidify in the pan, turning a rich, dark yellow in the center.

"When are they done?" Rue asks.

"Keep folding and turning them until you can no longer see any liquid. And the second that happens, pull them from the pan and plate them."

She stirs with a laser focus, eyes transfixed on the pan. I bring my arm around her shoulder and grab a pinch of salt from the jar to the right of the stove. I breathe in her intoxicating scent of vetiver and violet. I sprinkle the salt over the eggs, then move slightly away from her.

"Now?" she asks innocently.

"Now," I confirm.

She pulls the pan from the heat, uses the spatula to plate them, and then looks at her handiwork. "Now what?"

I laugh at her confused expression. "Now, you eat, Rue. Enjoy the fruits of your labor. They are best when they're hot. Try a bite right away."

She takes her fork and stabs into the fluffy eggs. I watch as she brings them to her soft lips, feeling a certain amount of envy for that fork.

As her mouth wraps around the bite, the moan it elicits is instant and decadent. "Oh my, Grim. These are incredible."

I smirk, loving the look on her face and the sound she just made. "I'm glad you like them."

"I wish you could have some too."

"I'd want you to practice a few more times before I deign to try your attempt at a soft scramble."

I smile at her and move to a seat in the kitchen. She devours her plate, inhaling three eggs almost entirely before I've even taken a seat.

Good, I think to myself. *You're gonna need the energy.*

"Maybe I'll make some more right now. Those were incredible. I had no idea eggs could have that much flavor."

"You can coax wonderful flavor out of many things, if you're willing to take your time with them." I pause briefly, seeing if she clocks the innuendo. I can't be sure based on the look on her face, but we have more pressing matters to attend to, so I change topics. "Now sit down. Take a load off your hoopity-floopity slipperdoos. I have something I need to tell you."

"You mean hippity-hoppity flippity-floppities? Okay." She smiles and parks her ass in a chair at the small breakfast nook in the kitchen.

My lip curls as I stare at the monstrosities on her feet. "Hippa floppa what?"

The vibration of my Tombstone Phone pulls me away, and I glance down to see a message from Big D.

> **Big D: Hey there, Kane. Just popping in to say how excited I am to be hosting you and your plus-one at this year's gala. It's going to be a scream. —Big D**

A second later, he follows up with an image of his face in place of the central figure in Edvard Munch's *The Scream*.

I take a deep, steadying breath so as not to scream myself.

The silence stretches. Rue fills it.

"First off, don't look at my hippity-hoppity flippity-floppities like you're better than them."

"Noted," I mumble, still staring at my phone.

"Second, what?"

"I just received an event reminder."

"Reapers have a Calendar app?"

"No, this was a personal message from Sleep's brother himself. Death."

"Oh. What did he say?"

"We have to go somewhere," I say, voice lower now.

"We?" Rue queries suspiciously. "You mean I'm actually invited somewhere?"

"Not willingly, Mayday, I assure you," I grunt. "It's a formal event."

Her brows shoot up. "Formal?"

I nod. "OtherWorld masquerade. Hosted by Big D."

"Are you telling me that Death throws … parties?"

I glance sideways, already regretting this conversation. "Big D's Devilishly Deviant Dress-Up Dance."

"That sounds like the world's worst prom theme."

"You're not that far off."

"So, skip it. Call in sick or whatever."

"You really don't have a sense of the hierarchies in place, do you?" I bite out.

"You could have just said it was mandatory. You don't have to be a dick about it."

"I'm not trying to be a dick. I'm trying to teach you how things will be for you in the eternal hereafter. And now, on top of that, we have to get you a dress."

A slow, devious smile spreads across her face. "Oh! No worries on that. If it's a ball, I have a dress."

"You what?"

"I have a dress."

Chapter Twenty-Three

BUT NOT THE SHOES

RUE

"YOU HAVE A DRESS?" KANE PARROTS, TURNING OUR CONversation into a low-rent Abbott and Costello routine.

I try to jump off the carousel before he starts asking me, *Who's on first?*

I blink at him. "Yes, Kane, believe it or not, I do own a dress."

"Right," he says, narrowing his eyes. "A dress that would suit a ball in the OtherWorld? Or anywhere for that matter." He mutters the last part, but I hear it. "And where is this dress?"

"It's in the attic," I say, not quite meeting Kane's eyes as I gesture upward. "You know, that room three floors up from here, with the creaky stairs, cobwebs, and window leading to the roof." I toy with the hem of the shirt I'm wearing, suddenly feeling too small inside my own skin.

"I know what an attic is, Rue. I've been inside a multilevel home before." His lips twitch as he stares down at me. "And I'm very aware of where your attic leads. Believe me, it's not something I'll soon forget."

"Oh," I answer meekly, not sure exactly what to make of his response.

"Are you ashamed of what happened between us, Ms. Chamberlain?"

I meet his energy with confidence of my own. "No, I am not."

"Good. Neither am I. So, don't turn all meek on me when you mention it, if you mention it. Though I'm not entirely sure there's a need to mention it at all, if I'm honest. We have loads to do before your official crossover."

"Do you not want to talk about it?" I ask, unable to keep the hurt out of my voice. Unsure what I'm even truly asking.

He clears his throat, as if he's trying to stall before giving me an answer. "We've got bigger issues that concern us presently, Rue. Tell me about this dress." The pivot is sharp, surgical.

I can see by the steely look of his eyes that there's no sense in pursuing that topic right now, so I press on with a story from my childhood I've had very few opportunities to tell.

"When I was a kid, I wanted to be a theater girl. Shakespeare, musicals, the whole thing. I used to dream about it every night. From Roxie Hart to Rosalind, I wanted to play them all." I pause, swallowing past the tightness climbing my throat. "But *Fate* had other plans, evidently. I didn't 'look like a leading lady.'" I air-quote the refrain heard from countless directors and mean classmates alike.

Kane scowls, but makes no move to speak; in fact, he makes no move at all. He stares at me, still as a statue, eyes locked on my mouth.

Before I can continue, the family clock intones the top of another hour. Kane and I stare at each other silently.

I have never been more aware of the passage of time, I think to myself during the aural backdrop of the metronomic gong.

After the tenth tone, I return to my story. "In my mind, I knew. Culture and time dictate a community's sense of beauty and expectation. A Renaissance queen would be laughed off of a Miami beach, but in her own era, gorgeous. Try explaining that to Mr. Gladwell or any of the kids at Crestview High. Anyway, the point was moot in the end. My sophomore year, doctors advised against pursuing activities that would put undue strain on my heart, so that was that. The only gown I ever got to wear came from a hospital." My voice cracks, and I hate it. I force a small laugh, brushing it off like it doesn't still carve into me.

Kane exhales slowly and deliberately. "That's awful, Rue. People can be the worst kind sometimes."

I smile softly at his simple but effective distillation, then press on to my conclusion. "My dad started buying me dresses. Said I'd always be his princess, and if I couldn't be Juliet on a stage, I could still be her in our backyard."

My throat clogs. I feel Kane's stare, heavy and raw.

"Rue ..." he says softly.

There's something in the way he says my name that makes everything inside me splinter a little more. I lift my chin and give him a smile that feels a little too sharp at the edges.

"Anyway, that was my dad. Always meeting me where I was. Always giving me space and encouragement to dream." After another lengthy silence, I ask, "So, do you want to see it? The dress?"

"No," Kane answers, taking me by surprise.

"You don't want to see it? Make sure it's suitable for a party in the OtherWorld?"

"No," he says, his voice a gavel. "If your father got it for you, that's good enough for me."

"Okay." I blush. Then a new thought occurs to me, and a small smile creeps onto my face. "However, I do have one problem ..." I say, dragging out the word.

"What? I don't like that look."

"I don't have any shoes."

"You don't have any shoes?" he repeats.

"Let's not do this again, Grim. No, I do not have shoes appropriate for an event of this magnitude."

"There must be something you have here."

"Unless you want me to wear my hippity-hoppity flipp–"

"Do not finish that sentence," he cuts me off forcefully, which has me giggling under my breath. His next sentence comes out extremely quickly. "Where does one procure footwear in this town?"

"The mall, Grim."

He stiffens. "We are not going to the mall," he declares adamantly.

"Oh, we absolutely are. Now, I've got to get dressed and then order us a ride."

"I'll open a portal," he states.

I raise a brow. "You said that portals are for official reaper business."

"Desperate times, Mayday."

"No," I say, crossing my arms over my chest.

"No?" He raises a brow. "Rue, let's be realistic here. A portal is faster."

"It's also nauseating, disorienting, and altogether too draining for a simple trip to get shoes. Sorry to burst your bubble, Grim, but we're doing this the human way."

"You're overexaggerating the portal and romanticizing getting into a stranger's vehicle, smelling their odor, and trusting them not to kidnap you."

"I'll be dead in a couple of days anyway, so what does it matter?" I shrug, and he scowls, not enjoying my remark. "Besides, the only romanticizing I'm doing is the part where you, a centuries-old reaper, are about to set foot in a mall with food courts, crowds of teenagers, and fluorescent lighting."

He looks at me, genuine pain and discomfort in his voice as he says, "Barbaric."

"You'll get over it."

Kane groans. "Rue ..."

"Don't *Rue* me," I say, forcing back a laugh while reaching for my phone. "We're doing this." I tap through the app on my phone before smiling up at him and heading to my room to get dressed. "Steve will be here in three minutes. Gotta love these modern conveniences."

"Steve? Is that the name of the car or a person?"

"The driver, silly. Now let me get ready. He's almost here!"

Kane follows me to my room, leaning on the doorframe while crossing his arms. "And what *car* will I be forced into?"

"Can you not stand there while I'm trying to get dressed?" I huff, slipping into my skirt.

"I've seen you naked already," he points out annoyingly.

"And now is not the time for a repeat viewing," I state while turning my back to him, removing my baggy shirt, and chucking it at his face. "And it's a Prius." I turn back around after slipping my tank top on.

"A what?"

"A Prius," I repeat. "It's good for the environment."

"Wear pants," Kane states sharply.

"Excuse me?" I laugh lightly. "Now you have something negative to say about my skirt?"

"No, I just … never mind, I'll be in the living room."

I watch him stalk away, and I cock my head to one side.

"What was that about?" I wonder aloud.

"Prolly not wanting others to look at you!"

"Seek!" I gasp, clutching my heart as the small ghost pokes his head through my wall. "We've gone over this. I have a heart condition!"

"Sorry." He smiles cheekily as I walk to my dresser and pull out leggings. For no other reason than the fact that malls in the summer in New Orleans are cold. And that's the *only* reason.

The lie I tell myself gets interrupted by a series of cheerful beeps from outside. I look out the window and see a silver Prius parked at the end of my gravel driveway under the weeping oak.

I head down the stairs and stop in the living room to grab Kane.

"Our noble steed awaits," I say cheerily.

"Oh joy," Kane grumps before I grab his hand and drag him outside.

The Prius rolls to a stop in front of the mall's south entrance. Kane is already straightening his coat like he's preparing to step onto a battlefield instead of a linoleum-tiled food court.

I open the door and slide out. Kane appears beside me the moment my feet hit the concrete.

Steve leans out his window with a grin. "Stay spiritual, Rue. It's been real." He places his hand over his heart and nods with a soft smile.

I give him a salute. "You're a legend, Steve."

Steve shoots us the *rock on* gesture with his left hand, completely unaware of the immortal entity he just shepherded to Atrium 88, New Orleans' finest mecca to merchandise.

"We should have transported," Kane grumbles at the retreating vehicle before he turns his glare to the grey structure in front of us, like a general assessing the enemy's battlements. "So, this is where we make our stand," he murmurs, voice low and grim.

"Yes. Watch out for the escalators. Avoid the perfume sprayers and try to be brave." I look directly at Kane with as much seriousness as I can muster.

He ignores me and steps forward with all the reluctant dread of a condemned man. "This entire building is vibrating with chaos and monosodium glutamate."

"It's called capitalism," I whisper, looping my arm through his—just for the comfort of pretending he's *here* in a way that people can see. "You'll be fine."

The sliding glass doors part, and the fluorescent glow and buffed floors beckon us toward the light. But before we enter the space, Kane clears his throat and removes his arm from mine, stopping me in my tracks.

"Don't you remember?" he asks condescendingly.

"What?"

"Don't loop your arm around the spirit no one can see. Put your earbuds in and keep your eyes forward. Otherwise, it looks like you're talking to a brick wall."

"Sometimes, I feel like that's what I'm doing," I mumble to myself while looking up at the ceiling to deliberately piss him off. I push the buds into my ears. "Better?" I snark.

"Just remember, you're the one they're going to whisper and point at." He smirks.

"Just walk, reaper."

We make our way down the first hall, and I find a kiosk with a map.

Kane takes in his visual surroundings with wonder

and derision, if his tone is any indication. "Fascinating. Reminiscent of a medieval village."

"They're about to be just as extinct too," I reply scanning the business names along the bottom of the display. "Shoes, shoes, shoes. Ah, here we go. HPSW."

"What is *hupsswuh*?" Kane strings the letters together in a mess of sound.

I laugh. He does not.

"It's not a word, Kane. It's an acronym. Half-Price Shoe Warehouse," I say, emphasizing each first letter.

Kane looks appalled. "Don't be ridiculous. You're not getting heels for a ball hosted by the lord of the OtherWorld on clearance. Show me on this map where FILTH is located."

"What the fuck is *filth*, Grim?"

"FILTH, an acronym that's also a word, Mayday. The best kind of acronym."

"What does it stand for?"

"Fine Italian Leather-Topped Heels. Take us there, Rue."

I notice a couple of teenagers staring at me from the entrance to a hat shop and realize I look as though I'm talking to air again. I've got to get better at this ghost chatter. I scan the map and speak to Kane, pressing my fingers to my ear, as though starting a phone call.

"Hello? Yes? Can you hear me? I don't think they have a store like that. They do have a high-end boutique with women's designer wear."

"Laying it on a little thick there, Mayday, but I appreciate the effort. Nice work."

"Shut up, ass," I whisper under my breath without moving my eyes from their spot.

"Yes, take us there."

I track the route from the *You Are Here* marker on the map and make my way. "Okay, Mom," I say with a bright, fake laugh. "Heading there now."

Kane rolls his eyes as I take the lead, but he follows close, like an overly opinionated shadow.

We pass the firing squad of perfume slingers, who look disappointed when I refuse to make eye contact, and Kane mutters something about "chemical warfare disguised as citrus blossom."

I ignore him until something glittering in one of the jewelry cases grabs my attention. I pause briefly to stare at the beautiful piece. The teardrop diamond pops against a pair of sapphire rectangles, housed in rich eighteen karat gold.

"That looks just like a necklace my grandmother wore," I murmur, caught in the gleam of memory.

Kane cuts against the wistful note in my voice with an acerbic tone, "Move it along, little lady. They're called accessories for a reason. They're not necessary. Shoes are. You can't show up to a party barefoot."

Kane continues toward the shoe section, and it's the first time I am able to take in the fact that no one else can see him. As I trail behind him, I watch him walk past customers and store clerks. To me, he looks as real as anything; to them, he is invisible. They take no notice of his towering height. No one balks at his immaculate, though decidedly outdated, wardrobe. To them, he simply does not exist. It is disorienting.

We reach the leather couches in the back, where the women's shoes are located. Can lights highlight walls full of flats while tabletops display more luxurious pumps and heels. Kane dismisses the shelves on the wall immediately and prowls purposefully around each of the table displays.

While he inspects, I am greeted by a young woman with enough vocal fry to zap a mosquito. "Hi," she states, managing to make the word contain about thirteen letters. "My name is Paloma. Can I help you find anything?"

"Yes. Hi. I'm Rue. I'm looking for some shoes for an event."

Kane interjects, speaking directly at a table rather than looking up. "You're not looking for shoes, Mayday. You're looking for heels that will stop the dead in their tracks. You're looking for lift and line and elegance. You're looking for sex in a stiletto."

"Ma'am?" Paloma asks, looking at me askance. "Did you hear me?"

Shit, Paloma must have said something while I was listening to Kane's admittedly hot diatribe on heels.

"Yes, sorry. What was the question?"

"Did you have anything in mind? Color? Style? Design?"

Before I can answer, Kane chimes in again, hands clasped behind his back, like a judge inspecting evidence. "Black and lifted. With something that ties or wraps around the ankle to highlight and accentuate the gentle curve of your calf muscle and the softness of your pale skin."

"That's awfully specific." I shoot daggers at him.

Paloma's eyes pop out of her head, and Kane shakes his head at me, a disappointed dad. He points to his ear, reminding me about my earbuds.

I touch my finger to my ear and say, "Mom, I'm not asking the clerk for that!" Then I whisper, turning my attention to Paloma, "Sorry, on the phone with my Mom, who's helping. I don't do fancy events or dress up often."

"You don't say," Paloma sneers.

Kane sighs audibly, though it sounds like he's covering a laugh. "Just ask her if she carries Manolo Blahnik."

"Fine!" I yell at Kane, though this time at least, I remember not to look directly at him.

"You don't need to yell, ma'am."

"Okay, Mom. I'll ask." I turn to Paloma. "Sorry, she's a handful," I say, pointing to my right ear while trying to find any semblance of composure. "And please don't call me ma'am. I'm on the phone with my mom. I'm not actually my mother though." I give a half-hearted laugh.

"Okay," Paloma returns, making this four-letter word even longer than her initial greeting.

"Do you have any Manolos?" I ask without a trace of confidence in my voice.

Paloma's face lights up. "Yes, we do. Right this way."

When we arrive at the small white table with six pairs of shoes on display, Kane hums as he surveys the footwear. His focus is unwavering, his gaze bordering on obsessive. The silence stretches, and since these are my shoes anyway, I take a look at the table and make a pick. I point to a black patent leather heel with a single black strap over the toes and a thin black ankle strap with a small gold clasp.

Kane moans a low rumble in his throat as Paloma oohs audibly at the same time.

"Not bad, Mayday, but not quite it."

"Great choice," Paloma says. "What's your shoe size?"

"Seven," I say as Kane speaks only to me. "Those, Rue. The ones to your left."

He points to an open-toed sandal-style heel with a soft curve to the arch, a single strap in smooth leather, and a bow to secure it around the ankle in a rich crushed velvet of the purest black.

As Paloma begins to walk to the back, my eyes break from the shoe in my hand to Kane's. His sinful smile is damn near edible.

"Wait," I shout after Paloma. "On second thought, could I see this one too?"

"Ooh, the Chastanas," the clerk says reverently. "Yes, queen."

I take a seat as Paloma disappears to the back. She returns with two cream-colored boxes that reveal some of the nicest shoes I've ever seen, let alone tried on.

Paloma kneels and helps me slide into one of each– left foot in the patent heel, right foot in the Chastana. I stand to my full height. The contrast is immediate.

Kane says nothing. He just observes for a moment. His silence weakens my knees.

Finally, he breaks the tension. "Hmm," he appraises with a delicious growl to his voice. "You're more bows than straps, Mayday. A gift to be tied up, not a danger- ous creature to be strapped down."

My face floods with heat. "I'll take the Chastanas," I say, my voice rushed as I sit back down.

Paloma helps me remove and then box the shoes, and we head to the counter. "You're going to turn a lot of heads in these."

I glance briefly at Kane, and like he's not standing right there, I answer honestly, "I'm only hoping to turn one head, Paloma."

"Ooh, okay, girl. That's a lucky person then." The clerk scans the side of the box and looks up at me. "That will be eleven hundred dollars."

"I'm sorry, what? Eleven hundred?" I exclaim, my voice hitting an octave I did not know I had.

"Mayday, calm down," Kane says.

"These are more than shoes, girl. They're a feeling, a statement, a purpose," Paloma preaches.

"You can't take it with you," Kane reminds me with a smirk as I take a deep breath.

He's right. The price tag doesn't matter much since money won't mean anything in a few short days. I ignore the pit in my stomach that realization invokes and offer Paloma my credit card.

"Wrap 'em up, Paloma," I say, handing her the plastic rectangle.

Kane smiles and offers one more piece of encouragement. "And you can't put a price tag on feeling good about yourself, *ma chère*."

As we're walking out of the store, bag in hand, I glance down at the box, then up to Kane. "I do feel decadent," I admit, surprised by the weightless grin tugging at my lips. "It does not suck."

Kane stops in his tracks and turns toward me. His voice is low, reverent. Like a vow. "Your father might have treated you like a princess, Rue Chamberlain," he says as he traces my cheek with his thumb, "but I intend to make you a queen."

Chapter Twenty-Four

NOTHING IS IMPOSSIBLE

KANE

EXITING THE FLUORESCENT JAWS OF THE SHOPPING MALL, WE step out into the open air, and the difference is immediate–no more synthetic oxygen, no more perfume traps, no more cursed overhead music trying to reanimate my soul through nostalgia.

Just warm New Orleans sunlight filtering through centuries-old oaks, the faint aroma of powdered sugar from down the street, and the constant hum of life pressing in from every direction.

I hear a low rumbling noise coming from my left and glance that way. A sound I thought had come from the throat of an angry beast seems to have come from Rue's stomach.

"You're hungry." It is not a question.

"I'm fine."

"Don't do that, Rue," I insist while surveying my surroundings. "Your body just made a sound that startled pigeons. You don't have to be polite about survival. You're clearly in need of food."

"Sorry about that," she whispers, evidently embarrassed.

"You don't need to apologize, and don't act like needing something is shameful. You are allowed to take up space in this world. You want food? We'll get food. That's it."

She exhales, her mouth twitching toward a real smile. "Okay. Yeah. I'm hungry. But you don't eat. I can just get a slice or something."

"A slice?"

"Yeah, like a piece of pizza?"

"A slice of pizza?" I make a face like she just proposed she drink bathwater.

"No. You live in the heart of one of the most culinarily blessed cities in the world. You're not eating something that's been coagulating behind an exposed glass window for hours." I shudder. "I've got nothing but time, Mayday. And since I don't eat, I'm going to need you to indulge enough for the both of us. Let's get you a proper lunch."

She squints at me. "Who are you, and what have you done with my broody reaper?"

"I've decided to expand my brand."

"Fun." Rue laughs, the sound bright against the dull hum of the street. "That sounds great actually, but I don't really know what's around here."

"You're in luck," I say, lifting a finger. "I have just the place. About a century ago, I was here for a reap. Some odious land developer who spent most of his life bull-dozing historic blocks and replacing them with buildings shaped like tax write-offs."

"Charming."

"Oh, he was detestable. Spent the first moments of his postmortem trying to bribe me."

"Did it work?"

"Rue, I'm incorruptible."

"You're full of it." She snorts.

I ignore that.

"As his soul began detaching–tendrils of energy separating from his decaying ego–he had one final thought. One last pitiful wish before slipping out of existence."

"This story had better be going somewhere, Grim. I'm not getting any *less* hungry over here."

"Hold your horses, Rue. I told you to stand up for yourself, not be an impatient nit who doesn't have time for a little backstory appetizer."

"Fine," Rue says, rolling her eyes sardonically. "Fill me with your big words, Kane. I want them all."

"Watch that mouth of yours," I warn, though there is

no denying the allure of her sass. "Anyway, this man's spirit is separating from his body, wispy tendrils clinging to this place as his essence becomes less like him and more like a cloud. And then his voice croaks–and I quote–'I wish I'd had one last étouffée from Simone's. Nothing brought me joy like that first bite. Nothing in this life or the next.' Then he dematerialized."

She blinks. "That's his legacy? Shellfish regret?"

"I don't think there was anything selfish about it actually. Probably the only unselfish thing that man ever thought about. Goes to show you, in the end–"

"Shell-fish, you dolt. As in crustaceans and mollusks. Not selfish."

"You're a mollusk."

"Wow." She shakes her head. "You're shrimply the worst."

"Then it seems we have something in common. We're both shellfish. Anyway, where was I?"

"Shellfish regret."

"Yes. Precisely. But fortunately for us, he left behind valuable culinary intelligence."

"And please tell me, where do we find this meal that was a dying man's final regret?"

"Make a left right up here."

We walk deeper into the French Quarter, where the streets are a fever dream of wrought iron balconies and faded signs, jazz notes floating from cracked-open windows like ghosts with good rhythm. The air smells like cane sugar.

Rue's steps slow as we round the corner onto a cobbled alley. Her eyes flick to the storefront ahead–two stories tall, painted deep green, with weathered shutters and gold-lettered signage in script: *Simone's.*

"This must be it," she says.

"What gave it away?" I deadpan. "The giant sign

bearing its name? Or the fact that we stopped walking? No, don't tell me. It was both. It had to be both."

She turns toward me, already reaching for the handle. "You can wait outside if you're gonna be rude."

I press a hand to my chest, scandalized. "Me? Rude? Never. I'm far too excited to live vicariously through you. I do intend to behave."

I mime locking my lips and tossing away the key before solemnly crossing my nonexistent heart.

Rue arches a brow. "You're not as charming as you think you are."

"I'm exactly as charming as I think I am," I say, stepping aside. "After you, Mayday," I state, extending my arm and ushering Rue into the two-hundred-year-old family establishment.

The moment we step inside, everything shifts.

Gone is the humidity of the New Orleans streets–the brass-band chaos, the soft rot of history humming in the pavement. Instead, the air inside Simone's is rich with spice and stories. The walls are deep green, trimmed in weathered gold.

Rue's boots cause the polished wood floors to creak. I, on the other hand, am silent, to the living at least. The living-adjacent girl beside me carries all the weight of this world, and I... well, I carry the weight of the rest.

"Good afternoon and welcome to our home. Table for one today?"

We are greeted immediately upon entering by a genial old gentleman behind the host stand. His soft Cajun accent is as authentic as the aromas pouring from the kitchen.

Rue doesn't miss a beat or even flinch. "That would be lovely," she replies, her tone graceful.

I watch her closely as he leads the way to a small table by the window, warm sunlight breaking through the warped old glass. He pulls her chair out with a flourish. I slip into the seat across from her, unseen.

"Pretty little thing shouldn't be eating alone," he says softly as Rue settles in. "But that's not this old man's business. What brings you to Simone's today, darlin'?"

"Heard from an *old* friend that you have the best étouffée in Louisiana."

The way Rue emphasizes the *old* in that sentence makes me smirk a soft laugh.

"You heard wrong, I'm afraid," he retorts gravely.

"Oh, perhaps I heard my *friend* wrong." This time, she emphasizes *friend* while staring subtle daggers my way.

He leans in, all slow grin and secrets. "It's the finest étouffée in the *world*, darlin'."

I sneer back at Rue defiantly, but the icy resolve doesn't leave her eyes.

Feisty.

Rue grins like she's won something. "That's what I'll have then."

The old gentleman shoots back to the kitchen before returning with a glass of water and an amber liquid, adorned by a twist of lemon.

"Your meal will be right up. In the meantime, enjoy a Sazerac, on the house."

Rue blinks. "Oh, I don't drink very often."

"Live a little," I say, leaning in, while at the same time, the older man says, "Good thing now isn't often."

That riddle leaves us both speechless.

"Care for a story?" he offers.

Rue glances toward me, looking slightly unsettled. I can almost feel the chill running down her spine. She forces a small smile and looks up at the man.

"I love a good story."

This seems to please the man, his dark eyes dancing under the lights as he sets one steady hand on the table—scarred, heavy-knuckled.

"Jean Simone and his wife founded this place in 1834," he begins, voice dropping like an incantation. "Four years later, a Creole apothecary and friend of the family, Antoine Peychaud, created this drink in the back with his favorite French cognac and a splash of absinthe. He would make small batches of it that the owners would share with their favored guests after operating hours." He pauses, and Rue leans in, completely engrossed with his story. "Legend has it that some of the first imbibers saw ghosts. When Jean went back to Antoine with the news, Antoine looked decidedly unsurprised. 'Why, of course, *Monsieur* Jean. The spirits speak the ultimate truth. That's why I've devoted my craft to learning how to summon them.' "

The silence lingers after this story.

He slides the drink forward gently. "I'll leave this here for you. In case you feel like summoning any spirits," he continues with a gentle smile.

Rue and I stare at the glass, then to each other, countless unspoken questions hanging between us.

I wonder the name of this man, and so must Rue because she voices the question with a small shake in her voice. "What's your name, sir?"

"My mama calls me Charles. So, everyone else does too."

"Nice to meet you, Charles. I appreciate the story. And the drink," Rue says, eyeing the glass.

"Go ahead," I encourage. "It ain't gonna kill ya."

"And the company," Rue says by way of a toast as she raises the glass to the affable Charles before he walks off. She sets the glass down and looks at me.

"Well," I say, voice low, "you can't say he didn't set the mood."

She lifts the drink again, staring at it cautiously. "He's either the best host or the most charming soul stuck here on Earth."

"I'm undecided," I mutter jokingly.

She raises the glass in a soft toast. "To amazing stories."

Rue takes a small sip of the drink, winces immediately, and starts coughing.

Charles's full-bellied laugh floats from the kitchen as he calls out, "Well, spirits aren't for everyone, darlin'."

Rue takes another pensive sip of her cocktail with similar results before she switches to water. Then she makes a show of putting her earbuds back in while pulling out her phone.

"Should probably call my mom," she murmurs while pretending to push a contact on her screen.

"Probably wise," I muse. "I'm sure she'll have plenty to say about your alcohol-induced hauntings."

Rue rolls her eyes. "Shut up, Grim."

"Wouldn't dream of it, Mayday." I smirk before

resting back against my seat and surveying the restaurant while we wait for her meal.

The inside of Simone's feels less like a restaurant and more like a relic.

Candle sconces flicker against old brick walls, their flames casting soft gold light over velvet-backed chairs and dark wood floors that creak like they remember every footstep. The air is thick with garlic, bay leaves, and the weight of stories no one bothers to tell anymore.

Above us, iron chandeliers drip with fractured light while portraits of the long dead watch from the walls with eyes gone soft from age. No music plays. Just the gentle hum of voices and the low hiss of something sacred happening in the kitchen.

The scent of roux mingles with something sweeter—bourbon maybe. Even the quiet here feels intentional, like the building is listening.

And Rue—alive, luminous, entirely unaware—sits at the center of it like a flame at the heart of a candelabra.

"This place is so warm and inviting," Rue says, glancing around with a soft smile.

"Timeless, I would say."

"Yes!" she exclaims, and a couple at another table glance over. She grins sheepishly and buries her face back in her phone. "*Timeless* is a great word for it. I feel transported."

"And now you see why the Sisters are so protective of their domains."

She looks a touch confused. "Why?"

"Because time is a construct in many ways. A human invention to demarcate a type of travel we cannot always see. Oh, sure, we notice it in the wrinkles on our skin, the leaves on a tree, or the setting of the sun. But what is that? Movement, surely. But is it linear? Forward or backward only? Trees grow new leaves. The sun rises again the next day. Here anyway," I add, thinking about the constantly waxing and waning OtherWorld moon.

She stares out the window, her voice soft as she speaks. "Well, I'm about to die, so I'd say time seems to be marching pretty far forward. A line that goes right off the end of a cliff."

"Look around you again. The candles in the wall

sconces, the lace in the curtains, the soft browns and dusty veneer. We are here now. In a place that exists in multiple times at once. Kinda takes the sting out of capital-T Time's punch, wouldn't you say?"

Rue's eyes dance in the reflected light coming through the window. She answers with a beautiful smile.

"But shh," I say while bringing my finger to my mouth. "Don't tell the older sister. She gets very upset when holes are poked in her symphony. She likes her sheet music to be read in order."

The double doors to the kitchen swing open, drawing our attention to a boisterous Charles bringing over a steaming bowl of red stew.

"*Bon appétit, ma chère,*" Charles says, setting the dish in front of Rue.

"Hey, that's my line. And I thought I liked you, Charles," I state to the man who cannot hear me.

He waddles off, and I turn my attention to Rue, who's absorbing the steam and rich, salty aroma of her lunch.

She lifts her fork and scoops a mound of amber-colored rice and broth, then spears a succulent piece of shrimp onto the end before lifting it to her delectable mouth. I watch her, enrapt, as the bite disappears into her mouth, and she moans. Her eyelids flutter closed as she chews softly, and her face morphs into a portrait of pleasure.

"Good?" I ask dryly.

"Sweet fuck, Kane. I feel like I've snorted a line directly from the heart of the ocean."

"Disturbing metaphor, but based on the sounds escaping you, I'd venture to say it's delicious."

"It's the best thing I've ever eaten. Ever. Not even close." Rue purrs again as she scoops another forkful and devours it.

"Careful there, Mayday. Keep making those noises with that look in your eyes, and I'm liable to get insanely jealous of a stew."

Before Rue can answer, we both look over to find a woman in a white dress and matching hat hovering next to the table. "How is everything?" she asks, her French-accented lilt warm and gentle as she smiles fondly at Rue. "You enjoying that étouffée?"

"I am. Thank you, ma'am," Rue says, smiling at the middle-aged woman.

"*Mon plaisir.* I will have to let my husband, Jean, know. We do so love to hear our guests are having a nice time."

"Please pass my compliments along to the chef."

"I will indeed." She then turns her gaze my way. "My Jean works so hard back there. It means so much to me to be able to meet with our guests and do all I can to make you feel right at home."

"Well, I certainly have felt very welcome. I'm sorry. Did you say your husband's name was Jean? What a coincidence. Didn't Charles tell us that the original owner's name was Jean?"

The woman nods, pleased. "Isn't Charles delightful? He's been with us for almost forty years now. Started as a busboy when he was just a boy himself."

"His energy is infectious," Rue says around another mouthful of food.

"And, yes, Jean is the fourth generation of Simones to man the helm back there. And I, of course, am proud to call him my great-great-great-great-grandson too. I'm Claire. Claire Simone."

She extends an elegant hand toward Rue, and my eyes narrow as I scan the room. No one seems to be looking at her or reacting.

"*Enchantée*," Claire finishes as Rue awkwardly shakes her hand.

We share a silent conversation across the table. Before Rue can ask what's on both our minds, the woman turns her attention my way.

"And what about you, young man? Why aren't you eating? Can't we get you anything?"

I freeze, unable to move, let alone speak.

"I am not that hungry. Thank you." The words finally form as the color drains from Rue's face. "Did you say your lineage has been serving patrons in this place for four generations?"

"I surely did, handsome."

"So, that makes you the original owner then? *The* Claire Simone?"

"The one and only."

"Which would make you no longer living."

"Oh, I am very dead, dear," she says with such cheerful conviction that it's nearly startling. "But I can't leave this place. Our legacy, our passion, our family—it's still here. The warmth and love we've built are here in these walls. There's nothing for me out there."

Rue assesses the situation and decides to have another sip of her drink as she mumbles, "Another lost soul."

Claire snaps in Rue's direction, "Watch your tongue, girl. I am not lost. I have a purpose that ties me to this place. My babies are here. And we've built a refuge from the cold, dark world out there. Our doors are open, and our hearth is warm. Ready to fill up any road-weary traveler who may happen by."

Rue smiles softly, dabbing her napkin to her lips before setting it next to her plate. "It must be nice to bear witness to all these moments, to see what a legacy of hospitality you've left behind."

"It is, darlin'. I knew you would understand. I could see it in your kind eyes the moment you came in here."

"Your family—can they see you? Charles? Any of the other staff?"

"Oh, no. I've been invisible for longer than I can remember now. Sometimes, I think about the promenades through the glades Jean and I used to take. Or the games of cards I would play with my sister Daisy in her courtyard. But every time I try to exit the building through the windows or a door, I simply cannot get beyond. Seems I was meant to stay here. Forever. *C'est la vie*, as they say."

I scan the room again and see that Rue's conversation has still not drawn any unwanted attention. I step into the conversation. "Forgive me, Claire, but when you died, wasn't there a reaper? Someone to offer passage?"

"Oh, yes. When I choked on that pesky salmon bone at that table over there, a handsome gentleman in a suit not dissimilar to yours came to me and was so kind. Offered to help me 'cross over,' as he put it. But the restaurant, you see, and our family and the spirit of hospitality ... I was scared and could not make it. Eventually, he said I missed my window and disappeared."

"Do you regret it?" Rue asks gently.

Claire offers her a knowing smile. "Live long enough, my dear, and you're bound to regret something."

"Or in your case, unlive long enough," I mutter without malice.

Rue glares at me and returns her attention to Claire. "It can be hard to let go. But moving on does not erase what you created. I mean, look around you, Claire. This place has left a lasting legacy. Your family's name, your gracious hostess spirit. The flavors and aroma of this incredible food. It lives on, so you don't have to."

"I wish it were that simple, my dear. Some decisions change the entire trajectory, it seems."

"Are you settled here, Claire?" Rue asks pleadingly. "Do you wish to still be here?"

"Rue," I interject. "Apologies, ma'am," I say to Claire. Then I mumble to Rue across the table, "The worst thing you can give a lost soul is hope." Then, louder, "Let's pay our tab and head back to the house, shall we?"

Rue's face takes on a hard edge. "We can always cling to hope, Grim. Not you or anyone else can take that from a single soul. Living or lost."

"I do miss my Jean," Claire says wistfully.

"There is no guarantee that you would see him, even if you could go to the OtherWorld now." I inject some reality into this fantastical conversation.

How long do I allow this to continue? Sure, Claire seems calm enough–a peaceful lost soul. But they don't stay that way forever. Eventually, they turn angry, vengeful. And I don't need Rue to be what sets this soul off.

"Nothing can last forever, Claire," Rue states, seeming to ignore me. "Do you see that now?"

"And that is perfectly okay," Claire states warmly.

"Yes," Rue sings back, a simple call-and-response between them.

"I do. See that now. And that even in my fear of passing to the unknown, I was not able to keep my place in this world. Not in a way that has any real meaning."

"All you can do is observe now, huh?"

"A watcher in a doer's world," Claire hums forlornly.

"It must have been so hard to see all you built and all you loved be taken from you."

"You have no idea, child."

"I have more of an idea than you might think, Claire."

"Mmm," she moans, a note of wisdom. "I'll bet you just might."

"I know what you've been going through, watching the world pass you by while you're stuck, it must be painful. You deserve some peace."

"You think so?" Claire says softly and Rue nods.

"I do. I think Simone's has done fantastic and will continue to do so."

"I would love to feel some peace." Claire trails off and I furrow my brow. What is happening? Feel peace? Her time for choosing peace is over.

A sensation I have not felt in hundreds of years overcomes me as I swear I can feel my skin warm. The aura in the room around us seems to glow.

Rue's voice breaks the silence, calm and honest. "I hope you find the peace out there that's waiting for you."

My focus turns to the woman in the chiffon dress still hovering next to our table, and I notice that she seems to be going out of focus. Claire's form begins to blur, softening at the edges, like fog rising off a lake. Her eyes close as her features stretch, shimmer, and dissolve. The space around her hums and buzzes. It's a sound and sensation I've never borne witness to before. Claire releases a single sound, like the sustained final note of a mournful ballad. And then she disappears.

No portal, no reaper, no summons or rules—just gone.

My chair scrapes backward as I rise, voice trapped in my throat, disbelief rippling through every cell that remains fused to this form. I stare at the space she left behind, half expecting it to rewind. For the veil to close. For reality to reassert itself.

But it doesn't.

She's gone—and *Rue* did it.

Not a reaper. Not a Sister. Not Big D. A girl.

A mortal.

I can't make sense of it, not even in the quiet spiral of my mind that has held truths from a thousand dying mouths. It defies everything I know—everything I *am*.

My fingers twitch at my sides, some deep instinct screaming to take control, to restore the order I've lived inside for longer than most names have lasted. But there's no control here. There's only her.

And Rue ... Rue just picks up her drink, takes a sip, and swallows like she didn't just rewrite the laws of what's possible with nothing but her voice and her heart.

Rue blinks, smiles, and looks over to me. "Well, I hope that conversation put her at ease a bit. It must be awful to feel trapped in a world you're no longer a part of." She takes a deep inhale, reaching for one last pull from her drink. This time, she makes no grimace as she swallows. "I wonder where she went."

I can't speak. I don't trust what might come out if I try.

An elastic moment of silence stretches between us, broken by the tone of a message from my Tombstone Phone. I read the message to myself.

Big D: Get your ass to my office. Now. —Big D

Putain. This escalated quickly.

Rue stares at me, oblivious to the storm she just summoned, and asks with that casual grace that is becoming far more dangerous than endearing, "What is it?"

I look up from my phone and lock eyes with Rue.

I have a better question. "What are you?"

Chapter Twenty-Five

TOCK, TICK

KANE

BIG D DOESN'T NEED TO RAISE HIS VOICE. HE NEVER HAS. His anger comes wrapped in velvet and nails, slow and inevitable–like rot or taxes.

"To quote Ricky Ricardo," he says evenly, "you better tell me what the fuck you're up to."

I don't flinch, though my spine tightens. I give him a smirk anyway because, if I'm about to be flayed, I should at least go out in style. "I'm fairly certain that's not how the quote goes, sir."

His eyes narrow to slits. "Do I look like I give a shit?"

One clawed finger–growing by the second–pierces a piece of parchment on his desk like a skewer through meat. "Why don't you tell me what the fuck this is?"

I lean forward on the balls of my feet to get a closer look, not at all interested in stepping any closer to him in this state.

"That's a sheet of paper, sir," I state plainly. "Good texture, recycled stock, strong gra–"

"Look at it, you fucking idiot!"

I step forward with measured strides. "Okay."

I pluck the sheet off the desk, careful not to graze the talon embedded in it. The paper tears near the edge where his nail was. As I look up at him, his nail retreats, and his slithering tongue morphs back, and he closes his mouth.

"Uh ..." Clearing my throat, I read the information. "It looks like an intake form, sir. Sent to the desk of AfterLife Processing immediately following a successful crossover."

"Well, what do ya know? The doctor can read." Big D's eyelids close to razor-sharp slits. "Impressive." He pauses, clearly waiting for me to do something, then groans. His voice takes on that petulant-child tone. "Read the name, Kane. And the date."

I scan the paper more closely and realize that this is from Claire Simone. My brain short-circuits. If my blood wasn't already cold, it would be now.

This shouldn't be possible.

"*Típota den eínai adýnato,*" I mutter out.

Big D's head snaps up. "What did you just mumble, reaper?"

"Nothing is impossible."

"In Greek?"

"Yes."

"Why Greek?"

"What? I don't know. The language fit the mood. I know ten of them. Might as well use them. I'd hardly say that's important right now, sir."

"Important? No. Annoying? Yes," Big D deadpans, his thin eyes cutting into me from across the desk.

"So, she," I pause and look up, "crossed over? One hundred years after her portal closed?"

"Yes, Kane, she did. And now you've got a lot of fuckin' splainin' to do."

"That's the quote, sir."

"Shut the fuck up, Kane." His booming voice rattles me into immediate compliance. "Now, explain to me how a soul who missed her portal window by a cool century managed to cross over like she had the line-skip ticket at an amusement park!"

How can I answer that? I know what I saw, but it doesn't make any sense. Either way, telling him it was Rue seems unwise.

"I made contact," I lie easily. "Her soul connected. An opening appeared, and she moved on."

"Right." Big D sighs audibly as he falls back into his leather chair, the frame groaning in protest.

He reaches across his desk and grabs a human skull off the corner. The top of the skull is cut off and hollowed out, and inside ... more Twizzlers.

"Nana," Big D says softly as he looks at the skull, "I've been good to him, and he's repaying me with lies."

I close my eyes. I would rather him just punish me than make me witness him talking to his skull.

"Sir, I'm not–"

He holds the skull to face me, two pieces of the candy falling out in the process.

"Don't lie to Nana," he warns while gesturing to the skull.

"Sir–" I stop as he raises a brow in warning.

"Kane, I've been a fair boss. I've treated you well. I feel like when you've asked for things, I've done my best to deliver them. So, tell me"–he pops a Twizzler into his mouth and spins it around his tongue–"why do you hate me?"

"Sir, I can assure you, I do not hate you."

"But you must. Because you brought this mess to me." Before Big D can say anything else, a gust of shadow splits the room, and with it comes the arrival of Time and Fate, flanking him with amused looks on their faces. The ground shakes, and smoke coils into the office, causing D to lean back and groan.

"Wonderful," he mutters. "Now I get to deal with the Sisters too."

"Kane." Time smiles cooly while plucking a Twizzler out of Nana and biting into it. She curls her lip before finding a wastebasket to spit it into. "That is atrocious. Why would you put that in your mouth?"

"I like them," D mutters while taking the candy back. "Don't touch Nana without asking."

"Can we get back to the problem here?" Fate huffs. "I am very mad at you, boy."

"Not as mad as I am," Time hums while standing next to her sister.

Fate is thin with sharp features and a cold demeanor while Time is curvy with her golden complexion and warm aura. It's a trap. Time still oozes sinister ruthlessness. They are both vicious. While Fate is all about instant gratification, Time loves to watch the slow torture unfurl for the souls unfortunate enough to cross her. Like me currently.

"Oh, I don't know about that, big sister," Fate says in her silken voice. "This lowly soul shepherd has had his hands in my clay."

"Well, he's been messing with my perfectly crafted sheet music."

The Sisters face off, yelling at each other over Big D's head.

Fate continues, "He's been chiseling *my* marble."

"And he's been choreographing *my* dance."

"Not as badly as he's been weaving on *my* loom."

"Well, he's been directing *my* play."

"Oh, for fuck's sake." Big D rises slowly, deliberately, like a storm building behind stained glass. His voice doesn't boom. It seethes. "Enough with the bickering and the metaphors. This isn't a poetry slam, and you weren't invited, ladies. Show my office the respect it deserves."

The Sisters stop mid-spit, jaws snapping shut with audible clicks.

And like vultures sensing meat, all three turn to me.

It hits like a wrecking ball to the chest. Their attention isn't just a stare. It's pure suffocating judgment.

"You tampered with the weave," Fate hisses, eyes like shards of lava rock.

"You rewrote the tempo," Time snaps, her voice bending in unnatural time signatures, like it's folding over itself.

"You disobeyed a direct order," Big D adds much too softly.

I don't flinch. I've taken their orders. Followed every celestial command for hundreds of years–through plagues and wars. I've watched massacres unfold in crimson horror, taking the breath from thousands at a time. And I have heard desperate tyrants begging for one more breath of their own. And I have faced it all with efficient, dutiful professionalism. A good soldier to D.

And what did it get me?

Nothing but eternal mundanity. So, one time? After endless cycles of clockwise, I decide to try the other direction. What began as an impulsive moment to feel anything after countless moons of nothing became more than I'd ever felt in any of my days.

Because Rue isn't just another soul waiting to cross over into the AfterLife. She's the soul that I didn't know I'd been waiting forever to find.

She was the girl in the community center–black dress, orange-and-black hair, green combat boots, and a du Maurier novel. She didn't plead or scream or bargain. She just looked up and *saw me.* And despite trying with everything I have to stop her, she's found a way through my walls.

I look up, chin high. "This is old news," I say. "Yes, I gave her nine day–"

"You have no authority to *give anything,*" Fate spits like it's acid.

"Her time was up," Time says, eyes glowing too bright. "And you pulled her from the threads. You *ripped* her loose."

"And now look at all that's unraveling. You save one, and look."

"I intervene and give one human her allotted days, and what? The universe you so carefully constructed starts to crumble? I think that sounds like a *you* problem."

"You aren't paid to think," Fate huffs. "You aren't paid at all, so be grateful you still exist."

"Fate isn't your domain, reaper," Time says.

"It's mine." Her sister emphasizes, then continues, "And Time is none of your concern."

"It's mine," Time parrots her sister's earlier refrain.

"When mortals take their fleshly experiences too seriously, there are ramifications. And when they start intervening in the stories of lost souls, there are severe consequences."

"Punishment," Time interjects. "Cross over on our clock or face an eternity of regret."

"A forever of stuck-ness."

"Mortals move on our terms, or they remain."

"On our terms."

"No second chances. No do-overs."

"And no meddlesome nobodies altering our perfectly crafted world order."

"No one, reaper. Not a single, solitary soul."

"Not you. Not Rue. Not Cindy Lou Who."

I hold my tongue. I want to voice my disdain. I want to live in Rue's reality–a world where one mistake is not an eternal sentence, a universe built on forgiveness and growth.

I want to, but I dare not. This is not Rue's realm. I would only be signing my sad existence away to ages of pain and ruin.

"Did you have something you wanted to say, reaper?" Fate goads me.

"Does the cog in my perfectly tuned clock want to use his pathetic little voice?" Time piles on.

"That's enough," D says, his voice barely audible as he flicks some dust off the skull.

"My sister is right," Time states, ignoring D. "You've forgotten who you are, who runs this show, and who holds your leash. We say bark, and you say …"

The silence stretches for ages. The outer limit of my humility stretches near oblivion. The best I can do in this situation is maintain this lie and play my part. I can keep Rue safe by being the source of the Sisters' ire and playing at obedience.

Knowing I've accomplished all I can in this exchange, I swallow the last vestiges of my pride and softly murmur, "Woof."

The Sisters laugh while clapping and bouncing up and down.

"Good boy," Fate declares.

"Now get back to work and supervise that pasty pest until she's ours."

"And no more interventions from that importunate unfortunate, Kane. Or you both will pay."

"Are we clear?"

I grit my teeth, holding back a sea of invectives and insults. "Crystal," I manage to push the word past my locked jaw.

"Good," the Sisters say in unison.

"Then we'll see you both at Big D's ball. At least we know you can't get into trouble there," Fate finishes.

"Oh, we shall see about that." Time smiles.

"Something tells me Kane may already be in more trouble than he's letting on."

"His eyes do have that sparkle, don't they, sis?"

"They do, Fate. They really do."

"We'd better be wrong, of course," Fate says, boring her gaze deep into me. "Or you'll *Rue* the day, reaper."

With that, they both laugh and then disappear.

"Well," D says, his voice sounding like a tombstone tipping over, "isn't this going to be interesting?"

Chapter Twenty-Six

BOUND FOR THE BALL

RUE

I TWIST IN FRONT OF THE MIRROR, FROWNING AT THE CORSET as I try to yank the laces tighter with one hand. It's like wrestling a romanticized boa constrictor. "Why did I think I could do this alone?"

"Because you're a bit mad," comes Seek's chirpy little voice from the corner, followed by him flopping onto the bed like he owns it. "An' you ain't even had a proper fitting! That bodice is gonna pop off and take someone's eye out."

I glance at him over my shoulder, trying not to laugh. He's sprawled out like a Victorian ragamuffin, arms behind his head, ghostly boots kicked up in casual repose. Esther sits delicately beside him, tail flicking with exaggerated disapproval.

"Why don't you come lace me up then?" I say, spinning to face him. "Or are ghostly fingers only good for breaking dishes?"

Seek gasps with mock offense. " 'Scuse me! I was a really good helper in me time. I had the nimblest fingers in East London!"

I turn back around and feel the unmistakable cold presence of his hands fiddling with the corset ribbons.

"There," he says triumphantly, tugging the last loop. "All tight, like a sausage roll."

"Great. Just how every girl dreams of feeling in a corset."

Esther hops down from the bed and circles my feet with a grumpy *mrrrrow*, brushing against the hem of the dress. I look down at her and give a little twirl.

"Do you like it?" I whisper.

She blinks at me slowly, like I asked a foolish question.

Seek, however, whistles behind me. "You look like a right queen. Reckon if I still had a heartbeat, it'd be thumpin' like a drum."

"Thanks, Seek." I reach back to ruffle his hair, causing him to beam brightly.

"Blimey, Kane's gonna melt in his shoes when he claps eyes on you."

"Oh, Seek." I laugh as I feel my cheeks heat up.

Honestly, I don't know what's going on with the man. He got back from the OtherWorld a few hours ago, ordered me to get ready, and proceeded to leave again, saying something about having to make a stop before we left. He was brusque.

"It's true! He's got that look about him, ya know? Like he's on fire."

"Smoldering, Seek."

"That's the one."

Before we can say any more, the door creaks open behind me.

I glance up and catch the flicker of black as Kane steps into the room—and then stops dead in his tracks. He doesn't speak. Doesn't blink. Doesn't breathe.

His eyes rake over me, and I swear I can feel the tines in his gaze. Smoldering indeed.

I watch his throat work around a swallow.

Seek freezes next to me, then cackles. "Oi! Kane, you look like you've been struck speechless by love. I swear I see hearts in your eyes."

Kane's jaw tics. "Seek. Out."

"But I haven't even—"

"Out."

Esther huffs and leaps off the bed.

Seek throws me a wink and mouths, *Told you so*, before disappearing through the wall.

The silence stretches thick between us until Kane finally exhales a single word. "Fuck."

The corner of my mouth twitches. "Not the most articulate response."

"You're–" he starts, then abandons the sentence entirely. His eyes flick back to the curve of my waist, the corset cinched tight, the sweep of the skirt. "You look good." He swallows the compliment.

"Good?" I arch a brow. "Milk chocolate is good. Finding a dollar in your pocket is good."

"*Mais oui,* you are correct. I do not know why I said that. You look fucking incredible. Stunning." He drags a hand through his hair. "You are wrapped up like a present I want to take my time unboxing. Then I want to play with the pretty toy I find inside for a long time. Before wrapping you back up and taking you to this party. So, yes, you look good."

Heat creeps into my cheeks. "I could say the same about you."

There's an awkward silence in which Kane's eyes never leave me.

"You're staring," I say, my voice too light, too shaky.

He tilts his head, scowl fixed on my mouth. "Yes," he rasps, "I am. Would you like me to stop?"

"No," I admit easily.

"Good, because I'm not sure I could anyway."

His lips twitch, but the usual snark doesn't come. Instead, he just stares, jaw tight, eyes molten.

"Rue," he says, low and steady.

I swallow. "Yes?"

"I'm not sure how I feel about other people seeing you in this decadent outfit. I don't want anyone getting any ideas."

I smirk, lifting my chin. "Better stay close then."

Kane's smile is sharp as a blade. "Oh, I will."

He inches toward me with deliberate clicks of his heels on the wood floor.

"Lift the front of your dress up, Mayday. Now." His voice is rough, and it hits me low, curling in my gut like a match just struck.

"What?" My breath catches. "Why?"

His eyes drop to the hem of my gown. His gaze moves

like hands–tracing, claiming–and when it comes back to mine, it's not the usual simmer.

"Because a dish this delectable," he says, each syllable deliberate, dragged out like he's savoring them, "cries out to be eaten."

He closes the distance between us, the heat of his presence catching fire against my body. His stare makes my knees consider collapsing.

"I'm going to feast on your cunt," he whispers, so close that I feel the words slide down the slope of my neck, "until you come down my throat." His voice is low, dangerous, and somehow still calm, like a storm on course for land.

My pulse roars in my ears.

"And then," he growls, "I'm going to flip you around and fill you from behind. Hard. Deep. Until we are both writhing and shaking with a desperate release so primal and feral it'll echo in the walls of the OtherWorld."

"Oh." It's the only sound I can formulate. A pathetic, breathless vowel. Not even a real word–just the sound of surrender.

My fingers tremble slightly as I reach for the fabric. The air feels electric, like the moment before a thunderclap. Every nerve in my body is dialed to him. *To this.* To the weight of his words still ringing in my ears, dragging need down my spine like a blade made of fire.

I raise the dress up slowly, exposing the tops of my thighs, then higher still, until the cool air kisses my bare flesh, and I stand before him, open and waiting. My chest rises and falls in shallow little gasps. I don't dare speak.

Kane stares. And stares.

And then he slowly sinks down to his knees.

A silent act of supplication before he devours me.

The second Rue's fingers wrap around the hem of her dress and she brings her hands to her waist, I pounce.

Not like a man chasing hunger–no, I move with

purpose. A predator on the hunt who already knows his prey will surrender. My hands slide up her bare legs, my fingers tracing over her calves, her knees, her trembling thighs. An appreciative groan escapes me at the sight of her mound hiding behind a thin strip of black lace.

I glance up just once, locking eyes with her. She's flushed, breathing shallow, trying to stand still.

"These come off," I rasp, tugging at her panties. "Now."

She slips them down without a word, and I guide them the rest of the way—lifting her feet, one at a time—then toss the lace to the floor like a trophy.

There she stands, bare, beautiful, perfect. And I stare, just for a moment. Just long enough to commit it to memory.

My eyes flick to her cunt. Slick. Pink. Pulsing. A fucking masterpiece.

"Look at you," I whisper. "Shining for me already. Exquisite."

I lean in and kiss her inner thigh first before moving upward, continuing to stalk her body with my mouth.

I press my mouth to the bundle of nerves for a lick and some firm pressure. When I separate from her with a gentle kissing noise, a low rumble of approval emits from deep in my chest. The vibration causes Rue to let out a delicious moan.

"Eager," I muse while giving her clit a hard suck.

I explore her folds with precision, teasing her clit with the flat of my tongue, then licking up with just enough pressure to make her thighs shake.

"You're doing so well," I praise, knowing that Rue's pleasure is tied directly to her level of comfort.

She releases an appreciative whimper when I tell her, "Wider," while lightly tapping her thighs.

She obeys without hesitation.

I bring my tongue instantly back to her cunt, this time exploring deeper. The tip penetrates her tightness as the rest of my tongue massages and strokes against her clit. As her moans deepen and her thighs soften, she places her hand to the top of my head for support and possibly for a bit of control.

"That's it," I say without stopping my assault on her

pussy. "Bury me in your cunt, Rue. Use. My. Face." Each word quakes from my throat, sending vibrations along my lips and tongue.

I feel Rue's legs begin to shake, and my hands take firm hold of her ass.

She responds to the pressure by subtly bucking her hips upward. I reward her instincts with a low, deep hum as I shake my head savagely from side to side.

"Your desperation is delicious, Mayday. I want to drown in your pleasure." My voice comes out heated, like a popping, crackling fire. "Can you come for me now?"

She whimpers. Nods.

"I'm close," Rue says, though the way her body screams for me makes those words seem comically redundant.

I know, Mayday. Oh, I fucking know.

To emphasize my possessive thoughts, my tongue travels to her sensitive clit and I flick it greedily, coaxing her body closer to the cliff's edge of pure desire.

When the stimulation becomes too intense, she grips my hair firmly. I respond to her nonverbal request by placing my mouth fully over her wet cunt. Her voice rises, her legs spasm, and my hands lift her slight frame from her ass just a fraction off the ground, devouring her like the first meal after a fast.

Her orgasm rides out in waves, and my tongue doesn't slow—not until she's done shaking. I lick her clean reverentially, pressing open-mouthed kisses to her thighs, her mound, whispering between each one.

"*Douce.*"

"*Souple.*"

"*Paradis.*"

Her shaking subsides as I separate my mouth from her lips to drink her in. I take several steadying breaths as she tries to do the same.

I rise slowly, licking her off my lips like her essence possesses a power greater than any medicine. And when I finally meet her eyes, she glows.

We are both beautifully wrecked. I'm soaked in her. Lips slick, jaw sore, but she was worth every second.

"That. Was …" she mumbles.

"Just the beginning," I finish for her, which seems fitting, considering I did just finish for her.

Kane smirks, his green eyes burning with a dark desire. He grips me by the hips—hard enough to leave bruises, and I don't mind one bit. I let out a gasp as he spins me around like I weigh nothing, manhandling me until I'm bent over. I place my hands flat against the wall in front of me while arching my ass in the air. The front of my dress falls forward. Kane grabs the back of the fabric and brings the skirt up over the rise of my ass cheeks.

I hear the low, metallic *click* of his belt unfastening. The soft rasp of his zipper coming down.

And then silence—a breathless pause.

Without preamble, without warning, without a word, Kane pushes the head of his thick cock directly between my thighs and impales his length deep into the center of me. In one confident stroke, he's seated firmly inside my tight walls, filling every empty part of me.

He moans a multisyllabic, "Fuck," as his heavy balls press against my clit.

The pain of his size and the speed with which he fills me elicits a pleasure I've never felt before, and I crave more instantly. I greedily press my hands against the wall, seeking more of this big, beautiful man.

And then he slams inside me.

One brutal, perfect thrust that knocks the air from my lungs and nearly sends my knees buckling. My body seizes around him as he fills me completely. No easing in. No tenderness. Just raw, overwhelming stretch and the sound of both of us groaning at the sheer force of it.

"You're so fucking tight, Rue," he snarls at my back.

His length filling me, coupled with the squeeze of the corset, makes it difficult to breathe, to even think. My hands scrabble against the wall, looking for leverage, something—anything—to keep me grounded as he buries himself deeper.

He leans over me, his mouth hot against my neck, his hips grinding forward with slow, obscene pressure. "You like that?" he growls, tongue flicking over the shell of my ear. "Being split open by your reaper?"

"Yes," I gasp, but it comes out more like a moan. I'm already shaking.

Kane brings his mouth to the shell of my ear, licking the outside and nipping on the cartilage with just the right amount of painful pressure.

"Grim," I moan, feeling my walls pulse, and he slows his movements down.

"Take a deep breath for me, Mayday."

I do the best I can, filling my lungs like he's filled my core.

"Good. Because I'm going to pound you mercilessly until I explode inside you."

I moan involuntarily as I melt against him. My pussy clenches greedily around his cock, luring him deeper, begging for more.

"You think you can handle that, Rue?" he rasps, voice starting to fray with hunger. "Because I'm not sure I can be gentle right now. Not when you look like this. Not when you moan like that."

"Mmhmm," I manage to squeak as he slowly begins bucking in and out.

"Tap my thigh twice if you need me to stop. Do you understand?"

I moan again, and his hand comes down and grips the back of my neck, not hard, just enough to make me feel it.

"I need to hear you say it. Use your words."

"Tap your thigh. Got it."

"Twice," he says darkly, punctuating the correction with a stab of his cock deep inside me.

"Twice," I yelp.

He laughs. Not a kind laugh. A wicked one.

"Good," he growls deviously.

And then my reaper begins to fill me with long, powerful strokes. Pure, ruthless energy–his hips slamming into me, his cock dragging against every nerve inside me with a ferocity that feels intentional.

He's punishing me with pleasure. Owning me with every thrust. Using my body like it belongs to him.

"You like being fucked like this," he snarls, his hand wrapping in my hair to yank my head back just enough.

It's not a question, but I answer anyway. "Yes," I choke out, heat flooding every inch of my skin. "Yes, Kane–don't stop–"

"Does this feel like stopping to you?"

He continues his wild thrusting as I moan out, "No. It feels like ..." I run out of words as sensation takes over.

"Infinity," he growls, slamming into me harder.

My legs are shaking. My lungs barely work. And still, I press back into him greedily.

I don't care how dangerous this is. I cannot get enough of the way this delicious creature makes me feel.

With my hands gripping Rue's middle ensuring her dress is high up her waist and her ass is framed perfectly for my viewing pleasure, I pound deep into her tight cunt. In a slow, easy rhythm, I pull my dick out to the tip, then push all the way back in. Out and in, out and in, with long, brutal thrusts. I marvel at the pressure from her iron grip on my dick.

"That's it," I growl through clenched teeth. "Take every inch of my big, thick cock."

The view of me disappearing between the cheeks of her heart-shaped ass transcends art. The masters of Rococo wished they could have painted the purity of this pleasure.

"*Parfait.*"

"*Incroyable.*"

"*Maison.*"

I punctuate each word of praise with a pointed thrust, echoing my previous devotions to her pussy, but this time with more violence than reverence as I find an increasing tempo. Rue's ass shakes slightly at each full stab, and my balls make the most sinful sound each time they slap against her clit.

Another thrust—sharper this time. Her knees buckle slightly, and I catch her by the waist before she slips too far.

I feel a tingling in the base of my spine as my thighs begin to flex. My cock expands and lengthens as pleasure races up my spine.

Rue gasps out, "Kane. Your cock is ... ah!" She cries out while trying to match my speed.

"That's what you do to me," I rasp against the back of her neck.

"You're ... so—mmm ... so much," she confesses, her voice pitched high.

"It's all for you, Mayday. Only you do this to me," I snarl.

I grab a fistful of her hair and yank her head back just enough to make her arch perfectly. Her spine curves like a perfect bow, her ass pressed against my hips as I slam forward again, harder now, faster.

"You like it rough, don't you, Rue?" I grate, my voice dark and jagged, all edges. I demand an answer with an emphatic slap to both of her rounded ass cheeks.

"It hurts," she yelps, half broken. "And I love it."

"There can be so much pleasure in pain, *ma chère.*" I pound into her like I'm trying to stake a claim. Every stroke a promise she'll feel me tomorrow. And the day after. And every one after that until she begs me to stop.

Which I hope she never does.

"You want more?" I grunt, dragging my hands along her instantly reddened ass. "Say it," I demand with another firm two-handed smack to her backside.

"More," she gasps. "All you can give me, Kane."

My teeth bare in a snarl, and I drive into her with a pace that borders on cruel.

"*Tout de moi,*" I hum. "*Avec plaisir.*"

She brings her hand off the wall and reaches around behind me, clawing at my thigh, coaxing me deeper inside her. Her breath stutters. Her walls pulsate and clamp down.

"You're gonna come again, aren't you?" I groan. "Do it. Come all over my cock while I fill you up."

She whimpers, voice raw, "Kane–I–I can't–"

"Yes, you can," I growl. "You need to. Don't hold back. *Maintenant, jouir avec moi.*"

Her pussy grips me tighter as I thrust as deep as physics will allow, and we both come. Together. I slam in one final time, so deep I swear I can feel her heartbeat from the inside, and release into her with a sound that physically tears itself from my throat.

I take a moment to ensure her dress is still well clear of the space where our bodies are joined, then bring my hand around her front and grip her neck delicately. I monitor her pulse while massaging her shoulder. Parachute deployed, I hold her as we gently come down.

When our breathing regulates and the world begins to come back into focus, I whisper behind her, "My monstrous side wants you to keep all that cum inside you and have my juices dripping down your thighs all night long. However, the practical gentleman knows that would be unnecessarily uncomfortable, so stay right there, *ma chère*, and I will clean you up."

Kane's breath drags across the back of my neck, warm and heavy, before he pulls out of me. I groan softly, my body clenching around nothing, desperate to keep him inside just a little longer. The ache of his absence is immediate. My thighs tremble. My cunt throbs. And when the painful thickness of him disappears, I crave its punishing return immediately.

I make a wounded little sound I didn't mean to. He laughs behind me, low and wicked.

"Where are you going?" I breathe as I hear his shoes clop toward the bathroom.

My thighs continue to gently pulse, my knees decidedly weak. Kane ruined me, and it was divine. He's left me here with my thighs spread, ass on full display. I can feel the cool air tickling my cheeks. I feel vulnerable and exposed like this, helpless in a way that feels somehow empowering.

I focus on my breathing, feeling my heart rate slow as I replay the intense moments that preceded this delicious calm.

The measured click of Kane's shoes portends his return, and moments later, I hear him growl lustfully. Without warning, he licks and firmly kisses each of my ass cheeks before I feel a wet washcloth travel slowly up my inner thigh.

"It's warm."

He warmed the cloth to clean me? It's so caring, so intimate that I almost choke on a small cry.

"*Bien sur, ma chère.*" His voice is velvet and full of smug satisfaction. "I would not dream of cleaning you with a cold cloth."

He peppers several more kisses to my ass and the backs of my thighs as he takes his time caring for me. He expertly cups my pussy with the towel, gently ensuring a thorough clean. The vulnerability of my position to him, coupled with the care he's applying to my body, makes me feel like a porcelain doll–beautiful yet so very breakable.

He blows gently on my center, which may have the opposite of its intended effect. Shivers run down my legs as he softly declares, "*Finis.*"

He then folds the towel and places it on the edge of a nearby trash can. I turn just enough to see him pick up my panties. He doesn't even pretend to be subtle. He lifts them, presses them to his face, and inhales like he just stumbled into a field of wildflowers.

"Are you serious?" I gasp, scandalized.

He turns those wolf-green eyes on me and smirks unapologetically.

"You smell like fresh rain, Mayday. And I will never miss an opportunity to drink you in. Now, step into these, and let's go to a party."

Chapter Twenty-Seven

DANCE OF THE DESCENT

RUE

CROSSING INTO THE OTHER WORLD HITS LIKE A FEVER DREAM, where you wake up freezing, sweating, and shaking simultaneously.

The air is cold and crystalline. Icy particles assault my throat and lungs on each fractured inhale. The sky is an endless swirl of color and movement, shot through with violet and silver. The ground beneath my feet isn't earth, but something that feels like stone carved from glass and fog. This place feels like it's breathing, and we exist inside its breath. For being the home of the dead, it sure does feel alive.

My gaze flicks to Kane. He hasn't really spoken since the bedroom. Not that there was much time to do more than clean up and head out. Still, he seems on edge. Though taking a living woman to the Other World is probably fraught with anxious potential.

I look around, wondering if this will be my home after tomorrow. Will I live here? I want to ask Kane. I want to ask him if he'll be with me through the intake process, but I'm also scared to know the answer. Kane has told me he has no idea where I will end up once AfterLife Processing is complete and if we will ever even see each other again.

The thought of never seeing Kane again after tomorrow makes forever feel like a very long time.

Maybe that's why he's so quiet. Perhaps this is his way of dealing with the fact that he and I are essentially ships passing in the night.

Kane turns and looks at me, his eyes dragging over my body like he's memorizing every inch.

"Hold still," he says, voice low enough to make something flutter deep in my belly.

From inside his coat, he produces a delicate black mask. Unlike the metaphorical one he wears at almost all times, this mask I can touch and hold.

It is made of lace, leather, and whisper-fine mesh. The edges are etched in silver detailing that catches the ambient light like frost catching moonlight. It's shaped to hug the face closely, arching up at the temples in curling designs that remind me of thorns and wings. There are thin feathered accents, not soft or dainty, but sharp—sleek black plumes that fan up like a crown of raven quills. It evokes an immediate sense of danger and beauty, like the mask itself could harm someone and it would be impossible to look away as it happened.

I reach for it instinctively, but Kane stops me with a slight tilt of his head.

"Let me."

He steps in closer, and both my breath and spine tighten. The space between us feels like nothing at all, like we fill the empty air in the gap between our physical connection. His scent lingers with hints of cold night air, laced with charred wood.

His fingers brush my cheekbones and then the mask is against my skin. It feels momentarily cold against my flesh.

"Close your eyes, *ma chère*," he murmurs, and I do.

His knuckles graze the curve of my jaw as he cinches the mask into place. Instantly, it feels as though it were molded perfectly to the contours of my face, like it was only ever meant to belong to me.

Cinderella had her glass slipper. I have my black leather-and-lace mask.

The ribbons slide behind my head like satin serpents as he knots them patiently. He moves slowly enough to make me hyperaware of every breath in my lungs and beat of my heart.

When he's finished, he doesn't step back. Not yet. His fingers linger near the hollow of my throat, hovering just above my collarbone.

"You're shaking," he says softly.

"You're doing this on purpose," I whisper, breath catching.

"Of course I am." His voice slides against my skin like warm smoke. "You should see yourself." He steps back and stares at me like I'm the only flower in bloom.

I shift under the weight of it, suddenly more aware of the dress, the mask, and the way my chest rises and falls beneath the corset.

Kane clears his throat and breaks the moment like he's snapped a whip.

"Something's missing," he says, scanning me appraisingly.

"Missing?" I lift a brow. "You're not about to suggest glitter, are you? Because if you bedazzle me, Grim, I swear I'll–"

He cuts me off with the barest twitch of his mouth. "Hold out your hand, Mayday."

I hesitate momentarily, then comply.

He reaches into the inner pocket of his coat and pulls out a long thin black box that looks an awful lot like a jewelry box.

"Is that?" I ask, eyeing it suspiciously.

"Just open it," he grumbles with an expression on his face that I have not seen before. There is a crack in that confident veneer as he hands over the box.

I open the lid of the felt box to reveal a gorgeous gold necklace inside. A delicate gold chain holds a pair of sapphires, set off by a stunning diamond in the center. This is not just any necklace. It's *the* necklace–the one I saw during our trip to the mall.

I blink away the moisture in my eyes as I wrap my head around the gesture.

"You ..." I trail off, looking up at him. "How did you get this?"

Kane shrugs nonchalantly. "I thought it suited you."

"You thought it suited me?" I repeat in disbelief.

"I thought you'd like it," he mutters with that slight

crack appearing again. He hardens in the next beat when he says, "Don't make a scene."

I blink again, trying not to let it show on my face how much this gesture means to me. The piece of jewelry is beautiful, but more than that, the gesture says that he saw me. He remembered something that mattered to me and found a way to make it mine. I lift the necklace, fingers brushing the cool metal, and Kane steps in again, taking it from my hands with a sigh.

"Turn around," he commands.

The moment his fingers touch the back of my neck, I forget how to breathe. He fastens the clasp, then lets his fingers trail just a second longer than necessary against my skin. Not enough to be overt, but just enough to make me melt.

"*Superbe*," he murmurs in French. "*Stupéfiant.*"

"Wait, did you just say it looks stupid?" I ask, a bit stunned.

"Stunning. Both words mean some version of stunning, but this looks so good on you that one version was simply not enough."

I am speechless as I watch the confident Kane re-emerge before me. He offers me his elbow like a man raised right, and I thread my arm through his, my fingers coming to rest atop his gloved hand.

The leather of his glove is cold beneath my fingers, but his presence at my side radiates with heat and a gravitational pull.

He leads me through the open arch of a long, crumbling corridor that gives way to a ballroom carved from midnight itself.

It is unnaturally, almost impossibly beautiful. Like walking through cracks in the mountains until you round the corner and gaze on the treasury at Petra, only this place has an ethereal quality to it that could not exist in the world I come from.

A black glass-and-mirrored dome ceiling reflect this singular sky—velvet dark, threaded with violet lightning and glowing embers, like stars on fire. The walls are lined with towering candelabras that burn with silver flames. Light shimmers across the marble floor, which looks wet, but doesn't make a sound underfoot.

Everything moves like it's part of the same dream—guests in masks, drifting across the floor in elaborate gowns and shadowy suits; laughter echoing in strange, slow rhythms that feel like music, even when none plays. Some of the dancers have no shadows. Some have too many.

Everyone wears some sort of mask. And yet I feel them watching me. Their attention prickles my skin like the eyes behind the masks are shooting invisible needles in my direction. Not entirely aggressive, but it feels invasively curious.

"Are they staring at me because I'm not a part of their world?"

"No, Mayday. They're staring at you because you are the most beautiful creature in this room."

My knees go weak, and I lean deeper into his steady arm. He smirks at the noticeable effect that line had on me, and then, like the smug bastard he is, he undercuts the compliment by adding, "Or perhaps it's because you're still alive. We don't get a lot of full-flesh humans down here. Who's to say? We could ask some of them if you'd like."

"Dick," I mumble under my breath.

We move deeper into the ballroom. A man made of smoke offers me a glass of something that looks like wine but smells like petrichor. Kane plucks it from the tray before I can reach it.

"Not for you," he murmurs, sliding the glass back.

"Is this the part where you tell me I'm too delicate?" I say, feigning irritation to mask the flutter in my chest.

"No," he replies simply. "This is the part where I keep you alive."

Before I can argue, he veers left, guiding me through the swirling chaos of lace and shadow until we stop at the far side of the ballroom.

To our right, pairs of spirits swirl and sway in timed rhythm to the music playing from the string quartet in the corner. Each instrument hovers in front of the smartly dressed musicians, the bows moving without the use of hands. It is another visual indication that this party is taking place in some other realm, somewhere that could not be Earth.

The music is haunting and flawless, minor chords strummed with deep pathos.

I'm just starting to relax into the shadows Kane picked as our temporary sanctuary when a ripple cuts through the air. It slices through the room like a cold gust through a cracked window.

And then I see him.

He moves like a predatory wolf. His liquid walk is full of grace and confidence. Sharp lines cut the air around the edges of his fitted charcoal suit with oxblood undertones and a paisley pattern that glints red when it catches the light. His mask is a sculpted slash of metal and shadow, curling up over his cheekbones like smoke, concealing half his face, but I know who it is. Even before he opens his mouth, I feel it in the static coil of energy radiating from Kane.

"Good evening, Asher," Kane growls, barely keeping the venom from his voice.

Asher doesn't flinch. Instead, his smile widens. "Well, well …" he savors each syllable as he speaks. "They let just about anyone into these little soirees now, don't they? Pity, that. Big D used to hold himself to such high standards." Asher delivers this insult directly to Kane, his legs wide and eyes locked on to his fellow reaper.

Kane does not dignify him with a response. He doesn't need to. His stance does all the talking–shoulders tight, jaw set, hands flexing once, like he's picturing them around Asher's throat.

Asher's attention turns to me. "You, on the other hand"–his voice drops an octave as he bows with a courtly flourish–"are a vision."

Before I can pull away, he takes my hand, sliding two fingers behind mine, lifting it just enough to press a kiss to my knuckles. The act is measured, intimate, and very deliberate.

Kane steps in with unnatural speed, and a split second later, he's squeezing Asher's wrist in a steel-clad hold. His voice is flat, but it simmers with threat. "That's enough," he rasps possessively.

Asher's brows rise in mock surprise. "Enough what, Kane?"

Asher and Kane square off, a pair of undeniably attractive brutes.

Asher continues, "Hospitality? Affection? I knew you lacked culture, but did they not teach you manners in France either? *Sacrebleu*." He butchers the word with a grin, teeth flashing behind the mask. He doesn't pull away. "Jealousy doesn't suit you, Doc. Thought you'd evolved past that particular weakness."

"And I thought you'd evolved past being a lecherous little leech," Kane mutters, releasing him with obvious reluctance.

"Ooh. An alliteration. How poetic." Asher's eyes flick to me again, teasing. "Tell me, darling, how does our Kane look when he's undone? All that brooding control–does it crack, or does it *shatter*?"

"Just leave the girl alone, Ash. Go find another of your forlorn souls to keep you entertained."

"And what if I want to play with this one?"

"She's off-limits," Kane responds.

"Why? Because she's wormed her way into what used to be your heart, Kane?"

Kane doesn't answer. But the look he gives Asher is a grey cloud warning of a powerful storm.

I don't like being spoken about like I'm not in the room, so I cut in, my voice sharper than I intended it to be. "You two know I have ears, right?"

Asher bows slightly. "Apologies. Just admiring your gravity. You pull focus in a room full of immortals, Rue. That's no small feat."

I glance at Kane. His hands are curled into fists at his sides.

"She's my responsibility," he says finally, voice like stone. "Until she crosses."

Kane doesn't look at me when he says it; he's too busy staring down Asher like he's ready to draw blood. And maybe he doesn't even realize the impact those words have on me.

The words land like a slap. Clinically clean and completely dismissive.

"Until tomorrow," I mumble, my voice quiet.

Asher watches me a moment longer–something devious flickering in his eyes–before turning his attention back to Kane. "Well," he drawls, stepping back with a mocking half bow, "you two enjoy the rest of your evening. I'll leave you to your *responsibilities.*"

He doesn't wait for a reply. He straightens his coat, tosses me a half smirk, half apology and vanishes into the swirl of masks and shadows.

The silence he leaves in his wake reverberates between the two of us.

I keep my eyes on the dancers still spinning through the last notes of the current sonata, refusing to look at Kane. If I do, I'm not sure what I'll say. Or worse, what I'll let show.

But of course, he's still watching me.

Still close enough that I can feel the heat of him. Still quiet in that maddening way of his.

"You don't have to keep following me around," I say, my voice flat. "I get it. The clock is ticking. I'll try not to fall in a hole or trip into a reaping scythe."

"Rue–"

"Or maybe you can give Asher the reins. Seems like he's more than happy to handle your *responsibilities.*"

That gets his attention. His shoulders stiffen. I meet his gaze now, mask to mask, daring him to argue. He does not. But his eyes flare, sharp and stormy.

"That's not what I meant," he says, low and tight.

"No?" I force a smile I don't feel. "Sounded pretty damn clear to me."

His jaw flexes. I watch the muscle twitch, that familiar mask of control slipping for half a second before he reins it back in. He doesn't speak right away, but instead studies me like he's searching for the right words in a language neither of us speaks fluently.

I don't wait for him to translate.

"That's not–" he starts, but I'm already shaking my head.

"Don't," I cut in. "Don't you dare try to soften it now. You meant every word. Until I cross. That's how long I matter to you."

His expression shifts–something wounded flickering behind the ice–but still, he says nothing.

And it hurts. Not the nine-day countdown. Not the

looming veil of death. *This*. The silence. The holding back. The refusal to name *us*.

"I didn't ask for any of this," I whisper. "Not a second chance. Not the dress. Not the dance. I sure as shit didn't ask to fall for someone who can't even look at me without reminding himself it's temporary."

He steps forward–slow, dangerous, measured.

"You think this is easy for me?" he asks lethally. "You think I don't want to tear this whole system down just to buy you one more wild and precious day?"

A voice cuts through the murmur of conversation, clear and commanding. "Ladies and gentlemen."

All eyes turn toward a spectral man who stands near the musicians, wrapped in layers of regally tattered silks. He claims the space he occupies. His belly protrudes slightly under his coat like a nobleman who hasn't missed a single banquet in several centuries.

He raises one hand. "Please clear the dance floor and make way for our performers," the herald calls out with a sharp, resonant voice. "It is time now for the Dance of the Descent."

Once the center of the room clears, the band strikes an ominous opening chord, the cello moaning notes through the room, the viola answering in a melancholy sigh.

Eight dancers take the floor in metallic shades of black and grey. They move fluidly to the sad music, a dance that feels more like memories collapsing in on themselves. Their movements evoke feelings of loneliness and loss in me, and I have to force down the lump growing in my throat.

The masked movers seem pulled through the space by each languid note. Their arms lift, as if stretching for something just out of reach–something they once had maybe. Something they'll never touch again. They circle one another in cruel harmony, never connecting. Always missing. Always a second too late.

They dance synchronously, though separate. Each a mirror of the other, yet neither seems to recognize its reflection.

They drift and fold, jerk and sway, like puppets unraveling from the inside out. Each motion holds the shape of grief. Throughout the song, each dancer fills their claimed space with gestures of struggle and motion that seem to almost whisper their foreshadowing–*this will all come to stillness soon; this will all inevitably end.* And end it does, on another heartbreaking chord, as each of the dancers melts down into broken piles on the floor. One collapses mid-step, knees buckling. Another stumbles and folds in half like she's been broken at the hinge. One by one, they crumble.

In the final moment, half of the dancers transforms, as if by a trick of the eye, into mounds that look exactly like grey dirt, while the other half turns into grey stone. I bring my focus from the individual performers to the tableau of the whole and see it immediately.

They have morphed into tombstones and piles of ash, echoing life's close in a haunting visual image. As the final note fades from the room, I feel a single tear betray me and begin its own descent behind my masked face. It snakes its way down, escaping off the bottom of my chin and colliding with the onyx floor below.

The silence in the room is broken by a resounding sonorous clap that emanates from a single source at the top of a staircase, made of iron and bone that spirals around the entire room. Atop it, alone, stands a being that could not be mistaken for anyone other than who he is.

"Is he–"

"Yes," Kane says under his breath. "That's Death."

He's clothed in a suit that shouldn't make sense–torn velvet, stitched shadows, gold thread crawling across the lapels like vines–but somehow, it works. His mask is bone white, like a blank canvas that could morph into anything he desired at any time.

He stands alone, above and apart, commanding the entire room.

Chapter Twenty-Eight

THE SEND-OFF

KANE

"CLAP WITH ME, YOU FOOLS," BIG D BELLOWS, THE SOUND of his voice ricocheting off the cathedral-high bones of the ballroom ceiling.

He's still the only one applauding. A beat of silence stretches just a tad too long for comfort before the entire ballroom erupts in a cacophony of celebration. Shouts roll in from every side, a wave of sycophantic noise. The dancers slowly return to their OtherWorldly forms and take a well-earned bow.

The herald, ever the show pony, takes his place near the base of the spiral staircase and throws his arms wide. "To all who revel, I introduce the Keeper of the Cup, the Ruler of the Roost, the indomitable, the indestructible, the interminable–"

"This introduction is interminable," Big D snarks petulantly. "Just say my name so they can cheer already."

The herald falters, eyes flicking toward the top of the staircase, hand gripping his velvet sash. He draws in a shaky breath, puffs out his chest, and finally booms, "The one and only, Big D."

The applause returns–louder this time, more relieved than respectful–as Big D descends.

He makes a meal of it, of course. One hand on the iron railing, the other swinging just enough to show off the glint of stitched gold running like veins through his coat. His movements are deliberate as he weaves his way slowly down the staircase that bends and stretches around the entirety of the ballroom. All masked eyes stay glued on him, and he soaks up every self-satisfying second.

I don't watch him; my focus is on Rue.

She stands perfectly still beside me, her gaze fixed upward in wonder. About halfway down the winding stairs, Big D catches Rue's gaze and stops mid-step. His head tilts ever so slightly, and even though I cannot see it, I can feel his smile behind his skull mask.

Fuck.

Big D never pauses. This cannot be good. His pleasure and intrigue radiate from him, and it makes something inside me twist uncomfortably. D scans the crowd, who are all still gawking at him. He finally shifts, gaze still tethered to Rue, even as he continues his descent.

Once he hits the ballroom floor, he doesn't raise a hand, nor does he bark an order. Just says, low and laconic, "Mingle."

The spell breaks instantly. Souls begin to stir, and motion returns to the ballroom. Noise resumes as the partygoers speak and the musicians strike up another tune, almost as though the assembled are trying to remember how to breathe, which, of course, none of them do anymore anyway. But D is still watching Rue. She notices, frozen by the intensity of it. Big D's unpredictability often comes across as cartoonish, though in truth, his arbitrary nature makes him dangerous. And I would be lying if I did not admit to a certain amount of fear of the unknown as he makes his final approach toward us.

"Kane." Big D's voice sounds like slowly dripping honey. He throws his arms in the air as though he might fold me in a bear hug, only to bring his palms together in front of his chest as he takes the final step, arriving directly in front of us.

"D. Wonderful party, si–"

He cuts me off before I finish, his interest in Rue evident.

"And you must be Rue Chamberlain, the melancholy mortal I've heard so much about."

Rue straightens. "And I, you."

"Yes, my child. I imagine you have. Don't believe everything you hear though, hmm. Unless it's fabulous. And then it's all true." As he says this, his hand lifts, and he touches her face. Not cruelly, but not kindly either. Just … strangely. A brush of his knuckles along her cheekbone, followed by a soft, theatrical *pat*. "Forgive me," he says though he's clearly not talking about the condescending contact he just made. "Where are my manners? Welcome to my party. I trust you have been offered whatever it is that mortals find pleasing?"

"We're getting on just fine," I assure D as Rue lightly rubs her cheek, more out of shock rather than pain.

His touch was light, but, in classic Big D form, highly unpredictable.

"And what about you, Miss Rue?" D says, cocking his head. "Did you enjoy the performance?"

"It was quite nice," she replies carefully.

"You wept, child."

The surprise is evident behind Rue's mask. "How did you–"

"It's kind of my thing." He smirks, grabbing a glass from a passing caterer and downing the contents in one quick pull. "Where did that emotion come from?"

Rue takes a moment to appraise Big D, then does the most curious thing. She mimics his earlier gesture by bringing her hand to his masked cheek. She runs her fingers along the ridges of his skull mask, as though she were reading a passage in braille.

Big D does not flinch or try to stop her, but he stills. "What are you–"

"What do you think about when you weep?" she asks softly.

He laughs awkwardly and swats her hand away. "I don't cry, child. I am the lord of the OtherWorld."

"You have a sadness in you," she says, unshaken.

"Watch your–"

"And that's okay," she cuts him off again. Her words land with eerie finality.

I may as well be a statue for all the good I'm able to add to this unimaginable conversation. Rue speaks with a mysterious strength while Big D looks like a boxer stunned by a left hook he did not see coming. He staggers–not physically, but something in his posture tilts, like her words hit somewhere beneath the bone.

Like any prize fighter worth his muster, Big D recovers and asserts his dominion over the moment and the mortal. His voice drops to a dangerously low volume, and the temperature in the room begins to fall. "You would do well to watch your words around me," he murmurs, tone sharp. "Your days on Earth may be numbered, but your time in my realm is infinite. And I am not a man to be trifled with."

Rue receives D's warning words silently, though there is a noticeable strength to her spine as she stands toe to toe with Death himself.

With a deft sleight of hand, Big D brings his index and middle finger up, filling the space between him and Rue. In his hand, he now holds a green shrub with small yellow flowers clustered atop the leaves.

"Rue," he whispers, leaning closer to her, eating up the space between them and slipping the herb directly between her breasts, which are tastefully displayed in her corseted top. The flowers obscure the diamond on the necklace I got her.

It takes every ounce of restraint I possess not to grab his hand and rip his wrist from his arm. Knowing the futility of any physical move against D on his home turf, I silently seethe. I know what he's doing. He's baiting me. Testing me. And I am not stupid enough to flinch in front of Daryl.

"For remembrance." He finishes the *Hamlet* quote with nefarious undertones.

Rue does her best to hide the shaking that's involuntarily creeping over her shoulders, but Big D's presence looms large.

He takes a small step back, squares his shoulders, and addresses us both with his pitch-black eyes. "Enjoy the rest of the party, you two. I'll see you for The Send-Off."

Big D spies another attendant walking away with a tray of the drink he downed earlier. He stalks the server with the tray, leaving me and Rue frozen in his manic wake.

"What is The Send-Off?" Rue asks, her voice thin. "Is

that about me? Is there"–she swallows–"a ceremony?" The question cuts through the noise, laced with fear and the quake of uncertainty.

I shake my head slowly. "There *is* a ceremony," I admit, my tone even and controlled. "But it has nothing to do with you, Rue."

Her shoulders don't relax, and I release a sigh.

"Rue," I murmur, just for her, "you're safe. You can relax. I won't let anything happen to you."

She nods, barely. But the tension in her spine is steel.

I add, softer now, just above the music, "You can breathe now, Mayday. I've got you." I look at her, hoping my nearness will serve as a reminder that I want to protect her.

She takes a steadying breath as her shoulders soften and asks again, "What is The Send-Off?"

I explain plainly, "After souls cross over, they're meant to enter AfterLife Processing–ALP. It's a bureaucratic purgatory, really. They get assigned roles, stations, purposes in the OtherWorld. Not everyone becomes a reaper, mind you. Most shuffle paperwork or hold down time loops or oversee spectral inventories."

She blinks at me, the confusion evident.

"But sometimes," I go on, slower now, "a soul can't detach. Not fully. They leave their bodies behind, but not their grief. Or guilt. Or bitterness. And if they can't release that weight, if they keep looking backward instead of forward, they fail onboarding."

Her brow creases beneath her mask. "Fail onboarding?"

"They become unfit for eternal service."

There's a long pause, and I can almost feel her forehead wrinkle behind her mask.

"And?"

I sigh, rubbing the back of my neck. "In your language? They're fired."

She quirks a brow. "Fired?"

"Try not to think about it, Mayday," I say, my tone deliberately lighter. "There's nothing you can do about it anyway. *Supra nostram potestatem.*"

She scowls, the line of her jaw flexing under her mask. "I really don't like it when you do that."

"What?" I arch a brow. "Use the languages I spent years learning? Keep stories and cultures alive? Seems a bit shortsighted of you."

"It would help if I knew what you were saying."

"I said, it's beyond our control. That's it." I cut my gaze toward the center of the ballroom, where the music is beginning to thin. "So, best to leave the machinations of the OtherWorld to the architects who built it. Keep your head down and survive the night."

Rue does not seem completely satisfied with my rationale. I can see the rebellion mounting behind her eyes. She's not the type to go quietly, even when she should– *especially when she should.*

"So," I continue, "what you need, milady, is a proper drink. Let's go find you something to wash down that bitter taste I can see swirling around in your mouth."

I offer Rue my arm and begin to scan the room for a libation station that could accommodate Rue's mortal tastes.

We don't make it far. A cold gust brushes over us, though there's no wind. And they appear–the Weaver Sisters–whose gazes snake their way over every inch of Rue's body.

They do more than simply tower over Rue as they take her in. They hover and undulate. Their limbs weightless and bending at angles that ignore the laws of flesh and gravity. Their silhouettes blur at the edges, like half-drawn ink sketches that never fully dried.

"There she is, sis," Fate sings to Time, her icy eyes slicing Rue in half. "Oh, look at that little dress, what do you think?"

"Not much to think about it honestly," Time cuts, causing a prickling sensation in my neck. "She can only work with what she has I suppose–which is very little."

"I certainly don't see what Kane seems to." Fate doubles down.

Rue catches my eye, perhaps wondering if I've said anything to them.

I meet her eyes, trying to tell her without speaking, *No, I haven't said anything.*

"All I see is a meddlesome little brat," Time hums,

"who thinks she's entitled to tinker with the very seams of the universe."

Rue speaks up for the first time. "I'm sorry. Have I done something to upset you?"

The Sisters cackle with derisive laughter.

"Upset? Hardly." Fate scoffs.

"A little speck like you can't upset us. You have, however, become a bit of a rough edge in desperate need of smoothing out," Time continues. "After all, we do not care much for you awakening old cases and finding new endings to stories we finished writing ages ago."

"I have no idea what you're talking about." Rue's confusion is evident.

"We are the authors of mortal tales, miss," Fate says, voice like a blade unsheathing. "Not you."

"When we write *The End*," Time adds, "it stays ended."

"Not an invitation for you to come along and pen some bleeding-heart epilogue."

"Lost souls are not meant to be found, Rue."

Awareness dawns on Rue's face. Her lips part as she quietly says, "Claire Simone."

Fate smiles like a shark. "Exactly, Rue."

"She made her choice," Time snaps. "She wanted to stay. Those decisions are final."

Rue bristles before raising her chin, defiant as ever. "Everyone deserves a second chance."

Their laughter returns—harsher this time. Less amused, more unkind. "No, my *pet*," Fate sneers, "they do not. That's not how life or death works."

"Everyone must play by the same rules, mortal," Time echoes.

"Our rules."

"Or everything descends into madness."

"And we can't have that. That's far too messy."

I see it then. The fire behind Rue's mask. It licks up the back of her spine and curls around her fists. I know what comes next, and I have to stop her.

I say, warning her softly, "Rue."

Before any of the women can say any more, the herald's voice rings loudly off the walls of the ballroom.

"Souls of the Other World, it is time. Cease your carousing and bring your attention to the center of the room."

The stillness is absolute. Even the shadows seem to hush. A hundred masked faces pivot as one, all eyes on the herald.

"The Send-Off commences," he intones. "Make way for Death and the Parade of the Pathetic."

Rue mumbles, barely audible, "He really does like his alliterations."

I would smile if not for what I know is coming.

Big D appears at the far side of the room. He drags behind him a massive chain that loops around his broad shoulder like some ceremonial sash—except the sash hisses and groans under its weight. At the end of it, a tangle of grey souls, bound at the limbs, necks, and torsos. Shackled to one another by memories they were never able to release.

They move like ghosts underwater, sluggish and resigned. They know what this is. They've seen it before. Some of them have probably watched from the sidelines during past Send-Offs, hoping they would never join the chain.

Big D walks theatrically, like a man headed for the podium at his own award ceremony.

He rounds the crowd and leads his condemned into the clearing. The herald's hand lifts, gloved fingers stiff, and just like that, every sound in the ballroom dies.

No final note from the quartet. No rustling of gowns or murmured gossip behind masks. No scrape of shoes on marble or glass on tray. Just absence.

Thick, unnatural, and cloying.

The kind of quiet that only arrives when something terrible is about to happen—and everyone knows it.

"Now we await the proclamation and decree from the ruler of Death's Door, LLC" the herald announces, drawing everyone's attention to Big D with a flourishing wave of his hand. "The crowd listens for your judgment."

A tremor moves through Rue's fingers, which remain locked around my arm, small and trembling and too human for this place. She doesn't say anything, but I feel the change in her. I feel the stillness coil inside her rib cage, like a spring pulled too tight.

And I know, without looking, that her eyes are on the chain.

Big D stands at the center of the ballroom like a war general surveying a battlefield carved from marble and smoke. Draped over one broad shoulder, a dark tether stretches behind him—shifting, alive, like smoke trapped in glass. It binds the condemned to him like the strings of a marionette. They shuffle after him like well-worn puppets, stumbling forward in jerks and spasms. Some are barefoot, others in the remnants of uniforms or gowns, all greyed out, muted by time and shame. They are spectral shells, each one collapsed in on itself. No longer screaming. Just breathing. Just waiting. Like they already know they are moments from obliteration, and the worst part is not the fear, but the understanding.

They were never going to make it.

Big D clears his throat and delivers the same speech many here have heard countless times before. Rue, however, has not, and she hangs on every word.

"Denizens of Death's Door, A Limited Liability Corporation ..."

His tone is syrupy. "You have failed me."

Rue's hand tightens on my forearm so hard it takes me by surprise. She doesn't look away, doesn't even blink.

"You have failed our system. Your inability to complete the tasks assigned to you is a direct result of your inability to let go of the past and focus on the present."

He pauses in front of a small grey woman, hunched beneath the weight of the chain.

"Memories," Big D spits, "of your former lives—your failures, your regrets, your insignificant longings—have corrupted your thoughts. Distracted you. Kept you tethered to a world that is no longer yours."

One of the souls falls to their knees. A broken, heaving sound escapes them—low and dry and void of any hope. Another tries to speak, but their mouth moves without sound.

"You crossed over," he says with sacred reverence. "And a new world opened before you. But you chose to turn around. To remain obsessed with what came before. And for that weakness, for that core-deep failure ..."

He spreads his hands.

"We now leave you to The Nothing."

The silence that follows cracks and splinters. It holds the sound of hearts breaking open and lives ending. A murmur rises–begging, pleading, promises strung together. But they're too little, too late.

"I didn't know–please–let me try again–"

"There's still something in me–"

"I remember my daughter's laugh–please don't take it–don't take it–"

Big D ignores their weak protestations and raises his hands in front of his face. Staring at the center of the room through the gap between his fingers, Big D grins as he slowly stretches his hands, and with a slow, parting motion, he pulls.

The ballroom floor groans. The chains writhe and flex like boa constrictors around each of the punished. The grey souls panic. One tries to flee, but the chain pulls taut and yanks them back with a bone-snapping force. Another begins to scream in nonsensical agony, but then the sound is swallowed whole by the chain's grip around his spectral throat.

A fracture rips through the center of the marble like a scream splitting a mouth wide open, and then the ground yawns apart like an earthquake contained inside a snow globe. The room around the middle remains eerily still as the bottom of the floor opens to the void below. The space created beneath the chasm has no features, no curves, no discernible markings of any kind. It is white, long, and flat. It is depthless. It is endless.

One by one, the so-called Pathetics descend into that haunting mundanity, released from their interconnected metallic yokes. The furious struggling from moments before gives way to a disturbing calmness as the souls cross over to their final destination. They move to their ultimate end of their own accord, a final stab at their tattered dignity.

Rue can't breathe beside me. She whispers, "Where are they going? Why isn't there fire or volcanos or something?"

"This is worse. This is pure Nothing."

"Nothing?"

"The opposite of pleasure is not pain, Mayday. It's boredom. Soul-crushing emptiness."

I watch realization dawn behind her eyes as she takes in the final moments of this spiritual massacre. This mass exodus to the waiting room with no end.

And then the floor closes back up, neat and seamless. As though it never happened.

The chains that hovered above the hole crash to the floor as it slams shut, and the heavy metal ignites and disintegrates in a puff of fire, like so much flash paper.

Ash floats in the air like confetti. It lands on my coat sleeve. On Rue's mask. On the hem of her dress. We both just stare at it, watching the memories fall like grey rain.

Big D claps a single sound that rattles. Those crystalline flecks in the air tinkling audibly.

Then, like puppets trained to mimicry, the rest of the room joins in. Polite, hollow, measured applause for the annihilation of those who couldn't forget what they lost.

Rue doesn't join them, and neither do I. The applause wanes slowly. A few scattered claps linger before even those fall quiet. I'm just beginning to believe it's over–that Rue might be allowed to slip back into anonymity for the remainder of the evening–when Big D lifts his head.

His gaze, veiled behind his mask, turns in our direction with unsettling precision. The crowd parts instinctively as his voice slithers out above them, slow and theatrical.

"Well, mortal," he calls, every syllable soaked in amusement and warning, "what did you think of our little ceremony?"

Rue stiffens beside me.

I don't look at her–I don't dare–but everything in my body screams the same thing, *Tell him what he wants to hear. Keep your head down. For the love of everything, Rue, just keep your head down.*

But I know better than to believe she will.

Rue Chamberlain doesn't bow. She doesn't flatter. She doesn't shrink. Even now, her spine is straightening like a blade being drawn from its sheath.

And when she speaks, it's not with tremble or deference. It's with cold, cutting honesty.

"Cruel and unkind," she says, voice even and deliberate. "With decidedly poor production values."

A ripple of black spreads outward from where Big D stands. It curls across the marble as if it were oil seeking a flame. Then, from either side of him, the Sisters appear.

Fate tilts her head, birdlike and venomous. "What did she just say?"

There's a lull. A single heartbeat of silence in which Rue could still possibly retreat, recant, and run.

She doesn't.

Instead, she takes a half step forward, chin lifted. "I said," she repeats, her voice growing louder, "that punishing people for remembering their stories is monstrous."

Her eyes flick toward the sealed floor, where the ash of the condemned still glitters faintly beneath the chandeliers.

"We remain alive in memory only. That's all we have left. So, forgive some of us if letting go of that is too hard."

"She speaks of forgiveness," Time spits out.

"I speak of mercy," Rue corrects, and the word lands in the room like a lit match in a dry field.

Everything stops. Every eye turns to her.

Every masked guest, ghostly warden, every reaper-in-waiting faces the girl who dared to speak *that* word in *this* place. The name no one invokes.

"Mercy," Fate hisses, as if spitting out poison. "That sounds so familiar, doesn't it, sister?"

Time bares her teeth in the opposite of a grin. "It sure does. Like a memory we *buried*."

"I wonder," Fate purrs, circling Rue now, "does our little twit of a mortal know what she's evoking?"

Rue doesn't move. She stands firm like a mountain, refusing to bow to the howling winds.

"Poor Mercy." Fate feigns a sob before smirking. "She was the ugly sister anyway."

"W-what happened to her?" Rue asks quietly, much to the Sisters' delight.

Fate squeals and clasps her hands together in excitement. "She was a weakness."

"She believed that souls could be redeemed," Time adds, practically snarling at the word. "That some endings *should* be rewritten. That pain could be unraveled with compassion."

"Basically," Fate snorts, rolling her eyes, "she thought she knew better than us."

"She was wrong," Time snaps.

"She was," Fate trails her fingertip just beneath Rue's jaw, barely grazing the skin, "removed."

Rue doesn't even flinch.

"So, that's your answer then?" she says, voice low and trembling with fury. "You destroy what doesn't conform? You erase what makes you uncomfortable? You make nothing of *anything* that dares to remember?"

"Of course we do," Fate replies as if it should be obvious. "Because feelings and memories are inefficient."

"They lack function," Time adds.

"Because if we allow every soul to embrace the past," Fate gestures to the masquerade around her, "we'd be incapable of moving forward."

"And that simply won't do," Time says, tilting her head with a smile too sharp.

They step back in unison, like the performance has ended and the curtain is about to fall on Rue's part in this play.

Fate turns toward Big D. "She's dangerously close to becoming a problem."

"Agreed," Time murmurs. "And problems must be dealt with."

Big D doesn't respond immediately.

Terror wraps itself around me in a most uncomfortable embrace.

Because they're right; she is becoming a problem. And they've made it clear what this world does to problems.

Fate grins dangerously. "Mercy."

The word hangs between them like a scent they thought long lost.

Fate leans in toward Rue, her voice gone syrupy with sarcasm. "I hardly knew ye."

"I wonder," Time glides behind Rue like a shadow, "do you know how long forever feels in darkness?"

"Mercy," Fate says again, this time turning to the room, to D, to the watching crowd, "banished to the Moonless Mountains."

"Those perilous peaks," Time says.

"Doomed, disposed of, and forgotten," Fate adds, fangs beneath her smile.

"And you, mortal?" Time tilts her head, as if considering whether Rue would look better as ash or stone. "You reek of her."

"Your sentimentality," Fate coos. "Your softness, your insipid belief in second chances. It's enough to make some remember."

"Which means you cannot stay."

"No," I state with decisive power.

Fate's head swivels, and Time's smile vanishes.

Rue turns toward me like she momentarily forgot that she wasn't alone. Which she never will be, not if I can help it.

"No?" Time questions coolly.

"She doesn't belong here," Fate adds.

"No," I repeat with steely calm. Then, fiercely, I state, "She belongs to *me*."

I step between Rue and the Sisters before they can reach her.

Rue's breath catches behind me. I don't touch her. I don't need to. The bond between us is molten now, threaded through every bone in my body, every thought, every instinct.

"She is *mine*," I say again, louder this time, darker, more final.

Her mind. Her body. Her soul.

All of it etched into me like a promise I never dared to make.

And I, in turn, am hers.

Bound not by contract, or duty, or design—but by the simple, unmistakable truth of pure feeling. The kind of conviction that can move mountains.

Fate sneers, "Such a disobedient little dog you've become."

"Your attachment is unbecoming," Time says, her voice dripping with disdain. "You were once one of our most efficient reapers. Now, look at you."

"Emotional." Fate spits the word.

"I'm taking her home," I say, taking one slow step forward. "She has time left on Earth. I'm going to see to–"

"No," Fate states, tapping her finger to her lip in mock thought. "No, I think not."

"What?"

"You were assigned to guard her crossover," Time reminds me, waving her fingers as if flicking away dust. "But you have failed. You allowed her to interfere. You indulged her delusions. You disobeyed."

"Bad dog," Fate scorns.

I grit my teeth. "She has time left."

"And that time will be honored," Fate replies with mock graciousness. "Just not by you."

"Asher," Time sings, and my stomach drops.

He steps into view from the shadows, always having to make a fucking entrance.

"Ladies," Asher says, voice smooth and unhurried. "You called?"

"You have a new assignment," Time states.

"Supervise and escort the mortal," Fate adds, already turning away from me as though the decision is sealed.

"With pleasure," Asher hums.

Fate snipes, "We don't give a fig for your pleasure, Asher."

"We only care about your fealty."

"Now do as you're told."

"Yes, Sisters," Asher concedes and makes a move toward Rue.

"No," I snarl.

Time's eyes flash a coppery gold. "Say that in any of your ten languages, and it will be just as meaningless."

"Grim," Fate taunts, using the nickname like a weapon.

"You can't do this," I snap, stepping toward Rue like I might pull her behind me and run. "She is mine to protect. That was *your* order."

"And now we are changing it," Fate declares.

"Because we've seen enough," Time snips.

"Felt enough."

"And because, and this is the most important part ... we can."

Rue steps forward, but I stop her with a hand. I don't look at her. If I do, I'll unravel. And I need to hold on. I need to fight.

"Kane?"

"Please!" I say over Rue's weak voice. "Please," I beg again, pride lost to reckless desperation. "Don't do this."

"Why not?" Fate tilts her head like a curious cat. "Because you care?"

"Oh, I don't know, sister," Time muses. "He's begging. That might be more than caring."

"Because everyone deserves to die with dignity. Everyone should be given the grace to end their life, surrounded by the ones that love them." The words pour out of me, no less true for the speed with which I spit them out.

"Love?" The Sisters hiss as Rue whispers the word in the same breath.

I lock eyes with Rue in what I fear may be our last moment together and say as simply and honestly as I can, "Yes."

"Oh, this is too good." Time smirks.

"And you have been very bad, Kane," Fate hisses. "Which is why …"

Before I can react, before I can reach out for Rue, the floor beneath my feet shifts. My wrists and hands are bound by invisible shackles. I feel the lock instantly, the helplessness of being caged inside my own skin.

"No!" Rue's sharp voice cracks like lightning—wild, raw, and real. She rushes forward, her footsteps frantic against the floor.

I expect one of them to stop her, but they don't. Maybe they want to watch me break.

Her small arms wrap around my neck before I can speak. She throws herself into me like gravity doesn't matter, like there's no dignity in distance. Like she couldn't care less who sees her beg.

"Kane—K-Kane please," she chokes, breathless and trembling. "Please, don't let them take me. Don't make me do this alone."

I lean into her as far as my bonds will allow. *Not nearly far enough.*

She's holding on like she thinks she can keep herself

tethered to this world through me. Her fingers fist in the back of my collar, her face buried in my throat, tears searing my skin.

"You can do this, Rue. You are brave. You are strong. You are enough."

"I'm not ready," she whispers. "I can't face this. Not alone. Not without you."

The crack in her voice at the end splinters me.

My heart—the one I thought I buried centuries ago—shatters. Shards so sharp they carve regret through every piece of me.

I want to hold her. I want to press my hand to the back of her head and promise her she will *never* be alone. I want to tear the room down around us and challenge them all to stop me.

But this is no fantasy. This is no one's fairy tale. My hands are bound and I cannot move.

"Mayday," I say, the word rasping from me like blood through a wound, "I'm here. I will always be *here.*"

"No, you won't," Time snaps.

Fate sighs. "This has grown tiresome."

"No!" Rue gasps again, louder this time, trying to twist her arms tighter around me, like she could make it permanent. "Please don't let them take me. *Please.* I'm scared."

"I know," I whisper, hating myself more than I've ever hated anything. "I *know.* But you're going to be so brave."

"I don't want to be brave," she sobs. "I want more time."

Our hopeless moment gets interrupted as Asher steps forward and the Sisters nod. The crowd watches in silence, their masks hiding whatever pity—or perverse interest—they might feel.

Asher does not speak; he simply reaches out.

"No, *no—*" Rue panics, trying to grip tighter. "Kane, don't let go. Please don't let go—"

"I'm *not,*" I snarl, straining with everything I have. "I'm not letting go, Rue—"

But it doesn't matter.

Asher touches her arm as a portal opens, and she's gone, ripped from me like a scream swallowed by a void.

"Kane!" Her final cry echoes off the walls, guttural and aching.

Then silence.

And I stand in the center of a masquerade, chains around my wrists, heart bleeding into the hollow of my chest, with nothing but the ghost of her body clinging to me.

"D," Time states after a pregnant pause, "take this philanderer away. He can wait out the rest of Rue's time in your office."

I don't fight as D grips me by my biceps and pulls me toward the stairs.

I say nothing. But I swear by every grave I've dug, every soul I've ferried, every curse I've ever muttered into the mouth of night, I will not forget this.

And I will not forgive.

Chapter Twenty-Nine

DOGGED AND DOG-EARED

ASHER

SHE'S SCREAMING BEFORE HER FEET EVEN TOUCH THE FLOOR-boards.

"Take me back. Take me back right now!"

The sound rips out of her high and hoarse. I barely manage to steady her as her fists collide with my chest, again and again. Her hits are ineffective, but she swings like she means it.

Her whole body shakes with the effort. A firm squeeze of her shoulders slows the punching, and then her fingers curl into claws, nails digging into the lapels of my coat.

"You don't get to do this!" she shouts, voice cracking like fractured glass. "You don't get to decide!"

Each word tears a piece off her—more gasped than spoken, more sob than sentence. Her face is wet and red, hair falling wild around her cheeks, and I swear I've never seen someone look more alive and more broken in the same breath.

"You're gonna hurt yourself," I mutter, hands bracing her shoulders, trying to keep her upright. "Calm down. Easy—"

"Don't," she hisses. "Don't tell me to calm down!"

She throws herself at me again, but her knees buckle the moment she moves. I barely catch her.

A wet cough racks her chest. It doubles her over, and

she curls in on herself like she's trying to hold her insides together.

"Rue," I say, my tone patient and pleading.

She twists out of my hold, creating distance between us again, like touching me burns her.

Her eyes are unfocused. She reminds me of a rabbit with nowhere left to run. Rage and heartbreak and raw terror rolling through her in waves. Her breath comes too fast, too shallow. Her lips have gone pale.

"I hate you," she whispers. "You're a coward. You let them take him. You let them take me."

"I didn't have a choice." I state the obvious, though I wish it lessened its sting.

"I *don't care*!" she wails. "I should've died with him!"

She sways.

I step forward, arms out, but she slaps my chest, one last useless hit before her hands slide off me.

The fight leaves her, or she leaves the fight. Whichever happens, the effect is the same. She drops like marionette strings have been cut, a piteous pile on the floor.

"Sad mortal," I sigh before crouching down.

She does not respond to my nearness or my touch. She has gone numb. Her back rising and falling sporadically indicates she is still breathing.

With one hand on her back, I bring the other to the top of her chest and pull her body upright. That hand travels to her sternum. Her heartbeat thrashes like a fly trapped in a glass jar.

Her eyes are open, but she is unresponsive. Without Kane, the fight has left her, and now she is simply a shell.

"Hey." I tap her cheek gently. "Where's that stubborn little spitfire the good Doc went and cracked his black heart open for? Hmm?"

She doesn't answer, still trapped in the middle distance. She sighs a ragged breath as I scoop her into my arms.

"Let's get you somewhere a bit more comfortable, yeah?"

I carry her down the hall, searching for her bedroom in this foreign place. My search is momentarily interrupted by a massive cat assaulting me in the hallway.

"Easy there, tiger," I say to the feral feline. "Just looking for the lady's chambers."

The fat grey fluff ball visibly relaxes and then, as though she understood me, turns slowly and walks straight to the door I've been seeking.

"Much obliged." I thank the cat, then tell it to get lost as I set Rue down atop her made bed.

Rue's brow twitches, a little furrow right between her eyes. There's the whisper of that fight left.

Good girl.

I touch her wrist, feeling her fluttering pulse beneath her pale skin.

Haven't felt a pulse in ages. I can see the allure, Kane ol' boy.

I should leave. But I don't. I have no reason to remain in this room. Yet I do. I stand there, staring down at her.

"What am I going to do with you?" I wonder aloud.

Kane may be a loathsome twit, but honor among reapers or something like that. I decide the path of least resistance makes the most sense for all involved. I will do what I can to make her crossover as smooth as possible. I only hope she's amenable. Because if she resists …

My fingers tingle at the thought like they can feel the weight of my blade.

She will rue the day, I think to myself on a smirk, then take in the room around me.

You can learn a lot about a person from their bedroom. Their passions and proclivities are on full display in that most sacred of sanctuaries. Rue's room screams of one thing–stories.

Glancing around, I notice all of her books. They are everywhere. Books on tables. Books under tables. Books in stacks beside the heater. Some with broken spines, others pristine because as any good book lover will tell you, there really are two hobbies–reading books and collecting books. I scan the titles, looking for themes and genres that might give me a glimpse into this fast-fading soul. The variety of subject matter speaks of a voracious mind, a tireless consumer of tales. The one through line I feel among all the dusty pages and chaotic stacks? Love. Rue adores literature. It permeates the room.

I stop when I spot one in particular, the familiar font making the bottom of my stomach drop out.

North and South by Elizabeth Gaskell.

I've seen this edition before. I inch closer as a more haunting realization dawns.

It can't be, I insist in my head, even as I reluctantly reach for the book.

I not only recognize this edition; I know this exact copy. Same worn leather. Same bruised corners that speak of much use. Same pages, still dog-eared, even after all these countless years. I finger the edge and open the book to the first flagged passage.

" 'I know you despise me; allow me to say, it is because you do not understand me.' " I read the words aloud, remembering them in her voice.

Madeleine.

"How did you manage to get your copy of this book back into my hands, Maddy? You always were the cleverest girl," I whisper, secretly expecting a response.

A torrent of long-lost memories pour forth. My head and heart are consumed with the overwhelming feeling of it all. The passion and power of us.

Ash and Maddy.

Forever.

But nothing lasts forever, does it?

Only pain.

Only ever the pain.

That is all that lasts, all that lingers, all that remains.

My fingers tremble as they stroke the letters, as though each spot of ink holds an ocean of memories. Unbidden—and I thought impossible—a single tear jumps off my cheek and lands on the page, blurring the words.

Visions of that old stone prison, of the stench of that place, and the crippling feeling of regret overwhelm me. I slam the book closed in my hand in a futile attempt to shut out the past.

The smoke and the screams echo inside me while the one thing I cannot remember continues to haunt me. Madeleine's last words.

I look over to the peacefully resting Rue, then back to the book in my hands. I open it to the other folded page.

" 'But the future must be met, however stern and iron it be.' "

I smile sadly as I continue my one-sided conversation with a ghost from my past. "How right you are, Maddy. How right you are."

Then I close the book and toss it unceremoniously onto the edge of the bed.

From somewhere in the house, an ancient clock chimes the top of the hour.

Chapter Thirty

SEEK AND YE SHALL FIND

RUE

I DON'T KNOW HOW LONG I'VE BEEN LYING HERE.

Time feels like a thread that's unraveled completely, tangled around my limbs, caught in my throat, dragging behind me like a frayed scarf. The walls have stopped creaking. The house–this strange, sentient thing that once groaned and shifted and sighed with me–has fallen silent. Even the wind outside, which used to whistle through the shutters and rattle the old glass, seems to have vanished. It's like everything knows. Like the house itself is holding its breath, waiting.

Or mourning.

I try to move, but my limbs protest. Every muscle aches. My lungs feel too shallow for this body. There's sharp pressure behind my sternum, like grief and gravity fused into one unbearable force.

Kane is gone. Another vital piece of me stolen, another sliver of my traitorously weak heart torn asunder.

The worst kind of separation because the distance remembers. The other soul still exists, but not for me. Not anymore. He's somewhere in the OtherWorld, and I'm here, entombed inside my own body.

My story's end has been foretold by the cruel twins, Fate and Time, while Kane and I have been cleaved from each other, just as he separated souls from bodies with his blade at that bus accident.

He promised me he would be here now.

Yet I am alone.

Not completely alone, but without him, which I am now realizing is worse than being alone. Because it holds the ache not of a mere emptiness, but a chasm that was once, momentarily, full. And that is when the void is truly felt.

I breathe as best I can. Each exhale a countdown, every heartbeat a drummer's march, one step closer to its coda. I can feel the inevitability of it all.

I try to sit up. My bones feel like they've been carved from ice and left to melt inside my skin. It takes more energy than it should, but I do it anyway. Because I haven't given up yet.

But before I lose myself to all my maudlin musings, I am comforted by the sight of a friend.

Seek.

He's curled beneath the window, knees tucked to his chest, his too-big coat wrapped around him like armor. He looks smaller than usual tonight. He's staring out at nothing.

And for a long moment, I think maybe he doesn't know I'm awake.

But then he speaks softly without looking up. "I had a sister once."

His voice sounds more mature than I have ever heard it.

"She was a couple years older than me. She wasn't my real sister, not by blood, but she pretended. For me. When I first arrived at the orphanage, I could barely speak, from fear and on account of my being so young and all. I did not have many words, certainly none good enough to describe my feelings." He shifts, pulling the coat tighter around himself. "But Sophia didn't need my words. She hardly even gave me any of her own. She just poured out kindness. I could feel it coming off her and wrapping around me like a blanket."

His fingers twitch against the fabric of his coat.

"I must have been standing there like a mouse in a shoebox, eyes as big as saucers. Sophia came right up to me and offered me her hand. I took it and squeezed, tight as could be. 'Come on. Let me show you where you're going to sleep.' She spoke so warmly to me. Always made me feel safe.

"The first morning I woke in that cold bed, my eyes opened, and there was this little stuffed bear sitting on the corner of the bed, staring back at me. I squeezed him so tight and kept him with me every day I was there.

"Sophia had given it to me. I know she did, though she never admitted it. That wasn't her way. She didn't need credit, only comfort. She's the only person I can remember in my life who made me feel safe and seen. Until you, Miss Rue."

Seek finally pulls his eyes away from the window and looks at me. I smile back at him, meeting his gaze.

"What happened to the bear?" I swallow, the ache in my chest suddenly magnified.

"I left it at the orphanage when I made my escape. Figured another scared little boy might find comfort in it too."

"And what happened to Sophia?"

"Same thing that happens to all of us in the end, I imagine. Hope it was peaceful for her anyway."

I try to speak, but nothing comes. He keeps going, like he has to say it now or he never will.

"She's the only person I can remember who made me feel safe. Who made me feel like I mattered." He hesitates. "Until you."

The simplicity of his declaration makes the impact of his statement hit even harder.

He tucks his chin to his chest, cheeks burning red even though he doesn't have real blood anymore. "I know I'm not always easy. I talk too much. I steal stuff. I'm a bit much sometimes. But you made me feel like I wasn't just a stupid little ghost. You listened to me. You saw me."

I bite the inside of my cheek. "Seek ..."

He cuts me off before I can finish, "Is it really gonna happen?"

I pause.

He still won't look at me.

"What do you mean?" I ask gently, though I already know.

"You," he whispers, "leavin'?"

I close my eyes. It hurts to lie. It hurts worse to tell the truth. "Yes."

Seek nods once, like he's known all along but needed to hear me say it. "Thought so." He stands, brushing invisible dust off his coat with complete earnestness. He mimes the action as though it's the most important thing in the world to do at that moment. And maybe to him, it is. Perhaps pretending to be clean keeps him from falling apart. "I want a story," he says quietly. "One last one."

I blink, caught off guard by the seriousness of his request. "Seek ..."

"Please." He turns to me then. His eyes are bright, but not with mischief this time. There's something else there. Something sharp. Fragile. "Your voice comforts me, Rue. Like how I felt, holding Sophia's hand."

The words hit me like a brick to the sternum and cause me to quietly break all at once. "I-I don't have it in me to make one up," I admit. "Not tonight."

"That's all right," he says. "Just read me one that's already been written."

My throat burns, but I nod.

I drag myself to my bookshelf, fingers trembling as they skim the worn spines. My eyes land on a weathered copy of *The Velveteen Rabbit*. I pull it free, the pages soft from love, the cover barely clinging to its hinges.

I sit on the floor. Seek nestles beside me, head resting on my shoulder, like he belongs there.

He fits.

I begin to read. My voice shakes, but I keep going. The words from the pages fill the room, keeping us company. And for a little while, it's enough.

I clear my throat, though it doesn't help much. I make it through the part where the Rabbit asks what it means to be real. I pause, voice cracking on the line about how it doesn't happen all at once. That it takes a long time. That sometimes, it hurts.

Seek doesn't speak. He just leans against me and listens.

I read aloud as the Rabbit is left behind, forgotten by the Boy he loved. As he becomes something real, though at great cost.

When I close the book, I realize I'm crying. There's a

trail of warmth down my jaw, and my shoulders shake from the effort of holding the rest of it in.

Then I feel something cool on the back of my hand.

Seek is crying too.

"I don't want to forget you," he says, voice small and shaking. "I don't want you to forget me either."

"I never could," I say, and I mean it. "You're inked into my story now."

"I don't think I want to be here anymore," he says. "Don't feel like I need to be."

I nod, even as my throat tightens.

"Knowing you, feeling like I belong, not to some-where, but to someone—I haven't felt that since Sophia. I forgot what it felt like. You made me remember, Rue. Made me feel real. Like that bunny did for a time. And you set me free."

He tries to smile, but it breaks into a million tiny pieces before it fully forms. I lose it then. All at once. I fold in on myself and sob. No holding it in. No being strong. Because I *can't* do this.

"You'll always be real to me, Seek," I say between sobs. "Funny and brave and kind. So real."

He lets out a shaky laugh, the smallest puff of sound. "You're gonna make me cry again."

"Can I tell you something?" I ask him.

"Anything," he answers immediately.

"I'm scared."

"I know. Me too."

He leans back just enough to look at me, and I swear I see his whole life in that one glance. All the missed birthdays and cold nights. And somehow, impossibly, the hope that something comes next.

"It's okay to miss someone," he says. "That ache means you remember 'em. And that's a good kind of hurt."

"I like that, Seek," I tell him plainly. "Then I hope I hurt you."

"And I hope I hurt you." His smile glows faintly. "But, you know, the good kind."

He doesn't say he's ready.

He doesn't have to.

It's in the way his shoulders ease. In the way his hand slips out of mine so gently I barely feel it.

I press a kiss to his temple. "You're not a lost soul, Seek. You're found. And your home will always be with me."

His answer is barely a breath. "Maybe I'll read a story to you someday."

I nod, unable to speak.

And then he's gone.

No flash. No dramatic wind.

Just gone.

The room doesn't feel lighter.

It feels lonelier.

I curl into the spot where his body used to be, and I sob. Hard.

For Seek. For Kane. For myself.

And for all that good hurt, which still hurts all the same.

I do not hear Asher enter.

The silence left in Seek's wake suffocates. It clings to the wallpaper and pools in the floorboards. It consumes and distracts.

I sit against the wall, my back pressed to the peeling paint, my knees drawn up like a shield from all that exists outside myself. The book lies in my lap, the spine worn, the corners soft, its weight unbearably light for something that feels like it holds the last real thing I have left. My hands won't let go. My fingers press so tight against the cover I worry the binding will give.

My cheeks are wet. My eyes pour forth a duality of emotion. One half of it feels the ache of loss, the sadness of a good thing now gone. While the other weeps in a joyous melancholy, where the heart can celebrate sweet surrender. I let out a sigh that releases some of that miasma of feeling.

"Where's the boy?" The voice comes from the doorway–gravelly, thick, low, and lazy.

I don't look up.

"I heard you talking in here."

"He's gone," I state numbly.

"What do you mean, gone? Like back into the walls? Has he blended with the ether? Or did he piss off to haunt the attic?" Asher asks.

I shake my head. "Gone," I repeat. "Really gone. Crossed over. Or moved on. Or whatever the technical term is."

His eyes bulge slightly, and then booted steps cross the floor–deliberate, unhurried. A sigh. Then the creak of worn leather as he sinks down beside me. He smells faintly of smoke and paper. Not unpleasant.

"That's not … that's not a thing," he mutters. "There are rules about this, you know? Whole bloody chapters. Reaper rule number nine: *'No soul can cross after its portal window has closed. Decisive action is required from the reaper to prevent consequences that ripple into eternity.'*"

"Haven't read that book." I state the obvious because the obvious is all I have right now.

"Well, you've read plenty of others," Asher mumbles appreciatively.

The closest thing to a compliment I've ever heard from the brute.

He glances at the old book in my lap. His voice softens, just a notch. "That one was always a bit of a gut punch."

"He wanted to hear it," I say, voice wobbling. "Said it made him feel real. Didn't peg you for much of a reader."

"Stick around a couple of centuries, you hear a story or two."

There's a weighted silence between us, the space between chapters.

Then, finally, Asher speaks again. "And now he's gone."

"Yes."

"Peacefully?" There's something cautious about the way he asks. Like he's never had the chance to see it done that way.

I nod. "I think so. He wasn't afraid at the end. He was ready."

"No one should be able to do what you just did."

"And yet here we are." I sigh, feeling Seek's burden lifting slightly. "His spirit is at rest now."

Another beat of silence.

Then, with something like realization creeping in at the edges of his tone, he says "So, that's why they don't like you."

I blink. "Who?"

He gestures vaguely. "Them. The suits and the strings. It's not just your feelings for Kane that have their knickers in a twist. It's this. What you did. Quite a mess you've created for yourself and the Doc."

"Yeah, well, life is messy sometimes."

"You mean love." Asher purrs the sentence.

"I didn't say that."

"Didn't need to, Rue." He smirks, taking me in as he returns to standing.

"Don't get smug," I say, not bothering to wipe the tears from my cheeks. "I didn't break any rules on purpose. I didn't even know it was possible. I just made space for his story, then provided some comfort in the form of someone else's story."

"Yeah, well …" He clears his throat, scratches the side of his nose. "Funny, isn't it? The whole machine built to keep souls contained. And all it took to rattle the order of it all was a tattered bunny and a young woman willing to listen."

I glance at him. He's staring straight ahead, jaw tight. I can't tell if he's impressed or unnerved.

"But this, what you just did, changes everything. For everyone."

"Doesn't change anything for me. All it's done is make me an enemy of Fate and Time and a burden to those around me."

"For an empath, you sure do manage to find the energy to feel sorry for yourself. You have a gift, Rue. A power I've certainly never heard of before."

"All I do is listen."

"And it would seem there's more power in that simple act than you will ever know."

"Well, my window for receiving stories in this world is drawing swiftly to a close. So, lotta good it's done to discover this gift so late."

"Never know what the future might hold. And it mattered to that one soul, didn't it? That ain't nothing, Rue."

"You going soft on me, Asher?"

"Don't tell Kane," my reluctant reaper deadpans. "Or anyone else for that matter. I have a reputation to uphold."

"Your decency is safe with me, Ash. I won't do anything to dissuade anyone from thinking you're a shit."

"Thank you," he concludes with a smile, then shakes his head in disbelief. "If only Mercy could see this. She would be beaming."

"Tell me more about her. Her sisters were so vague at the ball."

"That's because no one is meant to speak of her." Asher saunters to the chair, where he sits smoothly, crossing his legs in one fluid motion.

"She was banished after a huge fight with her sisters. Fate and Time always loathed her inefficiency and hated how revered she was by those on Earth. They were jealous of her, plain and simple. And jealousy makes us behave in the most peculiar ways." He voices this last sentence with the weight of personal knowledge in his tone.

He continues when I don't respond, "The Weavers felt that Mercy's emotional outbursts kept leading to complications–adjustments of timelines, reversals of fortune, change. And we all know that Fate and Time are anathema to change. So, instead of making room for the complexities of human experiences and working with Mercy to create a compassionate tapestry of time, they sent her to the Moonless Mountains, forever lost to the world."

"The Moonless Mountains?"

"Yes." Asher's expression darkens as he describes this place. "They exist on the outer edge of the OtherWorld. A place so dark it renders its inhabitants immobile. One wrong step, and the jagged edges of its rocky slopes can swallow you whole. Once someone is brought to the mountains, they are presumed lost forever. Destined to become rooted in rock, a part of the cold, dark landscape for all time."

"Something kind of beautiful about the idea of a Mercy flower."

"Yes, well, something rather ugly about a world without Mercy, wouldn't you say?"

"I would," I agree softly.

Silence folds between us again.

I lift my head at last. "I'm not her."

"Maybe not." He stands now, slowly, deliberately. "But you're starting to sound like her. And those who sound like her usually end up with the same bloody epilogue."

"I'm not afraid of endings," I say, facing him fully.

"You should be," he replies instantly.

"I'm afraid of not being remembered."

"We're all forgotten in the end, Rue. Merely a question of how long it takes."

"Wish I'd left something behind. Some words echoing after me somehow."

The tension in his shoulders eases by a fraction. "You're exhausting, you know that?"

I smile faintly. "So I've been told."

Asher continues to stare straight ahead, not at me. His jaw is clenched, thumb picking at a fray in his glove.

"You gonna go softly?" he asks tentatively.

I shake my head and answer plainly, "No."

"No?" he asks, eyes turning toward me. There's a crease between his brows, like he can think his way to the center of my truth.

"I've been told it's much better to rage."

"No offense, sprite, but you don't seem like the rage type."

"When faced with that good night, Asher, I plan to 'rage, rage against the dying of the light.' "

"Fucking poets," Asher mumbles. "Making it harder doesn't make it any more meaningful, Rue. There's a certain power in knowing when to give up, to simply give in."

"And when that moment arrives, I'm sure I'll be ready. But that's not now. And it won't be anytime soon either. Perhaps I won't go at all. Seek's gone. Someone has to look after the house now. Remember her stories. The love and laughter that my father and our family poured into these walls."

"I'm afraid that's not an option. If I have to, I can make you. I will make you, if need be."

My mind flashes back to the catastrophe, to Asher and his bowie knife in the field, cleaving souls with ruthless precision. He's not lying, and I know it.

"I thought all souls were given a choice."

"They are, unless they piss off three of the pettiest, most powerful creatures in existence."

I roll my eyes. "I won't give those girls the satisfaction. Punishing souls for believing in their dreams. Death eviscerating beings for clinging to memory. No. If I can't take control over the *when*, I can still have something to say about the *how*."

I rise defiantly from my spot on the floor, firm and resolute. "I'm going to bed. I need my strength for tomorrow. I've got a story to finish writing."

The clock strikes a discordant note. The gong sounds off somehow. I flick my gaze to a smug-faced Asher.

"You won't make it until the morning. You will be gone before the rise of the sun."

I look outside, staring down at my family's cemetery plot mournfully. Then up to the sky, seeking solace. All I find is grey. "There's no moon tonight."

"Now that's poetic," Asher says with a mixture of derision and futility.

I grab my notebook and pull it tightly against my chest. I hold it against the spot where Seek once laid his head. The same place Kane once kissed me. Where every story I've ever lived or loved echoes faintly in the final beats of my fragile heart.

I open the notebook to a piece I vaguely remember writing, my fingers finding the page instantly, as if they too know my time is short. I scan the words, my words. These captured moments of my mind.

I look over to Asher, who stares silently back at me.

I press the notebook closed. And I smile. My palms stay on the cover, grounding me to this reality.

I think of my mother.

Her hands in my hair when I was too feverish to

speak. Her voice, fierce and tired and full of love, even when we fought. The way she stood in doorways, arms crossed but heart open.

The way she told me once, "I'd rather have you for a short time than not at all."

I didn't understand what that meant back then.

Now I do.

I swallow the knot rising in my throat and say, more to myself than Asher, "I have to make a phone call."

Asher raises an eyebrow. "I imagine you do."

Chapter Thirty-One

THE SHOW IS ABOUT TO BEGIN

BIG D

I HOLD THE DOOR OPEN FOR KANE AS WE ENTER MY OFFICE—not out of sentiment, mind you, but because I believe in appearances. Manners, decorum, the little rituals that keep the wheels of the cosmos turning smoothly. Just because I am Death Incarnate doesn't mean I can't be civilized. The man's in shackles after all. Let the condemned keep what dignity they can carry.

Kane limps forward like a man walking into his own grave. Shoulders hunched, head down, he has become a ghost of a ghost. Piteous.

I snap my fingers, and the chair drags itself to the center of the room with a low groan. It's a beautiful Victorian-style chair, a real staple piece in my otherwise modern office. It's dark red, overstuffed, with a very showy carved back. I like aesthetics, and this one screams my name. The chair slides behind Kane and clips the backs of his knees, forcing him to sit. The smoky grey bindings rethread from his wrists into the arms of the chair, twisting in place like patient vipers. Another pair locks around his ankles–tighter this time.

I walk a slow circle around him, admiring my handiwork.

" 'Man is born free,' " I muse, hands clasped behind my back, " 'and everywhere he is in chains.' "

"Fuck you," Kane states flatly.

I let the insult roll off me like a stray breeze. "That's not very nice, Kane," I reply, drawing out the words, giving them just enough theatricality to needle him. "I thought you'd appreciate the reference. That's Jean-Jacques–"

"Rousseau. I know, Daryl. I'm French. And smart."

"That's a lot of attitude, coming from a man tied to a chair." I grace him with a smooth smile.

"Well, I figured my intelligence was one of the reasons you hired me. That and my good looks."

"Perhaps once upon a time, Kane. Now, look at you." I don't disguise the disappointment. "So eager to be more than what you are. A reaper playing the hero in someone else's tragedy. Honestly, it's embarrassing."

I move behind him slowly, the heels of my shoes clicking against the floor like a clock counting down. "You were designed to guide souls, not fall in love with them. You were built to serve balance, not break it. And yet here you sit–shackled and defiant–because a mortal made you feel something."

I lean close to his ear, lowering my voice. "She made you forget your place, my friend."

He doesn't respond right away, just stares forward. I double back around to look at him. He isn't looking at me, but through me. It's that hollow, unblinking stare that only grief sees through. I've seen it on the faces of countless mortals. The faces blend together over millennia, but the stare never changes.

"Send me back," he says finally, his voice cool and slow, almost conversational.

"That almost sounds like a threat, reaper," I say, brushing my lapel absentmindedly. "And I'd hardly say you're in a position to be making demands."

His jaw sets, a smoky fire settles behind his eyes. I see the familiar flicker in his expression–something perilously close to hope. That dangerous glint of belief that things might still be undone, rewritten. Mortals carry it like a disease. Apparently, reapers aren't immune either.

"The problem with people," I say, strolling toward the window overlooking the OtherWorld, "isn't that they die. It's that they think they should not. That they can somehow circumvent the inevitable. That their end is somehow negotiable." I roll my head to gaze back at him as he glares at me. "You know how I feel about negotiations, Kane. That look you're flashing me right now is giving vibes."

"I'd like to give you the inside of my—"

"I don't care for it," I cut him off. "As I was saying, things would all be so much more pleasant for so many more if they simply embraced that which is unavoidable. Tonics, regimens, 'practices.'" I air-quote, thinking of all those tiresome yoga poses and bendy meditators. "I've watched empires rise and fall on nothing more than the desperate need to live a little longer. But in the end, the clock always strikes."

I wait for Kane to argue, much preferring a conversation to mere monologuing, but he offers me no joy, so I continue on a sigh. "Immortality. Longevity. All these pathetic pursuits to extend their days, to run from that which is sure to catch all in the end. Man is free, Kane. But it is their futile attempts to change the unchangeable, their sad insistence on *hope*"—I mutter the word as if it's gone sour—"that becomes the very shackles of which Rousseau spoke metaphorically and of which you now find yourself quite literally bound by." I wave my hand lazily in his direction.

"Where is she?" he asks with forced calm.

"Back," I say simply. "For a time. Until her proper TOD in which she will be escorted, willing or not, to ALP. She'd make a good fit here but ..." I trail off and shrug my shoulders. "I think one of my brothers may have an opening. I know Famine needs a new assistant."

"Don't," he grits out, his voice desperate. "D please, I don't—why are you doing this?"

"I'm a fair boss Kane, I allow things to slip by without saying much. I can turn a blind eye to workplace fraternization even if it's grounds for serious punishment, Kane. I gave you two plenty of latitude. But that little mortal coming to my party and embarrassing me in front of my subordinates? What did you think I would do?"

"So, you're trapping me, exiling her, all because of your party?"

"Sounds kind of petty when you say it like that—"

"Because it is!" Kane yells. "She is a living, breathing human and you're treating her like…like…"

"Like she's a recalled product? That's because she is. Kane, the only thing special about her is her ability to stick her nose in where it doesn't belong and taking my best reaper with her. Consider this your correction whack on the snout."

His fingers twitch against the chair. "Give her time. Take whatever you want from me. Just let her live."

Oddly enough, the sentence pierces deeper than expected. For a single unwanted moment, I feel a pull on a string that hasn't been plucked in longer than I care to think about. I shove the memory aside.

"I think," I say instead, "if you listen closely, you might hear the chiming of her family's Hermle clock now. One hour less. Tick. Tock."

He struggles, predictably. The bindings hold. He slumps back, and the sound he makes is one I know well. It isn't the scream of a fighter or the silence of defeat; it's that brittle, tired release of someone who's realized he's no longer in control of anything at all. It's the kind of exhale Cobain released near the end of that haunting rendition of "Where Did You Sleep Last Night." The sound of release, of giving up. No, not giving up. Giving in. Which is what we all must do in the end anyway.

"Time," I begin again, annoyed by Kane's romantic insistence that these mortal moments matter somehow—*that she matters*—"wasn't made for beings like us. It was made for the mortals. To keep their minds from unraveling. To trick them into thinking they can measure something immeasurable. To give order to their chaos." I raise a brow, watching the storm churn behind Kane's eyes. "Did you even read your *Reaper Regulations Guidebook*?"

He says nothing. Pity. His body is slack, then slowly, he stiffens.

Kane lifts his head and speaks with deliberate, pointed calm, like he's moving his queen for the first time in a chess match. "Rule number eighty-eight," he intones, voice steady, " 'Wherever possible, meet each soul with mercy. Better to help a soul float across the threshold as on a cloud than to cleave it from its spot.' "

My jaw tics once. That word—*that* name—lands

between us like a splintered relic from an ancient place, sacred and reminiscent of past pain.

"Well," I say slowly, "look at this insolent little teacher's pet."

I can hear the shift in my voice before I feel it. I can feel the temperature of the room drop by several degrees as something tightens behind my sternum.

"Was that meant to impress me? Quoting outdated regulations, like a schoolboy hoping for extra credit? You must have studied under an earlier edition and never adjusted to the subsequent updates. Bad reaper."

Kane stares straight ahead, unblinking. "You gonna punish me, D?"

I pause.

There's something in the tone. The lazy casualness of someone who knows they've already struck a nerve.

I don't care for it.

The force of my next words cracks the molding of his chair.

Unfortunate. I really liked that piece.

"You do not speak of Mercy here," I snarl, the syllables tearing through the space like a blade through silk. "Not anymore."

The window to the right of me explodes outward. A gale of glass and energy bursts across the room in a sudden shock wave.

"She–*that*–has been written out of the story. Banished from the narrative. Stricken from the record."

My voice breaks on the last word.

A tremor of pain.

It barrels through me like a fist driven into the center of a hollow. I hate it.

"The Weaver triplets became twins," I finish, voice brittle now. "And that is the end of that."

I do my best to recover from the unrecoverable, but Kane's demeanor has shifted, and I am aware I have said too much.

"Where is she now?" Kane asks with the same obnoxiously empathetic voice he has been using this entire conversation.

"She is gone," I snap. "And that is all you need to know about that."

"Dead?"

"Mercy cannot die."

"Lost then?"

"Gone," I state after a pause that stretched longer than it should have. I can see the challenge behind his eyes before the acid words come out of his throat.

"You loved her." He slaps the truth across my cheek like a gauntlet.

"Love is for the weak, Kane. As you have now become painfully aware. And I," I lean in closer, my voice dropping to a thread of warning, "am anything but weak."

He doesn't flinch. "Love is the opposite of that," he says with a pestering sadness in his tone. "Love is why, D. Whatever the question is, love is the answer."

My patience frays.

"Not here. Not now. There is no *Mercy* in this story, Kane," I say, each word deliberate and final. "Not anymore."

The floor shakes under us at the finality of my tone. I turn our attention to the large abstract painting on the side wall of the office. At another thunderous snap, I fix my gaze on the image and bring up our viewing arena for Kane's final torments.

"You'll like this," I say with a wicked grin. "You like stories, don't you, Kane? Let's watch a few."

The first image flickers into focus–a strong young woman jogging in place, checking her heart rate. Her pulse spikes. Her body seizes, and just like that, she drops.

"She ran her PR marathon last week, Kane. That means personal record."

"*Je sais*," he replies dryly, his mouth tight.

I swipe my hand. The next scene plays out. A pediatric surgeon on their new boat, grinning, wind in his hair. Then gone. Aneurysm. No buildup. No suspense. Just one second laughing, the next lying cold.

"What are we watching?" Kane murmurs.

"Life." I grin. "Spoiler alert though: these stories all end with a TFE."

"*Qu'est que çe?*"

"A tragic fucking end, Kane. It's like an HEA, but you know ... not."

Kane's silence bores me. I snap my fingers and change the story on the screen.

"Ohhh," I squeal. I do love a good squeal. "Here's a two-pack-a-day smoker, fueled by whiskey and regret. He's just ridden out ninety-two spiteful years in a rocking chair on the front porch of a house he inherited from his parents. Gifted just enough comfort to squash any chance of ambition."

I look at Kane, whose gaze does not leave the screen.

"Would've been a great poet actually," I muse. "But comfort kills ambition, doesn't it? Poor bastard never even tried. Oh, Fate."

"She can be cruel," Kane mumbles.

"Now you're playing along! That's my boy."

I smile wickedly. Because I know what's coming next. I always do. Which can be tiresome, but it can also be exhilarating. I snap my fingers a third time, and the image on the frame in front of us changes yet again. An image of a large Victorian house comes slowly into focus. The shape, character, and patina of the home are immediately recognizable to Kane–Rue's house.

His reaction is immediate. His entire body tenses, eyes blown wide, muscles straining uselessly against the bindings.

"Recognize the place?"

"Fuck. You."

I sigh, shaking my head. "You said that already, Kane. Very unoriginal. Now, shh! Enough babbling. The show is about to begin."

Chapter Thirty-Two

INEVITABILITY CALLING

RUE

WALK DOWN THE NARROW HALL THAT FEELS TOO LONG NOW. Seek's absence trails behind me like fog. The paradox of my pain is not lost on me. I helped him cross. I offered solace. He found strength. Now he moves on. The dichotomy of loss aches. Shrouded beauty. It is, as we are, more than one thing at any given moment. The worn leather of my notebook anchors me to the present, to this moment.

The house groans beneath my feet. Old wood creaking out the sounds of even older memories. My bare soles pad along the cold hardwood, but I don't feel it. I'm too full of splinters.

The phone is exactly where I left it—half hanging off the edge of the table, like it's ready to make a break for it. The screen blinks, a weak pulse. Low battery. Ten percent. *Fitting.* Everything's running out.

I do not want to make this call. *Does anyone?* That's not a rhetorical question. I would really like to know the answer. I would like so many more answers.

What I do know is that if I don't make this call, I'll never forgive myself. And eternity is a long time to hold on to regret.

It takes three tries to unlock it. My fingers are shaking too hard. I keep hitting the wrong button. Before calling, I change the name on the Contact to read simply *Mom*. Sometimes, so little says so much.

My thumb hovers, then presses the green button.

How does one say goodbye without saying goodbye? How does one leave without letting those they love the most know they're going?

It rings.

How do I do this?

It rings again.

"Ruby Rue." The first voice I ever heard singsongs my name. "How's my only girl who's too busy to call her only mother?"

"Hi, Mom." I do everything I can to hide the break in my voice–or was that only my heart that broke on those words?

"And here I thought, I was going to have to buy one of those spirit boards to get ahold of you. After all, death is the only reason to avoid your mother's calls for days on end."

I let out a huff of air that might be a laugh. "To quote Monty Python, 'I'm not dead yet,'" I say in a poor imitation of a British accent and think instantly of Asher. His presence looming.

"Oh, you think you're funny." Her voice is tinny through the speaker, but familiar. Home, in the shape of sarcasm. "Do you know how many voicemails I've left? I almost drove down there. Had my keys in my hand and everything."

"I've been busy."

"Doing what? Staring at walls? Collecting dust like a haunted porcelain doll?"

Falling in love. Living. Dying, I think to myself.

"If I were a doll, I'd be made of something far tougher than porcelain," I say instead. *How often do we say what we really mean?*

"Rue." She sighs my name. Maternal worry bleeding through the cracks in her bravado, like liquid through cheesecloth.

I push away from the table and start pacing. Movement is easier than stillness.

"I'm okay, Mom."

"No, you're not. Don't insult me. I can hear it in your voice. You sound like you've been crying."

"I'm hormonal."

"You're terminal."

"I met someone," I blurt out. I'm not sure if I'm more interested in sharing this truth with her or if I'm simply trying to change the subject, but it's out now anyway.

"I take back my previous comment. There are *two* acceptable reasons to not call your mother. Tell me everything. Who is he? Or her? Where did you meet? What does he do? How?"

Juliet levels of pining for Kane take over as visions of him dance in my head at her enthusiasm. Her final one-word question pours ice water on that.

"Wow. Thanks, Mom," I reply dryly.

"I'm kidding."

"Turn it off," I tell D coldly.

If a tree falls in a forest and no one is around to hear it, then it does not make a sound. If he turns this off and I do not bear witness, it will not happen. Everything can change.

"Nothing can change now, Kane," the prick replies, reading my thoughts.

"Then let me out of these fucking chains and take me to her."

He cocks his head, considering, as a smirk forms across his face. "Can't help you with the latter," he says at last, almost cheerfully. "But I don't see why I can't accommodate the former."

He snaps his lithe fingers, and the grey chains instantly release me from the confines of the chair.

I roll my wrists and stare helplessly at the framed screen playing out this ghastly scene.

"Make yourself comfortable, reaper," D says behind me, almost bored.

"Fuck you." I seethe.

He sits back in his chair, propping his legs up on his desk.

"Shh." He presses his fingers to his lips. "This is my favorite part," he whispers, and we both turn our attention back to a conversation we should not be watching.

"His name is Kane," I tell my mother, deciding there can't be any harm in bumping up as close to the truth as I can.

"Ohhh," she hums, drawing the sound out. "Strong, vaguely ominous. I like it. What's he do?"

"He's a doctor. Wildly intelligent, and, boy, does he know it." I chuckle softly.

"Oh, confidence, bordering on arrogance? We do love that, don't we? Tell me more."

"He doesn't smile much," I admit softly. "But when he does, it's earned. And his eyes—Mom, his eyes speak volumes in a look." I pause for a moment before adding, "He's a bit of a sarcastic ass as well."

"Well, you're used to that with me," Mom interrupts. "You're welcome. Where did you meet?"

I smile wistfully, remembering the first feel of his mouth against mine. Remembering every beautifully imperfect moment we shared since.

"Dumb luck," I murmur. "The wrong place and the right time. Or maybe it was the right place at the wrong time."

"Sounds like the right place at the right time to me. Fate," Mom exclaims, and my heart physically shudders at the word. "Is it serious?"

Her continued litany of questions keeps dragging me back to the present. Guilt begins to creep in as I fear I might be misleading my mom or giving her a false sense of hope. But I want her to know this. I want her to have this.

"It is, Mom. Very. It's been fast and passionate and real. He loves me. He makes me feel it in the most extraordinary and mundane ways. And I love him. And it's just the best feeling, Mom. The best."

How can a single moment be the best and worst of my entire meaningless existence? Nothing has burned brighter or stung more sharply than this moment. Nothing has ever lifted me this high while simultaneously slamming me so hard into the cruel ground. Nothing sings and stings with as much potency as Rue Chamberlain's unknowing declaration of her love to me.

She talks about me like I'm the best thing that's ever happened to her. But I am not. I failed her.

The room feels like it's pressing in.

I feel the strength leave my body through the single tear that falls from my right eye.

"Ooooooooooh," D purrs from his perch in the corner, watching me and the screen simultaneously. "That was juicy." He extends his hand toward me. "Popcorn?"

My words are failing me in this moment, my vocabulary not doing justice to my emotions, even now, when the stakes are so high.

"I am so happy for you, baby."

I can feel the smile in my mom's voice. It feels good.

"Thanks, Mom."

I sink into one of the old chairs, wincing as it creaks beneath me. *I get it, chair; believe me, I get it.*

"Anyway," I say, changing the subject, "I just wanted to hear your voice."

The kitchen smells faintly like mint and mildew. The old kettle still sits on the stove. The chair across from mine still has the indents from a night I can't get back. My hand presses over my heart, and I try to memorize the sound of her breathing through the phone.

"Remember when I used to fake fainting to get out of math class?" I do not know where the recollection comes from, but I voice it back into being.

"You didn't fake it. You committed. Hit the floor like a sack of flour," Mom says with a light laugh.

"I was a theatre kid at heart."

"You were a menace."

"Your menace."

She exhales, long and shaky. "My fucking menace."

Now it's my turn to laugh. "You always did have a mouth on you."

"Didn't think you got your vocabulary from your father, did you?"

I chuckle lightly. "He was a fisherman."

"Yeah, and I taught him a few words that made him blush."

"Speaking of words," I begin, pressing my thumb deeply into the soft exterior of my notebook. This is my chance to share my work with Cerulean. I'm not sure I was wholly aware at the time, but this is the thing I need to tell her. I want her to know that I inherited more than just her foul mouth. I got Dad's broken heart and Mom's tortured artist soul. And I wouldn't have it any other way.

"Yes?" Mom asks as I realize I stopped speaking.

I thumb the notebook open to the same page as before. "May I read you some of mine?"

"From your little diary?"

I roll my eyes, but instead of getting frustrated, I own the space and claim this moment. "They are more than journal entries, Mom. I write prose. I have dozens of short stories about love and loss and adventure and regret. I write poems too. And I want to share one with you."

I can hear the cautious enthusiasm in her voice as she tells me, "Of course, Rue. I would love to hear your words."

"Okay. This one is called 'Rue's Lament.'" I clear my throat and take a fortifying breath. Then voice aloud:

RUE'S LAMENT

What begins in the light ends in the dark.

Heated wax melting into memory.
Liquid pools formed from that initial spark.
Every wick burns out eventually.
Fear not the candle's smoky finale
Celebrate instead the way it burned bright
Tendrils of grey-black smoke, the last sally
Of a flame that flickered with all its might.
The chandler crafted with wick and tallow
Each piece meant to serve an earthly purpose
So, burn your candles, lest they lie fallow
Trophies to obsolescence for the corpus.
Heat, light, and power dancing off the tip.
Snuffed out, brief candle. Sweet life, what a trip.

The silence punctuates the poem's final couplet fittingly. I wipe a stray tear from my eye. I hear a soft sniffle on the other end of the line.

"Beautiful, baby. Simply beautiful. What a haunting metaphor. I want to paint your words."

"Thank you, Mom. There are loads more in all the notebooks in my room. You're welcome to them anytime."

"Don't talk that way, Rue. They're your creations. Yours to share."

"Just know they're there, Mom. Yeah?"

I blink hard and press my palm to my chest. Everything is starting to ache.

"I think I'm gonna come visit this weekend," she says suddenly, the words tripping over each other.

I close my eyes. My throat tightens. "What?"

"Yeah. I'm tired of this long-distance shit. I want to sit on your porch and make fun of your neighbors."

"By neighbors, you can only mean the family cemetery–full of dead people."

"Fine, then we'll drink wine and mock the squirrels. I don't care. I'll bring that stupid rug you keep trying to steal."

"I bought you that rug."

"Details."

I press the heel of my hand into my sternum. "That sounds nice."

"Then it's settled. This weekend. You can read me more of your work. We can make art. Together."

Regret washes over me. *Why didn't we ever do this?* It sounds so wonderful.

"And maybe you can introduce me to this handsome mystery man."

"Ah," I sigh out. "Now your true motives are revealed. I knew something seemed fishy!"

"I'll bring soup," she continues.

"Oh, no, Mom, please not soup." I groan. "Spaghetti?" I offer.

"You hate my spaghetti."

"But you love making it."

That gets a laugh. "You little shit."

"My big tyrant."

"My perfect brat."

There's a pause.

"Well, I've gotta run, Rue. There's always something going on! But I'm so glad we had this catch-up. What a talent you are. And with a man. This weekend. I can't wait."

"I'll see you then," I lie.

"Wonderful. Until then."

"Goodbye, Mom," I tell her truthfully.

She ends the call.

And I sit there until the screen goes dark. Until my reflection stares back at me in the black mirror of the phone. Pale, small, and unraveling.

It's just me again. Me and the kitchen. Me and the ache. Me and all the words I couldn't bring myself to say.

"Brutal," Big D says before shoving another fistful of popcorn into his mouth.

My jaw tightens. I don't look at him. "She didn't tell her," I say quietly. "Her mother doesn't know. And Rue didn't tell her."

"Of course she didn't." D's voice is halfway bored. "That's the entire tragic point, Kane. These mortals, with their little soft bodies and their ridiculous insistence that what they do matters. That they can *do* something." He waves a hand, the popcorn in his palm scattering across the floor. "Rue didn't have it in her."

"She can do anything she wants."

D turns to look at me, raising one sharp brow. "No, she cannot. That's not how this works. Have you been paying *any* attention?"

"She wrote that poem. Those fucking words."

"Yes! Now you're on to something, Kane. *Art,* my friend. Art is the antidote to all that humans cannot control." He gestures wildly with his hands. "It's their most noble delusion. Their attempt to tame chaos with rhythm. To answer all those pesky questions that claw at the inside of the skull—*how, why, what if.*"

I interrupt his ceaseless musings with an earnest plea. "Take me there. There's still time." I lock eyes with him, hoping I can climb my way to some compassion beneath those obsidian orbs.

"In which of your ten languages," D says, his tone dripping with mock pity, "do I need to explain to you, that is not going to happen? Hmm?"

I cry out a guttural, hopeless sound.

"Oh look!" Big D replies gleefully as he points toward the screen. "She's on the move."

Each step feels taller than the previous one, and I cannot say if that's my body playing tricks on me or a design flaw of the house I did not previously detect. I feel like Alice trying to walk out of the rabbit hole. My legs quake beneath me, but onward they march. Halfway up the stairs, I stop. It all feels like too much. Too much effort, too much pain, too much to face. Lingering midway, I seriously entertain the thought of resting here, taking a seat for a minute. I need more strength, and then I can press on.

The power I lack is not physical. Though I am bone-weary and my erratic heart a jackhammer in my chest, I know I can make it up. What I lack now is the courage.

Most people don't know the *when* of their physical end, and most who have the best idea are too physically incapable to do anything about it. Resigned to petering out in an antiseptic hospital bed, plugged up with tubes and strapped to machines that monitor all that which keeps us alive, none of which makes us human.

The ancestral clock strikes again. This time, a single gong rips through the house, the death knell.

The soft vibrations of generations pulse off my skin and whisper in my ears on the sound. Spurred on now by my family, strengthened by my own determination to make *something* out of nothing, I take one more step up. My hand clings to the banister as memories of the passion shared with Kane and the pathos shared with Seek distract me from the fear and motivate my moment.

Oh, Kane, where are you now?

Her unspoken thought somehow pours from the screen, as though she said it directly to me.

"I am right here, Rue," I whisper aloud in D's office.

"Immersive stuff. This viewing technology keeps getting better. It's like we're almost there."

I ignore Big D's continued sardonic jabs and press my energy through the ether, willing my words to reach Rue.

"I am with you, brave girl. I am always with you. Even when I cannot be there. I am fused to you. Love knows not time and space. I am yours. In every way. In every place. In all planes of space and time, Rue, I belong to you.

"*Eros*: I love you passionately.

"*Agape*: I love you unconditionally.

"*Pragma*: I love you enduringly.

"*Mania*: I love you madly. *Je t'aime toujours. De tout le chemin.* I love you always. In all the ways, Rue Chamberlain."

"That was beautiful, Kane. Unfortunately, the viewing screen doesn't work in both directions," D says quietly. At least he has the decency to sound somewhat contrite.

We both get sucked back into the action on display in front of us as Rue makes her way to the roof.

"This is it," D says with far more solemnity than fanfare. "Bang and whimper time."

I conquer the final stair and peer back down to marvel at how far I've come. Something poetic about it all. A rugged ascent before my final descent.

I force open the attic door. The musky air escapes through the opening like a prisoner from an unlocked cage. Memories are trapped in every cobwebbed corner. I stumble across the floorboards and throw myself toward the dresser beneath the gabled window.

My heart flutters like a trapped bird in my chest, too panicked to take flight, too broken to stay still.

The latch sticks but eventually succumbs.

A cold rush of night air fills my lungs, a sharp contrast to the dingy confines behind me. A gentle rain falls, and a cool wind dances across my skin. The combination sends prickles along my flesh. It is not an unwelcome feeling, like nature knows. But then nature always does know, doesn't she?

I make my way cautiously up the slope to the place from which I can see as far out into the world as possible. The same place where Kane and I saw as far into each other as we ever did.

The potent memory distracts me, and I slip on a wet shingle. My heart rate spikes, and I claw at that air to regain my balance. Fear jolts through my body, and then I stabilize and steady myself. I almost fell off the roof and died. Just like I did that night up here with Kane.

His words right before we kissed echo in my chest. *"Believe me, it's very dangerous to fall."*

The utter absurdity of it all overtakes me, and I do something I thought impossible in this moment. I laugh. A giddy, dizzying mess of a laugh.

Eventually, the giggling subsides, and I come to

stillness atop my perch. My dress gets tighter against my skin as more of the misting rain accumulates. It makes it heavier. That feels right too. My hair knots around my face. Lightning bursts across the clouds, illuminating the landscape in the distance. Rolling hills and copses of trees dot the horizon, adorned with homes that look like out-of-place decorative cake toppers.

The wind slows, then completely dies. Portentous, invisible force. The rain softens, now mixing on my cheeks with my tears. Impossible to tell where nature's weeping ends and mine begins.

I open my mouth, but nothing comes out. No sound. *What is left to say? And who's even here to listen?*

"I am, Rue. I'm listening. Speak what is in your heart. Share your soul while it's still yours," I plead low in my throat.

These words belong only to her.

"Did we miss it?" Fate barks, materializing in the room and drawing my attention momentarily away from Rue.

"Did we make it?" Time chirps.

"Of course we did."

"We're right on time," Fate's sister concludes with a smirk in her voice.

Big D laughs at the Sisters, beaming at their entrance.

The powerlessness that I've been wearing like a blanket since entering this room lifts slightly as a bone-deep anger begins to bubble over. Each tickle of their amusement adds immeasurable fuel to my burning rage.

Daryl's voice booms over all other noise. "The climactic action. The big finish. The storm after the calm. It all leads to this."

He sweeps his arm toward the screen, and all our eyes pore over the vision of Rue in the rain before us. Visible yet impossible to touch.

Rooted to the most towering place in my home feels like a fitting spot for Rue's Last Stand. I do what I imagine many souls do when face-to-face with the end. Fears are generally best conquered with others. And there is no greater fear than the unknown. Though I do know that *something* awaits beyond this earthly realm, what it will mean for me, or even what's left of me, is a complete mystery.

Faced with the yawning abyss, I seek connection. Solace through symbiosis. And I know to whom I wish to be connected with in this moment. Though I know in my head it's futile, I seek my voice again. "Kane?"

" 'Fraid not, love. It's just li'l ol' me."

I do not know where he came from. He simply appeared, and his sonorous voice somehow fills all the open air around us. There is little of the smug brashness in his tone. Asher's voice carries the weight of the moment with appropriate reverence.

He is almost kind when he asks, "Will you cross willingly then?"

"Asher," I rasp, voice raw, "no."

"Shame that. Would have been a lot easier that way. And there's no other *Rue* running around to give you a second chance at this later. So, it's the easy way or the hard way," he says, resting his hand on the pommel of his bowie knife.

Flashes of his speed and brutality from the catastrophe fire in my brain, but I will not be moved.

"For a life I fought so hard to live, the only way to honor that legacy is resiliency to the last."

"In spite of its utter uselessness?"

"No, Asher. Because of it. Because the life I was living had so much more story to tell and the love I just found is far too young to die. So, if my truths have to conform to that bleak reality, then Fate and Time can extend some extra comfort where I'm concerned to answer for their cruelty."

"Still determined then?"

"Resolute. Let them know that for a life snuffed out with wax to burn and a love that could have burned forever, I fought to the bitter end. I refused to let go."

Asher's face seems to indicate he's coming to grips with the reality before him. A look akin to pride flashes as he quotes The Bard, " 'It is an ever-fixed mark.' "

" 'That looks on tempests and is never shaken,' " I continue the line with a stone-like set to my voice. I square my shoulders and face my reaper. "So, bring on the fucking storm, Asher."

Right on cue, the wind returns on a howling cry, the rain intensifies to a lashing ferocity, and the sky illumes with the staccato crack of lightning and thunder.

Asher remains silent in the ensuing torrent, but he slowly begins to unsheathe his blade.

And then I feel it. Again.

It. *The* it. The cessation of a beating heart. It doesn't hurt this time. Because when everything hurts, there is nothing to compare the pain against. It just is.

And I simply am ... dying.

Before I lose the last breath I have, I sing my final notes. Though my cadenza is not belted to the back of the balcony, but rather a softly whimpered, "Mayday."

Strengthened by my defiance, even in the face of death, my second utterance is a marble statue of my reckless madness. "Mayday," I declare with stony certainty.

In my final stubborn moment, I give in to hope and allow myself to believe. One more cry for help, and I shall be saved. Kane will appear, and all will be right. My dad will ride in on a phantom vessel and whisk us all away. My own words will leap from the page and protect me from being forgotten.

My story will end with the happiest of ever afters if only I can ...

The thought dies on the vine, never destined to become anything other than shriveled and dry.

I see the glint of Asher's blade against the moonlight before I can pronounce the word a final time.

Chapter Thirty-Three

IN THE PALE MOONLIGHT

KANE

*M*AYDAY.

I silently voice Rue's final word. A word that became an endearment, a battle cry, a lament. And now, those two sad syllables dig into the center of my hollow chest and burst back out, shattering me into a rainbow of agony.

The viewing screen ripples out from the middle in liquid obsidian, then goes dark.

I look down at my hands as they tremble. I watch as something wet lands in my right palm. A droplet, followed by another. Reaching up to my face, I touch the result of my heartbreak.

I am crying.

"And that's all you need to see of that!" Time declares.

"The End," Fate chimes in. She sniffles theatrically, looking at her sister. "Such beautiful writing. What a wonderful send-off. Some of your most dramatic work."

"Haunting," Big D growls, though there is no joy in his voice.

"Where is she?" There is nothing but steel in my throat.

"In Asher's very capable hands, Kane," Fate announces condescendingly.

"Take me to ALP. Take me to Rue. Now." I boom the

final word with enough force to rattle the walls of D's office.

"Thought only I could do that," he says to himself, though my attention stays locked firmly on the Weaver Sisters.

"Mortals' pathetic insistence that their feelings matter always makes me smile." Fate giggles softly.

"Time cares not for your moods."

"And Fate wrests final control. Always."

" 'Man is born free, and everywhere he is in chains.' " D repeats the quote from earlier with sad sagacity.

"No," Fate snipes. "Mortals belong to us. We are the only authors, and each soul but a splotch of ink on our pages. Freedom is a phantom. Only the chains are real."

I am no longer crying. My mind has cleared to a single thought. I have become the final sustained note thrumming at the end of a song. I am a hurricane with no eye. I am that most dangerous of creatures.

"If this place has taught me anything, it's that true freedom means having nothing left to lose," I declare in a menacing monotone. "And I have nothing left to lose. So, explain this."

I do not hesitate.

I pull out *Baiulus* from my pocket, depressing the silver button, releasing the shank from its center, and driving the blade directly into Fate's center. She gasps–just once–but that's all I allow. I rip my blade from her chest before replacing it with my fist. I feel bones crack and ribs splinter as her body collapses beneath the weight of my wrath. Her throat is in my hand before she can conjure another word, and I watch her squirm, watch her lips try to cry out for help.

"Feels pretty free to me," I whisper, voice trembling with rage and grief and the sharp edge of something I can no longer name. "You soulless monster."

I snap her neck just as Time tries to disappear into vapor. I reach into the mist and yank her back. My fingers curl around her throat, and she claws at me, eyes wide, lips forming my name.

"And you," I murmur, tightening my grip until she gags, "where does this fit on your precious timeline?"

I slam her into the marble once. Twice. A third time

until the floor gives way and she crumbles beneath me. I rip her hand that's still clawing my arm off her body and toss it across the room before looking over my shoulder.

Only he remains.

Daryl.

"Huh," he grunts in surprise.

I stalk toward him, then spy the faintest flicker in his expression, the subtlest twitch of his jaw.

"That was dramatic."

"Their part of the story is finished now, D. Rue is a part of your domain now. And she is mine."

Big D snaps his fingers, and his scythe flies across the room into his hand. "Are you threatening me, Kane?"

I continue my march toward him. My knuckles white around *Baiulus's* pommel.

"Only if you refuse to do as I say."

His menacing snarl matches his predatory eyes as he eyes my weapon, then glances at his. "Mine is much bigger, Kane. Don't start a war you cannot win."

"I just told you, D. I have nothing left to lose."

With that declaration, I lunge toward D, *Baiulus* extended. He sidesteps my first attack and brushes me aside.

I step, turn, and strike again. Madness and menace controlling my motions. D brings his scythe across his center and knocks my blade away. *Baiulus* skitters across the floor. We both watch it bounce away.

On a primal scream, I raise my arms and grapple D around his throat. His hands aren't fast enough to stop the contact, and I lean in with all my might, managing to move the ruler of the OtherWorld back a step as my nails dig deeply into his neck. The retreat is infinitesimal but feels significant.

Our eyes lock, and those blue-black flames spark in his. They redden, and a force emits from D, unlocking my arms and sending me flying across the room. My back lands flush against a stone wall, and I'm not sure which breaks harder—the rock or my spine. I lie limply, moaning, seeking the strength to continue my fight.

D walks over slowly, now dragging his scythe behind him, the metal grating against the ground. As I crawl to a sitting position, I notice the pile of flesh that was Time, rent limb from limb just moments ago, begins to swirl, morph, and coalesce back into her full form. She cracks her neck from side to side with a lascivious smile.

I glance to my left and see Fate, her stab wound fading into nothing, her eyes popping open. Not even her dress retains any indication of the pain I inflicted, the blood I shed.

All my efforts are futile in the face of their ferocity. Love should be stronger than all of this. I have read the stories. I have heard the songs. I have felt the power of that fierce infinity.

But those are just that—stories. And this is reality. And in truth, nothing lasts forever. Heroes and cowards alike, it does not matter, for in the end, we all die.

"I am capable of delivering to you unspeakable pain, Kane," D grinds out, placing the tip of the scythe against my carotid artery, against the scar that was my greatest shame and deepest loss. Until now.

"The pain you could inflict is nothing compared to the torment I feel now. Your power pales in significance against the magnitude of a lost love's ache."

"How very poetic, reaper," Fate says. "Some of Rue's writings must be rubbing off on you."

At the mention of her name, a surge of energy tries to course through me, but I am well and truly defeated. All of Rue resides in me, but that is still not enough. Only Hercules could wrestle lives back from the dead, it would seem.

"Did you just call me weak?" Big D presses the tip of the blade harder against my skin.

"I misspoke. You're nothing but a coward."

He pulls the blade off my neck, twists it a quarter turn, and then smacks the flat edge across my face.

"End him," Time snarls.

"He has no more use to you, D. He has no place here."

Big D sucks in a lungful of air, contemplating a fate I no longer care about—my own.

"No," he begins, the pompous judge handing down his final sentence. "An ending would be too merciful for you at this point, Kane. I made allowances for you. I trusted you to obey me. A small price to pay for the quality of the AfterLife I've afforded you as a reaper."

"Quality?" I scoff. "Ripping the souls from the loved and loving. Watching children mourn their parents. Or the unthinkably worse, witnessing parents mourn their children. I buried my humanity underneath your ledgers and regulations. And for what? For this? Do your worst, D." I spit on the ground at his feet.

He stares down to the mark I made on the floor and then travels his gaze up my broken body to my eyes. "Even in pain, you still were given a gift, Kane. Even in suffering, you could still feel. But now, I am taking that away from you. No more suffering. No more pain."

"And certainly no more joy," Fate pipes in over his shoulder, rankling Big D.

"Shut up." D punctuates without averting his gaze from me.

"No more feeling at all, Kane. You will still be of service to me. And you will feel nothing at all. For eternity. It's not an end for you. It's an end*less*. You will receive your new assignment shortly. And soon, Rue Chamberlain will be nothing more than a faded memory."

"Where are you taking me?" I ask weakly.

He looks at me with decisive finality. A wicked gleam sparkles in his eyes as he slams down his metaphorical gavel, sealing my solitude. "Clerical."

Chapter Thirty-Four

THE BEGINNING

RUE

"Hello?"

Chapter Thirty-Five

LIKE SANDS THROUGH THE HOURGLASS

KANE

Later . . .

THE OVERHEAD LIGHTS HUM THEIR ENDLESS TUNE. A DRONING insectile buzz that chews at the back of your skull. The incessant noise makes time ooze from moment to moment in a sea of sameness. As though Nietzsche's eternal recurrence of the same has been made manifest. What even is time? The monotony of it all fogs the mind, like watching sand pour through a frosted hourglass.

Sometimes, the lights flicker. Brief, stuttering moments where the world goes dark, and I think that maybe it's all ending. A literal glimmer of hope in an otherwise endless numb. A proper end would be better than this. Anything would be better than this.

But they always come back on. No one ever fixes them. No one fixes anything here.

My official title is Oversight Officer for Problematic Sortings, or OOPS. I am not amused. I sit at desk thirteen of who knows how many in the back corner of some windowless, nondescript room. The same grey metal surface, the same squeaking chair, the same stack of files that never seems to get smaller. Cubicle thirteen–unlucky for some, meaningless to me. I didn't choose it. Choice is the prerogative of the living. Sort of.

After a lengthy stretch of silence, where I was just

sitting, someone finally brought me a tabbed manila folder. They handed it to me. Inside was a single sheet of white paper, which made the folder feel a bit redundant, but that was the least of my concerns. The paper read simply, 'Reclassify old records. Begin at the end. You'll know when you're finished.'

What kind of cryptic bureaucratic nonsense was this? It read like a broken fortune cookie.

That was three months ago. Or three years. Or three centuries. Time doesn't move in any one direction here. It just oozes outward all at once.

The work brings new meaning to the word *meaning-less*. Old paperwork from botched transitions, files that got lost in middle-management black holes, death certificates that were filed under the wrong dates. I read them, verify the details, stamp them 'Approved' or 'Requires Amendment' and move to the next. My fingers have developed permanent indentations from the stampers.

Nobody speaks unless protocol demands it. I prefer it that way. It is easier to get lost inside the silence.

But once, at the start of this purgatory, a clerk named Beth decided to be friendly. She was new, still had that eager shine in her eyes that hadn't been ground down by the weight of endless futility. Turns out, nothingness is pretty heavy. She leaned over my cubicle wall during her break, chin propped on her hands.

"You know, you always look like you're in mourning," she said with the kind of casual observation that was meant to start a conversation.

I looked up. Let her see what was behind my eyes—or what wasn't. The absence. The echo. The hollowness.

She stepped back from my cubicle wall like I'd slapped her. Since then, she takes the long way around my desk when she needs to file reports.

They call this echelon of labor "rehabilitation." The supervisors say this is a stepping stone back to field work or full passage to the Final Beyond. I'm not holding my breath though.

This feels like permanent erasure. With one meaningless task at a time, they're wearing away the edges of who I used to be until there's nothing left but this—a shell that shows up, does the work, and goes home to an empty room.

The soul I was before commanded respect. My jobs in the mortal realm and the AfterLife demanded precision and perfection, and I delivered. I had a path and a purpose and was highly regarded by all who knew me.

But that man died the same day Rue did. As did my true purpose.

"Kane Deveraux?"

The voice cuts through my thoughts. I look up to find Marcus Holt, one of the junior leads, standing beside my desk. He's holding another manila folder like it's the Rosetta Stone. He lacks his usual supervisor swagger.

"You're behind on your quarterly submissions," he says, his voice pitched carefully neutral. "Pages twenty-two through thirty-seven weren't included in yesterday's batch."

I stare at him. The words register, but don't connect to anything that feels important. Pages. Numbers. Deadlines. All of it might as well be written in a dead language. Huh. Maybe it is the Rosetta Stone.

Marcus shifts his weight from foot to foot. "The forms need to be completed by the end of business today, or I'll have to file a deficiency report."

Still nothing from me. The silence stretches past uncomfortable and straight to excruciating. I watch him struggle with it, watch him try to figure out if I'm being deliberately difficult or if something's genuinely wrong with me.

"Look," he says finally, lowering his voice, "I can submit an override form if you're having difficulty completing the work. Maybe you need a personal leave?"

I blink once. Slowly. That's all the response he gets.

His Adam's apple bobs as he swallows. "Right. Well, I'll give you some more time then. Two business days. That's the best I can do."

He walks away quickly, like his mother just used his full name to call him into the house for dinner.

I turn back to my screen. The cursor blinks at me, patient and impatient at the same time. A digital heartbeat in a body that's forgotten how to live.

When break arrives, I avoid the gathering room

with all the other clerks and head outside the beige intake wing for a walk.

The same route every day. Down corridor C, past the maze of identical cubicles, where other sad souls shuffle papers and pretend their work matters. Past Reaper Dispatch, where the bulletin board still displays my old assignments like museum pieces. Past Records and Filing, where the sound of stamping and sorting creates a rhythm that might be soothing if you don't think too hard about what it represents.

I pause at the wall that's been cracked for as long as anyone can remember. The fissure runs from floor to ceiling, a jagged lightning bolt frozen in concrete.

My eyes trick me into seeing a bolt of pure yellow filling the space, transporting me back to that rooftop with Rue. The way her cheeks glistened in the rain and the moonlight danced over her skin. A rush of exhilaration overtakes me momentarily before it's replaced by a sharp pain, followed by the sting of nothingness. I try to get her image back into my head, but it retreats as quickly as it arrived.

I stare at the crack in the concrete. Some say it happened during the Mercy Riots, when half the department staged protests over stricter clerical regulations. Others insist it was just the building settling, or maybe Big D had a fit.

Nobody knows, and even fewer care. That's the theme here–apathy. Nothing gets fixed because fixing implies that something was worth preserving in the first place. When everything is broken, it almost makes it all feel functional.

When the workday ends–marked by a bell that sounds like a death knell–I make my way to my quarters. The walk takes seven minutes if I don't stop to think about where I'm going. Twelve if I do.

My room is a study in institutional minimalism.

Concrete walls painted the color of old bones. A cot with sheets that smell like industrial detergent. A sink with a single cold-water tap. A shelf built into the wall for personal effects storage. I use it to display the only two things of value in this place to me. Rue's belongings that Asher managed to smuggle back for me. Perhaps he's not a total nob after all.

I begin and end each day staring at the necklace I gave her and her slippers.

I eye the oversize, rabbit-inspired indoor footwear when I can't sleep. I can't sleep often.

Recalling the ridiculous name Rue gave them gets me closer to cracking a smile than anything else nowadays. *Hippity-hoppity flippity-floppities.* The sound of her voice uttering the words fades slightly each time though, an echo running out of vibration.

I'm sitting on the edge of my cot, staring at the shelf, when I hear footsteps in the hallway. Heavy boots with a slight drag on the left foot. I know that walk.

The door opens without a knock. Asher fills the doorframe. Asher fills most doorframes. His coat is rumpled, his usually perfect hair mussed. He looks like he's been running, or fighting, or both.

"You look like death," he says.

I almost smile. Almost. "Fitting."

He steps inside. Closes the door. "You haven't checked in for eight days."

"I don't have a need to check in anymore."

"And you've moved into this shithole."

"When's the last time you minded your own business?"

"Been a couple decades." He crosses his arms. "Talk to me."

"About what?" I snap.

"Her."

The word cuts clean through my rib cage.

"Don't."

"Ru–"

"Don't say her name again," I grit out.

He doesn't flinch. "Rue wouldn't want this."

I stand, grabbing him by his coat and slamming him

against the wall. "You don't get to tell me what she'd want. You didn't know her."

"I know what love looks like, mate. When it's been carved into someone's bones. You can't spend another eternity mending a broken heart. You will be on the chain with the souls refusing to forget."

"Then so be it!" I shove him back. "She's crossed into oblivion," I say. "She said, 'Mayday,' and I wasn't there. I was locked in some office, forced to watch her cry for me. And now she's gone. I've been stripped of my blade, my abilities. I can't look for her. I'm trapped. I was supposed to be there with her."

"For what it's worth," he drops into my chair and suddenly looks tired enough to crumple, "I was as gentle as possible."

"It should've been me."

Silence fills the space between us. Not empty. Just full of things neither of us wants to touch.

"I can't feel anything," I say.

"Maybe that's your mind trying to keep you going."

"I don't even dream about her anymore."

Asher exhales slowly. "Maybe that's your soul trying to remember how to carry on without her."

"I don't want to go on like this."

"Then don't."

I look at him.

"Do something," he says. "Go to your home. Go to D and demand your job back. Fuck, come with me to Casualties and get that anger out. But stop sitting here, waiting to disintegrate. You're Kane Deveraux. Don't vanish."

"I've already started."

"Bullshit." He scoffs.

"I held her! I–I loved her."

"And you think that's where she ends?"

I don't answer.

He stands, walks to the door. "Love never ends, Kane. It's the only thing more enduring than death. That doesn't vanish just because she did."

"I don't know."

"Yeah," he says quietly. "You do. And here's something

else to think on. How would she feel, knowing you're using her memory this way?"

The door closes behind him with a soft click. I'm alone again, but the silence feels companionable somehow. Like Asher left the soft hum of hope when he left.

I lie back on my cot and stare at the ceiling, then my eyes are drawn to the shimmer of the gems on her necklace. As the light dances off the facets, I catch glimpses of Rue in each pinpoint of light. The stubborn set of her jaw when she was angry. The fall of her hair over her shoulders. The softness in her eyes after we kissed. The visions are faded, but I can see them.

I smile as I look at her slippers. Unlike before, her voice returns in my head. I recall the way she named them.

Bunny and Cher. I can hear her. It's faint, not much more than a whisper, but I can still hear her.

Chapter Thirty-Six

SHOWING SOME MERCY

BIG D

THE BATHHOUSE REEKS OF EUCALYPTUS. SOME EAGER INTERN thought I needed to 'find my vibe'. I'm about to help her find a new career.

Steam drifts across the ceiling while I sip my cocktail through a Twizzler straw, floating in a pink flamingo. Sorry, not in a flamingo. On a flamingo. This isn't an inflatable floatie. This is an actual bird with real eyes and incredible balance. The string quartet in the corner has been butchering *Clair de Lune* for two hours straight. I told them not to stop until I forgot how to feel. They're doing a terrible job at both music and memory erasure.

"Sir?"

I ignore the voice. I'm busy contemplating the water and trying to figure out where I go from here. Losing Kane left a sour taste that even this top-shelf daiquiri can't wash out. My subordinate assaulted me, sure. A reaper attacked the boss—not a good look. But banishing one of the best to the bureaucratic basement doesn't sit well with the boss, even in alliteration.

"Sir ... there's a visitor."

"Can't you see I'm busy, Clarence? Not now."

"Tell him I've traveled a really long way to be here, Clarence."

My body stiffens harder than rigor mortis at the sound

of that voice. That particular blend of honey and razor wire I haven't heard in ages.

The intern squeaks, "It's Mercy, sir."

"Thank you, Clarence. I can fucking see that, can't I?"

"Don't mind him, Clarence. You've done a great job." Mercy pats my assistant on the shoulder and ushers him out of the room.

I eye the lost triplet, agog.

"What's the matter, D? You look like you've just seen a ghost. And that seeing ghosts isn't an occupational hazard for you."

Mercy stands at the edge of the tile, as if she owns the place. In a different timeline, I imagine she does. Arms crossed, coat dusted with ash, wearing a hardened expression that spells a most deviant form of trouble. Her eyes–still that same electric blue, like a live wire submerged in the ocean. I am rendered as shocked as I was the first time I dipped my toes into her depths.

She looks exactly like she did all those years ago, though she's taken on an aura that speaks of hard-earned knowledge. It gives her an unmistakable and devastating patina.

Her auburn hair is braided thick, showing off a jawline sharp enough to cut glass. Pale skin, scattered with freckles I used to count when we had nothing but time. Silver scars trace her exposed skin, like cave drawings that tell the story of hard-fought battles, those waged both internally and externally.

"Nice float," she says sarcastically. "Really brings out your ego."

"You're supposed to be gone." I have no time for flippant comments. I want answers.

"I was." She strolls in like she still has keys to the place. Like I didn't spend decades trying to drink away her memory. "Funny thing about being gone–sometimes, you come back."

"You were banished."

"Not as permanent a fate as Fate seems to think. Just ask Oedipus or Perdita. You'd think my sister would learn her lesson, but she never was the sharpest pencil in the drawer."

"Your story should be over."

"Trust me, if it were possible, my charming siblings would have managed it by now. But this stubborn little girl never did like a stand-alone. I'm here for the whole series."

I haul myself out of the pool, water streaming off my bare chest and torso. I dry my chest, then cinch the towel around my waist. "You were sent to the Moonless Mountains."

"Yes. One of several bones I have to pick with you. Definitely not a prime vacation spot."

"I didn't know."

"Didn't you?" She closes the distance between us.

"That wasn't the plan. I would never—"

She cuts me off sharply, "I know grace is kind of my thing, but do me a favor, Strawberry."

"Don't call me that."

"Don't forget who you are."

"I have not. I know exactly—"

"Next time," her voice is cool as she interrupts, "show me enough respect to stab me in the front, yeah?"

She punctuates the question with a single sharp poke to my sternum. I look down at the place where her finger is touching my bare chest.

"Your sisters ..." I falter on the rest of the sentence.

"Are conniving shrews, I know. And you are just the hapless fool that signed the contract, looked the other way, and collected your shiny new title." She pauses, and the silence stretches between us. "*Death.*"

Disdain drips off each letter as it rolls off her tongue. It drips acid.

We both go still. The quartet mercifully stops their musical torture.

"Tell me," she says, breaking the quiet, "how are you enjoying your promotion? Are all those benefits paying off?"

"I stay busy."

She looks me up and down, taking in the flamingo, the cocktail, the general state of my existence. "Evidently."

There is so much she does not know. So much she is assuming, but none of that matters right now. She is here. That is all I care about. That and the exhilarating and terrifying consequences that accompany that truth.

"Enough about me. How the fuck did you get here?" I demand, settling back into my own skin. Remembering who the *fuck* I am.

"That's a story for another time, Daryl. But I can give you the highlights."

"No one has ever escaped the Moonless Mountains."

"And I can understand why. It was not easy. As I'm sure you can imagine."

"Yes, I can imagine." The words fall out of my mouth, but my focus has shifted entirely to the figure before me. Even more alluring than I remembered. I've only been in her presence mere minutes, but the change is unmistakable. This experience has given her depth and richness like a thick, supple leather.

"So, I was on the cliff's edge. Free to move around, but with nowhere to go. I could not see. You know, on account of the–"

"Lack of any light source. One might even say, the *moonlessness* of it all."

"You've got it. Quite dark, and wherever I would put my foot or hand anywhere around me, all I felt was air. One step in any direction seemed a certain doom. Jagged rocks and steep descents did not seem like my idea of a party, and where would I go anyway? I couldn't see centimeters around me, never mind the full landscape beyond. So, there I remained, with nothing but my mind and my memories. The former I used to devise a plan to will more compassion into the OtherWorld. The latter fueled the former."

"You're losing me."

"This is my surprised face." Mercy flashes me a deadpan expression. "Then, a short while ago, something incredible happened. A light flickered to existence directly in front of me. I could see. The illumination danced in the air around me, giving me a glimpse of what perils and promises lay all around me. *Yada yada yada.* Now I'm here."

"Did you just *yada yada* an epic quest?"

"Like I said, D, story for another day. Right now, I want answers."

"I can't tell you what I don't know."

"I haven't asked you anything yet, you brick."

"It's a preemptive strike."

"Has anything strange been going on recently? Anybody messing with anything? Maybe showing a little more grace or compassion than usual?"

My silence hides nothing. Mercy has always been able to read behind my eyes and directly into my soul, the damnable vixen.

"I knew it," she exclaims.

"It's nothing. She's no one."

"She?"

"Rue," I say on a sigh, knowing there's no way to hide any of this from Mercy.

"Go on," Mercy coaxes, rising on the balls of her feet in anticipation.

"She's sort of been inadvertently locating lost souls and reopening their portals. We have had a series of crosses from dead cases."

Mercy speaks slowly and reverentially. "We have been waiting for this. Her energy must have created a spark, allowed me to navigate out of banishment from the strength of her light." Then another thought hits her, and she finishes sadistically, "I'll bet my sisters are super pissed!"

"They are. There's a reaper involved too. It's messy, Merc. Very messy."

She takes a sauntering stride toward me, and the sway of her hips hypnotizes. "And you're just the boy to clean things up."

"No. I'm not getting involved. And when your sisters find out that you've come back from the darkness, there is going to be no stopping the mayhem."

"And that's why they won't find out."

"Not from me they won't."

"You let me worry about staying out of sight. I need you to do something for me."

"Depends on what it is. VIP seats to next year's Send-Off? Done. You want–"

"Don't get smart with me, D. I may show mercy, but even my patience wears thin."

"I am the one who decides when mercy is shown now, *pet*." The way the term of endearment makes her shoulders stiffen paints a grin across my face. "However, it happened; I'm in charge now. And with great power comes a great ME. So, speak your mind, but don't forget who's making the rules here."

"Careful, D," she warns. "You're starting to sound like your father."

"And you're starting to piss me off."

"We had plans." Her tone shifts, soft and inviting. "AfterLife Processing doesn't need efficiency. It needs compassion. You wanted to change things. You wanted to be different."

"I'm not helping that mortal mess up the system that we have fine-tuned so precisely. Adding complexities and nuance to something best served with blunt force trauma." I speak with finality, but the ensuing back-and-forth only escalates in pitch and intensity.

"You will, D."

"Why?"

"Because the greater good demands it. The needs of the many outweigh the wants of the few."

"Your utilitarianism smacks of naivety now, Mercy. The world is harsher than that. Putting the self before the herd just makes sense."

"And your objectivism is disheartening and nauseating. This isn't you, D."

I roll my eyes. "You don't know me."

"I did. I do. I know the real you." Her gaze penetrates, more invasive than a polygraph. "Besides," she coos, "you owe me."

"Oh, yeah?" I huff. "How do you figure?"

"Ousting me elevated you. All of this in exchange for my eternal darkness." She gestures to the room around us, eyeing me up and down to punctuate her point.

"I didn't ask you to help me."

"I wanted to."

"Yeah, well, I never wanted you to leave." The traitorous crack in my voice betrays my hard exterior.

"It had to be. It was the only way."

"You sound like your sister," I grumble.

Her upper lip curls. "And you sound like a different man from the one I used to share the moonlight with."

"Enough talking," I demand.

"Why?" She looks at me, dumbfounded.

"Because I don't have the words for this."

I take her in with one long breath, and the inhale burns. My hand lifts as I wrap it firmly in her auburn tresses.

She gasps at the firmness of my grip.

There is a moment of stillness you could fill with a galaxy. Her sapphire eyes glint, the spark shoots straight into the center of me. Zap.

I desperately pull her to me, and our mouths crash roughly, like thunder before the rain. It's a kiss full of promise, longing, and all the what-ifs, colliding in the press of lips and teeth and breath. It's a kiss hundreds of years in the making and one I wish would last that long to make up for all the time we lost. Her body flush to mine, I bring my other hand to her lower waist. If I squeeze just a little tighter, I am quite sure I can fuse her to me. Press her soul into mine and keep her there forever.

I run my tongue along her lips, and she whimpers against my mouth. It undoes me.

She molds to me like she never left. Like no time passed.

Her hands are on my chest, her nails dragging down me like she wants to mark me. Fuck, I want her to. I want—no, I need her to leave marks, scars to prove she was here. That I'm not passed out on that fucking flamingo, dreaming.

Her lips part, and I take full advantage, tongue sweeping into her space. Her moan is soft, broken, and carnal.

My knees nearly give out.

I tighten my grip on her waist, in her hair, like I can keep her if I don't let go. If I just keep her here, everything else can wait. Collapsing systems. Angry Sisters. Depressed reapers. Let it all burn.

This is the moment I've been starved for. A taste of what we lost.

The ground trembles beneath us, a low rumble that vibrates through the tiles and into my bones. I know what it means. I know what this costs. Us together like this—touching, tasting, feeling—it's a threat to the order. To the balance.

To everything.

Then so fucking be it.

But even as I think this, I know better. I know better than to chase what I can't keep.

This, whatever this is between us, is as strong a force as a natural disaster. As dangerous too. The thought has me pulling away from the kiss. The action is a lie. I could stay there for a thousand moons. But instead, I break it off quickly, both of us panting for air.

"So," I say, clearing my throat, "tell me your plan, and I will take it under advisement."

Mercy's face stretches into a giddy grin. The strings begin in on Mozart, and Mercy steps closer to whisper her plan into my ear. When she finishes, she bites playfully on my lobe, sending shivers running not just throughout my body, but the entire room.

"You're in charge," she says, looking me in the eye. "No one else tells you how to do this job. It's your name on the gilded nameplate. Make it your own."

"And don't you fucking forget it."

"I won't." She smiles. "There's no rule anywhere that says that the act of death can't be a merciful one. There is no time limit on forgiveness and understanding. Compassion over convenience. Think about it."

"I will." Then, after a beat, "No promises."

"I'd never want you to make a promise you couldn't keep."

She stops speaking, and I wish she wouldn't. The band crescendoes as she makes her way back out the door.

"Merc," I say, stopping her. "Where are you going? When will I see you again?"

"When Time and Fate allow."

She laughs at her own joke; I do not. I don't speak, waiting for her to give me a real answer to those questions.

"I'll see you around, D," she says instead and walks out of my bathhouse and into a new kind of darkness than the one she was immersed in on the Moonless Mountains.

I stare at the ceiling, and feel the weight of every choice I've ever made pressing down on my chest.

"Well," I whisper to the empty room, "this is going to be a disaster."

Chapter Thirty-Seven

CLIMBING THE ALPS

RUE

WHERE AM I?

It's not a poetic question. It's not rhetorical. I genuinely have no idea where I am.

I've looked around at least fifty times now, each scan as fruitless as the last, though that hasn't stopped me from repeating the motions like a nervous tic. The room is vast with rows of chairs that stretch in both directions like a pair of infinity mirrors. Every chair is filled, but no one's talking. Not in a frightened way, more in that deadened, post-waiting-room-eternity way. There's a vacancy in all the eyes here.

Across the room is a long row of desks, like a Department of Motor Vehicles designed by someone with a real flair for the mundane. Behind each steel station, workers in stiff charcoal uniforms shuffle papers, stamp forms, and speak just loud enough to be irritating without being intelligible.

How long have I been here?

I check the window for the fifth? Seventh? Twentieth time? Hard to say. The outside looks identical to the inside–same dull shades of grey and purple. There's a sliver of a moon suspended in the sky, hanging there like an old fridge magnet. Every time I glance at it, it seems a fraction larger than it was before, but if I stare at it to witness its waxing or waning, it doesn't move at all.

I cannot quite figure out if I have been sitting here for a matter of moments or many hours. I am somehow no longer connected to time in a way I am familiar with. I cannot feel it. Its passage does not resonate anywhere in or around me. I do not seem to be accumulating the memory of each minute, and so they do not seem to exist. Like each second is the only second, and they all paradoxically hold the magnitude of everything and the weightlessness of nothing in each of them. It is difficult to describe. It is disorienting.

What is this place?

The line at each station never diminishes. One by one, souls are processed, papers are stamped, badges assigned, and then herded off through one of the glass doors behind the desks. I haven't seen anyone come back. No one looks confused, nor do they protest. They just accept it.

I cross my arms over my chest and stare at the nearest clerk, who doesn't look up. I consider grabbing a pen or something and throwing it to get their attention. But I have no pen, no paper, nothing at all.

I try not to fidget, but it's hard when you don't have a sense of whether you're supposed to be fidgeting. Maybe this is all part of the test. Or maybe they're waiting for me to crack. I'm not sure what they want from me, but I'm starting to think I'm the only one here who didn't attend orientation.

Before I have an opportunity to begin to unpack any of these mysteries, I hear my name called from one of the desks. I stand and look around, unable to discern exactly where the sound is coming from. On the third intonation of my name, I spot the source of the sound and move toward the tiny, bespectacled woman sitting behind mountains of paperwork.

"Rue Chamberlain?" Her round eyes peek over the rim of her glasses as she looks up from her paper at my approach.

"Yes," I say, not remembering the last time I spoke.

"Sit down." Her clipped tone offers no room for discussion, so I slide into the seat opposite her desk.

"Where am I?"

She sighs the sigh of a person who's been asked the same question too many times to count. A dull exhale, followed by the same answer she's clearly given over and over again. "Welcome to the OtherWorld. This is AfterLife Processing. My name is Zandra, and I will be your ALPer."

"Helper?"

"ALPer, as in AfterLife Processing."

"ALPer?" I repeat. "What do I need ALP with?"

She doesn't blink at my attempt at levity. "Despair. Mostly."

Zandra clicks her pen and begins scribbling on a form. "Here you will be given your status ranking, placement, and temporary assignment. Once assigned to your designated sector, you will begin your tenure for Death's Door, LLC. At the end of your term, you may be relocated and cleared from additional service, or your contract may be extended."

The fog begins to clear from my mind as visions from my recent past return. A beautiful man with a dark soul that matched his dark suit. Spirits and stories and adventures. My house, my heart, my home.

"Kane," I whisper, then lock eyes with the clerk. "Where is Kane?"

Zandra's pen pauses. She peers over her glasses with a tilt of her head. "Who is Kane, lady?"

"He was my reaper." *He was my love.* The sensation sparks in the center of my chest, but I do not voice that truth now. "He is supposed to be with me," I offer instead.

"No one belongs to anyone else in the OtherWorld. It's just you and eternity now." Zandra eyes the sheet in front of her. "Also, says here your reaper was an Asher Bennett. Cause of death: heart failure from a genetic condition. Poetic passing, smooth soul extraction."

"No." I lean forward, my hands gripping the edge of the desk. "No, that's wrong. I need to see him. Kane Deveraux. Please, you have to help me."

"No one can help you now, Rue. No one can help any of us. Not anymore."

There is an eerie darkness to Zandra's declaration. They are the first words she's spoken with anything resembling emotion or feeling. And the haunting senti-ment sends a chill rushing down my spine.

She continues, scanning the sheet in front of her, "According to your paperwork, you will be assigned to ..." She trails off, picking the paper up and bringing it closer to her face. "Huh. That can't be right. I've never seen that before," she mumbles to herself.

"What? What's not right? What is it?"

"Your account has been flagged." Zandra squints as she looks over the papers, and my stomach twists. "Your file's been marked 'Classified'. No assignment issued. *Directive: escort subject to Main Office for evaluation.*"

I stare at her, dread creeping over me. "To see Big D?" I ask, the rest of my memories from my final mor-tal days flooding back.

Zandra looks up again. Her mouth opens. Closes. "How do you know we call him that?"

An odd sense of confidence replaces the cold in my back, and I arch my shoulders as I stare straight at my curly-haired ALPer. "I've been here before, Z. Now show me to the boss's office."

She studies me, her expression finally cracking into something resembling emotion. Bewilderment maybe. Or caution.

"I need the big stamp," she mutters, rifling through a tray of ink pads and oversize labels. Her hand lands on a red one the size of a dinner plate.

A loud *chunk* sound echoes off the steel table as the red ink slams onto the page. The word 'Assigned' splat-tered atop the black ink.

Zandra shoves the paper aside and nods toward the far corner of the room. "Door's over there. You'll know it when you see it."

And I do.

Now that it's been pointed out, I can't unsee it—a tall, oval archway that shimmers like the surface of water trapped in a mirror. It hums, just low enough to feel in my molars. The air around it smells floral and toxic.

I take one last look at Zandra. She doesn't smile, nor does she wave.

"Good luck," she says flatly. "You'll need it."

Then she's gone again–absorbed back into her fortress of red tape and resignation.

I walk toward the door.

I don't look back.

I step through the inky center of the arched door and am instantly transported to the end of a long red carpet. I take in the high ceilings, ostentatious art adorning the walls, odd pieces of furniture in mismatched period styles. I don't know Big D well, but even without context clues, I'd know who this space belonged to. I scan the length of the red carpet before me and see a tiny desk at the end. The desk probably isn't small, but its distance from me makes it seem so.

There is nothing tiny about the booming voice that echoes from behind it though. D intones with all the bravado of a cartoon villain, "Rue Chamberlain. We meet again."

"To my great disappointment," I mumble to myself.

"I heard that," he snipes, though there is a hint of delight in his undertone. "Come here."

This time, he snaps his fingers, and I find myself immediately opposite his desk, gold name placard pointlessly announcing the owner of the room to a world that doesn't need the reminder.

"Neat trick," I deadpan with a hint of venom in my tone.

"I think you'll find I'm full of surprises today, girl," he replies with a too-wide smile while leaning back in his chair. The way he says that last word gives the sensation of spiders crawling on my neck.

I shiver, and he continues, "Also, rude. Nana heard you talking ill of me."

He gestures to a human skull sitting atop a carved lava rock coaster. Red candy ropes jut from the top, along with a blue umbrella, like the ones found in those tropical vacation cocktails.

"Care for one?" he asks, pulling the candy out and offering it to me. "Twizzlers straight from Nana. The purest ambrosia."

"I would sooner eat a stranger's toenails. Thanks."

"Suit yourself." He pops it into his mouth and leans

back, giving the skull a pat. He looks so amused with himself.

"What do you want with me?" I ask, not bothering to hide the bite in my tone.

"Straight to the point. I like it! So, we're skipping over the *hard feelings* thing then?"

"Oh, by 'thing,' are you referring to the whole separating me from the mate to my soul during the single moment in human existence that mated souls should be together?" I stare at him, my gaze stone-cold. "Fuck. You. Daryl," I spit.

He holds up both hands. "Still a bit raw. Okay, I get it. Listen, my hands were tied. I think you'll see that in time."

"I don't care about time," I finally snap. "I care about what you did!"

"Patience, peaches." He laces his fingers together on the desk. "You see, I forgot myself for a while. I let Fate and Time run too much of the show. Gave them creative control, which was clearly a mistake. They tried to hogtie me with my own rules—and that isn't as fun as it sounds. Then," he shudders theatrically, "do unspeakable things to my executive authority."

"What are you talking about?"

"I'm talking about power, Rue. Hierarchy. Who makes the rules and who has to follow them. Those Weaver Sisters sing a siren's song, but my head is clear now. They overplayed their hand and didn't think I'd see the puppet strings. But I have, and I have cut them down."

"That's a second rope analogy, and I'm just as lost as I was after the first one."

"I don't answer to Time, Rue. Death isn't beholden to Fate. Everyone whines about choice. *Choice, independence, free will.*" He mocks in an odd whiny baby voice. "Well, no one and nothing escapes death. Fate can tell any story she wants, as long as it ends in death. Time can strum a tune for any soul, but the final note will always be silence. I am the period at the end of a book. I am the rest at the end of a ballad. I am the only inevitability in a world full of mystery. And I will be obeyed." During this diatribe, D rises from his chair, placing his palms flat on the surface of the desk, punctuating his last sentence.

"Ooookay." I stretch out the word, taking the wind out of his sails. "Well, congratulations on your rebranding. What does this have to do with me?"

"Everything, fool."

Flames light behind his eyes, and I pause. He's a bear in a cage, and perhaps I'd better not rattle it. He may act like a sitcom villain with a sugar addiction, but he is still the current incarnation of Death and de facto ruler of the OtherWorld. Unhinged or not, he is still the boss.

He continues in a much more composed manner. "I am feeling, shall we say, a bit merciful at the moment, Rue. So, I come to you today with a choice. According to your intake forms, you qualify for a fast track to PTO."

"PTO? Paid time off?"

"No, Rue. Passage To Oblivion," he corrects. "It's a bit like The Nothing, which I'm sure you remember from my recent soiree–which everyone loved, by the way–but much nicer. An all-expense-paid eternity in a dream state of your own making. No work, no souls, no pain. Just you, your imagination, and an infinity pool of peace."

"Can I bring anyone?"

"Oh, you won't remember anyone or anything there, Rue. That's the Oblivion part. Blissful ignorance, a mind free of those pesky memories."

"So, a lobotomy in a luxury suite?"

He gives me a wink. "It has an amazing view."

My brain floods with a sea of memories I cherish, each like one of the precious crystal animals in Amanda Wingfield's menagerie. "And what's the other option?"

"Well, Rue, it turns out, that tiresome empathy of yours, that annoying willingness to *listen* and *understand* people, has proven a pretty powerful tool. Who knew?"

"This is my surprised face," I mumble.

"What did you say?" D's voice cracks like a whip.

"I said, this is my surprised face."

D gyrates behind his desk as though shaking the phrase off him somehow.

"Anyway," he begins, "I turned a blind eye to the potential in this pathetic, and frankly meaningless, compassion."

"It's not meaningless to the souls receiving it."

"Yes, I understand that, but in the grand scheme of things, when you take a macro view, *mortal*, each of your stories mean very little in the end."

I bury my ire for the moment and allow him to finish his explanation.

"But we have been missing an opportunity. More souls mean expansion, growth, increased productivity. So, I'm offering you a once-in-an-AfterLife chance to continue what you started. Return to the mortal realm and help shepherd more of those long-abandoned cases back across the threshold. Punishing beings for eternity because of a poor choice made in one high-stakes moment is perhaps a bit draconian. Now, with your gifts, we have an opportunity to make room for …"

"Forgiveness?" I supply, and D bristles at the word.

"Something like that," he deflects.

"Mercy?" I drop the word like an anchor straight to the bottom of the deep blue sea.

His black eyes shoot to mine, but the flames inside them don't dance. Instead, they turn the deepest shade of blue I've ever seen. A fire burning at its hottest point.

"In my infinite generosity, I offer you a choice. An eternity of peace or an AfterLife of purpose. PTO or a job as the founding head of the Lost Souls Division," he says, plucking another Twizzler from Nana's dome and biting it in half.

I stare at the skull between us with her hollow sockets and furrow my brow. "Did Nana just wink at me?"

"Probably." D shrugs. "She must like you. She's an excellent judge of character."

D pauses and appraises me, perhaps trying to guess at which direction I'm leaning. This is my red pill/blue pill moment.

"So, what'll it be?" D leaves the question hanging in the air.

I don't hesitate. "I only have one demand."

Chapter Thirty-Eight

REASSIGNMENT

KANE

THE WEATHERED BEIGE STACK OF PAPERS REMAINS A HEAP ON my desk. I pull, verify, stamp, and sort sheet after sheet, yet still, the pile remains. Like Sorites paradox of the heap, I wonder futilely if this task has an end, if this mass of dusty pages will ever stop being a heap.

Pull. Verify. Stamp. Sort.

Pull. Verify. Stamp. Sort.

The air smells stale. The words on every page look as though they were printed on the last dregs of ink in the printer. The only reprieve from the endless mundanity of it all comes in the form of the occasional papercut–an annoyance in life, a welcome distraction in the OtherWorld.

A cool blue fluorescent light emits half of its potential illumination, giving me just enough to see by, if I remain hunched over my nondescript desk. Somehow, this is worse than the days before electricity. Candles at least give off some warmth.

I look up to the wall opposite my desk, where a clock should hang. But time is nothing more than a loop, an eternal recurrence of the same nothingness. Moments blur together, much like the pale words on the page I'm currently trying to decipher before applying the appropriate stamp and shuffling it off to its correct outbox stack.

I used to shepherd souls. I used to have a purpose. Now I shepherd paper. And have no *raison d'etre*.

I reach for the next page in my never-ending pile as the little light I have becomes drenched in shadow. A soft ruffling noise draws my attention away from the monotonous routine, and I look up to see Big D himself standing there.

This is new.

I've never seen him in all the time I've been here. He looks every bit the absentee boss, reluctantly making the rounds, as he hovers over my desk.

"Well, don't you look like a pathetic sack?"

"How am I supposed to look, *boss*?" I do my best to turn the word into an insult.

"Where did your passion go, Kane? Your *joie de vivre*?" When I don't respond, D fills in the blanks for himself. "Lost somewhere in these stacks, I imagine." He runs his finger down the side of a stack, causing dust to billow in the air around me.

"My passion died when she did," I mumble.

"Don't be dramatic, Kane. You're so grim."

D's use of Rue's nickname for me, whether intentional or not, sparks the last kindling of rage inside me. I pull my shoulders back and lock eyes with him.

"You made me watch her end, powerless to stop it. Your cruelty knows no bounds. You enjoyed it. You watched her final moments like it was some sick form of entertainment to you. You had fucking popcorn."

D's blank expression tells me nothing of how my words impact him. "That might have been a bit crass of me, Kane," he admits. "I see that now. We're all works in progress, you know? Molded from clay that never fully dries."

"You're molded from something," I mumble without much feeling behind the jab.

"Your eyes, Kane." He sighs. "They look like a pair of stars that have burned out. Sad."

"What are you doing here?" I change the subject, not interested in pursuing this line of interrogation any further.

"Ah, yes. I came to deliver the good news personally."

He smiles, and I do not trust it. "You have been reassigned, Kane."

"I didn't put in a transfer request."

"And I wouldn't have cared if you did. You go where I tell you to go. And I am telling you that you are the newest member of our newest division. You're going back in the field, big guy! Now, let's hurry this along. No time for a going-away party, I'm sorry to say."

His jocular tone grates on every last nerve I've managed to cling to during this nauseous nothingness.

"I thought Clerical was my punishment."

"It was. It is. And that's over now."

"Why?" I ask skeptically.

"Because I'm not wasting the talents of the man who broke all the rules for love. I'm putting him to work for the business."

"Why?" I ask again like a petulant child.

"Because the most interesting stories have the audacity to believe in redemption, Kane. Mistakes pave the way for greater success and, in our case, an opportunity to build a bigger, better OtherWorld. So, welcome to your new assignment, reaper."

D tosses a business card on the desk. I see my name embossed in silver against a matte black background and read its inscription aloud. "*Kane Deveraux. Second-in-Command. Lost Souls Division. 'May those who are lost be found again.'*"

I look up at D, a thousand questions dancing on the tip of my tongue, but the only one that matters escapes. "Who's my boss?"

"I thought you'd never ask." Big D smiles and snaps his fingers, instantly transporting us into a conference room, where a single figure stands sentinel at the head of the table.

And I stare directly into the stormy eyes of my orange-and-black-haired eternity. My forever.

Rue stares right back. "There's my anchor in the infinite. Good to see you handsome. You're late."

Epilogue

WELCOME TO THE LOST SOULS DIVISION

RUE

I STARE DOWN AT THE DEVICE IN MY HAND. KANE STANDS BE-side me, angled slightly to read over my shoulder. His chin just grazes my temple as he tilts to get a better view of the back of my Tombstone Phone.

"*Rue Chamberlain. Loving daughter. Cat mom. Writer. Always Home.*"

He looks at me, brows slightly drawn together as he repeats in question, "*Always Home?*"

I nod. "It's from a sonnet I wrote to my dad. My mom must have found my notebooks and actually read them."

There's a beat of silence.

"Wonders never cease," Kane mutters dryly.

I nudge his elbow. "Sometimes, people can surprise us."

The soul outlives the body, and stories outlast our days on Earth. If even for a short time, that's not nothing. I don't say it aloud, but a silent thank-you floats some-where out there in the direction of my mom.

"Hey," I say, remembering something I asked Kane ages ago that he never answered. "Your Tombstone Phone. You never told me what it says."

He pulls his device from his breast pocket and hands it to me to see.

"The real version is in a small cemetery in the ninth arrondissement. It says *l'amour guérit.*"

When I give him a blank stare, he translates, "Love heals."

I think about Kane's story, the parts he has shared and those he has been more reluctant to reveal. I bring my hand to his neck and gently touch the raised flesh above his vein.

He rests his hand outside mine as I ask him, "Does it?"

"When administered in the proper dosage, yes. Yes, it does."

He guides our hands to his cheek and pulls us together for a kiss, which is cut annoyingly short by the repeated notification from my Tombstone Phone. The same gong from my old family clock chimes on the device.

Looking at the screen, I scan over the alert. My face lights up when I read the message.

"Here it is," I say, failing to contain the excitement in my voice. "Our first case!"

I click the button and read the details aloud to Kane. " 'Katherine Sinclair. Initial Crossover: Failed. Current Status: Tied to Titan Media building.' "

The words hang for a moment. I look up and see a stricken expression on Kane's face.

My smile slips.

"Nothing," he says in response to the unvoiced question in my glare.

"Kane."

"Rue–"

I step in front of him and narrow my eyes. "Your beautiful mouth says, 'Nothing,' but those eyes are screaming a story, Grim."

He sighs, pinching the bridge of his nose, as if I'm giving him a migraine. "She was my final reap. Before you. She insisted that the business could not survive without her. Tied to her career. Could not let go."

"Until now," I say with a smile in my voice. "Nothing like our first shot at a second chance. I'm not naive enough to think this will be easy, but let's try to set things to rights, yeah?"

"Your enthusiasm is infectious," Kane says flatly.

I beam. "Yeah? You're feeling the energy?"

"No, it's making me sick."

"Awww." I place a hand dramatically over my chest. "Are we entering our grumpy-sunshine era?"

He exhales slowly. "I imagine it's more like an eon, but, yes, I suppose we are."

"Well, come on, Grim. Let's go 'lead with love.'"

I ignore Kane's broody grimace and press the Transport button at the bottom of the case report on my Tombstone Phone. In the literal blink of an eye, we are in a busy conference room. Executives sit around a long oval table, droning on about strategy and budgeting.

I look around, surprised at how quick and painless our transition went. One second, we were standing in the ALP Hub, and the next, we're planted on the sixteenth floor of Titan Media.

I blink. "Well, that hurt a lot more when I was living."

Kane stands beside me, hands in his coat pockets, looking supremely unimpressed.

My attention turns to the soul we must be here for. Katherine Sinclair flits about the conference room, flailing her arms and shouting insults at the staff, all of which fall on deaf ears. No one can see or hear her; they make no reaction to her rantings whatsoever, but it doesn't seem to deter her meddling one bit.

"This is pointless," Kane begins.

"No, it's not." I sigh, sensing he might make this way harder than Katherine will. "I taught you the system. You know the mnemonic. You can do this."

Kane grunts, the sound somewhere between annoyance and dread.

I press on gently, "Repeat after me."

"No."

"*Distract* the subject. *Ingest* her story. *Ease* her to the OtherWorld."

He scowls. "Look at her. She's even more invested in this business than when I last saw her. She's not ready."

"Help her die, Grim. D.I.E. Die."

"I wish I could die," he grumbles, which I choose to ignore.

I clear my throat and speak, which, of course, only Katherine and Kane can hear, "Ms. Sinclair, you're needed immediately in your office. There's a critical update on the merger, and we need your input now."

"Merger?" Kane whispers from behind me.

"There's always a merger," I whisper back. "Corporate America runs on the fantasy of reinvention. Everyone wants to be somebody else, especially when they've already sold who they were."

Katherine stops berating one of the seated suits and turns her attention to me. "The merger?" she exclaims.

"See?" I side-eye Kane.

"Beginner's luck," he returns.

We follow swiftly after Katherine, who is beelining for the corner office. The name *Frank Davenport–CEO* is etched into the frosted glass, but that does not deter our lost soul, who turns to us immediately after entering the room.

"Talk to me. Get me up to speed. What's the latest?"

I look over to Kane, silently telling him to take the lead.

His expression says, *Absolutely not.* The cant in his hips screams, *I'd rather be reaped myself.*

Still, he knows this is supposed to be his moment.

"Ingest," I coax.

He sighs exaggeratedly and then explains, "There's no merger, Ms. Sinclair." He says bluntly, "You're still just dead."

I close my eyes and count to three. "Soft landing, Kane. Real soft."

"They've taken my blade, Rue. Now all I have left is my cutting frankness."

Before I have a chance to respond, Katherine's voice pitches up, and she moves closer to Kane. "Wait. Do I know you? You look familiar."

"We met a while ago, Ms. Sinclair. I was tasked with helping you cross over to the OtherWorld, but you were reluctant."

"Yes. I remember. It's fuzzy, but yes."

"Did you ever finish that turkey sandwich?" Kane asks more smugly than I might have liked.

The stricken expression that paints itself across the media mogul's face lets me know that awareness has sunk in.

"Your time to affect change in this plane has come to an end. I'm very sorry," I tell her gently.

She turns to me. "I built this company from the ground up. Over two decades of my life was devoted to this enterprise. My first love, my longest love. My desire to become a mother didn't happen until I was almost thirty years old, but I've wanted to tell stories since I was a little girl."

Kane looks on, attentive and somber. I lock eyes with him, silently willing him to give Katherine the permission she needs.

His mouth softens at the edges and he turns to her. "It's time to tell your story, Ms. Sinclair. We are listening."

She sighs, her spectral form coming to stillness for the first time since we arrived. "My ambition was always my largest appetite. No matter how much I fed it, it never seemed sated. When I was a girl, I wanted to sing. I wanted to act. I wanted to perform. By the time I reached my twenties, the writing was on the wall. I was not good enough. Simple as that. It wasn't the thing I was put on this planet to do. It wasn't my *why*. You know?"

"But you found your *why*, didn't you?"

Her face lights up. "I did. I had a friend who was so talented. She had everything. The looks, the drive, that intangible *it* factor. We would audition opposite each other constantly. She would hit on occasion. I never would. I was frustrated that my own career wasn't taking off, but I simply didn't have the talent. She deserved to make it, and it just wasn't happening. *Finally*, I said to myself, *the world can ignore her gift, but I won't.* I spent the next six months working with her on a one-woman show. I produced it, directed it, and promoted it for her. She performed, and I made sure the world watched.

"We became so close. Friends. Business and creative partners. We were unstoppable. Then I got an offer to show run a new series with this hot young writer. I made my deal contingent on the team casting Lizzy in the pilot. But when they balked, I turned my back on her and went on without her. She never spoke to me again. Twenty-two years."

A silence falls over the room that feels as long as the one that descended on her friendship.

"So, it's not the business." It's a statement, not a question. Kane puts the pieces together out loud. "It's regret. You miss your friend. You never got reconcilia-tion for that perceived betrayal."

"I built my own media network. Twenty-four hours of programming a day for two decades. I sent so many straight offers to her agent. She rejected every single one." Katherine huffs out a beleaguered sigh. "She would never let me forget."

There's a pause that neither of us fills because it feels like Katherine has more to share. She does.

"And now I'm the one who will be forgotten. If I leave this place, no one will remember me."

"That's not true. Diane in Accounting made a down payment on her first home from the money she makes working for your company. Jack Pendleton–"

"I don't know who that is," Katherine cuts me off.

"But he knows you. He's a new hire, and when he told his parents that he was working for your company, his parents beamed with pride and said how happy they were to see their child pursuing his passion and building a name for himself."

Katherine's expression still holds a defensive edge to it. "And what happens when I leave? What if it all crum-bles? What if it all ends?"

"It will. Eventually," Kane answers darkly. "Everything ends, Katherine, and we are all forgotten. All of us."

"Is that helping?" I ask quietly.

"And that's okay," he continues without acknowl-edging me. "It is inevitable. We can fight an unwinnable battle against our own impermanence, or we can face our own minuscule place against the backdrop of time and celebrate the moments that matter for as long as they matter."

"But was it worth it? To lose one of the best friends I ever had?"

"You'll have plenty of time to wrestle with that ques-tion, I promise. Whether it's right or it's wrong isn't nearly as important as the fact that it *is*. Accept it and move on."

"Easier said than done."

"Might be easier than all this energy you're putting into hanging on," I put in, floored by the power of Kane's words. "Release yourself from what you cannot control. Give yourself the grace to be imperfect and to be comfortable with your flaws."

"They are as much a part of you as your victories," Kane finishes.

Katherine releases a sigh that ends with a soft whimper. "I tried," she cries softly.

"And that is enough," I encourage. "You are enough."

Katherine's wispy form begins to lighten. The smoky edges of her grey form stretch and thin and dissipate.

Kane asks her, "Are you ready now, Ms. Sinclair? Let go of what's tying you here and move on to the next part of your story. Wherever that may lead."

"But last time," Katherine begins meekly, "you told me that was my only chance."

Kane looks to me, a flash of warmth behind his penetrating gaze. "Turns out, I was wrong. No mistake should cost a soul forever. Everyone deserves a second chance."

She looks between the both of us, then turns to Kane and says with conviction, "Then, yes, I am ready."

"Then you shall," I assert.

On her next soft sigh, Katherine's ghostly form pinches into its center and then winks out. *Poof.*

Kane pierces the silence that follows with a question. "Is that it? Has she crossed?"

Four measures of Philip Glass's String Quartet Number Three chime from my Tombstone Phone, and I glance at the screen.

" 'Lost Soul Found,' " I read out loud.

A profound sense of satisfaction washes over me. I feel the tear wet my cheek before I'm aware I've even started crying. I do not wipe it away. I am not ashamed of this response. I think about the freedom Katherine now has. I wonder at all the lost souls we have yet to meet.

Then I look up and gaze on that beautiful, broken soul by my side. I celebrate that sublime, overwhelming feeling of connection to others, that transcendent stillness that accompanies the power of purpose, and the euphoric weightlessness of being in love.

"Are you okay?" Kane asks softly, perhaps misunderstanding the source of my tears.

"Never better." The smile that spreads softly across my face speaks louder than words. "Grim?"

"Yes, Mayday?"

I turn to him fully, taking in the man who fought Death for me, the man who fought himself for us, and I smile softly. "You ready to go home?"

"*Avec toi?* With you? Always."

The End

Acknowledgments

To honor death, a central theme in this story, DJ and Joe would like to acknowledge all the beautiful souls who will never get a chance to hold a copy of this story in their hands.

That list includes, but is most certainly not limited to: DJ's sister Leslie, Joe's mom, Joe's grandpa, and Joe's grandma. His old music teacher Dr. Falconer, his English teacher Ms. Creasy, and his friends Felicia, Raven, Rhea, John, and Brandi.

About the Authors

DJ KRIMMER

International Bestselling Author, DJ Krimmer is known for crafting emotionally immersive romance stories with grit, heart, and heat. Her books blend slow-burn intensity with sharp banter, found family, and characters who feel achingly real. Whether it's a dark romance set in a twisted afterlife, or a small-town love story stitched together with grief and healing, DJ writes for the readers who crave depth behind desire–and a love that hurts just a little before it heals.

When she's not writing, you can find her crying over fictional characters in audiobooks, drinking way too much iced coffee, or plotting emotionally devastating storylines from her office with her support pup curled at her feet. She's powered by angst, redemption arcs, and readers who say, "this book ruined me–in the best way."

To learn more, follow her on
Instagram: @djkrimmer
or visit www.authordjkrimmer.com

ALSO BY DJ KRIMMER

Hel's Ink Series:
Fox, Atlas, Ash, Derek, Stevie & PS I'm With You

Rowe Ranch Series:
Stray

The Fallen Series:
Beatitude

Standalone:
Closing the Distance
Must Love Cat
Remnants
Slap Shot
Jolly & Jaded

JOE ARDEN

As a voice actor, Joe Arden's deeply emotional performances and character connectivity have made him a fan favorite. Over the years, he has brought hundreds of memorable characters to life. Joe's passion for the art of storytelling have propelled into more areas of creation as an author, a musical artist, and a performer.His solo writing debut, The Chameleon Effect, was shortlisted by Audible's Editorial Staff as "one of the Best Audiobooks of 2022," earned an Earphones Award, and was voted one of the "Top 100 Romance Audios of All Time."

Joe's entrepreneurial spirit and thirst for creativity can be seen almost daily in his original works and community engagement inside The Audio Attic. On the stage, on the page, and in the booth, Joe finds places and spaces to share his love for words, language, and human experiences.

ALSO BY JOE ARDEN

My Soul To Take: Bound (2025)
The Rest of Me EP (Musical Release 2025)
shadow.self. (2024)
The Chameleon Effect (2022)
How To Get Lucky (2021)

Stay Connected

To join a community of lovers of love
and celebrate all things storytelling,
check out The Audio Attic :

patreon.com/JoeArden

For exclusive merch, info on upcoming live
appearances, and much more, visit :

TheRealJoeArden.com
MySoulToTakeShow.com

SOCIALS

@TheRealJoeArden

BOOKISH

www.bookbub.com/authors/joe-arden

www.goodreads.com/author/show/20682028.Joe_
Arden